THE MARATHON CONSPIRACY

Also by Gary Corby

The Pericles Commission

The Ionia Sanction

Sacred Games

THE MARATHON CONSPIRACY

Gary Corby

First published in the United States in 2014
Soho Press, Inc.
853 Broadway
New York, NY 10003

Library of Congress Cataloging-in-Publication Data

Corby, Gary.
The Marathon conspiracy / Gary Corby.
p. cm
ISBN 978-1-61695-387-4
eISBN 978-1-61695-388-1
1.Nicolaos (Fictitious character : Corby)—Fiction. 2. Diotima (Legendarycharacter)—Fiction. 3. Hippias, –490 B.C.—Fiction. 4. Private investigators—Greece—Athens—Fiction. 5. Girls—Crimes against—Fiction.6. Missing children—Fiction. 7. Skull—Fiction. 8. Greece—History—Athenian supremacy, 479–431 B.C.—Fiction.
I. Title.
PR9619.4.C665M37 2014
823'.92—dc23 2013033925

Interior design by Janine Agro, Soho Press, Inc.
Map illustration by Katherine Grames

Printed in the United States of America

10 9 8 7 6 5 4 3 2 1

For my own Little Bears, Catriona and Megan

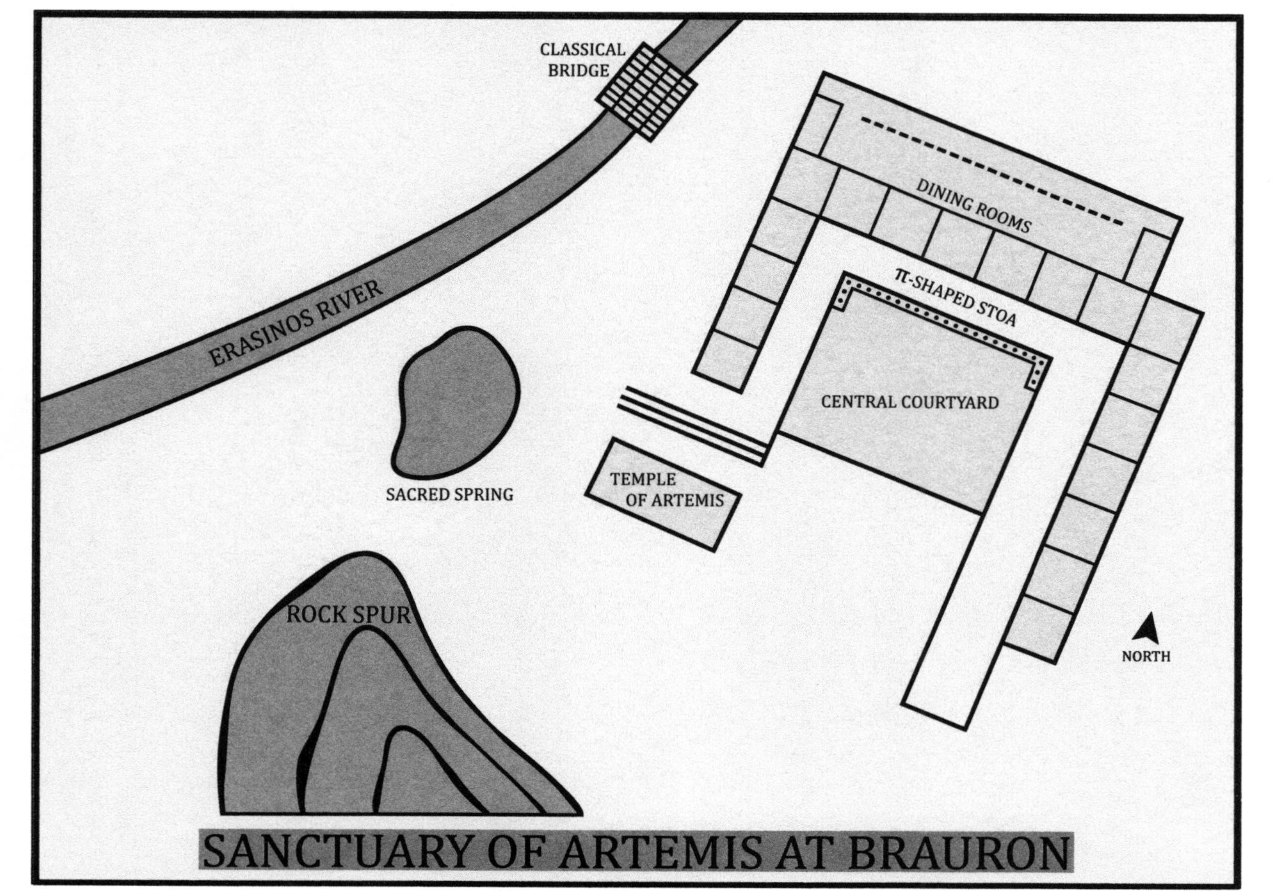
CLASSICAL
BRIDGE
DINING ROOMS
ERASINOS RIVER
π-SHAPED STOA
CENTRAL COURTYARD
SACRED SPRING
TEMPLE
OF ARTEMIS
ROCK SPUR
NORTH
SANCTUARY OF ARTEMIS AT BRAURON

A Note on Names

SOME NAMES FROM the classical world remain in use to this day, such as Ophelia and Doris. Others are familiar anyway because they're famous people, like Socrates and Pericles. And some names look slightly odd, names such as Antobius and Gaïs. I hope you'll say each name however sounds happiest to you, and have fun reading the story. For those who'd like a little more guidance, I've suggested a way to say each name in the character list. My suggestions do not match ancient pronounciation. They're how I think the names will sound best in an English sentence. That's all you need to read the book!

The Actors

Characters with an asterisk by their name were real historical people.

Nicolaos NEE-CO-LAY-OS (Nicholas)	Our protagonist	"I am Nicolaos, son of Sophroniscus."
Pericles* PERRY-CLEEZ	A politician	"I suppose you're wondering why there's a skull on my desk."
Socrates* SOCK-RA-TEEZ	An irritant	"Nico, I don't think this can be right."
Diotima* DIO-TEEMA	A priestess of Artemis, fiancée to Nicolaos	"I'll just hit him again, shall I?"
Allike AL-ICKY	A dead schoolgirl	"Allike was one of the smart ones. She could read anything."
Ophelia The modern Ophelia	A missing schoolgirl	"Why did Ophelia say someone wanted her dead?"
Zeke The modern Zeke	A handyman	"It's obvious I'm too old to be any use."
Thea The modern Thea	High Priestess of the Sanctuary of Artemis	"Age does terrible things."

Doris The modern Doris	A priestess of Artemis (the nice one)	"What are you doing with that goat?"
Sabina The modern Sabina	A priestess of Artemis (the bossy one)	"No immorality in front of the girls!"
Gaïs GAY-IS	A priestess of Artemis (the naked one)	"Do you know what they drink in Hades? They drink dust."
Hippias* HIP-IAS	A tyrant	He's dead. Very dead.
Aeschylus* ES-KILL-US	A veteran of Marathon. Also, he writes plays	"I write military adventure. That, and family drama like this trilogy I'm doing now. Dysfunctional families slaughtering one another. You know the sort of thing."
Callias* CAL-E-US	A veteran of Marathon. Also, he's the richest man in Athens	"Don't push the limits of my bodyguards, Nico. Just point and say 'kill.'"
Pythax PIE-THAX	Chief of the city guard of Athens, future father-in-law of Nicolaos	"Dear Gods, boy, didn't I teach you anything?"
Sophroniscus* SOFF-RON-ISK-US	Father of Nicolaos	"I see you're bent on self-destruction. Well, most young men are, I suppose."

Phaenarete* FAIN-A-RET-EE	Mother of Nicolaos, future mother-in-law of Diotima	"It's a good thing Diotima is joining us. It's going to take the two of us to keep you alive. You obviously can't do it on your own."
Euterpe YOU-TERP-E	Mother of Diotima, a social climber	"I was thinking for the wedding guests, something along the lines of all the best families in Athens."
The Basileus BASS-IL-E-US (origin of our word "Basilica")	The city official in charge of religious affairs	"Don't you have anything better to do than take up my time?"
Glaucon GLOW-CON	Assistant to the Basileus	"Record tablets are paid for out of public monies. There's plenty more where that comes from."
Melo	A forlorn fiancé	"I'm not going to shirk my duties just because they're not official yet."
Sim	A farm manager	"If it weren't for me, Pericles would be broke."
Ascetos the Healer AS-KET-OS	A doctor	"I've lost count of how many people have died on that couch . . ."

Polonikos POL-ON-IK-OS	Father of Ophelia	"Take my advice, young man, and avoid both borrowing and lending. These new-fangled bank businesses seem to be springing up all over the place, but frankly, I see no future for Athens in banking."
Antobius ANT-O-BIUS	Father of Allike	"Get out of my way!"
Aposila AP-O-SILA	Mother of Allike	"What can I do? Tend the grave of my daughter and care for my family."
Malixa MAL-IX-A	Mother of Ophelia	"I pray to every god that will listen that I will not soon wear my hair like Aposila."
Blossom	A donkey	If someone called me Blossom, I'd probably bite him too.

The Chorus

Assorted thugs, slaves, agora idlers, dodgy salesmen, wedding guests, and uncontrollable schoolgirls.

THE MARATHON CONSPIRACY

CHAPTER ONE

PERICLES DIDN'T USUALLY keep a human skull on his desk, but there was one there now. The skull lay upon a battered old scroll case and stared at me with a vacant expression, as if it were bored by the whole process of being dead.

I stood mute, determined not to mention the skull. Pericles had a taste for theatrics, and I saw no reason to pander to it.

Pericles sat behind the desk, a man of astonishing good looks but for the shape of his head, which was unnaturally elongated. This one blemish seemed a fair bargain for someone on whom the gods had bestowed almost every possible talent, yet Pericles was as vain as a woman about his head and frequently wore a hat to cover it. He didn't at the moment, though; he knew there was no point trying to impress me.

In the lengthening silence, he eventually said, "I suppose you're wondering why there's a skull on my desk."

I was tempted to say, "What skull?" But I knew he'd never believe it. So instead I said, "It does rather stand out. A former enemy?"

"I'm not sure. You might be right."

I blinked. I thought I'd been joking.

"We have a problem, Nicolaos." Pericles picked up the skull and set it aside to reveal the case beneath, which he handed to me. "This case came with the skull."

I turned the scroll case this way and that to examine every part without opening the flap. It was made of leather that looked as if it had been nibbled by generations of mice. Clearly it was very old.

The case was the sort that held more than one scroll: five, I estimated from the size, five cylindrical scrolls held side by side. The surface on the back of the case was much less damaged than the front, but dry and cracked; this leather hadn't been oiled in a long time.

I said, "The case has been lying on its back for many years. Perhaps decades. Probably in a dry place such as a cupboard."

Pericles tapped his desk. "The skull and the case were sent to Athens by a priestess from the temple at Brauron. Brauron is a fishing village on the east coast. The accompanying note from the priestess who sent it said that two girl-children had discovered a complete skeleton in a cave, and that lying beside it was this case. For what macabre reason the priestess thought we'd want the skull I can't imagine, but the contents of the case are of interest. Open the flap."

Inside were four scrolls, and one empty slot. I removed one of the scrolls and unrolled it a little. I was worried the parchment might be brittle and crack, but it rolled well enough, despite its age. This was high-quality papyrus, no doubt imported at great expense from Egypt.

I read a few words, then a few more, unwinding as I did. The scroll was full of dates, places, people. Notes of obvious sensitivity. I saw the names of men who I knew for a fact had died decades ago. Whatever this was, it dated from before the democracy. In fact, if what I read was genuine, these notes referred to the years when Athens was ruled by a tyrant, and the author—

I looked up at Pericles, startled.

He read my expression. "I believe you're holding the private notes of Hippias, the last tyrant of Athens."

Hippias had ruled many years before I was born. He was so hated that men still spoke about how awful he was; so hated that the people had rebelled against him. He ran to the Persians, who sent an army to reinstate him, so they could rule over Athens via the deposed tyrant. The Athenians and the Persians met upon the beach at Marathon, where we won a mighty victory to retain our freedom.

I held in my hands the private notes of the man who forced us to fight the Battle of Marathon.

There was only one problem, and I voiced it. "But all the stories say that Hippias died among the Persians, after they were defeated."

"We may be revising that theory."

"Then the skull is—"

Pericles held up the skull to face me. He waggled it like a puppet and said, "Say hello to Hippias, the Last Tyrant of Athens."

"Are you sure about this, Pericles?" I asked.

We moved over to two dining couches Pericles kept in the room. He'd sent a slave for watered wine. Now we sat in the warm sunlight that streamed through the window overlooking the courtyard, sipped the wine, and discussed the strange case of a man who'd been dead for thirty years.

"I'm sure of none of it," he said. "That's why you're here. I'm not the only one asking questions. The skull and case were sent in the first instance to the Basileus."

The post of Basileus was one of the most important, his job to oversee all festivals, public ceremonies, and major temples. A priestess who wanted to bring something to the attention of the authorities would naturally go to him first.

Pericles continued, "The Basileus took it to his fellow archons who manage the affairs of Athens, and they in turn brought it to me."

I nodded. "Yes, of course."

It was a strange fact that Pericles, who wielded enormous influence, held no official position at all. The source of his power was that melodious voice, and his astonishing ability to speak in public. Men who would otherwise be considered perfectly rational had been known to listen to Pericles as if bewitched, and then do whatever he said. In the *ecclesia*, where the Athenians met to decide what was to be done, Pericles needed only to make a mild suggestion, and every man present would vote for it. Conversely, if Pericles disapproved of someone's proposal, it had no hope of passing a vote. It had reached the point that no one bothered to introduce legislation without first getting his backing. That a man with no official position wielded so much power had become a source of unease among many of the better families, as well as among the elected officials, who were intensely jealous of his easy command.

Pericles said, "It was agreed this had to be investigated, and incredible as it may seem, your name was mentioned. The recent events at Olympia have gone some way to repairing your reputation."

I'd been unpopular with the archons for some time, ever since I'd accidentally destroyed the agora during my first investigation. One archon had even called me an evil spirit sent to harass Athens, which I thought somewhat cruel.

"Reputation matters," Pericles said, echoing my own thoughts. "Your standing with the older men will be particularly important."

I puzzled over that, then asked, "Why, Pericles?"

"Because they're the only ones who can tell you anything about Hippias. The tyrant belonged to their generation. Not ours. So don't do anything to annoy them, Nicolaos."

"Of course."

"In particular, show the greatest respect to those who fought at Marathon." Pericles paused before going on. "You know that Hippias was at Marathon, on the Persian side?"

"Yes."

"The Persians tried to reinstall Hippias as tyrant over us. The veterans stopped them. You must treat the veterans with care, Nicolaos. They're old men now, and respected, and powerful. The veterans tell a story, that after the battle at Marathon, a signal was flashed to the enemy from behind our own lines. The rumor of a traitor among us has persisted ever since. They say one of the great families of Athens secretly supported Hippias the tyrant."

"Is it true?"

"How in Hades should I know? That's your job. I tell you only because this discovery is sure to revive the rumors. We don't need men finding reasons to accuse each other of treason. We especially don't need it when the elections are due next month."

No, we didn't. The other cities closely watched our grand experiment with democracy. It was in everyone's interest, not only Pericles's, that the voting go smoothly and without trouble. If there was any problem at all during the elections, the other cities would say it was because our form of government was unnatural.

Pericles said, "When word gets out about this body—and it will!—everyone will demand answers."

"Will they? This happened thirty years ago, Pericles. It's ancient history. Nobody cares."

"That's what I thought too. But I was wrong. I'm afraid, Nicolaos, that I've made one of my rare blunders. I've sat on this skull and these scrolls for ten days and done nothing about them; I didn't call you in because I thought, like you, that they didn't matter. But somebody cares. Somebody cares a great deal." Pericles shifted in his seat and looked distinctly uncomfortable. "I told you two girls found the skeleton."

"Yes?"

"One of them's been killed. They say the child was torn apart by some terrible force—"

"Dear Gods!"

"And the other girl's missing."

WHY WOULD ANYONE care about an old skeleton, let alone kill a child over it? It didn't make sense.

I contemplated this as I made my way home. Pericles had

no more to tell me. He'd arranged for one of the priestesses—the one who'd walked from Brauron to Athens to report the disaster—to see me at my home that afternoon.

My family lived in the *deme* of Alopece, which lay just beyond the city wall to the southeast; Pericles lived in Cholargos, beyond the city wall to the northwest. I had to cross virtually all of Athens to make my way home.

I knew these city streets like most men knew their wives. I knew which of the dark, narrow, muddy paths between the houses were shortcuts—these I slipped down, sometimes forced to edge sideways where owners had extended their houses into the street. I knew which routes ended in the blank wall of a house where some builder had encroached a step too far. Most important of all, I knew which alleys afforded the deep, dark shadows, the ones where the cutpurses and the wall-piercers liked to ply their trade. Those streets were good places to avoid.

I knew these things because for a year now I had been an agent and investigator, the only one in Athens. It was a job that didn't pay well. In fact, so far, it hadn't paid at all—Pericles still owed me for my very first commission. Despite my occasional prompts, he'd never quite gotten around to delivering on his end of the bargain. That was Pericles all over. Though he was liberal with expenses when the crisis was upon us, Pericles was a different man when all was calm and the bill arrived. I'd managed to survive so far because my needs were few. I lived in my father's house, as all young men do, and when I was on a job, I could extend the definition of "expenses" beyond its usual borders. Soon, though, I would have no choice but to corner Pericles and force him to cough up my fees, and for a very good reason: when the night of the full moon after next arrived, I would become a man of responsibilities. I would become a married man.

I entered the city proper through the Dipylon Gates in the northwest corner of the city walls, then walked down the Panathenaic Way, which is the city's main thoroughfare. The road is paved, which keeps down the dust, and is so wide that two full-sized carts can pass each other without touching. The Panathenaic Way runs like a diagonal slash through the city. I passed by the Stoa Basileus on my right, the building in which the Basileus who had first received the skull and the scrolls has his offices. Opposite it was the shrine of the crossroads, which confers good luck on all who pass through the busiest intersection in Athens. I hoped some of the luck might pass to me; I would probably need it.

The Panathenaic Way continued along the northern edge of the agora, then down the eastern side. I came to the temple of Hephaestion, which is surrounded by statues of heroes and gods, and then finally to the marketplace, the perfect opportunity to stop for a cup of wine, to sit in the shade of one of the stoas where men liked to congregate, and to watch the crowds as they haggled. I bought the cheapest vintage I could find and walked away with it in a clay cup. I sipped the wine and stood back to watch the chaos that is the agora of Athens.

Any man who wished to sell his wares that day had paid a permit fee to the state official who oversaw such things, then set up his stall. Each stall was a rickety affair, with a crate at each end and a plank across for a bench. The stalls had to be put up with a minimum of fuss at first light, and come down when it was too dark to trade any longer.

Many of the stalls were manned—if that's the word—by women: the wives of the men who had rented them. The fishwives sold the catch, and swore loudly as they did. Their fish-smelling husbands had already worked a full day and now had to tend their boats and mend their nets back at the port at Piraeus before they could sleep. Likewise the farmers' wives had walked into town with their husbands, in the dim dawn light, to sell the farm's vegetables. The men erected stalls for their women to work from, and then returned to tend the farms. So too for the pottery and the bronze ware: the women of the family traded while the potters potted. In Athens, every business was a family business. I reflected that this was true for me as well. My fiancée Diotima had been my work partner from the moment we met, and that wouldn't change after we married.

The children of the traders ran in and out among the legs of the shoppers. Sometimes a child might run into a leg, and then an irritated shopper might give the child a whack about the head, but for the most part the men and women in the agora were tolerant of the children at their feet. And no wonder, because these children were our future. In Athens—in all of Hellas—to survive to adulthood was a minor miracle. There were too many diseases, too many infections, too many ways for a child to die.

There'd been an explosion of babies after the Persian Wars. I'd been one of them. Soldiers who'd fought throughout the duration came home to their wives, and ten months later the midwives had more work than they could handle. It was a good thing, too, because the loss of life had been fearful. Athens desperately needed to renew her citizens. Athenians prayed to Hestia, the goddess of the hearth, that not too many of the children would die before they grew.

I returned home to find my fiancée and my mother together in our courtyard. Diotima stood on a statue plinth—my father being a sculptor, we had plenty of spares—with her arms stretched out to both sides. She was a woman of extraordinary beauty, two years my younger, with long, dark tresses that lay curled that moment over her shoulders. My mother, Phaenarete, held a measuring stick to her side and frowned in concentration.

"What are you doing?" I asked.

My mother, with several sewing needles in her mouth, mumbled, "Measuring her for the wedding dress, of course."

"You want a new dress for your wedding?" I said to my intended. "Don't you already have enough dresses?"

Both of them gave me scathing looks. My mother continued with her measurements.

"How did the meeting with Pericles go?" Diotima asked, quite deliberately changing the subject.

"Interesting," I said. "I have more work." I told her the tale of the strange skull. Diotima listened and didn't move a muscle, which was most unlike her, but she probably didn't want a needle stuck in her while my mother fussed about. When I came to the dead girl and the missing one, my mother gasped and almost choked on the needles. After she'd spat them out, she said, "That's awful!"

I'd known Mother would be displeased. Phaenarete was a midwife and had strong views about children.

But Diotima's reaction astonished me. She staggered backward. She almost fell off the plinth, but managed to step off at the last moment. There were several dining couches in our courtyard. Diotima collapsed onto the nearest and put a hand to her head.

"Diotima, what's wrong?" I said. "Are you all right?"

"Nico, they killed these girls at the sanctuary at Brauron?"

"Yes. Why? Have you heard of it?"

"Of course I've heard of it," she snapped at me, but I could hear the tears forming. "I spent a year there. Nico, I used to be one of those girls. *That was my school.*"

At that moment the house slave walked in to tell me there was a man at the door, demanding to see me. He couldn't have sounded unhappier if he'd been announcing a plague victim. The house slaves had never reconciled themselves to my chosen trade.

"Something about a dead man," the slave said, and jerked his thumb at the front door. "He says he wants to confess to murder."

"MY NAME IS Glaucon. I've come about the death of Hippias," the visitor said.

We spoke in the andron, the room at the front of every house reserved for men to talk business. I'd directed the slave to take Glaucon there.

Glaucon was an older man, perhaps fifty. Well, that was no surprise. Fifty was the minimum age for anyone who might have information about a death that had happened thirty years ago.

"How did you hear about me?" I asked.

"Word is passing among all the veterans of Marathon. They say the body of Hippias has been found."

"That's supposed to be a secret. Only Pericles and the archons and their assistants know."

"Oh, word gets around," he said vaguely.

"I see." I guessed the assistants to the archons had been talking.

"I've come to confess," Glaucon said. "I killed Hippias."

I blinked and waited for the punch line, but then I realized he wasn't joking.

Glaucon said, "When I heard you were on the case, I realized there was no hope of hiding my crime. My best chance was to throw myself on the mercy of the Athenian people."

I rubbed my hands and tried not to look too gleeful. This was going to be my fastest case yet. Pericles would be amazed. But still, I had to make sure. There was one vital point.

I asked, "What of the girls, the dead one and the missing one? Is she still alive? Where is she?"

Glaucon looked at me with an odd expression. He said, "What girls?"

It was my turn to be perplexed. "You don't know?"

"I'd appreciate it if you could announce my guilt as soon as possible," Glaucon said. "Could they schedule my trial for this month, do you think?"

The door slammed open. There stood a complete stranger, an older man with gray hair, who if his straight back and wide shoulders were anything to go by was in good shape. The house slave stood obscured behind him, jumping to see over the intruder's shoulder. Our slave was beside himself with anxiety. "He pushed his way in, master! I couldn't stop him. I'm sorry—"

"What has this mountebank been telling you?" the stranger demanded, glaring at Glaucon.

"Who are you?" I said.

"My name is Hegestratus. I'm a candidate for the post of city treasurer in the next election."

"So?"

"So Glaucon is running, too."

"I fail to see the relevance," I told him. "Glaucon has this moment confessed to the murder of Hippias, the last tyrant of Athens."

"That's utter bull droppings," snapped Hegestratus.

"How do you know?" I challenged him.

"Because *I* killed Hippias. I've come to confess."

AS THE DAY progressed, a small queue of men lined up outside our door, all waiting to confess to the murder of Hippias. They had one thing in common: every one of them was a candidate in the coming elections. Every one of them wanted to enhance his chances by being known as the killer of the most hated man in the city's history. There wasn't the slightest danger to the men in confessing. No jury in Athens would convict them.

There were so many I had to enlist Diotima to take notes.

"It's ridiculous," I groaned. "Why are we doing this?"

"Because everyone wants to know the name of the man who killed Hippias," Diotima said. "So they can congratulate him."

"We'll have to work out who really killed Hippias, and then announce the lucky winner."

"That will be tricky, since it probably happened thirty years ago, and we don't even know how he died," Diotima pointed out. "The skull's nice, but a body would help, even if it's only a skeleton."

"Yes, it would." I'd taken the remains with me, Pericles not having any use for an extra skull. I set it on the table, and Diotima and I had stared at it in fascination. The one thing we knew for sure was that the victim hadn't been knocked on the head: the bone was all in place.

"How many confessions does that make?" I asked Diotima.

Diotima ran her finger down the list and frowned. "Thirty-six," she said.

"It must have been a crowded murder scene."

"Very," Diotima agreed. "Especially since four of them claim to have decapitated Hippias with their swords. Ten knifed him in the chest, eight used spears, and most of the rest strangled him. I wonder if that was before or after the first four had cut off his head?"

There was nothing we could do about it now. We heard a banging on the door, huge resounding thumps. I'd recognize that ham-fisted knocking anywhere: it was Pythax, Diotima's stepfather, and with him would be Diotima's mother, Euterpe.

Diotima and I looked at each other in despair. We were scheduled to marry at the next full moon; our fathers had signed the agreement. Now our parents were about to meet, all four together, for the first time.

CHAPTER TWO

I LIKED THE IDEA of *being* married, I just didn't like the idea of *getting* married.

Getting married meant a ceremony. I disliked ceremonies at the best of times. But worse than that, planning our wedding required my family to talk to Diotima's family, and that was a disaster of such epic proportions as to make the Trojan War look like a mild disagreement.

"A small, private affair, with close friends attending," my mother, Phaenarete, said.

"I was thinking more along the lines of all the best families in Athens," said Euterpe, the mother of my bride. Euterpe was a former high-class courtesan and desperate to establish herself in respectable society.

"I'm afraid that's impossible," said my mother. She'd been quietly respectable all her life. "We couldn't possibly find room for that many people."

What she left unsaid was that we couldn't possibly afford to feed them either.

"We gotta have my guardsmen there," said Pythax.

"You want to invite *slaves* to a citizen wedding?" said my father, Sophroniscus, utterly aghast.

"They're my buddies," Pythax growled. "They'd be insulted if I didn't." Pythax was a new-made citizen, who through his enormous merit had risen from being a slave himself to command of the Scythian Guard of Athens, the men who enforce the peace. Pythax had a foot on each side of the social divide:

not comfortable in his new milieu, but no longer at home in his old.

"I forbid it!" said Sophroniscus, his face purple.

"Who's paying for this?" Pythax demanded.

"We both are," Sophroniscus replied.

It was part of the wedding contract. Each of our fathers thought the other was the richer. They both thought they'd gotten a good deal in the marriage contract. Little did they know they were each as poor as the other, and Diotima and I weren't about to tell them. It meant both our fathers were constantly thinking of reasons why the other should pay for things.

"Pythax, dear husband," said Euterpe. "We couldn't possibly have your friends at the ceremony. Think what the good families would say."

"My friends aren't good enough for you?" Pythax said to his wife.

All four parents fell to arguing.

Diotima and I stood to the side, listening to this disaster in the making. "They can't agree on one single thing," Diotima whispered to me.

"No."

Diotima looked close to tears. This was her wedding day they were destroying. I caught her hand and led her from the house. Even when we stood outside the house, we could still hear the raised voices. So we walked away.

Diotima and I sat, disconsolate, on a low wall at the end of the street. Beside us was a herm, a bust of the god Hermes with an erect phallus carved into its base. The city was dotted with herms; they were meant to bring good luck to those who passed, but I doubted they could do much with difficult parents.

"This is going to be the worst wedding ever," Diotima said. I'd heard men condemned to death sound more cheerful.

I put an arm around her. "No it won't. The worst wedding

ever was the one we performed for ourselves, when we were stuck in that prison."

Diotima looked up at me. "There's not a day goes by that I don't look back on what we did in that prison as the happiest moment of my life. No, that was my true wedding."

"We thought we were about to die," I pointed out.

"Irrelevant."

I didn't recall thinking so at the time, but I wasn't about to argue.

Some small boys had been sidling up to the herm beside us, obviously wondering how they could vandalize it without us noticing. I picked up a handful of pebbles and threw them at the junior criminals. "Go away."

They scattered.

"That was cruel, Nico."

"Nah. There's another herm on the corner they're running toward. They can vandalize that one. But they won't be able to break off its phallus."

"Why not?"

"I did it myself, when I was their age. No one ever fixed it."

A woman walked up the street. She stopped outside our house, hesitated for a moment, then knocked on the door. She looked up and down the street, then started to walk away. At that instant the house slave opened the door. The slave and the woman talked. The slave shook his head.

I said, "That's odd. I wonder who she is?"

"Who?" Diotima had been watching the boys run down the street.

"That woman just knocked on our door, but then she walked away."

Then I remembered that Pericles had sent a priestess to tell me more about the mysterious skull. This must be she. In the excitement of Glaucon coming to confess, I'd forgotten all about it, forgotten even to tell Diotima.

Diotima looked, and looked again, and then her jaw dropped.

The lady came our way. She stopped in front of us.

"Hello, Diotima," she said. "You've grown since I saw you last."

"You know this lady?" I said to Diotima.

With the muffled voices of our parents arguing in the background, which surely the lady could hear but was too polite to mention, Diotima said, in slightly strangled tones, "Nico, I'd like you to meet Doris. She was my teacher."

"I AM THE priestess Doris, from the Temple of Artemis in the deme of Brauron," she said to me.

The priestess Doris was a lady of late middle age. Her hair was gray, held back with a simple clasp of silver that was designed for practicality rather than display. The chiton she wore was of heavy linen and the oldest style; it covered her from shoulders to ankles, respectable and unpretentious. Her sandals were heavy-duty and very dusty, as well they might be since that same day she had walked to Athens.

It was obvious from her carriage, her gentle accent, and the manner of her speech that here was a well-born lady of a certain age; everything about her was simple and composed. I found myself liking Doris, and I was deeply intrigued that she had known Diotima long before I had.

We had escorted Doris to the town house that had once belonged to Diotima's birth father, and which Diotima had inherited a year ago. At the town house we had privacy. The alternative was to take Doris to my home, where our parents continued their long, loud argument over the wedding plans.

Diotima was an heiress. Technically, once we were married, the town house would become mine to manage on her behalf. In practice, I didn't know if we could afford the upkeep. Although Diotima was coming to me with property, there was no income to speak of at all; we would have to rely on my earnings as an agent—those would be the earnings Pericles hadn't paid—and the upkeep on a city house is expensive. Besides which, the pressure on us to move in with my parents was enormous. That was the tradition for newlyweds.

Diotima's town house was empty but for three slaves to maintain it. The chief of these was Achilles, a dapper little man with crippled ankles, whence his slave name.

I had promised Achilles his freedom if Diotima survived our first assignment, an adventure in which he'd had some minor involvement, but Diotima had preempted me by herself offering to free him. Achilles had refused; a slave doesn't have to accept freedom if he doesn't want it. Achilles had explained with these words: "I'm an old man, Mistress Diotima," he'd said. "I wouldn't know what to do with myself if you freed me now. Please don't send me away."

What he'd not said, in his slave's pride, but which Diotima had divined at once, was that a free man can starve, while a slave will be cared for so long as the family has food to put on the table. It's a sacred obligation. So Diotima had sworn an oath to Achilles, that she would care for him to the end of his days and never sell him, and Achilles in his gratitude had become her devoted servant.

Thus it was that Achilles opened the door to us, and we led Doris the priestess into the inner courtyard of what had once been Diotima's father's home. Achilles hobbled off to bring us wine. Diotima took his arm as he went and whispered to bring the best her father had stored. I knew the quality of the cellar in this house, and that told me as much as anything the high esteem in which Diotima held this priestess.

I said, "It's an honor to meet you, Doris. Pericles said you can tell us what happened at the temple."

"Do you know about the sanctuary at Brauron?" she asked me.

I shook my head. "It's a girl thing."

Doris laughed. "And therefore men don't need to know about it? Wait until you have daughters."

Achilles brought in a tray of food and set it before Doris: olives and bread and sliced quince and a bowl of lentils. He returned with a krater of wine mixed with water. Achilles ladled a cup for each of us.

Doris was hungry. She dipped her right hand into the lentils. "I haven't eaten since breakfast, and that was before first light. I hope you'll excuse me."

"That's why the food is there," I said.

Diotima said, "It's wonderful to see you, Doris. I often think back to my time at Brauron."

"For our part we've been following your career with the greatest interest. You made quite a spectacle of yourself in that court case last year—our High Priestess wasn't entirely pleased about that, by the way; she felt it might reflect on the temple—and the word we hear is something happened at the last Olympics. The truth is, my dear, that in the small world of our sanctuary, you've become something of a celebrity."

Doris spoke between mouthfuls.

"Our temple has always been a haven for girls," she said to me, licking her fingers. "The wealthiest and most powerful families in Athens send their daughters to us. The girls are called the Little Bears. For most of them, it's the first time they've ever lived away from home. It's good training for marriage." Doris paused. "In fact, the reputation of the sanctuary for turning out young ladies of quality is unsurpassed. Fathers have been known to offer bribes and even fight to have their daughters admitted."

"Yet *Diotima* got in?" I grinned.

"Thank you very much!" Diotima said, in mock anger. She threw a cup at me. I caught it easily, as she intended, and I set it aside.

Yet the question was genuinely asked, because although Diotima was a perfect lady in her manners and her education, and although her father had been a statesman of the highest regard, it was all too well known that her mother had also been at the top of *her* profession. Which was, unfortunately . . . prostitution. Or more accurately, until she married Pythax, Diotima's mother had been a courtesan.

Diotima's birth was as irregular as you could get. It meant she wasn't even a citizen: Diotima was a metic, a resident alien, in the city of her birth.

"Diotima was something of an exception," Doris said.

No surprise there.

Doris said, "Her father's influence made a place for her, and though I have no knowledge of it, I wouldn't be surprised if there'd been a significant donation to the temple treasury."

I wouldn't be surprised either. That's how things were done in Athens, and her birth father was no longer around to ask.

"The girls stay with us for a year, usually when they're fourteen. It's the age right before their marriages are arranged. That was the situation with Ophelia."

"Who?"

"The child who's gone missing. Friend to Allike, the poor girl who died." Doris wiped her brow and grimaced. "This is the worst I've ever known the sanctuary to be. You've no idea how distraught everyone is."

"Could you start from the beginning, Doris?" Diotima said. "We need to know what happened, in the order it happened."

"Yes, of course. I'm sorry, dear. I'm upset about the children. Who wouldn't be?"

"Understandable."

"I begin, then, with that accursed skeleton, the source of all our woes." Doris turned to me. "You must know first of all, Nicolaos, that we allow the girls considerable freedom; well, you'd know that, wouldn't you, Diotima dear? But not your Nicolaos, who knows nothing of daughters. We play outdoor games. The girls exercise, hold running races, sometimes cross-country runs that take them into the woods. It's perfectly safe, I assure you—or at least, it used to be. There's been talk of bear sightings recently—I don't know if I believe it—and now of course there's the murderer out there somewhere . . . but it used to be safe.

"Last month, two of the girls, Allike and her friend Ophelia, returned from the woods to say they'd passed by a cave. Well, Greece is hilly and there are many caves, but they poked their heads into this one, and there they saw a human skeleton."

I interrupted. "Doris, you said this happened last month. What day, do you remember?"

"I can tell you exactly. It was *hena kai nea*."

Old and new; the last day of the month, meaning the end of the old moon, with the new moon to follow.

"Go on."

"The girls ran home to report it, very properly, in much excitement. It's not the first time someone's found a body, but usually it's a traveler who's died on the road, or an aged farmer who's expired on his land. There was one of those only recently; he lived alone and nobody noticed for months, poor man. But a skeleton in a cave was a new one for all of us. I'm afraid Allike and Ophelia made the most of their notoriety. Their story enlarged with every telling."

"Weren't they afraid?"

"Children don't fear death. They don't understand that one day it will happen to them."

"Oh."

"The priestesses assembled as a group—after Ophelia and Allike managed to convince us they weren't making this up—and the two girls led us to the cave. It was slow going, because the High Priestess insisted on accompanying us, but we got there eventually. Sure enough, there was the skeleton. The cave was large, as caves go, but to spot it one had to round a large rock and squeeze through a gap. It was no wonder no one had discovered the place until now."

"What did you do?"

"The first problem was the lingering *psyche*."

Diotima and I both nodded. A dead person's psyche lingers on earth until the body has been buried according to the proper rites.

"We left offerings to placate the psyche, then gathered the bones and carried them back to the temple. To give whoever it was a proper ceremony, you see. At least, that was the plan. But the next day was Noumenia, and it would have been terrible bad luck to perform any ceremony during the new moon."

Noumenia is a particularly sacred day, when no Hellene would willingly conduct business of any importance. Little wonder that the women of the temple had recoiled at the idea of a burial.

"The day after that, two of the girls came down with high fevers—"

"Not Allike and Ophelia?"

"A different two. It's not like we're short of girls to fall ill. Fever in a place such as ours can spread like wildfire, and children are much more likely to die than adults. Whenever a girl in our charge is sick, we drop everything to treat her and make sure the others don't get it. The girls survived, I'm happy to say, but days passed before anyone thought of the bones.

"That was when we discovered that Sabina had gotten it into her head to tell the Basileus. She'd read the scrolls in the case—I think she was the only one to do so—and sent him the material."

"Sabina is?"

"One of the priestesses, and an interfering little busybody, if you ask me. The High Priestess was furious. She felt that whatever this was, whoever it was, it was all in the past, and the publicity would do no one any good, and I must say I agree. But what was done was done."

"Did you bury the bones?"

"We planned a cremation, but there was no point until the skull was restored, or we'd only have had to do a second ceremony."

"I have the skull. Would you like it?"

"No, thank you very much! You can bring it with you when you visit Brauron. You *are* coming to Brauron, aren't you?"

"Of course. We have a murder to investigate."

"I'm very sorry about Allike," Diotima said. "How did she die?"

Doris hesitated. "She was . . . badly hurt. I don't like to think about it."

"Beaten?" I asked. "Stabbed?"

Doris hid her head in her hands and wept deeply. Hellenes like to declare their grief with lavish display, but it was clear that Doris's was from the heart.

Diotima left my side, to put her arm around Doris. "I'm so sorry," she said once more.

I said, "But Doris, we need to know what happened. Can you tell it now?"

"Yes." Doris used the hem of her chiton to wipe her face. "The girls take it in turns to do the after-dinner chores. We insist they do it themselves and not rely on the temple's slaves, because when they're grown and mistresses of their own households, they'll need to know everything about running a house, or how will they manage their own slaves? That night, Allike carried the bucket of scraps out to the compost, and she never returned."

Which probably meant that the killer had been stalking the sanctuary grounds.

"When did you notice she was missing?"

"When we sent the girls to bed. It's hard to keep track of who's where in the evenings, but an empty bed in the dorm rooms is obvious. Someone said, 'Where's Allike?' We searched, we walked all about with bright torches and called her name, but she never appeared."

"Go on."

"We mounted a major search the next day. Every adult, even the slaves. We found her body that afternoon, some distance away, beyond several hills."

"Then whoever took her knew the area."

"Or carried a torch," Diotima said.

Doris said, "We thought there was some madman out in the woods. We didn't connect Allike's death with the skeleton. Not until Ophelia disappeared two days later."

"You didn't lose her the same way, did you?"

"It's inexplicable! After the disaster of Allike, we ringed the sanctuary with guards and forbade all the girls to be alone. But Ophelia just disappeared, overnight."

"Maybe she ran away on her own?"

"Ophelia wasn't the type. I can spot them. That was when we realized Allike and Ophelia were the two who'd discovered the skeleton. The coincidence was too much."

It was too much for me, too. I said, "You think she was taken too, then."

"It seems the obvious answer, doesn't it? When our problems came upon us, and we didn't know what to do, someone suggested we call for you. The High Priestess resisted at first—she has a horror of publicity and thought your presence might call unwanted attention to our problems. But when time passed and the child Ophelia didn't appear, well, it was clear what had to be done."

So that was why my name had come up. Not because of the archons, but because the High Priestess of the sanctuary had asked for me by name, because one of her former pupils was my betrothed.

"Then my client is the sanctuary," I said.

Doris shrugged. "If you think of it like that. I'm more inclined to think of a child who needs your help, if she's still alive. But I'm very much afraid that her body's out there in the woods, somewhere. And now I wonder, who else might die?"

CHAPTER THREE

NEXT MORNING, BY the time I had finished breakfast, there were already men at our door, all wanting to confess to murder, every one of them a candidate for a post in the new democratic government. Every one of them looked confused when I asked about dead and missing girls. Not a single one of them knew anything useful.

I was considering putting a CLOSED FOR BUSINESS sign on our front door when I was saved by a slave boy with a message from Pericles. He wanted to see me.

I found Pericles at his desk, bent over piles of notes and papers. He held a stylus in his right hand with which he scribbled notes on a wax tablet. He looked up as I entered.

"I hope you're not about to confess to killing Hippias," I said.

Pericles put down the stylus and looked at me strangely. "How can you say such a thing, Nicolaos? I was only a child at the time."

"Thank goodness for that."

"No," Pericles continued. "It was my father who killed Hippias. I admit it in the interests of justice."

I groaned.

"After you left yesterday, I gave it some thought, and looked through the papers of my father Xanthippus. Imagine my surprise when I came across a note in which he says he killed Hippias."

"I'm imagining your surprise."

"I can certify the authenticity of the handwriting—"

"I'm sure you can."

"So you see, Nicolaos, you'll be able to stop the investigation early. I'll take the note to the courts tomorrow and explain everything."

"You'll have to stand in line."

"What do you mean?"

I told him of the queue of wannabe killers. Pericles looked chagrined. No doubt he was thinking he should have thought of the scam earlier.

"You're not standing for election, by any chance, are you?" I asked.

"As it happens, by sheer coincidence, I am," he said. "I'm running for the office of *strategos*. The advantages of the post will be immediately obvious to you."

"Yes, of course," I told him, while desperately trying to think of the advantages. A strategos is a commanding general of the army. The Athenians elect ten *strategoi* each year, one from each of the ten tribes, to command the armed forces of our city on both land and sea.

"Er . . . why don't you go for archon instead?" I asked. "I would have thought a civil administration position would be more your style."

Pericles sighed. "You don't understand, do you? The archons run Athens, which I'll grant you is a post of great importance. But the archons have no say in foreign policy, a subject in which I must have influence if I'm to guide Athens. The voice of a strategos, on the other hand, carries weight in any subject concerning other cities. Furthermore, an archon holds the job for only a year, and then can never hold it again. A strategos, on the other hand—mark this closely, Nicolaos—a strategos can be re-elected year after year, with no limit to the number of times he holds the post."

Pericles's grand vision swam before my eyes. Every public role was to be filled by election. Pericles had selected the *only* position of influence that a man could hold repeatedly, because whereas the city can survive an incompetent archon for a year, an incompetent general in charge of the army could destroy us in a single battle.

Pericles intended to control Athens for the rest of his life by getting himself elected to strategos and re-elected year after year, which given his abilities he surely could.

"That's brilliant. It's almost like being a tyrant, without being a tyrant," I mused.

"It's no such thing!" Pericles shouted in horror. "And don't you dare say those words outside this room. I tell you this only so you will understand the importance of your actions. With all this talk of Hippias and Marathon going around, people's minds are fixated on the older men, the heroes who fought at Marathon. It means the old men are more likely to be elected. Again. That's wrong, Nicolaos. Athens needs younger men to guide her. Men of the next generation."

By which he meant himself. Apparently, being the son of one of our greatest war heroes wasn't enough. Xanthippus, the father of Pericles, had died three months before. I'd attended his funeral, and not out of politeness. I'd come to like Xanthippus, and was sad to see him go. He was a crusty old war hero, demanding, difficult to get on with, but honorable as few men are. I was glad he'd lived to see his son become leader of Athens.

"I need all this talk shut down. As soon as possible. So voters will stop thinking about the past and start thinking about the future."

"There's another problem, Pericles," I said. I told him the evidence of Doris the priestess. "So you see, your suspicions about the girls are almost certainly correct. Whoever killed Hippias probably attacked the children."

"But Nicolaos, a gap of thirty years? No killer hangs around the scene that long."

"Then they must be associated, somehow. Nothing else makes sense. Either way, as long as there's a chance she's still alive, finding the girl must be the priority."

"She's only a girl. Affairs of state come first."

I barely prevented myself from shouting, only by grinding my teeth and reminding myself that Pericles's attitude was normal. I'd known he'd take this view and come prepared. I said, "Then think of it this way, Pericles. The death of Hippias is so old, it's almost impossible to trace. I could beat my head against that case for months and get nowhere. The recent action against the children must be an easier path, and will surely lead to the same person."

Pericles paced for a moment, as he liked to do in private, while he thought about it. "Very well, I can see the logic of that. Yes, the girls are the quickest route to the mystery of Hippias, which has implications for the coming elections. I see your plan. I suppose you intend to go to Brauron?"

"Yes. But I'll need some fast transport. I must be back and forth to Athens. I have an appointment with fate."

"Oh?"

"I'm getting married," I said proudly.

Pericles pursed his lips in distaste. "That Diotima woman, no doubt."

"Of course."

"You're young to be marrying," he said.

I shrugged. It was true, but I was happy. Most men married at thirty. I would be wed at twenty-one.

"A man of your station, with your prospects, you could do better."

I knew Pericles had never liked Diotima, but his words made me angry. So much so that I raised the thorny issue between us. "There's another matter we must discuss, Pericles, before I continue. My pay."

"You'll be paid," he promised.

"I meant payment for the *first* commission you ever gave me." If Pericles had any skill greater than his rhetoric, it was his ability to avoid spending money. "You offered me a small, steady income if I succeeded. Well, I succeeded, but you never paid me. This can't go on, Pericles. Soon I'll be a man with responsibilities. If I'm to take on this new commission, I must have payment for the first."

"Oh." Pericles sat down and drummed his fingers on the desk. They made a loud sound in the silence. I waited, knowing he couldn't rightly deny the debt, especially not when he needed me now. Eventually he said, "I admit there's been a certain amount of inadvertent tardiness. Very well, Nicolaos. I'll see to it."

"When?"

"Before ten days have passed. Does that suit you?"

I'd heard such promises before, but I could hardly call Pericles a liar to his face. "Yes," I said reluctantly.

"Good. I'm glad we have that sorted. Now, what is your next course of action?"

"I must discover who knew about Hippias. Only someone who knew that we had the body, or what was left of it, could have committed these crimes. Tell me, Pericles, how long between the Basileus receiving the package and the archons coming to see you?" I asked.

Pericles hesitated. "I didn't ask," he said. "I should think it rested with the Basileus for at least a day before he got around to it. He's a busy man. Then he had to arrange a meeting with his fellow archons. Then they had to come see me next day. All together it would be . . . three days? Five days?" he hazarded.

"Plenty of time for someone to learn of the rumor of a skull and scroll case," I said. "It would mean nothing to anyone who didn't know the story, but to the true killer, it would mean his crime had been discovered. Plenty of time, too, to send an agent to deal with the rest of the evidence, including the children who found the body."

"You may be right," Pericles admitted. "If so, it means something else. Whoever killed Hippias still has something to hide."

"What, with everyone else lining up to confess?"

"Don't you see, Nicolaos? Upright citizens want to be known as his killer. But the true killer . . . remember I told you, there were rumors, at the time, that someone or some people within Athens were secretly dealing with Hippias and the Persians."

The implication was clear. Those traitors, identity unknown, were still among us, and they'd turned to killing.

DORIS HAD DEPARTED early, to let the sanctuary know we were on the way. Before we left, I had to convince our parents that it was all right for Diotima and me to be a mere half-day's travel away. I expected our parents would be happy to have us out of the way while they arranged our lives for us, and Diotima and I were as happy not to have to watch it happening.

Diotima's stepfather, Pythax, had grunted his agreement while he drilled his Scythian Guard at the barracks and told me to stay out of trouble.

The mothers proved more difficult. For some reason neither of them trusted us. I had to promise to return my bride whenever necessary for wedding arrangements. Or as Phaenarete put it, "We've already sent out invitations to our friends. If I find out you two have disappeared to some foreign city, I'll send your fathers to hunt you down and kill you." And Euterpe had nodded grimly at those words and offered in such an eventuality to supply the instruments of torture. It was the only time I'd ever seen the mothers-in-law-to-be agree on anything.

My surprise came when I asked my father for permission. Sophroniscus had been in his workshop as usual, chiseling marble for his latest piece. He put down his chisel and turned to face me with an expression as hard as any I'd ever seen upon my sire.

He said, "Son, I understand that this dead man is Hippias the Tyrant?"

"It's not certain, Father. But probably, yes."

"Then the man you seek once supported Hippias?"

"It's one possibility."

"You didn't live through the days of the tyrant."

"No, sir."

"You can't know what this means. I was only a young man myself," my father mused, recalling those days. "Hippias was evil, beyond a shadow of a doubt. I don't know how many men he killed, merely on suspicion that they might be plotting against him. Your grandfather—my father—do you know they came for him once?"

I was startled. I'd never known my grandsire. "Sir? No, why?"

"For the crime of saying a good word about a man who'd been arrested, a friend of my father's who had spoken out against the tyranny. He was an honest man who paid for it. Other men were killed merely for looking at the tyrant with the wrong expression."

"Then . . . how did my grandsire survive?" I asked, perplexed. Father had never spoken of this before.

"By bribing the guards who came for him. He gave them almost everything we owned to leave him alone, a man who was entirely innocent. I was present. I saw my own father beg for his life. He fell upon his knees before men in his own courtyard. He died shortly after. I don't think he ever recovered from the shame of it."

"I didn't know," I said.

"And I've never forgotten. It impoverished us. We've never regained the wealth we once had. Do you know why I fought the battle at Marathon?" Father asked.

"To defeat the Persians, sir."

"Wrong! I fought, and I killed, to keep Hippias from returning. The Persians brought the old tyrant with them and, if they'd won, they would have restored Hippias to power."

He looked off into the distance, and I knew he was remembering.

"I was sure, as we marched in, that it was my last day on earth," he said quietly. "I was never a good soldier, but I had to do what I could. You know we were outnumbered ten to one?"

"Yes, Father."

"I fought anyway. Because anything, *anything* was better than life under Hippias."

He picked up his hammer and chisel.

"Very well, son. I didn't approve when you took up this investigation work. I thought it was foolish, a waste of time. But I've changed my mind. Not only do I give you permission to hunt down these traitors, but I do *not* give you permission to do anything else until you have. If that means your marriage must wait, then so be it.

"Because *anything* is better than allowing the supporters of Hippias to live."

Sophroniscus brought down his hammer in an angry arc. It struck the workbench beside him. The wooden top splintered under the force of the blow. My father barely seemed to have noticed.

I swallowed back the lump in my throat. There was only one thing I could say to that.

"Yes, sir."

I'D ANTICIPATED WE'D be back and forth to Athens while the investigation at Brauron went on. I was determined travel time would not slow us down at either end, and nor should my bride have to wear down her feet with a lot of walking right before her wedding. Diotima couldn't ride a horse, but anyone can drive a cart. Incredibly, my father didn't even own a cart, so I had to hire one.

There are many roads out of Athens, and almost every one of them has a cart-rental place just outside the gates. The Sacred Way, which leads out of the Dipylon Gate in the direction of Eleusis, has a whole row of them. These people make money by renting wheeled carts to casual travelers, and the beasts to pull them: donkeys, mules, and even horses. If a man doesn't own a country estate, then he doesn't need such things every day, and a beast is expensive to keep in the center of Athens. Cheaper, then, to hire transport when you need it. The only problem is, the men who rent out these things have a reputation for dodgy practices. No one ever accused a cart renter of excessive honesty.

It just so happened that the deme we lived in—Alopece—was outside the city walls to the south, and therefore lay along the road from Athens to Brauron. We could have gone straight on to Brauron from my father's house, but I had to walk back toward Athens, to the Diomean Gate, to find a cart to rent. Diotima insisted on coming with me.

"I don't trust you not to come back with a racehorse," she'd said.

There were three rental businesses beside the Diomean Gate, one after the other. The first, directly outside the city gate, was clean, well swept, immaculate. A cart had been placed out front to advertise the business, well painted and polished until it gleamed. Tethered to the cart was a horse: sleek, fit, alert. I knew a little bit about horses. I could see at once this was a fine beast. But to be sure, I raised a hoof to inspect the underside. I wanted to know how much distance the animal had covered, which I figured I could tell from how much the hoof had worn.

"Can I help you, sir?" A man appeared beside me from nowhere. He was dressed in a chiton of fine white linen, and his hair was cut and swept back and oiled until it gleamed. He smiled at me with perfect teeth.

"I want to hire a horse and cart," I said.

"Of course, sir."

"This one looks interesting."

"Sir has an eye for quality transport. The horse is a proven performer, well trained for cart work and with nothing but praise from previous drivers. The accompanying cart, as you can see, is in top condition and was repainted only last month. The wheels are solid-oak rims with no wear or tear; the axle is newly greased.

I see sir has his lady with him. We offer complimentary feather cushions for her traveling comfort."

It sounded perfect. "How much for a month?" I asked him eagerly.

The salesman named a sum.

I staggered back in shock.

"I could *buy* a horse and cart for that much," I choked. "I tell you what, I'll pay you half that."

"I'm afraid sir is under the misapprehension that we're a charity."

"Don't you have anything cheaper?"

The salesman pursed his lips. "Well, if sir wishes, we do have our economy stock, if you would care to inspect."

I looked about, but all I could see were other horses and carts like the ones we stood beside.

"Where is it?"

"Out the back. We keep the lower-rent animals where they're less . . . visible. One doesn't wish to advertise."

He led us out the back. Behind the pristine road-facing building was a stable made of dull-gray, weathered wood that was so termite-riddled it was probably hollow. The manure from the horses out front had been shoveled and heaped beside the stable. I wrinkled my nose and waved at the buzzing flies.

Ancient leather harnesses were draped over a small paddock fence. Within the paddock, a small herd of ponies watched us with an utter lack of interest.

"Where are the carts?"

"Over there." The salesman pointed to a row of small, serviceable carts. If you squinted hard, you could tell what color they had once been painted.

"What about this one?" Diotima was inspecting a scrawny animal, not within the paddock, but tethered to the fence. It stood on thin legs and seemed about to collapse.

"Diotima, that's a donkey."

"I'm aware of that, Nico." Diotima patted the animal's neck. The donkey was all patchy skin with bones sticking out. It wore an old straw hat that had been eaten by something. I wondered if it had some terrible disease and whether Diotima should be touching it.

I said, "It's the worst donkey in the whole yard."

"That's because it's the only donkey in the yard, Nico."

"It may be the worst donkey in the whole world."

"But Nico, he's *so cute*!"

I inspected the animal for any sign of cuteness. The donkey looked back at me with large, soulful eyes. They seemed to be the only functioning part of the creature.

Staring at the knobbly knees, I said, "That wretched thing can barely stand, let alone pull a cart with you on it. Aren't you the one who came along to make sure I didn't waste money on a racehorse?"

"I'm fairly sure this isn't a racehorse, Nico," she said, then she turned to the salesman and said, "Have you people being mistreating this donkey?"

"By no means, madam. In fact he only arrived the other day. It's a very sad story." The salesman rubbed his chin. "The animal's only had one owner, a little old lady who used it to carry herbs to the agora on market days. The old dear died peacefully in her sleep, but I'm afraid no one noticed for some time—her son was the neglectful sort—you know how it is—when they finally found her corpse, somewhat mummified, the beast was in the yard, tethered and almost starved to death. The son had no use for the animal and sold him on to us. Unfortunately he's proven impossible to rent. Well, you can see why. If we don't find a customer for him soon, he'll have to go to the knacker's."

The donkey looked up at Diotima in utter despair.

"We'll take him."

"Diotima!" I said.

"Nico, we can't let this poor creature suffer a moment longer."

"You can't save every donkey in the world."

"I'm not. I'm saving one donkey. This one. What's his name?" she asked the salesman.

"His name, madam? I believe the little old lady called him Blossom."

The donkey wouldn't be as fast as I wished, but it would still be faster than walking, and Diotima's feet mattered more than a few coins. I sighed. "Does he come with the hat?" I asked.

"I'm sure a new hat could be thrown in with our compliments."

I nodded.

The salesman called, "Philippos! Get your ass out here. We got a customer."

A head that was gray enough to match the surrounding wood appeared from within the darkness of the stable.

"Philippos is our back-of-house manager. I'll leave you to sort out the details with him. He deals with all the donkeys, mules, and asses."

The salesman walked rapidly away, to the front yard.

"What he means is, I'm a slave," Philippos said, unnecessarily. I'd already worked that out.

It didn't take long to negotiate. At least the price was inside our budget. The only problem was the deposit. Philippos demanded three times what Blossom was worth. When I protested he said, "Look, mate. The problem is, half the donkeys we hire out don't come back. You know why?"

I looked at the row of miserable-looking beasts in the paddock and took a guess.

"They died of terminal mange?"

"Very funny. No, people steal them. But it's never the clients, mind you. Oh no! They always claim they left the donkey tied up outside a tavern, and when they came out, it was gone."

But a deposit is money you get back later, so I didn't mind so much. We concluded the deal, hitched Blossom to a cart, and with a certain amount of pushing got the contraption going.

WE DISCUSSED THE case as we walked home. Or rather, I walked while Diotima sat proudly in her new cart, pulled by Blossom, who plodded along beside me. Diotima had carefully placed a new straw hat on Blossom's head, cutting two holes for the ears, and tied a string to the hat and around the animal's neck. "So the hat doesn't fall off and he doesn't get sunstroke," she explained. She was more worried about the donkey getting sunstroke than me.

Now she held the reins as Blossom plodded, and we talked about murder.

"It's really quite simple," Diotima said. "Thirty years ago, Hippias died. It might or might not have been murder. You'll notice we don't know for sure how he died. For all we know, it could have been disease, or old age."

"We'll have to read those scrolls," I said. "There's no telling what's in there."

"Yes," Diotima conceded. "But the situation with the girls is entirely different. There we have a very real crime, and a very current murderer. The priority must be the missing girl, Nico."

"The three crimes are linked," I insisted. "The death of Hippias, the murder of Allike, and the disappearance of Ophelia."

"Maybe. Think how her poor parents must feel, Nico. Her father must be frantic."

WE ARRIVED AT my parents' home to be told there was a man waiting to see me in the andron; he'd arrived while we were out. I was rank with sweat and the smell of donkey, so I quickly stripped in the back courtyard and poured a bucket of water over myself before I went to see the stranger.

He rose to greet me when I entered, still damp and dripping in the material of the fresh *exomis* I'd hastily pulled on. The exomis covered my body but ended at the shoulders and thighs, leaving my arms and legs free to move. It was the standard working dress of any artisan. It had also become my favored wear as a working investigator. Maximum freedom of movement in a crisis could be the difference between life and death.

My visitor was dressed in the most formal of ankle-length chitons, with a *himation* of pure wool draped about his shoulders. His black hair was graying at the temples, though thick enough, and his skin had the dried look of a man who spent long days out of doors. He was clearly a wealthy landowner and a man far above my station. I was relieved to see the house slaves had given him food and wine, and that he sat on the most comfortable couch. I invited him to sit once more and placed myself opposite. Was this a new client?

He looked me up and down. His eyes didn't miss my workman's clothing, nor the obvious fact that I was half his age. I knew that in his thoughts, he'd halved my importance.

"My name is Polonikos. I'm the father of Ophelia."

Of course. Ophelia's father was in Athens. That's where the families of most of Brauron's Little Bears came from. I should have thought of that before.

"I'm glad you came to see me," I said, and meant it. I was lucky I hadn't gone all the way to Brauron only to discover I had to return to interview the missing girl's father. "But how do you know about me? How did you know where to find me?"

"The priestess Doris visited me this morning to tell me there was no news, and that you'd been asked to look for Ophelia. I came to see you at once."

"Did you already know your daughter was missing?"

"Of course. The High Priestess wrote to me on the day she disappeared."

"You didn't go to Brauron at once?"

"Urgent business matters held me in Athens."

"You sent your own agent, then?"

"No."

I struggled not to show surprise. If I had a missing daughter, I'd be tearing the hills apart looking for her.

I said, "It was the priestess Doris who asked us to find Ophelia."

"Us?"

"My fiancée and I."

Polonikos frowned.

"I realize you've never heard of me, Polonikos, but I'm an experienced investigator, and my fiancée's been of the greatest assistance in the past. Also, she was once a Little Bear herself, and her knowledge will be invaluable in finding your daughter." It wouldn't hurt to mention that. Polonikos was acting like he doubted our qualifications. "Rest assured, sir, we'll find your daughter."

"Yes, very kind of you both, I'm sure. But there's no need to trouble yourselves."

It took me a moment to realize what he'd said, and then I thought I must have misheard. "Huh? What did you say?"

"I said, you don't need to bother searching for Ophelia. I have the matter well in hand."

"Er . . . sir . . . didn't you just say you'd done nothing?"

"I'm sure my daughter merely ran away from a situation she disliked," he said, in a tone that suggested no other thought was possible. "You know how children will do these things. She'll find her way home eventually, take her beating, and then all will be forgotten and life will go on."

"You're asking me to stop?" I repeated, unable to believe what I was hearing.

"I don't think you've quite understood, young man. I'm not *asking* you anything." His tone moved from polite to angry in one breath. "I'm *telling* you that your services are not required."

"Doesn't it worry you that your daughter's friend Allike has been brutally murdered? Sir, we know that for sure. Are you not afraid your daughter has met the same fate?"

"I think it more likely this other girl's death spooked my

daughter—understandably—and she's run off to hide. Trust me, I know my own child."

Polonikos was clearly a man not used to having his will opposed.

He continued, "I appreciate your concern, young man, and also that until this moment you didn't know my wishes in this matter. Please send me a bill for whatever actions you've taken to date, and I'll pay you."

"I'm afraid you're not my client, sir. I'm acting in the interests of the Sanctuary of Brauron, and they want Ophelia found."

"You refuse me?" he said, incredulous.

"I must. Only the temple can ask me to stop."

"Then I shall write to the High Priestess at the temple and require her to sack you, in which case there will be no compensation from me whatsoever."

"I never asked for it, sir," I said, becoming angry. I certainly couldn't stop him writing to the High Priestess. "I must say, sir, you seem to have a relaxed attitude to missing children."

"If it were a first-born son, that would be different," he said. "Losing a mere girl isn't the same thing at all."

I was suddenly glad that Diotima wasn't with us.

He stood. "I must go. My final word is this: you are not wanted and I will thank you not to poke your nose into my business. I expect to see your settlement bill in the morning. I'm prepared to be generous."

I saw the father of Ophelia to the door, where two slaves waited to escort their master home. Like many men of dignity, Polonikos wouldn't have been seen dead in the streets of Athens without a couple of slaves in attendance. He was obviously a man who liked to do things the traditional, old-fashioned way. I watched Polonikos walk down the street until he turned the corner before I shut the door.

One thing was certain. I'd been dubious about taking on this job, but now that I'd spoken to her father, I was absolutely determined to find Ophelia.

—

DIOTIMA SAT IN the courtyard, chewing her lip and reading the four scrolls from the case.

"Anything there?" I asked her.

"Plenty, if we want to blackmail men who were dead long before either of us was born." Diotima threw down the scroll she was holding in disgust. "These are all Hippias's private dealings. He couldn't stop himself writing down all the sordid things he did. This one"—Diotima picked up the scroll in front of her—"this one is all about when he first became tyrant. He expresses hope for the future, even tells himself he wants to be a fair ruler." Diotima touched the next two scrolls. "In these, the tyranny's in full swing. He mostly records who's vulnerable to what pressure, who he can blackmail, who hates whom so he can use one man against another. It's depressing.

"This final one," she said, picking up the fourth scroll, "begins with the death of his brother. There was a plot against them. The brother was killed, but Hippias survived. Hippias becomes paranoid . . . well, I guess if everyone hates you, it's not really paranoia, is it? He writes copious notes about who his enemies are. Imagines plots everywhere." She sounded distraught. "It's the arbitrary way he decides life and death that's simply horrific. Listen to this." She rolled through to the end.

> *Have discovered from local source that the girl was hidden near my own estates. She will go on the next execution list. The last thing I require is another Elektra.*

Diotima put down the scroll. "Then in the next section, he wrote her into an arrest list." She looked up at me. "He was killing people on a whim, Nico, or if he feared them, or if he merely disliked them. He was even executing *children*. Athens was right to rebel against him."

I said, "I don't understand the reference to Elektra."

Diotima shrugged. "Elektra was the daughter of King Agamemnon of legend. When he was murdered, Elektra grew to avenge him. Perhaps Hippias had killed this girl's father and he was afraid that, like Elektra, the girl would come to avenge the father."

There were tears in her eyes.

I put an arm around her. "That's why we're a democracy now."

"Yes."

"What did he write after he was exiled?"

"Nothing. The fourth ends with the growing rebellion against him. He saw it coming, Nico, but he couldn't stop it. Then it ends abruptly."

"Hippias was exiled twenty years before he died."

"There's a spare slot in the case. You're thinking what I'm thinking, aren't you?"

"There's another scroll. I wonder where it is."

THAT AFTERNOON, DIOTIMA and I rode to Brauron. Or rather, she rode and I walked. To my surprise, Blossom proved capable of pulling the cart over a long distance. He was stronger than he looked. There was only room for my girl on the driver's bench. I tried riding Blossom, but from the way he staggered it was soon apparent Blossom was more likely to need me to carry him. I got off and walked alongside and thought longingly of the high-performance racehorse.

The wheels on the cart had creaked and squealed with every turn on the way home from the rental yard. I'd turned the cart over with the help of a slave and coated the axle with lavish amounts of the pig fat we kept in barrels for the statuary sledge. If there was one thing our family knew about, it was how to move large blocks of stone, for which we kept a heavy sledge and many barrels of grease to ease its way. By the time I'd finished, both I and the cartwheels had been smothered in grease. Which is probably why Blossom was able to pull it. The rims of the wooden wheels were chipped, but sturdy enough to get us to Brauron and back. While I worked on the cart, Diotima had washed the donkey and then fed him so much hay I thought he might explode.

At first Blossom wasn't in any hurry, possibly because of his full stomach. I prodded him a few times and discovered he had more spirit than appearance suggested. But then, if someone called me Blossom, I'd probably bite him too.

I grumbled all the way. I'd spent much of the last six months out of Athens, but I hadn't realized how much I'd missed the place until I returned. Now here I was leaving my city once again, though it was the job I'd accepted, and we weren't going far. Still, I hated the idea.

Diotima, who had made this trip with her birth father when she was a girl, treated it like a happy outing. She took great delight in pointing out the sights she remembered and prattled on like a delighted child. I grunted from time to time in reply.

She eventually became exasperated by my surliness.

"You should have more appreciation for nature, Nico. There's so much to see: the birds and the flowers—they're pretty, aren't they? The trees and the small animals and—"

"And the naked woman running through the woods," I said.

"And the naked woman running through the . . . what?"

I pointed. Diotima gaped.

Running alongside the road, weaving between the bushes and moving at impressive speed, was a naked woman. At least, if she was wearing a shred of clothing, I couldn't see it. She ran like an athlete in training, slim and trim and in tip-top condition. She leapt a fallen log with an easy stride, and her breasts bounced.

"You're right, Diotima, the local wildlife is fascinating. I'm looking forward to seeing more of it."

The running woman turned away from the road and sprinted out of sight, back amongst the trees, without slackening her pace for even a moment. She'd shown no sign of noticing us.

Diotima whispered, "Dear Gods. What's she doing here?"

"I assume that's not the girl we're looking for."

"Did she look fourteen to you?" Diotima said.

"Not even close," I said happily. Her hair had been long and straight, not at all like a pampered lady's, but her skin had been as clean as could be while running through the forest. "Do you think there might be a flock of women in the hills around here somewhere?" I asked in hope.

Diotima didn't deign to answer.

The road split ahead of us. The main road curved right. It would soon take us to Brauron if we stayed on it. Our path, however, was to the left, down the narrow, tree-lined road, where we would come to the sacred sanctuary.

I heard the arrow before I saw it. Before I could even react it had thunked into the side of the cart, a mere hand's breadth from Diotima's right leg and right in front of me. If I'd taken one more step before it came in, I'd've been a dead man.

I shouted, "Ride!"

I kicked Blossom so hard up the behind even he got the message. Or perhaps he'd heard the fear in my voice, because Diotima was a target, high in the cart. Either way, the donkey took off as fast as a donkey can while pulling a protesting woman in his wake. I screamed, "Stay low!" at her rapidly disappearing back, and then took my own advice and flattened myself on the ground. Diotima pulled on the left rein, and the cart sped around the curve and out of sight on the road to the sanctuary. She was no longer a target. I breathed a sigh of relief. I would just have to hope there was no one waiting around there for her.

The attack had come from the right, from a copse of trees a hundred paces away, at the point where the road forked, and that was probably what had saved us. The ground between the road and the trees was clear of all but barley plants, knee-high, not nearly tall or thick enough to hide a man who must stand to shoot a bow. The trees were the closest a shooter could approach. The good news was I couldn't see a band of brigands. If it had been highway robbers, they would have rushed me, and I wouldn't have stood a chance. This had the look of a single assassin.

I was in the middle of a road, with no cover about me and a bowman within range. I considered running away, but rejected the idea. It would expose my back to a lucky shot, and besides, I wanted to know who was trying to kill us, and why.

I felt beneath my exomis for my knife. It was the only weapon I had. I could have borrowed my father's spear and shield and short sword before I left home, but who goes armed to find a missing girl?

There's a technical term for a man who charges a bowman wielding only a knife. The term is *corpse*. I couldn't run away, I couldn't charge without being hit, but I could crawl. I dragged myself off the road, in the direction of the trees, flat to the ground, until I was by the roadside amongst the first of the barley. Here I had some minimal cover. Another arrow flew overhead, in the right direction and barely above me. That would change in a moment, when he found his range. I dragged myself, I hoped out of sight, not forward or backward, but sideways, parallel with the road and going back in the direction of Athens. I moved slowly, careful not to make the knee-high plants sway against the breeze. I'd moved five paces when an arrow embedded itself in the ground, exactly where I'd been hiding. I moved farther to the right. Carefully.

A few more shots came in, falling in a cluster about where the shooter had seen me disappear into the grass, and I thought myself lucky that he and I were on the same level. If he'd been higher—on a hill, for example—I'd've been totally exposed.

If he were on a hill. Or if he were up a tree. And the bowman was hiding in woods.

At that moment the shooting stopped.

What were the odds my attacker was climbing a tree? If he got a decent purchase on a high limb then I was a dead man. But while he was climbing, he couldn't shoot at all. He might not even see me if I rushed him.

I prepared myself to run, then was assaulted by fear: What if he wasn't climbing? What if the shooter was merely waiting to see what I did? I'd take an arrow through the head the moment I raised it.

Which was he doing: climbing or waiting?

I had to do something. No decision was worse than guessing wrong.

If he was climbing, then my only chance to survive would be gone within heartbeats.

I grabbed a handful of the local dirt in my left hand—it was gray, dry dust that I scraped from the surface—because there's nothing a bowman hates worse than grit in the eyes. Then I took a deep breath, tensed my legs, and pushed off.

I ran five steps before I remembered to zigzag. I thought to myself, irrelevantly, that my old army instructor would have been ashamed of me if he knew.

Well, if I died here, he'd never find out.

It was lucky I remembered when I did, because at that instant an arrow whizzed by exactly on the line I'd been charging. I'd gotten it wrong. He wasn't climbing a tree at all. He was waiting for me, and now I was committed.

I yelled a blood-curdling scream, hoping to put him off his aim, and changed direction again. Another shot went by. I remembered that old sergeant telling us to change direction at random. "Otherwise the enemy will guess where you're about to be and shoot there," he'd said grimly to us raw recruits, and we hadn't paid the slightest attention because none of us had ever expected to be pinned down in a barley field by a deadly bowman.

I swore as I ran that I'd never get caught like this again, but my fervent promise to correct my inadequate life planning wouldn't be worth spit if I didn't make the next fifty paces into the trees ahead. If only I could get some solid wood between me and my attacker, we'd be on an even field.

I scanned the woods as I ran, but I couldn't see him. That meant he was further within, perhaps behind some shrubs. I changed direction for the last thirty paces, to approach on a broad curve. I hoped that by moving sideways I'd put trees or at least bushes between us from time to time to interrupt his sighting. Also, a man moving across the field of vision is harder to hit. The expectation of feeling an arrow in my side at any moment was a wonderful goad.

There were no more shots until I made the first of the trees. I wanted to stop and gasp for air—in fact I did stop for the briefest moment and heaved in the extra air I desperately wanted—but I had to keep moving. I dodged from tree trunk to tree trunk, searching for the man I now had the advantage over. Unless he had a sword, in which case I was in big trouble.

But I couldn't find him at all. There were no more shots, and all was silence.

I searched all over, stepping carefully from cover to cover, constantly aware of the danger of ambush, but the shooter was gone.

"WE HAVEN'T EVEN arrived yet, and someone's already trying to kill us," I said. I'd caught up with Diotima along the path to the sanctuary. Or rather, we'd found each other, because she'd tethered Blossom out of sight and pulled out her own bow and quiver of arrows, and was running back to help me. She'd had to retrieve the bow from where we'd cleverly packed it: underneath everything else in the cart. There was another lesson learned.

"It does seem a little premature," Diotima agreed. "We've hardly had time to annoy anyone yet."

"That's a good point. Who *have* we annoyed?"

"Polonikos, the father of Ophelia, seems to be the only candidate." Diotima paused to think about it. "He wouldn't seriously try to kill us to stop us finding his own daughter, would he?"

"Also, he's back in Athens," I said. "Come to that, anyone we might have annoyed is back in Athens. Whoever that attacker was, he must have run out the back of the woods as I entered from the front. The woods are smaller than they look from the roadside. There's another open field beyond, then more trees. I was slow moving through, for obvious reasons. He had ample time to reach the next copse."

"You didn't follow?"

"Across another open field, when I knew someone on the other side was armed with a bow? No thanks."

"He'd probably run out of arrows. That's why he retreated."

"I wasn't keen to test that theory."

Diotima sniffed. "Whoever he is, he's not so good. I could have hit us at that range."

"Maybe," I said. I doubted whether she could pull a flat trajectory out to a hundred paces. Diotima's bow was a custom-made marksman's weapon in reinforced bone. It had been the gift of her birth father, crafted by a master bowyer at mind-boggling expense. Diotima hadn't the strength of a man, so the bowyer had cleverly scaled down the pull to the level of a healthy woman. Her bow had inevitably lost power, but within her range, Diotima was an absolute dead shot. I'd seen her consistently bullseye at fifty paces.

Diotima frowned. "The shooter must have been someone from Athens who got ahead of us on the road. Who else knew we were coming?"

"Doris, and everyone at the sanctuary," I pointed out. "Plus anyone *they've* told."

"So you think the sanctuary called us in to help them, and then tried to kill us to stop us from helping them. Yes, I can totally see that."

"No need to be sarcastic. But you have to agree, the attack happened much closer to Brauron than Athens. In fact, we're almost there."

Indeed we were. We'd traveled as we talked, with a wary eye to each side of the road for any more ambushes. After we rounded a blind corner, there lay before us a small river crossed by a stone bridge, almost as wide as it was long. On the other side was a temple, new-built in good stone and brightly painted, and beside it, another new building in stone. We'd come to the Sanctuary of Brauron, where lived the most marriageable girls of the highest families of Athens.

Some of those girls saw us before we reached the bridge—I guessed they'd been sent to look out for us, since the sanctuary knew we were arriving today—and they quickly ran off, to return with a figure I recognized: Doris the priestess.

"Welcome," she said as we pulled up.

"Did you know there's a naked woman running around in the woods?" I said, by way of greeting.

"A naked woman?" Doris said, surprised. Then, "Oh! That's just Gaïs. Don't mind her. She's one of our priestesses."

"Oh, really?" I said, my interest quickened. "I may need to meet her. For the investigation, you understand—"

"Did you know there's also someone out there with a bow? He tried to kill us." Diotima quickly blocked any attempt to meet naked women. Instead she told Doris of the encounter with the bowman.

"Oh no!" Doris said. "It must have been robbers. We do get them on the main road from time to time. I'll warn Zeke to keep an extra lookout though, in case they come this way."

"Zeke?"

"Our chief maintenance man. There he is." Doris pointed to a tall, thin man loping across the green grass.

If Zeke was the sanctuary's first line of defense, then they were in big trouble, because he was sixty if he was a day. Maybe even older, with white hair and white whiskers and skin that had seen the sun every day of his long life. Zeke smacked his lips and looked thoughtful when Doris told him our story. "Sounds to me like a poor attempt at highway robbery. Not a professional. Probably some local who thought he'd try his luck." He shrugged. "It happens. There are poor folk in these parts. Too many of them are desperate."

"Then why didn't he try to waylay us on the much narrower tree-lined path to the sanctuary?" Diotima asked. "He couldn't have missed us there."

"'Cause most folk are on their way to Brauron town," Zeke answered. "Besides, the sanctuary's too well respected, even by cutthroats."

"So you're not worried?" Doris asked.

Zeke shook his head. "Not now this feller's had his taste of highway robbery and failed. I doubt he'll try again, not if he ran away. He'll go back to scrabbling in the dirt for a pittance, like all the other poor folk."

I could see Doris's shoulders relax with Zeke's very reasonable explanation. I couldn't fault him, but somehow I doubted he had it right.

"Come," Doris said. "The High Priestess commanded me to bring you to her private office as soon as you arrived."

THERE WERE ONLY two buildings at Brauron: a small temple to Artemis, before which Doris stood when she greeted us, and a larger stoa—that is, a covered porch—surrounded by rooms. Doris led us past the temple and across a courtyard of well-kept green grass to the other side of the stoa. She stopped at a closed door, where she announced our arrival by calling out, "It's me. They're here!"

The door opened to reveal an overweight middle-aged woman, and I thought this must be the High Priestess until I saw another beyond, an old lady sitting on a dining couch.

Thea, the High Priestess, was a woman of delicate features, gray, frizzy hair, and a determined set of the mouth.

She rose from the couch when we entered, Diotima leading.

The High Priestess took her by the hands, looked up into her face, and said, "Diotima, it's good to see you again. So few of our girls return to see us. You've grown."

Diotima wasn't a tall woman, yet she had to stoop to be on a level with the High Priestess. Diotima said, "The last time I stood in this office, I was a scared little girl."

"Not any longer," Thea said.

"High Priestess, I wish to present Nicolaos; son of Sophroniscus, who is to be my husband."

Thea looked me up and down. Her only comment was a non-committal, "Hmm."

I felt like I'd failed a test.

The overweight woman spoke up. "I'm Sabina," she said.

This was the woman who'd sent the original package of skull and scroll case to Athens and started all the trouble. I made a mental note to interview her later, and noted too the way Doris and Thea tried to ignore Sabina.

I said, "I understand you're a priestess here too?"

"I'm the treasurer of the sanctuary."

"Is that permitted?" I asked. For a woman to manage accounts was almost unheard of.

Sabina said, in a voice that bristled, "Administration of the Sanctuary of Artemis Brauronia falls within the office of the Basileus, who is back in Athens. The Basileus trusts me to manage things here."

Doris, in the background, rolled her eyes. Thea chose not to comment. I guessed Sabina's claim to manage the sanctuary was a sore point.

"I see." The Basileus had more than enough to do in Athens without having to worry about a small complex on the other side of Attica. He probably sent an assistant once a year to sign off on the books and approve funding for the next, and then tried to forget that Brauron existed.

"What can you tell us about the missing girl?" I asked.

Thea the High Priestess said, "She's the daughter of a wealthy landholder named Polonikos—"

"I've met him. Are all fathers that unconcerned when their children go missing?"

"We don't lose many girls, so I can't form a general opinion. But to answer your real question, I wrote a letter to Polonikos the moment we knew Ophelia was missing. I sent the letter by runner and instructed him not to stop for anything but water. A return message arrived next day. Polonikos asked me to let him know when the girl showed up." Thea grimaced. "Since then, I've had no news to send him."

"Have children gone missing before?" I asked.

"Yes. They always turn up the next day, usually in the company of a passing merchant who found the child walking the road back to Athens. They get homesick, you see. But I knew right away that Ophelia's case was different."

"Why?"

"She liked it here. Besides which . . . You said you met the father?"

"Oh. Right." It was hard to imagine the girl would be welcomed home.

Sabina said, "Of course, the whole matter might be much simpler than everyone thinks, given the unusual state of Allike's body."

Thea glared at her treasurer. "Sabina, there's no need to bring that up."

"Anything might be relevant," I said. "What unusual state?"

"Didn't Doris tell you? I thought she told you everything."

"Tell us what?"

"That Allike, when we found her, she wasn't just dead—"

"Sabina!" Thea shouted. Doris had turned green.

"She was ripped to little pieces. Torn limb from limb. Like some wild animal had gotten her. It took ages to find all the bits."

Chapter Four

NO WONDER DORIS had been upset, back in Athens, when we asked her how Allike died. Doris had been first to see the body of Allike. She must have been one of the ones who had to pick up what was left of her former student and put the pieces in a sack.

After that revelation, no one was inclined to say anything more.

As we emerged from Thea's room, a skinny, naked woman with hair flying behind her leaped over the fallen logs that served as a boundary to the sanctuary. She skidded to a halt. She was breathing heavily, and not merely at the sight of me. Her hair was straggly and unkempt, her face thin and dripping. She was the runner from the woods.

We all stopped dead; it was that or walk into each other in the narrow corridor. She eyed me up and down. A slight smile crossed her lips.

"This is Gaïs, the youngest of our priestesses," Doris said helpfully. "Gaïs, do you remember Diotima? You were both children the last time you met. And Gaïs, this man is Nicolaos son of Sophroniscus. Nicolaos and Diotima are to marry next month."

"I remember her, and no, they won't marry," Gaïs said at once.

They were the first words I ever heard Gaïs speak, and I was taken aback by her strange ferocity. It was like I'd been dropped into a conversation whose first half I'd missed.

"What did you say?" I said.

She ignored me. Gaïs transferred her attention to Diotima. "The Goddess will stop you."

"That's ridiculous," Diotima said. "Nico's the most important thing in my life. Nothing will stop me marrying him." But somehow, though her words were strong, my betrothed didn't sound as confident as I expected.

Everyone but Gaïs turned to look at me. I blushed. Why were we suddenly having this conversation about our private lives with a stranger? What did she care about our marriage?

Gaïs stayed fixated on Diotima. She said, "If that were true, you'd have given up everything else, wouldn't you? But I know you didn't. She'll stop you, somehow. Maybe she'll kill one of you. Arrow-shooting Artemis can't be denied."

Diotima stepped back as if Gaïs had struck her.

"Are you threatening us?" I said, confused and angry at the effect these words had had on my girl.

Gaïs turned to me, but her eyes looked right through me, and it was clear her mind was in another place.

I said, to bring her back to reality, "Allike's dead, and Ophelia's missing. What do you think happened to them, Gaïs?"

Gaïs said nothing.

I repeated, "Gaïs, what happened to the girls?"

"Do you know what they drink in Hades?" Gaïs asked.

"What?"

Gaïs crouched to scrape her hands across the ground between us, then she raised her cupped hands in front of my face.

"They drink dust."

She opened her fingers, and the dry, dry dust fell between us.

GAÏS HAD WALKED off, after that extraordinary statement, leaving the rest of us to stare at one another. Thea and Doris were obviously embarrassed by their young priestess but said nothing. Sabina seemed to enjoy their discomfort. We made small talk before Diotima pointed out that the sun had fallen below the horizon.

In a single day, we had hired a cart and donkey, traveled the breadth of Attica, interviewed men, women, and a crazy priestess, and been attacked by an unknown archer. I reflected that this job didn't pay enough. In fact, since I was still waiting on Pericles, it didn't pay anything at all. But now it was evening, there was nothing else we could do, and Diotima and I were exhausted.

Sabina had assigned us sleeping spaces.

"You're not married?" was the first thing she asked.

"No. Not yet."

"Then you certainly won't be sleeping together."

I protested, "But—"

"I don't care what you do back in Athens," Sabina snapped. "Though I'm shocked to hear one of our own, a former Little Bear no less, could so forget herself as to descend into debauchery. Did we teach you nothing about proper conduct, girl?" Sabina glared at Diotima, who blushed bright red.

Sabina said, "Here, you will conform to the proprieties. We have standards to maintain before the girls."

Diotima said, "Please, Sabina, we *are* betrothed, and soon we'll be—"

"I'm not interested in your rationalizations either. That's for your own conscience. Now where was I? Oh yes, accommodation . . . beds. You can sleep with the maintenance men," she said to me. "There's a wooden hut out back."

"Is there a bed there?" I asked.

"I'm sure you'll make do. I've never looked inside, myself. The smell of all those unwashed men drives me away." Sabina turned to Diotima and frowned. "Normally a visiting priestess would be housed with the rest of us, in the east wing, but there are no spare beds at the moment. We could make up a pallet, of course, but you'd be sleeping on the stone floor. We do have two spare beds in the west wing, if you don't mind sleeping with the girls in a dorm room."

"That might be better," Diotima said at once, and I knew she was thinking the farther away she was from Sabina, the better.

She probably didn't realize when she said it, but the two spares must surely have belonged to Allike and Ophelia.

Dinner that night was an interesting affair. Diotima ate with the women and girls, while I ate with the men. The conversation among the men was, predictably, about the women. Not that much of what they had to say was useful, nor repeatable if it came to that, though the speculation about what Sabina might do in her lonely bed was amusing and, based on what I knew of her, quite possibly correct.

There were eleven men, some of them slaves, some of them free men so poor they had to work at the temple for the few coins it paid. The slaves were the better off; they at least had guaranteed food and a place to sleep at no cost.

Zeke puzzled me. Normally you can tell which city a man is from by his accent, but Zeke I couldn't place at all. He wasn't from Attica, of that I was certain. I wasn't even sure whether he was a slave or a free man. His job was menial; normally a foreign man with a menial job must be a slave, yet Zeke neither behaved nor was treated like one. He was clearly the leader, by age, by experience, by force of personality. Zeke kept apart, spoke little, except to tone down with his soft voice any argument that threatened to become a fight, treated slave and free man alike, and let the men have their way. He reminded me of Pythax, my future father-in-law: a man who lived outside the system, while supporting it to the core.

Diotima and I met after dinner on the lush, green grass of the courtyard. A quarter of the girls had set about clearing up, while the others sang and danced in the moonlight. We sat and listened to the girls' voices. The moon was beautiful in the sky, and a soft, warm breeze blew across the sanctuary.

Lying back on the grass, I said, "It's hard to believe such a lovely place could harbor evil."

"Clearly you've never been to a girls' school before," Diotima said.

I looked over at her. "You didn't like it here?"

"I loved the place. I didn't like the other girls."

"Did you really know Gaïs when you were children? Was she always crazy?"

"Yes to the first. She was here before I arrived. She was still here when I left. But she's changed a lot."

"You mean she wasn't always crazy."

"I don't remember her like this," Diotima admitted. "She was always something of a loner. But then, so was I."

"You didn't become two loners together?" I asked.

Diotima snorted. "Not with her. I remember she was arrogant even back then. She always pushed people away."

"How come she's still at Brauron? I thought everyone stayed for a year."

"The sanctuary takes in a few orphan girls, ones with nowhere else to go. Gaïs was one of those. She grew up here."

"It's a wonder she isn't married," I said. "She certainly should be."

"Yes, I wondered about that too," Diotima said. "I never expected to find her still here."

It was the norm for girls to have marriages arranged for them by the time they were fifteen. Any significant age past that, and eyebrows were raised: people would start to wonder what was wrong with the girl. Diotima had been preserved to twenty because of her unorthodox parentage, but that was all to the good, because it had saved her for me, who otherwise would never have met my perfect girl. Gaïs had no such excuse.

I thought about the temple complex. Although it was beautiful, it was also very small; a world totally enclosed, with the same priestesses, who never came or went, and children who were replaced every year. A child who lived here had no chance to make any permanent friends. It was no wonder Gaïs went crazy. Then I thought about what the crazy woman had said. I hesitated, slightly afraid to ask, but I wanted to know.

"Diotima, why did Gaïs say that Artemis would prevent you from marrying?"

"I'd rather not talk about that, Nico."

"Oh." I was taken aback. I'd thought we had no secrets.

"Didn't we just agree she was crazy?" Diotima said. "Crazy people say crazy things."

I asked, "What was she going on about, with all that talk of the dead drinking dust in Hades?"

"It's true," Diotima said.

"The subject doesn't usually come up in casual conversation."

Diotima hesitated. "I don't know. It sounded to me like she thinks Ophelia's dead."

"Or she *knows* Ophelia's dead."

"You might be right," Diotima admitted. "I don't like Gaïs, but I'd hate to think she had something to do with this."

"Let's find out." I nodded in the direction of the Sacred Spring. Torches had been set up there, the spikes of their long, thin wooden poles pushed into the soil. In the flickering yellow-red light, I could see only silhouettes, but the shape of Gaïs was distinctive, even when she was wearing clothes. She was taller than the girls, but thinner than every other priestess. No one could miss her as she jumped and spun. A handful of the Little Bears were with her. They all weaved in and out of the light, and as they moved they sang. I could barely hear the words, but it sounded like a hymn to Artemis. Gaïs seemed to have a thing for Artemis even above what you might expect of a priestess.

I helped Diotima to rise, and together we walked to where the girls danced. I noticed that though the spring was nearby, the torchlight didn't quite extend to its edge. I hoped nobody would fall in.

Diotima and I watched the dance for a few moments. It was something you'd never see in Athens, where girls are mostly kept inside, and certainly never allowed out on their own. It occurred to me that the only girl-children I'd ever seen in Athens were either slaves or the daughters of citizens out on errands in the company of their mothers, or on special ceremony days when the girls would lead the public processions. But girls playing in the street? It never happened in the city. Only boys played outside. Here, it happened every day. I wondered how a child might react to such sudden freedom. It was a good thing they had a sensible woman like Doris to keep them in line, like the mother she was. Gaïs, I could see, being so much closer to the girls in age, was more like a big sister. She danced with every bit of the same energy as the children, as she laughed and sang to her Goddess. There was nothing now of the oddness that we'd seen in Gaïs that afternoon.

I waved to the leader of the pack. "Gaïs! Can we have a word with you?"

Gaïs started. She hadn't noticed us, standing in the dark. She told the girls to keep going and walked over to us. She was dressed in a priestess chiton, but one she had torn down to fit her slimness. She stood before us and said nothing.

I said, "Gaïs, did you shoot an arrow at us this afternoon?"

"No, was I supposed to?" She looked at us as if we were the mad ones.

"They say Allike was torn apart," I said to her. "I'm sorry to mention it, but I must. They say there's a bear out there. Do you think a bear might have killed Allike?"

Gaïs almost recoiled. "Never! The Goddess would never allow the greater servant to harm the lesser."

"Huh?"

"She means a bear wouldn't have hurt Allike," Diotima translated for me. "When Artemis walks the earth, she's attended by the wild bears of the wood, who are her sacred servants. That's why the girls here are called the Little Bears, Nico, because they're the little servants of Artemis. Gaïs is saying that the larger servant—the bear—wouldn't harm the smaller, Allike."

"Then why couldn't she just say so?" I said, exasperated. I turned back to Gaïs. "Are you by any chance related to the

Pythoness?" I asked, because the Pythoness at Delphi is the priestess who speaks for Apollo, and she always speaks in riddles. I'd never been to Delphi, but I imagined dealing with her must be as irritating as having to talk to this woman.

Gaïs shook her head. "I'm a child of the temple."

"So I heard. Have you no idea who your mother and father might be?"

"The temple is my mother." Gaïs looked over my shoulder at the marble building behind me. "It's beautiful."

Indeed it was. With the crickets chirping and the still night under the stars, and even just enough disruption from the noisy girls to give the place some life, the Temple of Artemis Brauronia was a good place to be, if you liked a quiet life.

I said, "With all this running you do, if there were a bear, do you think you might have seen it?"

Gaïs shrugged.

"Have you seen anything unusual out in the woods?" I asked.

"No," Gaïs said. "Not unless you count that strange man."

"*What strange man?*" Diotima and I said simultaneously.

"He follows me." Gaïs seemed utterly unconcerned. "When he sees me in the woods, he runs after me. I get away every time." Gaïs shrugged. "I think he might be crazy."

Well, she'd be in a position to know.

"EVERY TIME WE interview a suspect, they give us someone else to suspect," I moaned as we walked away, leaving Gaïs to rejoin the dance. "This can't go on."

"If only because we'll run out of people," Diotima said coolly. "The problem is that we're so removed from everything that's happened. We haven't been anywhere near a fresh crime, we haven't even seen a body! All we have to work with is what people tell us. It's frustrating!"

A gaggle of girls sat on the lawn, playing games and talking nonstop. We remained silent while they were in earshot. "What do you think of this bear everyone keeps talking about?" Diotima asked me in a quiet voice when we'd passed.

"It's obviously rubbish," I said. "There haven't been bears in Attica for decades, maybe even a century or more."

"What happened to them?"

"People hunted them to extinction."

"And by people, you mean men."

"Well, yes."

"What about the fathers?"

"No, they haven't been hunted to extinction."

"I mean, why aren't the fathers of those two girls down here with us, looking for their children?"

"Polonikos seems to be shifty. He has some reason for staying in Athens but wouldn't say what it was. The father of Allike I don't know about. But I'm not sure talking to him will help. Why would he have anything to do with this?"

We stopped outside the dorm rooms for the girls, where Diotima would sleep for the night. I had another hundred paces to the wooden shack out the back where the slaves slept on pallets on the dirt floor.

I said, "We'll have to talk to this stranger in the woods."

"We'll have to find him first."

I DREAMED OF Allike screaming as she was torn apart. The nightmare wouldn't let me rest. I rolled over into the man beside me. He snored and blew hot air straight into my face.

That woke me up.

But the screaming didn't stop.

I scrambled up, tripped over the man beside me, got up again, and banged my head into the door. My hand fumbled in the dark for the handle, and I finally got out. The stars were bright and the moon brighter. The noise was coming from the girls' dorm, where Diotima was. I reached for my knife, realized I'd left it on the ground in the dark shack, and decided to go without it.

I ran to the stoa, down the corridor, and into the girls' room, ready to grapple.

Diotima stood in the middle of the room, a knife in her right hand, the point red with blood. But for the knife she was naked. The girls in the room were backed up in their beds. They were the ones screaming.

Diotima pointed with her left hand. "He went that way."

Exactly the way I'd come from. No, that was impossible. I ran out, looked around quickly, and realized the intruder, whoever he was, must have turned left and headed toward the river. I instantly knew what he'd done. He'd entered the sanctuary by walking down the riverbed, where the banks hid him from view, then climbed up when he was closest to the stoa.

I padded softly along the top bank, in the hope of catching him. Well ahead I saw a silhouette scramble up the gentle slope that rose behind the sanctuary. I picked up to a run. He saw me and ran too, over the top of the hill that separated the sanctuary from the bay before I did, and then he was out of sight.

I stopped. Diotima caught up. She said, "He's hiding behind the bushes on the hill. I saw him bend over, and he's moving right to left."

If this was the man who'd shot at us the other day, then we were terribly exposed where we were, in this moonlight. I said, "Does he have a bow?"

"If he does, I didn't see it," Diotima said. "But then, I wasn't exactly looking. He crept into the room and leaned over me. I don't know what made me wake up, but I did. I opened my eyes, and I was staring straight into his."

"So it was your scream that woke me."

"No, it was his. Good thing I keep a knife beside my head. I think I only sliced him, though. If that's our bowman, he can still shoot."

"Diotima, go back to the sanctuary. I can stalk him."

"Not with this much moonlight. I've got a better plan. I'll divert his attention while you rush him."

"I said to run back to the sanctuary."

"No." Diotima turned away to run up the slope, not toward the target but well to his right. She made no attempt to hide herself. If the intruder was watching, he couldn't miss her.

This wasn't the time to argue, but I could see I'd have to deal with her lack of obedience later. I moved as quickly as I could to the left. This put me behind the creeper. When I felt I was far enough behind, I turned and ran up the slope. For the first time, I looked for my target.

I couldn't see him, but I could see a clump of bushes that swayed *against* the breeze.

Our creepy character had his eyes fixed on Diotima. I was relieved to see he held no bow. But that was my future wife he'd crept up to in her bed, and for that reason alone I was going to kill him.

He was crouched behind a bush, almost kneeling and with his hands on the shrubbery to create a gap to peer through. I knew now why he'd slowed down. The soil here was extremely soft and my feet sank in, the one advantage being that it made me silent. I bent low and walked rapidly. Now I was above and behind him, and I crouched to watch. He was a man I guessed to be thirty—certainly older than me. He had short hair and wore an exomis. He didn't have the look of a highwayman. He might be an artisan, or he might be the son of a wealthy man. Or he might be a well-paid assassin.

Diotima stood on the crest. How she had the nerve I don't know, knowing a stranger was watching—maybe the one who'd shot at us the day before. She was exposed as a silhouette. A silhouette with wide hips and perfect breasts.

That got our attention, both mine and the intruder's.

I had to tear my gaze away from my fiancée—swearing as I did that I'd do something about that beautiful woman that night, no matter what Sabina had to say about it—and turned back to the stranger. He was still staring at her. There was no bow, but hanging at his side was a short sword. That was an expensive piece of equipment.

From my crouch I began running, then straightened up as I got faster.

He heard me coming. He turned, saw me, and gave a startled cry. Then he drew the sword.

I dove into him. Hard. My shoulder went into his chest, and he grunted as I wrapped my arms around him and we both went flying downhill in an untidy ball. Somewhere on the way down, he lost the sword. I knocked my head on something and saw stars. We struggled to strike at each other as we rolled down the slope and onto the hard dirt.

The gravel stopped our movement. We finished with him on top of me, legs straddling me. I couldn't get up, or get out of the way. Then something large and brown seemed to descend from the sky and whacked him in the side of the head. His eyes rolled up, and he slid sideways off me to reveal Diotima standing behind him, holding in her right hand a large and rather nasty-looking lump of wood, which was now spotted with blood and a few tufts of hair.

She tossed the wood aside. "Are you all right?" she asked me.

"Never been better," I groaned.

The same couldn't be said of the stranger. His movements were confused, and his arms and legs jerked about. As we watched he rolled over onto his front, pushed himself up onto his hands and knees, and then threw up. He was heartily sick for some moments, then with a final heave he fell back to a sitting position and stared hatred at us.

"What did you do that for?" he said in an aggrieved tone.

"Who are you?" I countered.

"My name is Melo."

"What are you doing out here, Melo?" I asked.

"I don't have to tell you," he said.

"I'll just hit him again, shall I?" Diotima suggested.

Melo glared at Diotima, eye to eye, but then his gaze traveled south. So did mine.

"Diotima, you're dressed like Gaïs," I told her.

"What?" Diotima said, confused. "But Gaïs doesn't wear—" Diotima suddenly realized she might be missing something, such as clothes. She blushed. "Whoops."

Diotima ran back to the sanctuary. I heard the loud voices of Doris and Gaïs as they calmed the girls, the deeper and even louder voice of Zeke, demanding to know what was going on, and Diotima's equally loud voice doing some quick explaining.

"I'll ask you again," I said to Melo. "What were you doing?"

"I was looking for a girl," Melo admitted.

This Melo must be one very sick character. Whoever had taken Allike and Ophelia must have crept into the sanctuary, exactly as Melo had done.

He must have read my thoughts, because he said in a defensive voice, "Look here, it's not what you think it is. The girl I'm looking for is missing. Her name is Ophelia." He put his head in his hands. "Did you have to hit me so hard?" he moaned as Diotima returned, now dressed in a chiton that she'd thrown on. She was barefoot, and her hair was still in the single braid she put it in for sleep.

"Who *are* you, Melo?"

"I'm Melo, as I said, the son of Thessalus. I'm the man who's betrothed to marry Ophelia."

This was the first I'd heard of a marriage!

"What are you doing here?" I said warily. "Why did you creep up on my fiancée?"

"I wasn't creeping up on her. When I saw, through the window, someone in that bed, I thought Ophelia must have returned. I was happy! I crept in to see if it was her."

"Staring through a window at sleeping children isn't exactly a good way to prove your fine intentions."

"I guess you're right."

"How old are you?" I asked.

"Twenty-nine. I'll be thirty in three months."

That was the usual age. As a man approached thirty, pressure mounted on him to marry. Melo might be almost thirty, but his actions and manner made him seem much younger. I wondered if he might be a trifle simple.

Diotima had brought back a cup of water from the sanctuary. She gave it to Melo. He took a mouthful, swirled it in his mouth, then spat out the sand and grit and leftover vomit that was in there. He took another mouthful, and this he drank.

"You're in search of a girl you barely know," I said as he drank.

"That doesn't matter. She's my responsibility."

"She's her father's problem until you're married," I said.

"Have you met her father?" he demanded.

"Yes."

"Well, then."

"All right, point taken," I conceded. Thea—or was it Doris?—had said the same thing yesterday. Polonikos, the father of Ophelia, seemed to make a bad impression on everyone he met.

"I'm her only hope," Melo said. "Besides, the way I see it, soon I'm to be married. That makes me a man with responsibilities. I'm not going to shirk my duties just because they're not official yet."

This was so close to how I felt about Diotima that I could only agree with him. Suddenly Melo seemed a lot more mature. I switched my evaluation of him from simple to just plain dumb.

Diotima said, "So you're a concerned friend, are you? If you want us to believe any of this, you'll have to tell us everything you know."

"Why? Who are you, anyway?" he said.

I explained who we were, what our mission was, and finished, "So you see, you're not the only one looking for Ophelia. Are you from around here?"

"My family has an estate not far from Brauron. My father lives in Athens, of course."

That was normal. Wealthy landowners always kept a city house and lived there as much as possible; anyone who spent all their time in the country was dead to civilized life. Besides, the agora at Athens was the only place to hear the latest rumors and stay close to the political action.

"What are you doing out here then?"

"What do you think? When my father told me he'd found me a wife, I wanted to meet the girl. He said why bother, when he'd already checked her out and decided. I insisted I meet the girl before I'd agree to marry her. He was angry. He said I should trust him."

"You didn't, of course," I said.

"No, of course not. What son in his right mind trusts his father's judgment?"

Melo and I shared a moment of empathy.

"So I found an excuse to come down to Brauron—I told Father I was worried the slaves might be slacking off, and he believed me (the truth is, our farm workers are excellent); anyway he praised me for my care and I hurried to Brauron as quickly as I could to meet my fiancée." He paused, then admitted, "I might have been somewhat brusque when I demanded to see Ophelia."

"Oh?"

"I still bear the bruises from that old man of theirs."

"Zeke?" I said.

"Yes, him. Of course, you two just added to them."

"*Zeke* hit you?" Diotima said, amazed.

"Twice my age, but he packs a mean punch. I'm glad I didn't have to face him when he was young."

"I wish I'd been there," Diotima said with feeling. "Nothing like that ever happened when I was a Little Bear."

Melo said, "Imagine the disgrace if I struck a man older than my grandpa. There wasn't anything I could do but go away."

Two hundred paces away, the lights went out one by one at the Sanctuary of Brauron. Diotima's assurance had done its work, and the priestesses were getting the girls back to bed. But I knew we'd have some explaining to do when we returned. Somehow Melo didn't come across as the crazed homicidal type. He spoke like a fine citizen.

"What's your plan?" I asked.

"I'm sure Ophelia's not far from here. She said she would be. I'll search until I find her."

Diotima snorted. "She *said* she would be? You don't know the girl, not even slightly."

"That's not true! I know lots about her."

"What?" Diotima demanded.

Melo looked abashed. "I have a confession to make. Tonight wasn't the first time I crept into the girls' room."

"Dear Gods."

"After the slave punched me and the High Priestess sent me away, I crept back that night. I really wanted to meet her," Melo said in a rush. "I woke her up and we talked. Ophelia was as curious about me as I was about her. Ophelia and I managed to meet a few times. We met beside the pond, where no one would hear us."

To our accusing stares, he said, "It was only talk, you know? We didn't . . . well, you know . . . do anything else. I swear it. We just talked."

"What about?"

"What do you talk about, with a complete stranger you're supposed to marry?"

"Beats me."

"You two didn't go through the same thing?"

"We arranged matters the other way around."

"Lucky you. Ophelia and I spent all our time asking each other dumb questions. What do you like to do? What's your favorite food?"

"And?"

"Her favorite food is apples."

"No, I meant, what did you decide about each other?"

"Oh. I decided I liked her. She was nice. I was shocked when I realized she was more scared of me than I was of her." He paused. "No, that's wrong. We were both scared of marriage. That last evening, when they caught us—"

"*They caught you meeting*?" I said, aghast.

"Didn't I mention that? It was because we were arguing. Our voices were raised." He looked abashed. "Our first argument. I told her she had to do something about it, and she refused."

"Do something about what?"

"Ophelia told me someone was trying to kill her. Those were the last words she said to me, before the temple staff found us." He beat his fists on the ground until his knuckles bled. "She told me, and I didn't do a thing to save her."

There was a sudden silence between us. I broke it with one word.

"Why?"

"Why what?" He looked at his knuckles and winced.

"Why did Ophelia say someone wanted her dead?"

"It was when I told her to be careful—because Allike had been killed by the bear, you know."

"No, we don't know," I said. "Doris the priestess said there were sightings, and Sabina told us Allike's remains looked like she'd been torn apart, but everyone knows there are no bears in Attica. Have you seen this bear?"

"Well, no," Melo conceded. "But other people have seen it."

"Who? Name them."

"I can't. But everyone says it's out there." Melo paused, then added, "Ophelia was like you. She didn't believe in the bear story either."

"What?"

"We were talking about it. Ophelia said it couldn't be the bear.

She told me she knew a human had killed Allike. She said it was something to do with a scroll."

Diotima and I shared a look.

"Did she tell anyone else this?" Diotima asked.

"She might have said something to Gaïs. Ophelia liked Gaïs."

"Have you seen Gaïs?"

"I think so. Is she the thin one with the small breasts and the nice legs?"

"That's her," I said. "Shame about the face though."

"A little horsey," Melo allowed.

Diotima gave us both a sour look. "Is that really how men describe women?"

"Sorry about that," I said to her.

Melo said, "I've seen her running around. A couple of times I approached her to ask her about Ophelia, but she saw me and ran away."

"Where did Ophelia go, Melo?"

"If I knew that, I wouldn't be looking for her!" The tone of exasperation in his voice seemed genuine to me.

"She said she had a friend who'd protect her," Melo continued. "When I pressed her she wouldn't say more. She just said that she'd stay with the friend."

It seemed to me impossible that Ophelia should have a friend with a house in Brauron. It might be different if her family lived locally, but I knew they were in Athens.

I said, "If Ophelia's in hiding, why are you skulking about the sanctuary?"

"I was investigating, or rather, I was wondering how to go about it. How do you investigate?"

"Mostly you ask people questions. You look for the contradictions in their answers."

"What if there aren't any?"

"There always are," I said confidently, and hoped I was right. "Melo, if you want to help, you can do it best by continuing your search. But not near the sanctuary, all right? Stay away from this place. People might get the wrong ideas."

"All right."

"If Diotima gets together a search party, will you guide it?" I asked.

"Me?" Diotima said, surprised. "What will you be doing?"

"I'm off to Athens," I said. "Somebody needs to trace that missing scroll," I told her. "The question is, how many scrolls were in the case when the Basileus opened it? He'll talk to me, but not to you."

Diotima nodded reluctantly. She knew that was true.

"You can talk to Thea," I said. "Get her to assign the slaves to cross the countryside."

Melo nodded. "I know where to look," he said. "I know every farmhouse, every hut, every estate within walking distance. I can ask if they have her."

"Would they tell you the truth?"

"Yes. I'm her betrothed," he said simply. "They can't deny me. Besides, I'm a local, sort of. They'll support me, I know it. But . . ." He paused, a long time. "If Ophelia was at a farm, she'd have contacted me by now. I fear she may have been on her way to that safe place she talked of when she was stopped."

"Stopped?"

"By whoever killed Allike." Melo picked himself up. "I'll help you with your search, if you tell me what you know about what's going on at the sanctuary."

"Agreed."

He ran off, over the hills and to the north. I worried about that bash to the head we'd given him, but he was a man, and he knew his own business. It was better to leave him be.

Diotima watched him go and said, "Poor fellow."

"Do you believe him?"

Diotima looked down to where the blood from his knuckles had stained the sand. "Don't you?"

I got up and dusted off my knees. So did Diotima.

"He's not exactly bright. But yes, I believe him," I said. "This means Ophelia wasn't abducted. She's out there somewhere."

"Nico, if Ophelia trusted Melo like he says, why didn't she go to him for that safe place?"

I was thunderstruck. "I didn't think of that."

Diotima's face was troubled. "It's hard to know whom to trust. Except for Doris. I trust Doris."

"Let's try something different."

"What?"

"Everyone agrees Ophelia disappeared overnight, don't they?"

"Yes."

"And they said that guards had been set around the sanctuary, after Allike died?"

"Yes."

"Then how did a child sneak past those guards?"

Chapter Five

NEXT MORNING I got my first proper look around. The sanctuary at Brauron was much more than a temple. In Athens, all the temples are within walking distance of home. At Brauron, the temple complex *is* the home.

The center of the sanctuary wasn't the temple, as you might expect, but the courtyard in which Diotima and I had sat the night before. It was covered from side to side in thick grass that had been watered and scythed over and over until it felt like walking on a soft rug. Not once in all the time I spent at Brauron did I ever see that courtyard empty if there was light to see by; there was always a priestess or two, girls sitting on the grass and weaving, or singing, or dancing, or running or playing or doing all of those things at once.

Surrounding the courtyard was a stoa—three covered walkways with columns to support the roof and rooms behind—the whole built using stone blocks and constructed in the shape of the letter *pi*: Π. Four small dorms for the girls on the left, each room six paces by six, and workrooms at the top. The right-hand eastern side was twice the length of the other two sides and contained rooms for the priestesses and temple administration. The stoa was open to the south to let in the sun, which made the courtyard and the surrounding rooms all the more pleasant and meant that girls who had spent too much of their lives indoors rapidly became sore with sunburn.

The temple to the Goddess lay at the left foot of the stoa. We stepped past the altar, up the steps and into the temple.

The *pronaos* was small, its only purpose to lead into the main temple space, but it had one remarkable feature: hung on the left-hand wall was an enormous mirror of beautifully polished bronze. It was so large that I could see all my face and chest merely by standing before it.

"What's that for?" I asked.

"This is the temple where, at the end of their year, girls perform their coming-of-age rite," Diotima said.

"So?"

"So a girl wants to look her best. She stops here to adjust her clothing and fix her hair before she walks into the temple proper." Diotima brushed away a tear. "I stopped at this very spot, Nico, on my own initiation. Doris held my hand. I remember I watched in the mirror while she threaded the flowers in my hair. My parents waited inside, to watch me perform the dedication."

"And then she cheated," a voice said from behind.

I whirled round to see Gaïs standing there. She'd been listening in.

"What do you mean?" I said. "Don't be ridiculous. You can't cheat a ceremony."

Gaïs tilted back her head. She pointed at Diotima with her chin. "Ask her."

Diotima said, "Go away, Gaïs."

The tension between the two women was thick enough to cut with a blade. It made me wonder if the history between these two was more complex than Diotima had let on. After all, they'd been children here together.

I said, "Tell me Gaïs, what was Ophelia like?"

"Ophelia's pretty," Gaïs said softly and wistfully.

"She's also betrothed to Melo," Diotima said.

Gaïs said angrily, "Don't you think I know that?" She turned and walked out.

"What is it between you and Gaïs?" I asked my own betrothed.

"Don't ask, Nico," Diotima said, in a tone that told me I shouldn't ask.

Instead I peered into the next room, to make sure no one else was listening in. No one was.

"Did you notice something, Nico?" Diotima said. "Something about Gaïs?"

"I certainly did," I told her. "I always do with women. The curve of her upper thighs is excellent—"

My betrothed hit me. "Did you pay the slightest attention to what she said?"

"Of course!"

"So you noticed her tense."

"Um . . ."

"That's what I thought. Nico, she said Ophelia's pretty."

"Well?"

"Gaïs is the only person in the whole sanctuary who talks about Ophelia in the present. Everyone else talks of her in the past tense, like she's dead."

"Maybe the wacky, naked priestess who talks in riddles is an optimist."

We passed through to the main room of the temple. The cult statue of Artemis stood at the end. Ancient temples almost always house an ancient statue, but to my surprise, this one was new, made in bronze, painted in brilliant colors, and a thing of beauty. Artemis stood tall and proud, a young woman in her prime. The Goddess was attended by a bear, her traditional servant. The bear crouched beside her, on all fours—not in repose, but ready to protect his divine mistress.

"The old statue was destroyed when the Persians sacked the sanctuary," Diotima explained. "I heard it was made of wood and it went in the fire."

"The sacking was that bad?" I asked.

"Everything you see here is new. The whole place had to be rebuilt from the ground up. Of course, you and I weren't even born when it happened. I can only tell you what the priestesses say."

On the wall behind the Goddess were hung row upon row of dedications. It's the norm in any temple for people to give to the gods that which they value most. A man will leave his spear and shield in the temple of his choice when he's no longer strong enough to hold them. But what I saw here was nothing I'd ever seen before on any temple wall. There were skipping ropes, and leather balls attached by straps, and tiny wooden pet animals that ran on wheels, and dresses that were too small to fit any person. Beautifully carved dolls hung from hooks; they sagged like sad little wooden corpses.

"What's that?" I asked.

"Oh, those are the toys," Diotima said. "The girls dedicate their toys when they become women."

"Like a warrior who dedicates his arms when he's too old to fight?"

"I suppose, except in this case the girl dedicates what was most important in her childhood. She walks in with her child's toys and walks out without them, a woman."

We stepped out into the day, and both of us had to blink away the sunlight when we emerged from the darkness. It brought us face to face with one of the girls. A scrawny thing, which seemed to be the fashion at the sanctuary. I wondered whether all teenage girls were this thin.

"You're the investigators, aren't you?" she said.

"Yes."

"I wanted to see what you looked like. They say you two have sex without being married."

"Who says that?" I demanded.

"Oh, everyone," she said vaguely. "My father would beat me if I did that. How come your father doesn't beat you?" she asked Diotima.

"My birth father's dead," Diotima said.

"Oh," the teenager said.

"Is my private life all that anyone talks about around here?" Diotima said.

"I guess. Everyone talks about you because you're so famous. They say you tore your clothes off in a courtroom full of men."

"No, that was my mother."

I could see that in the back of her head the teenager was wishing she had parents like Diotima's. Diotima's mother, Euterpe, had indeed made a display of herself, but that was before she'd married Pythax.

"I suppose you knew Allike and Ophelia," I said to the girl. "Do you miss them?"

"Not much." Then, realizing that didn't sound good, she added defensively, "We were in different groups of friends."

"What group was Allike in?"

"Allike was one of the smart ones," the girl said. "She could read anything."

"Can't you all?" I asked.

She shrugged. "They make us learn that stuff, but everyone knows it doesn't matter. Your husband can read anything you really need."

Diotima grimaced. "You have an opportunity most girls would kill for. Don't you care?"

The girl waved her arm with the airy, all-knowing nonchalance of a teenager. "Everyone knows the important thing's to get a good husband. Men don't care if a girl can read. You should know how it works; after all, you're old," she said to my twenty-year-old fiancée. "Men judge women by other standards." She puffed out her near-nonexistent chest. "I'm working on it."

"What about Ophelia?" I asked, before Diotima could explode. "Was Ophelia one of the smart ones too?"

"Oh, no! She was normal."

Diotima's skin turned an unhealthy purple color.

"But they were friends?" I persisted.

"I guess. Not everyone can be in the popular group."

"What did they do together, Allike and Ophelia?"

"I dunno." She glanced about for something more entertaining. We'd become bores. "Allike and Ophelia spent a lot of time walking about."

Diotima and I followed their good example. We walked away.

"Was it like this when you were here?" I asked.

"Yes," said Diotima shortly. "That's why I have no friends. Except for you." She reached out to hold my hand.

Sabina walked past us, going the other way. She looked down to see our hands linked. Without breaking step she glared and ordered, "No immorality in front of the girls!"

We let go sheepishly, and she disappeared around the corner.

AT THE REAR of the temple gurgled the Sacred Spring. Water bubbled in nonstop from some place deep underground. The source of the flow was probably the massive rock outcrop immediately south of the temple, an outcrop so large you could have built a small fort upon it. The water in the Sacred Spring overflowed into a runnel that went to the river that passed by the sanctuary—the river over which we'd passed when we arrived. In reality it was not much more than a large stream. I'd seen real rivers, such as the Meander when we visited Ionia, and the Erasinos River at Brauron didn't even begin to compete.

Diotima said to me, "This spring was blessed by Artemis herself in ancient times. It's the most sacred water in all Attica."

It was a very pleasant place to be, in the shade, with the sound of the running water. Thea was sitting beside the spring with a group of girls. She recited Homer to them, but as we approached she broke off and listened to what Diotima said.

"Don't fall in!" Thea called out to us.

"Does that happen?" I asked.

"Ten times a year. There's always some girl daring another to go closer, and of course we draw our water from here. Accidents happen."

"It doesn't look that dangerous," I said, toeing the edge and finding it firm. The Sacred Spring was shaped in a rough oval, with an indented curve along one side. Water flowed in from a large rock that rose out of the ground to the south. The earth was solid and well-grassed all the way to the edge, but the drop-off into the water was surprisingly sudden.

"Nor is it dangerous, in daylight," Thea said. "But you have to be careful at night. One morning many years ago, we found a thief drowned in there. It seems he'd come in the darkness to steal from the spring, slipped, and fallen in. But that's the only fatality we've ever had, and that was decades ago. All the other idiots who go in do it during daylight."

I asked, "Is there truly stuff in the spring to steal? You said a thief drowned, trying."

"Oh, goodness me yes. Before the temple was built, women made their dedications by throwing them into the waters. And, what's more, when the Persians sacked the temple, we priestesses threw as much treasure as we could into the deepest part, to save it."

"That was during the second invasion, ten years after Marathon."

"Zeke couldn't protect you?"

"Zeke was away, serving with the army. The old High Priestess declared that it would be better to die in our temple than run, so when the men went off to war, we women remained behind, and tried to carry on with normal life, and wondered what was happening in the outside world."

Everyone gathered—the girls and Diotima and I—and listened to Thea's simply told story in silence.

"Then one day a messenger-slave stumbled across the bridge and into the sanctuary with word. Athens had fallen, and the Persians were on their way to sack our temple. The High Priestess ordered us to throw everything of value into the spring."

She gestured to the middle of the waters, the deepest part, beyond reach of the shore.

"It was the one place we could be sure they wouldn't find it."

"We priestesses worked nonstop. We tore down as much treasure as we could and threw it into the spring. We dedicated ourselves to the Goddess, and then we waited. We thought we were about to die."

Thea spoke quietly, matter-of-factly, but I had no trouble imagining the fear the women must have felt.

"When the soldiers arrived, well . . ." Thea glanced over at the girls, who were listening to her words with open mouths. "Well, it was bad. But we lived. The soldiers took the statue of the Goddess and those heavy things we couldn't lift to safety. They also found the hole we'd dug, in which we'd salted pieces of silver. The High Priestess said if we hid something for them to find, then they might leave. She was right." Thea paused. "But before they left, they drove a sword through her heart. They killed our High Priestess."

"That was when you took over," Diotima guessed.

"Someone had to," Thea said simply. "We were all in shock. Women staggered about or sat in the courtyard and cried. There was one particularly beautiful woman, who'd been repeatedly abused; she walked into the woods and hanged herself. We found her the next day.

"I find it hard to describe, looking back after all these years, just how dire our predicament was. Our High Priestess was dead. None of us had ever known a time when she didn't command. Normally we would have sent to Athens for instructions. But Athens had fallen to the enemy, and for all we knew the Athenians might never return. We were on our own."

Thea sighed.

"The other priestesses did as I suggested—to do those things we did every day, to bake the bread and worship at the temple. The women obeyed me. By the time the Athenians had taken back their city and the enemy had been driven off, it was the settled order. The Basileus confirmed me in my position. I never thought to be High Priestess."

Doris walked up as Thea spoke those final words. "Your incumbency has been a time of remarkable peace," she said.

"I'm glad," Thea said.

We followed the river north. Doris chose to join us.

As we walked, I asked, "Have you been a priestess all your life, Doris?"

"Indeed not. I was married to a man for half my life. But he died one day—just collapsed without warning—and my children were grown. I suppose I should have retired gracefully to the home of my son—he's a good man with a decent wife and they would have been happy to have me—or perhaps I should have married some lonely widower—but I thought instead to remove myself to the Sanctuary at Brauron. I've always loved children, you see; I missed my own daughters dreadfully when they married. Moving to the sanctuary was my way of reliving those lovely years when my own daughters were young. Who would have known it could lead to so much death?"

I said, "Thea told us that Zeke served with the army during the second invasion. That was the year I was born. When *did* Zeke come to Brauron?"

"Some time after Marathon. That's all I know."

"What's that smell?" I asked. I'd smelt something I hadn't expected, something . . . "Is that . . . salt?"

"It's salt water, Nico," Diotima said patiently.

"Brauron is by the sea." Doris pointed northeast. "See that hill? The one with the shrubs and not much else?"

It was the hill where Melo and I had fought.

"Walk over that and before you know it, you'll be at a shallow bay that leads into the Aegean."

"I didn't realize we were so close. Is it a port?"

"The sea here's far too shallow for that," Doris said. "There's a jetty and a rowboat. Sometimes the men will take the boat to

Brauron town, to bring back heavy goods. Just row the boat down the coast, and you'll come to Brauron."

"Is the town far away?"

"Not even half a day."

"Could a child row it?"

"No," Doris said at once. "Not a chance."

We turned south to walk down the east side of the complex. Our tour ended at the most important room in the complex for us: a small room in the east wing of the stoa where the bones of the dead man had been placed pending a funeral.

"I'll leave you here," Doris said, and she looked uneasy. "I don't like dead bodies." Doris walked off quickly.

Diotima and I shared a look. I shot open the bolt, then slowly opened the door. I peered in.

The skeleton was laid out on a board, which in turn lay on the floor: arms, legs, backbone, pelvis, ribs . . . everything in the right position. Everything except the head.

A skeleton without a head looks wrong. Without it, the neck looked like a road that went nowhere.

Without saying a word, I reached for the cloth bag I had with me, which we'd brought with us on the cart all the way from Athens. I pulled out the skull. The bag I tossed aside; I knelt and carefully placed the skull at the end of the line of vertebrae.

"There," I said. In the silence of the tiny room, my voice was louder than I intended.

The skeleton had been laid out on the floor in the same position it had lain for decades in the cave. That wasn't to make our job any easier, it was because the psyche of the dead person might be angered if the remains weren't treated with due respect.

Diotima and I looked down at the now-complete skeleton. The middle part was a complete mess. The clothing had rotted to tatters, and the flesh beneath had been eaten—by rats, no doubt.

We both waited for the other to speak.

When I realized this would go on forever, I said, "What do we do now?"

"I was hoping you'd have an idea," Diotima said.

"You're the one who always has the bright ideas."

"Not this time. There's nothing we can deduce from a musty pile of bones. We can't even tell if it's a man or a woman."

"Obviously not," I agreed. "The priestesses said they moved everything *exactly* as they found it?"

"He was on this board when they found him. They moved the entire board."

"Does this fellow look to you like he was buried properly?"

"Not even slightly," Diotima said. "I wonder if the killer gave him a coin?"

The most basic ritual anyone will give to the dead is to place a coin underneath the tongue of the deceased, so that the dead can pay Charon the ferryman to carry their psyche across the river of woe. The observance is so fundamental to common decency that a man will pay this service to his worst enemy.

"We know he didn't. We have the skull."

"But a coin would have fallen through and remained in the dust beneath," Diotima said. "It'd be easy to miss in all this accumulated muck."

Diotima scraped her hand along the space above the vertebrae, where the skull had been. The lower jaw had fallen to the ground, no doubt when the sinews and flesh had decayed to dust. The upper jaw was still attached to the skull. With the skull returned to its proper place, it gave the skeleton the appearance of screaming for eternity. The muck Diotima referred to was thirty years' worth of blown dirt and rat droppings. Her fingers scrabbled in the bones and dirt and raised a cloud of dust that filled my nostrils and made us both cough. It put me in mind of what Gaïs had said before—that in Hades the dead drink dust.

Diotima sat back and said two disconsolate words: "No coin."

Now *that* was interesting. Whether the victim on the floor

was Hippias or someone else, the killer had really, really hated him. Hated him enough to deny his psyche access to peace in Hades.

Diotima asked, "Nico, do you think this man's psyche might still be around?"

I was sure of it. Without a coin to pay Charon, the psyche of the man was trapped in the living world, and everyone knew a psyche stayed close to the body it used to inhabit.

Diotima looked about us.

"There's nothing to worry about," I said, trying to sound more confident than I felt. "We're here to help. If nothing else, we can swear to observe the rituals for this man." But I, too, looked about nervously.

"You're right," Diotima said, and in a louder voice, as if to someone farther away, she continued, "Hear me, Artemis, my Goddess of Brauron and Athens, as I am your priestess, so I swear to observe the rites for this man. I will place the coin, and build the pyre, and carry the remains in a fine urn, and with my own hands I will carry him to the cemetery at Ceramicus, where dwell the Athenians for eternity."

We waited. Nothing happened. Which was exactly the response we both wanted.

Then an idea occurred to me. I lay down on the ground.

"You're feeling tired already?" Diotima asked.

"Would you say this skeleton is longer than me?" I asked.

Diotima stood back for a better look. She glanced from me to the skeleton and back again. "Yes," she said. "By a hand's length."

"That's what I thought. This is the skeleton of a man. Men are taller than women."

"Either that, or it's the skeleton of an unusually tall woman."

"You only said that to be difficult."

"Tall women do exist, you know. But you're right, I was only being difficult. It probably is a man."

"Where does that get us?"

"Nowhere. Did you know that half of all dead people are male? Besides, I thought we'd already agreed this was Hippias."

"All we know for sure is that scrolls that were probably written by Hippias were found beside this skeleton. Wouldn't it be nice if we could confirm it?"

"Bones don't come with names engraved, Nico."

I sat up. "There must be *something* we can discover. What about damage to the bones?"

"Like what?"

"Like . . . if someone killed him with a club, there'd be broken bones."

We both looked down. What we could see of the bones showed they were unbroken.

"What about nicks and cuts?" Diotima suggested.

"If he was killed by a sword? Good idea."

With enormous distaste, we peeled back the rags that had once been a fine chiton. We picked up the pieces between thumb and forefinger and dropped them on the floor, to reveal what was left of the body beneath. The ribs lay where they had fallen, flat on the bottom of the board. They formed an odd travesty of a human being.

We both got down on hands and knees to inspect the bones.

"There are cuts and nicks on most of them," Diotima said.

"Rats and mice," I said. "They ate him."

"What about these?" Diotima pointed to several cuts, deeper than the others, in the ribs, about where the heart would have been.

I squinted. "Maybe. Not a sword, though."

"A knife?"

"Or a really big rat."

"What's this?" Diotima pointed. There was something amongst the bones and muck at the bottom of the board. It had been covered by the tattered clothing, and even with the rags removed, it was almost identical in color to the dust and, like the bones, was long and thin. Easy to miss.

"I've done my bit, it's your turn," Diotima said.

I apologized to the psyche that surely was watching, then put my hand between the ribs to hold what looked remarkably like a very tarnished knife.

I removed it from the jumble of bones. It was a knife—not one for cutting food, but the long, thin type for killing people.

Diotima and I shared a triumphant look. This was progress. I rubbed at the dirt with the edge of my chiton, and though most of it came away, the deep, dark tarnish remained. My futile attempt at cleaning did, however, reveal something important.

"There's something scratched into the blade," I said. "I can feel it when I rub."

We both peered at the blade. The scratches appeared to be letters, but neither of us could see enough to read it. Diotima tried to trace the indents with her more sensitive fingers, but that didn't work either. Then, by dint of holding the blade up to the light at the window so that the sun reflected off the debased metal, we managed to make out these words:

ἉΡΜΟΔΙΟΣ ΚΑΙ ἈΡΙΣΤΟΓΕΙΤΩΝ

Harmodius and Aristogeiton.

"The names of the killers?" Diotima suggested.

It was a good theory. There was only one problem. "Unlikely," I told her. "Harmodius and Aristogeiton died twenty years before the Battle of Marathon."

Harmodius and Aristogeiton were famous. They had attempted to assassinate Hippias and had been executed for their pains. Though they'd failed miserably, they were credited with starting the movement that eventually succeeded. Their statues stood in the agora.

"Turn the blade over," Diotima said.

I did. On the other side, using the same method, we read:

ΛΕΑΙΝΑ

"Leana?" The word meant "lioness."

"It's also a girl's name," Diotima said.

"Who's Leana?"

"I've no idea."

What was important was that the men named Harmodius and Aristogeiton had died on the orders of Hippias. It made the death of Hippias look like a revenge killing.

"Did you find what you're looking for?" a voice said from the doorway.

We both looked up, startled. Neither Diotima nor I had paid the slightest attention to who might be listening in. There, standing in the doorway, was Sabina, the treasurer of the temple, the woman who had taken the skull from the skeleton and sent it to the Basileus.

I hid the knife behind my back.

"I'm glad you're here, Sabina," I lied. "I wanted to ask: What made you tell the Basileus about this skeleton?"

"Isn't it obvious? A find like this is far beyond the remit of the priestesses of Brauron. Our task here is to turn girls into young ladies. Clearly it was for the archon in charge of all the state's temples to decide what to do. That's the Basileus. My action was the only responsible one."

Her answer was perfectly reasonable on the face of it, and yet I didn't believe it for a moment.

"Didn't the High Priestess order everyone to let the matter rest?" I asked.

"She suggested something along those lines."

"You disobeyed your high priestess," Diotima pressed, making it clear what she thought of that.

Sabina lifted her chin. "Thea *advised* that it was better to ignore the matter. I thought otherwise." She sniffed. "I report to the Basileus," she said, making much of her once-yearly report. "In any case, Thea won't rule here much longer."

"What do you mean?"

"Thea's an old woman," Sabina said. "Old women die."

She spoke with relish. Naked ambition can be ugly, and Sabina's ambitions were written across her face.

"Did you look inside the case?" I asked to change the subject.

"We had to know what was in there."

"Did you read the scrolls?" Diotima asked.

"Only part of the first, enough to see that this was something that needed to be dealt with by Athens. I never even opened the other four."

"You mean the other three," I corrected her.

She looked at me with an odd expression. "I mean four."

"There were only four scrolls in the case."

"There were five, tightly packed."

"Are you sure?"

"Is this some sort of test to see if I'm telling you the truth? You're not going to fool me that way. There were five scrolls, as you know perfectly well. I'm not the only person here who saw them."

Diotima and I shared a look. I knew what she was thinking.

There'd been five scrolls at the sanctuary. There were four scrolls in the office of Pericles ten days later. Here at last was proof that the killer was among us: not a stranger, but someone trusted.

The scrolls had traveled from the priestesses at Brauron to the Basileus, then to Pericles himself. Every one of those people was trusted, and yet somewhere along the line, someone must have removed a scroll, because Sabina had sent *five* scrolls, and a skull.

"Why did you send the skull along?" I asked Sabina, genuinely intrigued. "It wasn't the sort of thing most people would think of."

"I thought no one would believe me if I didn't. I imagined some fool assistant to the Basileus would read my note and think it a case of a silly woman having the vapors, not realizing that I'm one of his trusted representatives. But you can't ignore a skull."

No, you couldn't. The skull had gotten exactly the reaction she wanted: attention from the men who ran things, so that when it came time to choose the next High Priestess at Brauron, Sabina's name would be the one everyone knew. Sabina was no fool.

OUR NEXT PORT of call was the jetty over the hill. Just because Doris said the rowboat couldn't be used by a child, didn't make it true. Sabina showed us the way.

In the north field, there was a burnt patch of ground. It looked like there'd been an intense fire, but isolated to one spot.

"What's that?" I asked.

"That's where we cremated Allike," Sabina said. "Her parents came to collect the ashes."

"Oh." I should have thought of that. "What did her father say?"

"The mother was very upset. The father seemed more put out, if you know what I mean. He demanded compensation from the sanctuary, but really it wasn't our fault. I pointed that out to him."

"It was you who spoke to the parents, not the High Priestess?"

"Thea apologized to them. She really has little understanding of legal process. I'll leave you here. The jetty is over that hill." Sabina pointed.

Our feet sank into the same soft dirt that had made my steps so quiet the night before. Now I saw why: the hill was built from silt that had heaped up over long years. It curled about the toes of my bare feet and was pleasant to walk upon.

On the opposite side, the bushes struggled to live, not because of the soil but because the hill protected the sanctuary from the strong, dry winds that descended from the north every summer. The side facing the inlet was windswept. And inlet it was: narrow, almost pointy where we stood, and no wider than a *stadion*, it slowly widened out as it stretched from us until the coast curved away to the left and right, fully into the Aegean Sea.

The jetty was plain to see, a small affair but solid-looking: pylons driven into the seabed and weathered timbers to walk upon. The boat that floated at the end was tethered by a thin line. It all seemed terribly peaceful. The craft was larger than the small rowboat I'd imagined, but smaller than a fisherman's workboat.

We stepped onto the boards, walked gingerly along in case one of the boards should be ready to snap, and stopped at the end. The oars had been shipped on board, and I saw at once that Doris was at least partially right. No child could have lifted those oars.

But an adult with a child could. If Ophelia had left this way, it could not have been on her own. It was possible, though, if someone had helped her. Or if an adult had kidnapped her.

"Have you found anything?" a voice shouted to us. Diotima and I turned to see Doris. She carried wicker baskets and trudged the same path we'd taken to the jetty.

"Did you come looking for us?" Diotima asked.

"No. I've come to take the boat to Brauron. It's easier than walking if there're goods to carry, and faster than the cart."

"You row?"

Doris laughed. "On rare occasions, when I can't avoid it. Usually I'd take a slave along to row for me and carry the purchases in town, but Zeke has them all busy today, rebuilding fences."

Doris bent to load the baskets into the rowboat, a somewhat undignified posture for a lady her age. I took them from her, to load them myself.

I said, "Doris, we need to ask about this marriage of Ophelia's. It's a complication for us."

"It caused us quite a problem, too!"

"Why didn't you tell us about it?" Diotima asked.

"Because it was all over and done with long before there were any skeletons. About a month ago, Ophelia's father came to visit. We don't encourage family visits, it only makes the girls homesick—or more determined never to return home, one or the other; both are a problem. But it's not unusual for a girl's father to make an unexpected call in the final months."

"Why?"

"Polonikos brought another man with him: the father of a young man."

"Oh, I see."

Doris shrugged. "Ophelia was within months of officially becoming of marriageable age. A graduate of Brauron is considered a superior catch. She wouldn't have been the first girl to return home to discover her future has been decided for her while she was away. It's normal too for the father of the groom to want to meet the prospective daughter-in-law before the contract is concluded. The High Priestess doesn't like such dealings to be negotiated within the sanctuary, she feels it upsets the girls, but she can hardly refuse when a girl's father insists."

"So Ophelia's father and father-in-law turned up to inspect the merchandise," Diotima said. She sounded bitter.

"*Prospective* father-in-law, my dear," Doris corrected. "These things are never certain until the contract's sworn, and there's no point getting upset with me, young lady. We all do our best, but the world can't be to our liking."

"Yes, Doris. I'm sorry," Diotima said, contrite, and for a moment I saw the adolescent girl that was, standing before her mentor.

"How did Ophelia take this?" I asked.

Doris shrugged again. It seemed to be her way of dealing with unpleasantness. "She didn't cry, and she didn't smile. Who can tell what a child truly thinks? Both fathers spoke with her. The second man asked Ophelia to demonstrate her skill at weaving with the loom, and at sewing cloth, and spoke a few words with the child. He went away happy, I think. There was no problem until the son arrived."

"That was Melo?"

"Yes. You may well be surprised. We certainly were. A young man rode in a few days later. He said he was Melo, the son of Thessalus, and that he was betrothed to Ophelia. Then, without even pausing for breath, he demanded to see his fiancée. In private."

"Had they ever met before?"

"No."

"Were they truly betrothed?" Diotima asked.

"Good question! We had no idea. We'd heard nothing from the girl's father, but then, there was no requirement for him to tell us. I'm certain Ophelia herself didn't know. She was standing right behind me when the young man announced their intended marriage. The look on the child's face told me this came as news to her."

"Tricky for you," I said.

"Very. Thea decided that, in the absence of a formal note from Ophelia's father announcing a contract, she couldn't possibly allow the couple even to see each other, let alone be together in private."

No, of course not. I nodded to show I was in total agreement with the High Priestess. If the man and the girl were alone for any appreciable time, it would call into question the girl's virginity. Not necessarily a problem if the couple were to marry, but if Melo was there on a pretense then it would be a disaster for the girl. Thea had done the right thing.

"Melo refused to leave," said Doris. "Never in my time at Brauron have I seen such rudeness. Thea told him to come back with the father's permission, which he should have obtained in the first place. He pushed past her."

"He *laid hands* on the High Priestess?" Diotima said. She couldn't have been more surprised if Doris had said that Zeus had descended from Olympia.

"That was when Zeke hit him. Goodness, it's been ages since I saw him move that fast." Doris laughed. "Melo's major concern seemed to be whether Ophelia was attractive."

And fair enough, too. Who wants an ugly wife? But I kept that thought to myself; I was fairly sure neither woman would appreciate the point.

Doris said, "He repeated several times, in the hearing of every woman present, that he'd refuse a wife who wasn't erotic."

That probably wasn't the most tactful way of putting it, especially to a temple full of women.

"Was Ophelia listening in?" Diotima asked.

"Probably!" Doris said, and she grimaced. "They're normal children; I wouldn't be surprised if every one of them returned and watched from around a corner."

"So Ophelia heard that her future husband was there to check her out." Diotima grimaced.

"She also saw her High Priestess order Melo off the sanctuary. The young man went away angry. And that was the end of that. The High Priestess wrote a note to Ophelia's father and sent it with our fastest runner. After that ugly episode, I expected to hear that the marriage negotiations had fallen through. But we heard nothing."

"Wait," I said. "Did you tell this Melo which girl was Ophelia?"

"No, but when he announced the betrothal many of the girls gasped, and every eye turned to Ophelia. That and the expression on her face must have told him which girl was his bride. I'm sure he knew."

"Then that explains how he knew to find Ophelia in the girls' bedrooms, and not some other girl."

"What's this?" Doris said, startled.

I explained that the intruder the other night had been Melo—something we'd withheld from the sanctuary, telling them merely that someone had tried to break in and that Diotima had spotted them.

It was Doris's turn to grimace. "Thea isn't going to like it when she hears this."

"Then don't tell her," Diotima said.

"Spoken like a true schoolgirl, my dear. Unfortunately, we adults have other standards. I fear . . ."

"Yes?"

"The thing is, Nicolaos, there's another possibility. This is a man who wanted to know his future wife was erotic. Those were his own words. I fear Melo waylaid Ophelia at night, raped her, killed her, and then hid her body somewhere in the woods."

WE FOUND ZEKE in the fields to the northwest of the complex. The sanctuary owned land about the place and used it to grow crops for food, plus a few goats, a cow for milk, sheep, and a hen house for eggs. As small farms went, this one was highly productive, which was a good thing considering the number of mouths that had to be fed. Zeke was obviously an accomplished farmer; his darkened, dry skin certainly attested to the days he spent out here. At that moment he labored at the hen house, where the fencing had been damaged.

"Foxes," he explained between grunts. "They didn't get in, but it was a near thing. The night guard chased those four-legged bastards away." Zeke had younger men to do the heavy work, but he insisted on resetting the posts himself. "'Cause they gotta be done right," he said.

"Is there always a night guard out here?" I asked.

"That's why we've still got our animals."

"But setting guards around the entire sanctuary was a new thing, wasn't it?"

"Yes. Since Allike. The guards settled the girls right down, made 'em feel safe."

I said, "The thing is, Zeke, we're not sure the sanctuary guards were entirely effective."

Zeke's eyes narrowed, and for a moment I thought he would shout at me. Perhaps I could have put it more delicately, but if Melo had told us the truth, then on at least one occasion after the guards were placed, Ophelia had managed to creep out of the grounds to meet her betrothed, and then had crept back to her bed. That was if Melo was telling the truth, of course. If the security had been solid, it would cast doubt on his word.

"Perhaps you could tell us how you set the guards?" I said.

"By talking to them," he said slowly, as if he were speaking to a village idiot.

"No, I meant *where* did you place the guards. How do you know someone couldn't have slipped through?"

The last post dropped into its hole with a satisfying thud. Zeke nodded. He gave the young men detailed instructions how he wanted the holes filled in. Then he rubbed his dirty hands on his dirty tunic and said, "Come with me." Without looking to see if we followed, he set off across the land. He led us to the stone bridge that crossed the river.

"This is the main road in and out of the sanctuary. In fact, it's the only real road. All the other routes are tracks you couldn't drive a cart down. I was short of men, but two guards I set here, both good men," Zeke said.

"Why two guards, then?" Diotima asked. "The bridge is wide, but one is enough to see all of it."

I knew the answer to that one, but I let Zeke answer.

"'Cause it's the most obvious route. If one man gets knocked out, the other can call for help."

I nodded. That's what they'd taught me in the army.

The bridge was wider even than the distance across the river, so that it resembled a square.

"Does this road go any farther?"

"No, this is the end."

The bridge was supported by long stone blocks that ran lengthways in the river. Those supporting blocks were two hands in width, and almost *ten paces* long! The stream ran smoothly between them. The road was made of heavy, thick pavers laid across the supports. Even the heaviest of wagons could have crossed with ease.

"This bridge would do credit to the main entrance of a major city," I said, impressed. "You could get an army across it."

Zeke shrugged.

"What in Hades is it doing on a dead-end road to a minor temple?"

"A *major* temple, Nico, thank you very much," Diotima said.

"Mind if I look underneath?" I asked.

"I won't stop you," Zeke said.

I hitched up my exomis and stepped into the running water. Holding on to the top of the bridge, I pulled myself across, stopping at each gap between the underlying supports to peer beneath.

"What are you looking for, Nico?" Diotima asked.

"Dead bodies," I said. "But no luck."

"You'd call that luck?"

"I guess not."

Zeke walked north along the river bank. He said, "The river's fordable for a man. I doubt a girl could cross it, not without risking drowning, anyways, so if you're thinking Ophelia crossed the water at night, you can stop thinking it." He stopped a hundred paces north of the bridge. "I set the next guard here. Everyone carried a torch. I walked it myself to make sure either the guards at the bridge or this one here could see me no matter where I stood. No blind spots, you see?"

I saw.

"This guard along the river was alone?" Diotima asked.

Zeke nodded. "Not enough men," he explained. "But I ran the same system all round the rest of the sanctuary."

I said, "An attacker could take down one of your guards, then get to the girls."

"But that ain't what happened," he pointed out.

"Did you set guards at the rowboat?"

"No."

"Why not?"

"Because we were keeping a killer *out*, no one thought we needed to keep a child *in*."

That sounded all too reasonable.

"So Ophelia could have rowed away."

"No. The boat's too heavy for a girl to pull. Besides, the rowboat's still in place."

How obvious. So Ophelia didn't leave that way.

Zeke knew his business. I said as much to him.

He shrugged. "I've been here many years. I've seen every way the girls have found to get in and out without being seen. There ain't no way a stranger's going to get in that I ain't already walked myself."

We thanked Zeke for his time. As we left, I said to Diotima, "One thing's for sure: Zeke's no ordinary maintenance man. There's military in his background."

"Yes," Diotima said. "Thea told us he served during the Persian Wars."

"That was in the ranks as a common soldier. I mean more than that. At one time or another, Zeke's been an officer."

"The way he set those guards?" Diotima asked.

I nodded. "There are camp commanders who are slacker than him." I hesitated, then asked, "Do you think he's trustworthy?"

"Zeke?" Diotima looked surprised. "He was here when I was a child. He was probably here when the gods walked the earth. If Zeke was going to do anything wrong, he'd have done it years ago. I can't imagine *not* trusting him. Why?"

"Just asking."

There was something about Zeke that made me doubt him, but I couldn't put my finger on it.

Gaïs approached us from the other direction, going to the north. It was one of those long and embarrassing moments when people who barely know each other are forced to stare and wave for ages before they're finally able to say anything.

Gaïs carried a wicker basket, the contents of which were covered with a small cloth. I guessed she was on her way to feed the men working in the field. Her hair was still straggly, but at least it was pulled back and held with a silver clasp. She may even have combed it, but if so it hadn't had much effect. She wore clothes now, one of the standard, highly conservative priestess chitons; on her slim frame it resembled nothing so much as a sack. Her bare feet poked out from beneath the material. It was clear that Gaïs didn't go naked to flaunt her body; to her, clothes were merely an impediment. As she passed by, Gaïs gave us a cool look and said, "Ajax pulled Cassandra from the temple." She didn't break her stride but disappeared through the narrow gap between temple and stoa.

I said to Diotima, "What was *that* supposed to mean?"

Diotima looked upset. "In the legends, after Troy falls, Cassandra goes to the temple sanctuary to seek refuge."

"So?"

"Ajax drags Cassandra from the sanctuary and rapes her."

Chapter Six

THERE WERE TOO many things to do and not enough people we trusted to do them.

I made ready to depart for Athens, because tracing the scroll was a top priority. Diotima was to remain at the sanctuary to organize a search across the countryside, because Ophelia might still be alive, and finding her was *another* top priority.

Thea agreed to release the temple slaves to the search, though as Zeke pointed out, somewhat acidly, he'd already led a search party days ago. Zeke gave his opinion that Diotima (an inexperienced young woman, in his view) and Melos (a foolish young man) had no hope of doing better than him. This view was met by everyone with embarrassed silence.

We'd had to report what Melo had told us, of Ophelia sneaking in and out of the sanctuary, in order to persuade Thea. That too had raised Zeke's ire. We'd made him look bad, because security was his business.

Zeke said, "You saw yourselves how I set those guards. There's no chance a man could have gotten past."

"But Ophelia was meeting Melo outside the grounds," I said. "It seems Ophelia had a regular route out."

"It's as you said before, Zeke," Diotima added. "You set guards to keep evil out, not to keep children in."

"Do you trust the word of that arrogant young man?" Zeke asked in a tone that suggested that if we said yes, then we were idiots.

Diotima and I looked at each other and wondered what to say. Because we weren't all that sure we trusted Melo either.

Diotima temporized. "It's not your fault if the girl knew how to beat the guards, Zeke."

"Do as you will with this search. It's obvious I'm too old to be of any use." Zeke turned on his heel and walked away.

"You must forgive Zeke," Thea said in the uncomfortable silence that followed. "He feels this situation extremely. He holds himself responsible for what's happened. The gods know he's not as young as he once was, to bear these shocks."

"How long has Zeke been here?" Diotima asked. "I remember thinking he was old when I was here."

Thea stifled a laugh. "That was only six years ago, *young lady*," she said. "That's less than one tenth his years." She paused. "At least, I think it is. I doubt if even he himself knows his own age."

"Was he here before you, High Priestess?" I asked.

"I was a young woman when Zeke arrived. I remember every detail of that day." Thea sighed. "These days I struggle to recall the names of the new girls, and every year everything seems to get harder, and I become more forgetful. Age does terrible things."

"Zeke's older than you, yet you came to Brauron first. Isn't that surprising?"

"It's no surprise at all, young man. I was raised at this temple. I was left here as an orphan, like Gaïs."

Doris showed no surprise at this news. I guessed it was common knowledge.

It struck me that Doris was much younger than Thea. Thea was well-grayed and small and carried a sense of serene tiredness. Doris had gray hair too, though more of it, and a stout, healthy demeanor. Thea and tall, thin Zeke were the only ones here who remembered the time before the sacking.

"Where's Zeke from?" Diotima asked.

"You'd have to ask him."

"He didn't say?"

"Zeke's grown old in this sanctuary. Perhaps he's a bit set in his ways because of it. He resents outside interference, no matter how well meant. I'll talk to him later. Meanwhile, the slaves are yours to use in a search. It would help me to mollify Zeke if you could make sure you find Ophelia."

THE INVESTIGATION HAD thrown up many leads that could only be answered in Athens. Not least of these was the strange attitude of Polonikos. Why wasn't he worried about his missing daughter? Why, in fact, was he anxious for us to not find her?

I thought about this as I bounced on Blossom's back. Every now and then, he would skid on gravel and my head would jerk back and forth. Without the cart he was able to carry my weight, but only a masochist could have enjoyed such a ride. Diotima's attempts to feed the donkey were having some effect—at least he didn't look like he was about to expire—but he still resembled a refugee from a slave camp. His spindly legs were sturdy, but there was something wrong with his muscles, and every step felt like a kick up my behind. I thought longingly of the smooth stride of a high-performance racehorse.

Every explanation for Polonikos that I could think of was suspicious. I wondered if we'd paid enough attention to his odd behavior. As I approached the outskirts of Athens, I realized that his property lay not far off my path. The land of Attica resembles nothing so much as a giant octopus, with Athens at the head and the roads her tentacles that spread across the landscape. Running from the major roads in all directions are narrow dirt tracks, and it is down these tracks that one find the farms and estates.

My bottom was sore, but I needed answers more than I needed comfort. When I came to the dirt track that led to Polonikos, I took it.

Polonikos himself was out in his fields when I arrived, supervising his slaves. They held sticks, with which they beat the olive trees. Children collected the fallen fruit in baskets.

Polonikos took one look at Blossom, who had carried me this far, and said, "What is *that*?"

"I believe it's a donkey, sir. It's a rental. My fiancée's choice."

The corners of his mouth twitched. "You didn't fall for the adorable donkey routine, did you?"

"The what?"

"How long have you been married?"

"Er . . . we're not quite . . . yet. We'll be married next month."

"I see." Polonikos sighed. "Take my advice, young man. For the rest of your life, never let your wife go with you to a sale yard. The moment those salesmen see a man coming with his wife in tow, they haul out of the stables the scrawniest, most underfed donkey they've got. They put an old straw hat on the beast, stick a flower in the hat, and wait for the woman to say, 'Oh, isn't he cute!' Usually the salesman comes up with some cock-and-bull story about how the beast belonged to a little old lady who only used it to carry her herbs to market, and how she's died and the stupid beast will be off to the knacker's that day unless someone buys the animal. By the time the salesman's finished, the only question the ladies ask is what color the hat comes in."

"Thank you, sir, I'll remember that. I wanted to ask you—"

He quickly held up a hand. "Stop right there," he said sternly. "I told you to drop the investigation."

"Yes, sir, you did. But Pericles, the archons, and the High Priestess of Artemis at Brauron want me to carry on. Another person who wants Ophelia found is her fiancé."

I paused, waiting for a reaction.

Polonikos signaled to a slave, who hurried over with a bowl of water. In this, Polonikos washed his hands. "Working with fruit always makes my hands sticky," he said absently.

"Is it true, sir, that a marriage had been arranged for Ophelia?"

"It's a lie!" Polonikos burst out with no warning.

He must have seen my surprise, because he said, visibly calming himself, "I'm sorry. I'm afraid this subject upsets me considerably. The truth is, there were negotiations. But Thessalus can say what he likes; I deny that anything was ever finalized. If he insists I'll have to take him to court."

"That would be Thessalus, the father of Melo?"

Polonikos nodded.

"I understand the two of you were at the sanctuary together."

"That was during the negotiations."

"And that Melo later went to visit Ophelia himself."

Polonikos looked startled. "He did? Not with my permission."

"So the marriage negotiation failed?" I prompted him. Melo had said nothing of this.

"Talks broke down for the usual reason: we couldn't agree on the dowry."

"Oh?"

"Yes. That's what marriage is all about, young man, merging the wealth of two families. "

A shout from the orchard, a hundred paces away, and a large number of olives fell to the ground. At once the children bent to put the fallen fruit into the baskets. The baskets would be sent to the agora, where the fruit would be sold.

"There's wealth, right over there," Polonikos said, half to himself. "Would that there were more of it." He looked back to me. "This is a strange trade you ply," he said in a voice more friendly than before. "Who pays you?"

"My clients, sir. I accept work on commission, like any artisan."

"You're a craftsman of crime then. Does it pay?"

That brought home a difficult question. One that I'd been keeping from my own thoughts. "I have a large sum due from a client any day now," I said with more confidence than I felt.

Polonikos smiled cynically. He'd seen me ride in on a scrawny donkey. That made me angry, so to prove my words I said, "The sum is substantial. So large that it will more than meet my immediate needs. I'll need to invest the rest," I lied with a deadpan face. "Or maybe I'll put my spare cash in a bank."

It was an idle boast, but Polonikos held up his hands in horror and said, "Are you mad? Take my advice, young man, and avoid both borrowing and lending. These new-fangled bank businesses seem to be springing up all over the place, but frankly, I see no future for Athens in banking."

"They do seem somewhat unethical," I said, thinking of my past experience with bankers. I rubbed my chin.

"Unethical? Who cares about that? I'm talking about making a profit, lad. Land, young fellow, that's the future. Country estates. Come with me." Polonikos had become excited. He took me by the arm to lead me out to his fields. "Do you see that?" He swept his arm to display his fields and the working slaves. "That's wealth. These banks you talk of . . . they're more than happy to take your money—money you earned by hard labor on your own land. Then those vultures, those dogs, they'll lose your funds in the blink of an eye—"

I was struck by an inspiration. "Sir, have you by any chance recently lost money on an investment?"

"Who told you that?!" he barked. Then, before I could answer, he calmed down once more. "Never mind. I suppose the news was bound to spread. As it happens, I do have a matter before the courts at this very moment."

"What happened, may I ask?" I stated the question with some care. Polonikos seemed a man of wild mood swings. He was a man on edge.

"You may as well. It'll all come out in court anyway. Last year, I joined a consortium to underwrite certain trading ventures. Ventures involving a merchant ship and several cargoes. Nothing could go wrong, they said. Everything was insured. The principals were two bankers, their names Antisthenes and Archestratus . . . they told me the cargo was insured. I believed them."

"What happened?"

"The ship sank with all hands and, of far greater importance, with the precious cargoes. Or so they say. I have my doubts. I demanded the insurance. That was when those two vultures admitted the insurance had been arranged through their own bank, the payout to be drawn as a collateral loan on the cargo—the cargo that had sunk, mind you—so they claimed the money was lost."

My head was swimming. I understood only half of what Polonikos was saying, if that. I decided to ignore the high finance and got to the nub of the matter. "I suppose you found yourself short of cash," I said.

"You may say so. But I'm certain to win my money back when the court hears the facts, I promise you!"

Suddenly I understood his problem. Polonikos *did* have a contract for his daughter to marry Melo, son of Thessalus, and every marriage contract involved a dowry to be supplied by the father of the bride. The problem was, Polonikos had lost the dowry money in a bad investment. If Ophelia was found, the marriage would proceed, the dowry would come due, and Polonikos would have to spend money he didn't have.

It was entirely in Polonikos's interests for Ophelia never to be found. Or at least, not until he'd won his court case.

I left Polonikos, the father of the missing Ophelia, to his fields, and walked back through the house gate. A woman of middle age watched me from the second-story window of the farmhouse. She waved, and I understood she wished me to wait.

The woman soon ran out the front door of the farmhouse, holding up her chiton to keep it out of the farm mud. As well she might, since the dress was clearly of superior make, in hues of red and black and patterned with a conservative border. She was well groomed and bore no calluses on her hands, and her face was smooth skinned. I had no trouble guessing who she was.

"I heard you speaking to my husband," she said. "I am Malixa, the wife of Polonikos and the mother of Ophelia."

Her eyes were red, and she clasped her hands in anxiety.

"My husband's not a bad man," she said. "But he is one with many problems."

"Like your daughter, then," I said. I couldn't hide my distaste for Polonikos from my speech. Whatever problems the father had, the daughter's were infinitely greater.

"When my husband has resolved these problems with his money, then he'll go to find our daughter. I'm sure of it."

"It might be too late then," I said. To emphasize the urgency, I added, "It will almost certainly be too late."

"I know." The stress was painted across her face. "I beg you to find Ophelia before then. Please. I'll pay you."

"How?" I asked.

"Any way I can."

I said, "Malixa, I will find your daughter because the sanctuary at Brauron has hired me to do so. But I can't do it without information, and so far, what I have to work with is hopeless. If you want to pay me, you can do it with information."

"But I know nothing."

I thought she was about to cry.

I said, "I'll tell you the truth, Malixa. I don't even know if Ophelia left the sanctuary of her own will or if she was taken. It could be one or the other, with equal odds. If she was taken, then she's in enormous trouble. If she went on her own, then perhaps she can be saved. Your husband tells me nothing about your daughter, because he doesn't want her found. See what you can find out. Does she have friends there? Bring me anything, *anything*, that might tell us where she went."

"I'll try," she said. And now her tears began to flow.

MY PLAN WAS to see the Basileus to discover what had happened to the fifth scroll. If possible, of course. The archons were the busiest men in Athens. It occurred to me as I trudged the roads home that a letter of introduction from Pericles would get me in to see the Basileus faster. So I tethered the donkey at our house—both my feet and my bottom hurt, and I stared longingly at the couches in the courtyard as I passed it by—and dragged my feet to the agora.

I found Pericles on the steps of the Painted Stoa, where he was talking with other men, all dressed in formal chitons, all with their himation stoles of fine wool draped over their shoulders. Their clothing declared them to be men who had no need to work to earn their bread. No doubt they discussed affairs of state. No doubt they were all wealthy landowners with many slaves. I looked at them with envy.

They in turn stared at me with mild disgust as I moved to join them. I was coated in the dust of the road, my feet ached, and I couldn't remember the last time I'd washed. The men's hut I'd shared with the slaves at Brauron was every bit as foul and smelly as Sabina had promised. No doubt I carried its aroma of goat and sweaty armpits.

Unlike every other man in Athens, Pericles never seemed to pass the time of day with his fellow citizens: to sit in the shade of the stoas and talk about the meaning of life, which is to say, women and sport. Pericles never wasted his time in such idle pursuits. If he'd ever speculated about what was under a woman's dress, or who'd win at the athletics, no one had ever heard him do it. If he was in the agora, it meant he had business there. In anyone else such standoffishness would have been considered arrogance, but in his case men admired him for his dedication, even if it did give him the air of a highly intellectual, elegant automaton.

As I watched, Pericles turned and saw me. He waved as if to say, "Stay there." He said something final to the people he was with, then joined me.

"How goes it?" he asked.

I brought him up to date on the state of the investigation. He summarized my perhaps slightly convoluted explanation with the words, "So you've come here to tell me that you've made no progress?"

"That's not fair, Pericles. There are lines of investigation, and we've made progress down every one of them. The problem isn't lack of leads to follow. The problem is there are *too many* of them.

The High Priestess, the treasurer, a young priestess, and the mysterious maintenance man all look suspicious."

"None of these people have a reason to murder," Pericles said.

"None that we know of," I agreed. "The lovelorn Melo might be perfect for the abduction of Ophelia, but he had no reason to harm Allike."

"What about this story of a wild bear?"

"Maybe a bear did kill Allike. But Melo says Ophelia told him she was certain it was a human murderer."

That was second-hand hearsay. Even to my ears, it sounded weak.

"There hasn't been a bear in Attica for generations," Pericles said. "Men used to hunt them, but they're gone now."

"I know."

"What else?" Pericles asked.

"The fifth scroll. It has to be important. Where is it?"

"Brauron or Athens. Obviously."

"Everyone in Athens denies having seen it," I said. "Everyone in Brauron says they saw it. Maybe Ophelia could tell us the real truth. Pericles, what do you think of this Melo?"

"Highly untrustworthy," Pericles said at once. "I don't know his father."

"We have to find Ophelia, and we have to discover what became of the missing scroll, and we have to check the histories of *everyone* involved in this case who might have been around thirty years ago."

"Why?"

"Because whatever caused this began thirty years ago. I must warn you, Pericles, this might take longer than we originally thought."

Pericles thought about that before he nodded. "I see your reasoning," he said. "Yes, your approach seems satisfactory."

I stood in the dusty agora, open-mouthed, astonished that Pericles was being reasonable. It was so unlike him.

Pericles continued, "Nicolaos, I've looked into the issue of your payment for the first commission you carried out for me. I was astonished when I looked it up to see that sorry affair happened a full year ago. How time flies. You're correct that I never did settle my account. Clearly I owe you, and the agreed sum is *sufficient to provide a small, steady income*."

"That's right."

"I've given this some thought, and I think the best way to acquit the debt is to give you a farm."

"*What!*"

"Only a small one," said Pericles, almost apologetically. "But a farm's good for a small, steady income."

"I thought you'd give me money," I said.

"So did I at first, but consider, Nicolaos, if I were to give you coins, how could you make a steady income from that? You'd have to invest it, wouldn't you? To take shares in a trading boat, or perhaps lend it to someone at a rate of interest. These are all risky ventures, and you specifically said a *steady* income. There's nothing steady about trade. But land, Nicolaos, land is always a solid investment."

I thought back to the words of Polonikos, who had advised me to avoid borrowing and lending and to stick with the one true source of wealth, stretching back to King Theseus: ownership of the land.

Me, a land owner. What would my father say when he learned that I'd brought a farm into the family? He thought I was doomed to poverty because no one could make investigation pay! I smiled to myself.

"Does this suit you?" Pericles asked, interrupting my thoughts.

"What? Oh, yes Pericles. It suits very well indeed. I agree." I couldn't wait to tell Diotima. She'd be proud when she heard how her husband was going up in the world.

"Good. I know you need to see the Basileus in the morning. Meet me tomorrow afternoon at my family estate. I'll take you to your new property."

THE BASILEUS HAS his being in the Stoa Basileus—the Royal Stoa, for Basileus means "king" in our language—in the top northwest corner of the agora, on the busiest intersection in Athens, where the Panathenaic Way meets the road to Piraeus. Displayed before the Stoa Basileus are the laws of Athens, chiseled into stone, that any man might see them. The Royal Stoa lies directly opposite the Crossroads Shrine, where dotted all around are busts of the god Hermes to bring good luck to travelers.

Clutched in my hand was the letter I'd begged from Pericles, which got me past the long, long queue of men who waited to do business with one of the busiest administrators in Athens. I ignored the dirty looks of those waiting and breezed right through the door to the outer office.

In the outer office, standing right in front of me, was Glaucon, who had been first to confess to killing Hippias.

"What are you doing here?" I blurted, before my thoughts could catch up with my mouth.

Glaucon looked sheepish. "I'm assistant to the Basileus," he said.

So that was how he'd known to come see me so quickly. When I'd asked him, Glaucon had said that assistants talk. What he hadn't said was that he was the assistant doing the talking. He probably knew I was to be given the assignment even before Pericles had spoken to me. In the race to be declared the killer of the tyrant, Glaucon had cheated. No wonder he'd cringed when I walked in.

"I've business with the Basileus," I told him, and handed over the letter from Pericles. Glaucon barely glanced at it—he probably knew my business better than I did. He set aside the parchment and said, "The Basileus has someone with him now." He made a mark on a wax tablet. "I'll squeeze you in."

"Thanks."

While we waited, I said, "Glaucon, when the skull and the case arrived from Brauron, did you open the case?"

He blinked. "Of course. I always check anything sent to the Basileus. Otherwise, how would I know to prioritize his business?"

"How many scrolls were in the case when you opened it?"

"Four."

"You're sure?"

"I'm fairly sure I can count to four."

"Did you read them?"

"Only the first. When I saw who'd written it . . . well, you know."

He'd had the same reaction as me.

"I took it in to the Basileus at once," Glaucon continued. "I even interrupted a meeting to do it."

"Oh? Who else was at the meeting?"

"Is this important?"

"It might be." Whoever had been there would also know about the scrolls and the skeleton.

"I'll have to check. If you're lucky I'll still have the appointments tablet for that day. Wait a moment."

Glaucon opened a cupboard, in which were stacked piles and piles of wax tablets.

"We keep appointment tablets going back two months, then reuse them," he explained. "You're lucky this happened recently." He mumbled to himself as he ran his finger down the stack, calling off the days of the month. "Noumenia, Second Waxing, Third Waxing . . . no, no, no, it was later than that . . . Tenth Waxing, Eleventh, Twelfth, Thirteenth . . . Ninth Waning, Eighth Waning, Seventh Waning. Here it is!" He pulled a tablet from close to the bottom. The whole stack fell out and smashed on the floor.

"Curse it!"

"Sorry about that," I said.

"Not your fault," he said absently. "That always happens when I try to pull one from the bottom. I'll get the slaves to clean it up."

He opened the front door and yelled for a slave. One came running. Glaucon gestured at the tumbled pile without a word, and the slave knelt and got to work, shouting as he did for another slave to bring a basket.

I asked Glaucon, "Can the broken tablets be repaired?"

"Not a chance. We'll have to buy new ones. It hardly matters." Glaucon shrugged. "They're paid for out of public money. There's plenty more where that comes from."

"What job did you say you were running for?"

"State treasurer."

"Terrific."

Glaucon ran his finger down the list in his hand. "Ah, here's the answer to your question. The meeting when I walked in with the skull and case was to do with the next big public festival—that's the Great Dionysia, where they put on all the plays. There was only one other man in the room. One of those writer types, a fellow named Aeschylus."

At that moment the door to the inner office opened. A busy-looking man marched out. He passed right between Glaucon and me without acknowledging either of us, opened the outer door, and slammed it behind him.

Glaucon and I looked at each other. "The Basileus will see you now," he said.

The Basileus is one of the three senior government officials whose job it is to run Athens day to day, the other two being the Eponymous Archon, who sees to citizen matters, and the Polemarch, who manages matters involving resident aliens in Athens. The Basileus sees to religious matters and public festivals. Basileus means king, but the man who holds the post is no royal. Like any other archon, he serves his year and then is done.

This year's Basileus was a stern man who, like most archons, had rapidly thinning hair. Hair loss seemed to go with the job description.

He didn't stand as I walked in. He remained seated on a wooden stool behind a small desk, his back ramrod straight. He frowned at the sight of me.

"Nicolaos, son of Sophroniscus, of the deme Alopece, sir," I said by way of introduction.

"I recognize you," he said. "You're Pericles's little attack dog, aren't you? The one he hired over the arrival of that bizarre skull."

The Basileus gestured to one of the three camp stools on my side of the room. The legs of all three stools had been carved identically to resemble the legs of horses, and all ended in horses' hooves. It was basic stuff, and it looked as if the Basileus had picked them up at an army-disposal sale.

I eased myself into the one he indicated, by no means certain it wouldn't collapse under me, and realized at once why one of the most important administrators in Athens used such furniture. It was excruciatingly uncomfortable. The Basileus was a man who encouraged short interviews.

"I have a few questions," I said, wriggling my bottom in search of comfort.

"Be quick."

"There was a scroll case that came with the skull, sir."

"Yes."

"When you opened the case, how many scrolls were within?"

"Four. I recall thinking it was odd; that there seemed to be one missing. But then I thought perhaps Hippias never wrote a fifth scroll."

"The space for the fifth scroll is marked like the others."

"I can't help you there." The Basileus leaned forward and pointedly looked to the door. I pointedly ignored the hint. It occurred to me the Basileus could give me some background about what had happened to Hippias.

I settled back into the camp stool and asked, "What was your reaction, sir, when you saw the notes had been written by the old tyrant?"

"Indifference. That was all in the past. My job's to deal with the present."

"So you're not concerned about tyrannies, sir? I would have thought anyone your age would be overwhelmingly concerned—"

The Basileus suddenly stood up, and though he wasn't a tall man, he seemed to tower over me. "I'm old enough to remember those days, young man," he said. "I was there. I may have been only a small child, but even I knew enough to be afraid. Do you know what it means to go to bed not knowing whether you'll wake to find your father has been taken away by soldiers in the night?"

"Er . . . no," I said.

"I knew if it happened, I'd never see my sire again. My father's fear was palpable, even when he sat in his own courtyard."

"I wonder that anyone supported the tyrant."

The Basileus snorted. "It's very simple. In that situation, if you want to survive, then you do what you're told. Especially if you're not overwhelmingly interested in concepts such as freedom. Enough men acted to save themselves, and it swept along the rest, until only those bent on suicide dared resist."

"Did your father resist, sir?"

"My father was one of those who valued his life. He saved himself by giving the tyrant mild support. Father held a few minor administrative posts under Hippias, and that's one of the reasons I'm here today. I'm not proud of it, but it's what happened. He was never actively involved in the killings, mind you! I want to emphasize that."

The Basileus stood there and waited for me to comment. I considered my words.

"I see," I said, slowly. "I suppose you might argue that the city has to be administered, even when the government's bad."

"Precisely. If you want the ones who freed us, then you need to speak to the Alcmaeonid clan."

"The Alcmaeonids?"

"You know them well. They're the family of Pericles on his mother's side. It was they who fomented the second plot against Hippias, the one that finally succeeded. You young men admire Pericles for his voice, but we older men tolerate him because he has the finest pedigree of any man alive."

I said, "Pericles's parents and grandparents are all dead."

"So they are. If you want to know about those times, the only man alive that you could ask is Callias."

"Callias!" I repeated, shocked. I knew him.

"Yes. The family of Pericles instigated the rebellion, but it was Callias who funded it. He was in thick with the whole plot."

THAT AFTERNOON, I took the road out of the Dipylon Gates, turned right, and walked to the family estate of Pericles. It was only a short distance, because the property had been there since time immemorial; the oldest families had the estates closest to Athens, and the family of Pericles was of the oldest, stretching back to the time of King Theseus and beyond.

Come to that, my own family was ancient too. Father claimed descent from Daedalus, the genius inventor who created the Labyrinth in far-off Crete, and who after the fall of King Minos had fled to Athens to begin a new life. The difference was, genius inventors don't make money.

The road I walked followed Pericles's land before reaching his farmhouse. I looked at the olive trees with interest, the sheep and the corn planted in the fertile soil, and I felt a glow of satisfaction that something like this would soon be mine. There was a shepherd boy trailing the sheep (of course, otherwise they would have wandered off), and I waved at him happily; he stared back as if no one ever waved at shepherd boys.

The farmhouse, when I came to it, lay off the road behind a

stone fence and a wooden gate. The house surprised me in its small size, but then I reflected that Pericles spent all his time in the city, as indeed had his father before him, and the farmhouse probably hadn't been updated for two generations. But the house and the barn beside it were well kept and spoke of proper care.

Pericles stood out the front, in conversation with an older man who was dressed in farm clothes, which is to say a loincloth and a broad-brimmed hat of straw. His skin was as burnt as my cooking.

As I walked up to them, Pericles said, without preamble, "Ah, good day to you, Nicolaos. This is Simaristos. He runs the estate for me. He'll be coming with us."

The older man nodded and said, "Call me Sim. Everyone does."

No one had to tell me that Simaristos was a slave. No free man would willingly work for another, and Simaristos—Sim—had that air of hard-won competence that comes with a man who knows his business.

Pericles excused himself to see to other matters before we set off. Sim and I waited outside.

"Do you know anything about farming?" he asked, in a voice that implied he already knew the answer.

"I'm eager to learn," I told him. After all, how hard could it be? Put seeds in the ground, watch them grow. If an uneducated farmer could do it, so could I.

Sim frowned. "Well, I hope you have more sense than my master."

I blinked. "Pericles doesn't have sense?"

"The man's insane," Sim said, and threw his arms up in disgust. "We lose money hand over fist. You want to know why? Because Pericles couldn't be bothered with his own estate. This place is the source of his wealth, and he couldn't give a rat's ass. If it weren't for me, he'd be broke."

This was interesting stuff. I'd never before heard Pericles criticized, and certainly not by a slave. But this was no ordinary slave; Sim was entrusted with the good running of one of the most important estates in Athens.

"What does he do that's so wrong?" I said. "I ask so I won't make the same mistakes with my own land."

"He insists we sell all our produce, at wholesale rates, mind you, and then buy what we need in the agora at retail prices. Can you believe it? May Zeus strike me dead if I lie. Dear Gods, I know of at least three occasions when my master has bought produce that he grew himself."

Pericles walked up beside us as Sim finished his tirade. I wondered if he'd explode at hearing himself criticized by his own slave, but Pericles merely shrugged and said, "Running an estate this size is a full-time job. I have more important things to worry about."

Sim said, "Master, I've told you before. You lose money every time you sell a basket of corn at wholesale rates and then buy another basket at retail. At least let me sort out what your family and the farm needs and set that aside."

"No," said Pericles. "Then I'd have to approve your choices, and I don't have the time."

This was a side to Pericles I'd never seen before: a man so engrossed in the running of Athens that he neglected his own business.

Pericles walked toward the fields. Sim and I followed.

I asked, "Where are we going?"

Pericles said, "I haven't explained how I intend to do this, have I? Naturally I don't have a spare farm in my purse, but this is a large estate, as you've seen. My plan is to apportion a part to you."

Which meant I would become neighbor to Pericles.

We walked across the fields, through lush fields of barley. Presently I noticed a change in the land. It became harder, a trifle stonier, the vegetation more sparse.

We stopped at the foot of a large, barren hill.

"Here we are!" Pericles said in a jovial tone.

"This is it?"

We stood on stony, dry ground, with few bushes, but with straggly olive trees dotted about, so gnarled they looked ancient and ready to die. Among the trees was a small hut, so ill kept you could see through it where the wooden planks had rotted and fallen off.

This had to be the worst farmland in Attica. Pericles had tricked me.

"It's not as bad as it looks," said Sim. He knew what I was thinking. "There are only the olive trees, no other plants, because we put lime here."

"Lime?"

"Like from building sites. We get it cheaply and cart it in. Lime's good for olives. Other plants don't like it, though, so they don't grow much."

"You said you carted in lime," I said to Sim.

"Yes."

"How did you get it here?"

"How about . . . on a cart?" he suggested.

I didn't own a cart. I'd have to get one. That would cost money. Of course, for the moment we had Blossom and the cart he came with, but Blossom was only a rental; we'd have to give him back.

"That stony hill's no problem, either."

I looked at him blankly.

"All these stones on the ground around us rolled down from the hill," Sim explained patiently. "It don't mean nothing about what the soil's like, though I'll grant you"—he gave Pericles a hard look—"I'll grant you it would stand a little hoeing. Also, the hill's to the north."

"That's good?"

"That's the direction the strong winds come from. That hill protects the land."

"The trees are old," I said.

"That's a good thing too. Do you know how long it takes before an olive tree even begins to fruit? Thirty years. These old trees have been making olives for a hundred years or more, and they'll still be doing it when your grandkids are climbing the branches."

Until this moment I'd given no thought to what *sort* of farm Pericles might be offering. I knew nothing about olives.

"I'm not sure about this, Pericles," I said, and rubbed my chin.

"You're not pleased?" Pericles said in a hurt tone, as if he were somehow shocked that I might be unhappy with the worst farm in Attica.

"What am I supposed to do with a bunch of old olive trees?" I said.

"Sell the olives, of course."

"How?"

"Don't be ridiculous, Nicolaos," Pericles said. "Athenians buy olives by the bushel every day."

I thought of all the olives my own mother bought, which we ate every day. "I suppose that's true," I conceded.

"There's always a market for olives," Pericles said.

"The master's right," Sim said. "Of course, olives are a low-margin crop."

"Now, Sim, we don't need to go into that," Pericles chastised his head slave.

"Lots of supply, you see," said Sim, ignoring his master. Or more accurately, not even hearing him. Sim was a complete expert on farm economics, and like any expert, once he got going on his favorite subject he couldn't be stopped. He said, "It keeps the price down when there're lots of sellers."

"Terrific."

"That's why the olive-oil market is so much more lucrative," he mused. "Olive oil's a value-added commodity, you see. Higher margin," he explained. "Now, if I didn't have much produce to work with, I'd strive to maximize my return per unit. With less fruit to work with, it doesn't take so much effort to process it."

"How do I make olive oil?" I said at once.

"With an olive press. It's a big machine with a huge stone for crushing olives."

That sounded expensive.

"As it happens," Sim went on, "we have an olive press over in our main buildings."

He looked straight at me, and rolled his eyes toward his master, Pericles. Sim obviously couldn't speak against his own master, but I divined his meaning.

"I'm sorry, Pericles," I said. "But I'm not going to accept this farm as it is. There's no way it could earn enough."

"We agreed a small, steady income."

"This is too small, and it doesn't look particularly steady to me. I don't know the first thing about growing olives. Besides, this looks like very hard work. How could I run a farm without help and still carry out commissions for you? I refuse your offer. You still owe me the debt."

This put Pericles in a bind. He couldn't force me to take the offered land, but obviously this was the cheapest way he could expunge his debt, and Pericles liked to do things the cheap way.

Pericles looked displeased, but he said, "I imagine we could rent you the use of our olive press. At market rates, of course."

"*Market rates?*" I didn't know the going rate, but whatever it was, I knew it was more than I could afford.

"Very well," Pericles said, exasperated. "I offer you the loan of the machine rent-free for the first five years."

"Ten years."

Pericles sighed. "Ten, then. But after that, it's a commercial arrangement. Are we agreed?"

"I still don't know anything about growing olives."

"I'll throw in a slave who does," Pericles said in desperation. "In recognition of our close and trusting relationship."

I had Pericles on the back foot, for the first time ever, and I was enjoying every moment of it. His only alternative was to pay me coins, which would have cost him far more. But I had to be careful not to overstep my advantage.

"Where will the slave live?" I asked. We all knew the answer to that one. We all three turned to look at the draughty hut.

"Perhaps some spare building material and use of the tools?" Sim murmured.

"Very well," Pericles said quickly, clearly in haste to get this unpleasant business over with. He was losing ground with every moment that passed. "Is there anything else?" he said through gritted teeth, and I knew I'd reached the limit. I had a feeling that the free use of the olive press alone was probably worth more than what he owed.

"I think that's it," I said. "I accept your offer."

With those words, I became a landholder. Perhaps not a wealthy one, but I had gone up in the world.

We began the walk back to the main buildings. As we crossed the line that was now the border between our properties, Pericles remarked, "You'll need to see to new *horos* stones."

"What?"

"The boundary markers. Surely you've noticed them. There's one over there." Pericles pointed.

I walked over. Lying in the dirt was a large stone painted white, with some words chiseled into it.

"I thought they were only for decoration."

"By no means. Those stones are the legal declaration of ownership. Most are inscribed with a standard legal formula and, usually, the name of the owner. We'll have to lodge notice of the sale, too, but there won't be any problems."

"How do we do that?" I asked.

"We see the archon in charge of land. He's one of the lesser magistrates. I must swear before Zeus and Athena that the land I'm transferring is truly mine. You swear that you'll assume all responsibilities as are due any landholder. The archon posts the notice of sale in the agora for all to see for a period of sixty days. If no one objects in that time, then it's official."

"Could that happen? Someone objecting, I mean?"

"It certainly could if I was trying to sell someone else's land! The real owner would see the notice and complain to the archon."

"Oh, I see." That put me in mind of something else: the investigation. "Pericles, does anyone record who owns what land?"

"No. That would be needless government interference in a citizen's private affairs. The horos stones do a perfectly adequate job."

"That's a pity. It seems obvious that Hippias went to Brauron for some reason: either to see someone or for help."

"That seems likely."

"Whoever helped Hippias must have owned an estate around Brauron back then. If there was a registry of lands, I could look up who owned the properties back then."

Pericles looked at me strangely. "What do you mean? Of course there's a record. All you have to do is walk about the countryside and check the boundary markers. It's written in the stones, Nicolaos."

Chapter Seven

I ARRIVED HOME EAGER to tell my father about our new property, only to walk into a family crisis.

WHEN WE'D RETURNED home from the Olympics, not so long ago, one of the first things our father, Sophroniscus, had done was to tell my twelve-year-old brother Socrates that he had to go back to school.

Every deme in Athens has its local school, usually run by some tired fellow who couldn't make it in the philosophy discussions at the gymnasium. Our deme was luckier than that. The local teacher was a man by the name of Karinthos, an old soldier who'd retired when he was too old to survive as a mercenary. It was widely rumored that Karinthos hadn't smiled for at least half a century. He'd been my own teacher when I was Socrates's age, and I believed the rumors.

Nevertheless, Karinthos knew his Homer—he could quote *The Iliad* from memory—and he knew how to beat his knowledge into the boys, and that was the important thing. Also, Karinthos knew from long personal experience how to comport oneself as a man, and the difference between right and wrong.

Most boys would have complained, whined, screamed, or threatened to run away from home in order to avoid school, but Socrates quite liked it. Except for having to wake before dawn every day. That he hated.

Every school in Athens begins at first light and ends at dusk. The teachers used to run the schools for even longer, sometimes from dawn to midnight, but after a few boys dropped dead from exhaustion, the parents complained, and laws were passed limiting school time to daylight. The teachers grumbled that modern kids had it too easy—things had been harder in their day—but they stuck to the letter of the law. So dawn to dusk it was.

That was why I knew something interesting had happened when I walked in to see Karinthos standing in our courtyard, during daylight, with an unhappy expression on his face and Socrates in tow.

Karinthos was shown into the andron, the room at the front of the house reserved for men. Sophroniscus was summoned from his sculpting workshop out the back.

It would, of course, have been rude to listen in, so in the moments it took Father to arrive, I ran up the steps two at a time to his private office, pushed through the door, threw myself flat on the floor, and put my ear to the floorboards. The andron was directly below me, and already I could hear every scrape, shuffle, and cough as Socrates and his teacher waited for the master of the house. Then I noticed there was a sizable crack between two of the boards; I put my eye to it. I had a perfect view from above.

I was just in time for Sophroniscus to walk in and greet Karinthos.

Karinthos got straight to the point. "I'm afraid, Sophroniscus, that Socrates can no longer attend my school."

Sophroniscus rubbed his chin, looked concerned, and asked what Socrates had done. Had he burnt down the school?

"It's worse than that. He asks me questions," replied Karinthos.

"I thought students were supposed to ask questions," Sophroniscus said, looking somewhat nonplussed.

"He asks *too many* questions," said Karinthos grimly.

Socrates stood between the two men. His expression said, "Who? Me?"

The conversation continued for some time, but Karinthos was insistent. Socrates had to go.

I cringed. When the neighbors found out that Socrates had been expelled, it would shame our father.

I jumped up, ran down the stairs, flung open the door, and strode into the room. "There you are, Father! I wanted to ask you, can I borrow Socrates for . . . oh." I stopped and stared at Karinthos. "I'm sorry. I didn't realize you had company. Am I interrupting?"

"You're interrupting," Sophroniscus grumbled. "But say what you have to say."

"I only wanted to ask, could I borrow Socrates for a few days?"

I waited for a reaction, but Sophroniscus and Karinthos merely stared at me. Then I told the greatest lie of my life. I said, "I need Socrates's help with my investigation."

Socrates beamed.

My stomach lurched. I'd be paying for this forever, but it had to be done, for my family's honor.

"It might be as long as a month," I warned them. "Then he'll be free to go back to school."

"That's impossible, son," Sophroniscus said. "We're discussing Socrates's schoolwork now, and I say he's not to miss a day of school." Father glared at Karinthos.

I said, "If that's the only problem, Father, then set your mind at rest. As it happens, there's a schoolteacher where we're going. She comes with excellent credentials."

"*She?*" Karinthos almost exploded. "You propose to replace me with a *woman*?"

I said, "The priestess Doris is a famous teacher. But if you're concerned, I suppose we could arrange a contest between you and the lady." I smiled innocently. "To see which of you can recite the most Homer."

"I won't be party to such a travesty," Karinthos said. "Everyone knows women can't teach."

"Does this concern you?" Sophroniscus asked Karinthos.

"Of course it does," Karinthos said. "If people think you

withdrew your son from my lessons to send him to a woman, I'll be a laughingstock. The other fathers would send their boys elsewhere." No pupils at the school meant no fees for Karinthos. He blanched.

"But didn't you just say Socrates couldn't go to your school?" said Sophroniscus.

"I must insist the boy return."

"I think we're finished here," said Sophroniscus. "Son, you have permission to take Socrates with you. Now I must return to my workshop. I have commissions to complete. For Olympia," he added pointedly, for the benefit of Karinthos. To sculpt for the home of the Sacred Games is a high honor.

Karinthos said, "Very well, Sophroniscus, but when the boy is ready, I insist he return to school. I won't have my hard work undone by some feebleminded woman."

"If you insist, Karinthos," Sophroniscus said. As he passed by me, he whispered, "Well done, son."

THE EPISODE HAD turned out well for everyone. Except me. Now I was stuck with Socrates for the rest of the investigation.

"Thanks, Nico!" Socrates said the moment Karinthos had stormed out. "Does this mean we're partners?"

"It means you tag along and don't say anything," I said firmly. "Come with me."

We were halfway down the street—Socrates had to trot to keep up—when two men stepped in front of us. Neither of them smiled, and both wore the leather wrist straps favored by the worst sort of street thug.

"Are you Nicolaos, son of Sophroniscus?" one demanded.

I'd been asked that question by men who didn't smile enough times on past jobs that I knew what I had to do.

"No," I lied. "Who, me? My name is . . . er . . . Markos. I'm a vegetable seller. Would you like to buy a box of quince?"

"But Nico," Socrates spoke up at once, "quince isn't a

vegetable. It's a fruit. Quince hangs on its branch, so it must be a fruit, you see—"

"Shut up, Socrates!" I said in desperation.

"It's him," the second man said. "The kid called him Nico."

I said, "Thanks a lot, Socrates."

Quick as lightning the first man punched me in the diaphragm. I doubled over and gasped for air. The other hit me with a swinging uppercut to the jaw and I went over backward, straight into the open drain. Most of Athens's byways consist of garbage, with an underlying layer of street. That's because they build the houses to overhang to get more floor space, and people toss their rubbish straight out. The open drains run down the middle of every path.

I sprawled in a puddle that stank of urine and ancient wash water and rotting food. Something I didn't want to look at floated beside my head.

I curled up in the filth, expecting them to start kicking me at any moment, hoping they'd leave Socrates alone, but instead they grabbed me by an arm each and hauled me up, faces screwed up in disgust. The vile liquid of the open drain had soaked into my exomis to stain it brown.

"Eww, you stink," the first man said.

"Well, whose fault is that?" I complained.

"Just following orders," he said in a friendly tone. "No hard feelings, right?" He punched me in the diaphragm again, just to make sure there were no hard feelings. I doubled but didn't fall, and gasped for breath.

They relieved me of the knife I kept inside my exomis. Then they patted me down and found the other knife I kept secreted at my back, beneath my belt. Socrates watched from the side, openmouthed at the sudden violence.

"We're all professionals here," the first man said to me, and I wondered if he was about to invite me to a conference. "Don't cause any trouble and we'll all be fine, right?"

"Let Nico go!" Socrates demanded.

My stomach tightened into a knot. I was suddenly afraid they'd beat Socrates, too.

"Who's the kid?" the first man asked. He appeared to be the leader.

"My brother. He's not involved. Let him go, all right?"

"Can't do that. He'd run for help. But this is very inconvenient."

"Tell me about it."

He turned to Socrates. "Listen here, kid. You see this knife?" He held up a vicious-looking blade, long and jagged.

Socrates stared at the knife with wide eyes. He nodded.

"You do anything to cause trouble, I'll stick this blade in your brother's heart. He'll be dead before he hits the ground. Got it?"

Socrates nodded again and said nothing. I hoped he didn't get it into his head to try to save me.

They led us through the streets of Athens, me in the middle, them standing close enough to return the knives they'd taken straight into my kidneys if I caused any trouble. Socrates trailed behind. We passed men going the other way. They looked at us strangely. The ones who could smell me kept their distance—but no one intervened. Someone would have come to my aid if I'd yelled, but I saw no point in getting some hapless random stranger killed.

They led me to a nondescript house on a nondescript street. From the look of it—the boarded-up windows, the unswept path, the door that creaked noisily when a man within opened it—I guessed they'd appropriated an abandoned building. The complete lack of furniture within confirmed it.

They led us through the barren courtyard to an old workroom at the back. It was dark within; these windows were boarded, too, and covered in black cloth. When someone behind us shut the door, it was black as night, but I heard the small sounds of men shuffling and breathing and I knew I must be surrounded. My eyes slowly adjusted until I perceived before me a table, and behind it, standing straight as a pillar, was a man.

I couldn't see his face, not because it was dark, but because he wore a helmet, a *hoplite* helmet that covered his entire face, the sort of helmet that went with a shield and spear and was worn by soldier-citizens of Athens. Yet the shadows in which he stood gave it another cast altogether. Two candles flickered upon the table between us. The yellow light shone upward into the expressionless metal face. I felt like I faced some remorseless automaton from legend. I'd thought Pericles had a talent for theatrics, but he had nothing on this man.

He said, "You are Nicolaos, son of Sophroniscus."

"I am."

His voice had the deep, muffled, resonant quality of a soldier at arms, a quality that came from speaking through the mouth slit of bronze armor. Somehow it always seemed to make a man sound more menacing.

He said, "I seek answers."

"So do I."

Socrates shuffled his feet beside us but said nothing. Even he was cowed.

I sensed rather than saw the two thugs who'd caught us at our backs, deep in shadow. If it weren't for them, I might have grabbed Socrates and run.

"The answers I seek relate to the death of the hated tyrant," our captor said.

"I'm with you so far."

"And those who perpetuate his plot. I greatly fear that you're one of them. I think, though, that you must be nothing but a hired hand; a bit player in this drama. Tell me the names of your employers, and I'll let you live."

I blinked. "The temple at Brauron." This was public knowledge.

"Not them. Tell me the names of your *other* employers. I have it on authority you've been bribed *not* to find the men who helped Hippias."

"Would it help if I said I have no idea what you're talking about?"

"I wouldn't believe you. I've been warned what a dangerous man you are, Nicolaos, son of Sophroniscus. The word is you've carried out three missions for Pericles, all executed with utter ruthlessness; that you're a master of deception; that your enemies were convinced you were a bumbling idiot, right up to the moment you destroyed them. Well, you might have fooled them, but you won't fool me."

"That's not fair!" Socrates protested. "Nico really *is* a bumbling idi—er . . . that is—"

"Who is this child?" the helmeted man demanded.

"My little brother," I said. "Try to ignore him; it's what I do."

As I spoke, I thought quickly. How could our captor know about my past missions? The first and third had been public knowledge, but the second was a secret. Whoever this man was, he had access to information that was supposed to be discreet. Information known only to Pericles and a select number of very senior Athenians.

"There's nothing you can say or do that will convince me you don't understand my meaning. Tell me who's behind the plot."

"What plot?" I said. "I genuinely have no idea what you're talking about."

There was something odd about the man's voice. Without the visual clues of his face, it had taken me this long to spot it, but when I looked at his arms—the part of his body most exposed to view—they were thin, and the skin had the looseness of age. This was an old man, with an old man's voice.

"Does this have something to do with Marathon?" I asked.

"Of course it does, you fool! Living among us still are the men who told Hippias they'd support him if he returned. The traitors who signaled to him after the battle."

"What signal?" I asked, confused. Then I remembered Pericles had told me, days ago, of a signal that was flashed after the battle. I said, "Do you know who sent the message to the Persians at Marathon?"

"That's what I'm asking you! They must be found. They must be destroyed."

"Look, I don't know who you are, but whatever this is about, it's all ancient history. Nobody cares," I said. "Trust me on this."

"It's not for me to trust you. It's for you to obey me, like any good soldier in an army, like any good citizen of the state." He paused. "You *have* served your time in the army, haven't you?"

"I've completed my two years as an *ephebe*," I told him, becoming a bit angry. To question whether a man had served his time as a recruit was to question whether he was fit to be a citizen of Athens.

"Then you know the importance of obeying a superior. Good. You should have no problem doing as I tell you, since I am clearly your superior."

"I'm afraid I can't, *sir*. I have no idea who you are. How do I know you're superior to me? Also, my duty is to the Sanctuary of Brauron. Duty's very important to me—"

"I fought at Marathon!" he shouted. "My brother died there! Don't lecture me about duty. I'll have you know I almost slew the tyrant!"

I blinked. "You did?"

"I did. He hid behind the enemy lines like a coward, but I pushed through and almost took him with a spear to his throat. I saw the blood gush, but somehow he lived. Does that change your attitude? Will you obey me?"

"I will not."

He drew his sword from the scabbard that hung on the left side of his belt. "Do you know how many men I've killed with this sword?" he demanded.

"No."

"Neither do I. I've lost count."

Or more likely his memory was failing with old age. I wondered whether his story of having attacked Hippias was even true, or whether it was the fond imaginings of an old man. If he'd fought at Marathon, he must be at least fifty years old. He swept his sword round in a great, looping arc, a smooth, practiced movement that spoke of years of hard drilling. The sword slammed edge-first into the table before him. Splinters flew. I recoiled out of sheer reflex. When I opened my eyes, the table had split in two, the destroyed halves lying to either side of him.

He held the sword pointed at me with his bony, but apparently very functional, arm.

"That will be you," he said. "Unless you bring me the names of the traitors who assisted Hippias, the worms that remain among us. Do you understand now?"

I gulped. "I hear you."

"Take him away."

A sack appeared from behind and went over my head. I knew better than to resist. I heard Socrates squawk as a similar sack went over him. I said, "Socrates, don't fight them."

They bundled us into the back of a cart, covered us with something that smelled like canvas, and drove out of a gate and through the streets for what seemed ages, before the cart stopped and I was rolled without warning into a ditch. At least it was warm earth and not sewage.

Then a body fell from the sky and dropped straight on me. Socrates went "Oof!" in my ear. He'd landed right on top of me. With no warning to brace myself, I thought my bones had broken.

"You can take the hood off now."

I did. Socrates struggled out of his. Our two friends with the wrist bands were still with us.

"Where are we?"

They pointed. There was the front door of my father's house.

"Be seeing you."

The delivery to my father's home wasn't a courtesy. They were delivering a message.

SOCRATES MANAGED TO stay silent for five steps. A new record.

"Nico, do you really get to do stuff like that every day?" he said. "Like getting kidnapped and threatened? That was fun."

I ignored Socrates and walked around the back of our house. Socrates trotted along behind. I skirted the workshop where our father was chiseling—I could hear his mallet strikes—and stopped at the first of the water buckets that our slaves were instructed to keep filled from the public fountain. I dropped my clothing on the ground where the slaves would find it for washing, then poured a bucket of water over my naked body. The grime and sludge of the street sewer flowed away.

Next I picked up another bucket and without warning threw it over Socrates.

"What did you do that for?" Socrates spluttered.

"We're going to visit quality. You need to be clean. Don't worry, Socrates, you can drip-dry while we walk."

I walked through the courtyard, stopping only to put on my last remaining clean clothing, then out the front door. Socrates hurried to catch up.

"Where are we going?" he asked.

"Where we were going before I was interrupted. To see Callias."

I'd known before that I needed to see Callias, but now I *really* needed to see him.

I had dealt with Callias on several occasions in the past. I had an idea that he rather liked me, or at least, he had helped me and asked nothing in return. What's more, Callias was quite possibly the most fervent democrat in Athens. Even more so than Pericles; even more so than me. It was a paradox; you'd think such a wealthy man would be against the power of the people, but his name was the gold standard for those who supported self-government. This was why I needed to speak with him: a man old enough to remember the days of the tyrant, who was well disposed toward me and at the center of things. Callias was my route to the past.

I arrived at his house at the same time as he did. Callias looked utterly exhausted. I was about to knock on his door when I saw him. He trudged up the road in a dirty chiton, with ten slaves in tow leading a chain of mule carts to which cases had been tied.

He looked at me in surprise when he saw me on his doorstep. "Nicolaos! *Chaire* Nicolaos."

"Hail Callias," I said in return. "Are you all right?" I was genuinely concerned for the old man. He was dusty, bent over, and noticeably out of breath.

"You see me returned from Sparta this very moment. I've been on a mission for Athens."

Not only was Callias our wealthiest citizen, he was also our premier diplomat and the *proxenos*—which is to say, the local representative—for Sparta, our rival for power within Hellas. Whatever it was he'd been there for, he clearly didn't want to speak about it, for he changed the subject.

"You wish to see me?" he said.

"I came to ask you for advice," I said. "But I can see this is not the time. I'll come back another day."

"What's your problem? Has someone died?" He said it with a tired smile. Clearly he thought he'd made a joke.

"You mean you haven't heard?" I said. But of course he hadn't. Callias had been in Sparta. "The skeleton of Hippias the Tyrant has been discovered. Within Attica. I'm looking for some background, Callias, and I hope you might be able to tell me about Harmodius and Aristogeiton. And have you ever heard of someone named Leana?"

Callias fainted dead away.

His slaves leapt to catch him before he fell. I lurched forward to grab his arms, and Socrates, being the shortest, got underneath him. Together we carried Callias through to his own courtyard and onto the nearest lounge. Slaves brought water in expensive coolers, and this we splashed on his face until the color returned to his cheeks and Callias came to.

"No, that's not possible," was the first thing he said.

Callias ordered the slaves to help him up. He asked—no, he demanded—that I wait, despite my protestations that he was obviously unwell. He ordered slaves to install me in the kitchen courtyard and begged a moment to wash and recover; he'd been on the road five days, and this was the reason he advanced for his "weakness." Not an excuse, mind you, but a reason.

"I'm not as young as I used to be," he said sadly. "I remember when I could march that route in three days. Now, I must have slaves to help me up the hills, and a mule train for my comforts. Old age is a terrible thing, Nicolaos. But it's no excuse. Give me a moment and I shall be with you."

I begged him to take as long as he needed, or longer even. He'd ordered that we be served one of the best wines in Hellas—it was imported from Lampsacus, a city across the sea in the land of Ionia; there was no hope that Socrates would appreciate it, so I drank his share—and sat us in the shade in the most beautiful garden in Athens. One of my father's own works was on display on the land beyond, and I was happy to sip fine wine while I contemplated it.

When Callias returned, clean, refreshed, and looking much brighter, he lay back on the dining couch beside me with a cup of wine of his own. I explained what had happened while a slave massaged his sore calves. He was astonished.

His first comment was, "Those poor girls. Certainly I must do everything I can to help." Callias had three daughters himself. He had famously asked each daughter, as she came of age, who she wanted for a husband, and then offered the father a dowry so large that no sane man could have turned it down. It was a complete reversal of the usual system and had been the talk of the town. Callias was a man who valued his womenfolk.

I said, "Did anyone have a motive to kill Hippias?"

"Not more than about ten thousand men," Callias said. "Nicolaos, the whole point of the battle at Marathon was to keep Hippias out of Athens. Don't you think any one of us would have gladly murdered the bastard to save us all that trouble? The man who got him would be a hero."

I said, "This is what puzzles me. Legally, it's not even a murder, is it? Anyone could kill him and not only get away with it, but be praised. That's why I had a line of volunteers outside my house all wanting to confess. Why would anyone cover up such a killing?"

Callias scratched his head. "That's a very good question. I can't explain it."

There was only one possibility that I could see. I said, "What if whoever killed Hippias wasn't supposed to? What if his killer wasn't one of us, but someone on his own side?"

"That might make sense," Callias said.

"Which means his killer must have been part of the conspiracy to return him."

Callias said, "It's no secret that there were Athenians ready to aid Hippias and the Persians. In fact, after the battle someone on the mountain behind us flashed a signal to the enemy. We all saw it."

"So I've heard." I told Callias of the strange encounter with the man in the helmet, and his odd talk of traitors and a signal. I finished with the words, "Do you have any idea who this strange man is?"

Callias rubbed his chin. "There were many who fought at Marathon. I'll think upon it. Someone whose brother died in the fighting—you said he mentioned it—and a patriot—you said he's determined to find the men who conspired with Hippias, the ones who sent the signal."

"Yes," I said. "But I think he must be crazy. This was thirty years ago, and even if there were men back then prepared to help Hippias, their cause died with him. I'll bet they've done their best to forget the past. I'll bet they've been solid citizens these past three decades."

"Logic says you must be right." Callias looked thoughtful. "And yet, the scars from that time run deep. So very deep."

Callias paused. He drank of the herbed wine, then set down his cup and leaned back. His slaves had placed his couch within the shade of flowery vines that grew across the courtyard. Two slaves had stood anxiously behind Callias during our conversation; one of these moved quickly to refill the cup. The concern they showed for their master was genuine, I was sure. Callias was known as a humane man.

"You wanted to know about Harmodius and Aristogeiton, and Leana," he said.

"We found a blade within the corpse that bears those names."

"Dear Gods!"

Callias stood without warning. Startled, I stood too. Callias said, in a determined tone of command, "I have something to show you. Leave your brother here. You, Nicolaos, come with me."

I supposed he wanted merely to go to his office, but he led me out of the house and down the narrow, twisty streets of Athens to the agora. Callias said nothing on this walk, until he halted at the north end, at the Temple of Ares.

Around the temple were statues of the heroes Theseus and Heracles, a statue of Ares himself, and another of Apollo, who rather oddly had been portrayed in the act of doing up his long hair. Apollo always had been a vain god.

A host of lesser gods and demigods accompanied them. This open ground at the north of the agora was the city's largest collection of statuary. Some were of marble, the latest were in bronze. All these works were as close to perfect as the hand of mortal man could make them, and painted to an appearance so lifelike that one almost expected them to walk away.

The temple and statues stood beside the Panathenaic Way. Thousands of people passed by every day: people in carts, people on foot, visitors to the city, all of them going about their business, most of them headed to the stalls of the agora. The noise of squabbling traders was loud in our ears.

Callias stopped beside two statues: a single work of two men who stood side by side; the right-hand figure a young man about the same age as me, and on the left a middle-aged man in the prime of life. They both wore expressions of excruciating nobility, and in each of their four hands they held a sword.

"The Tyrannicides," I said at once. The statues had been there since before I was born.

"The Tyrannicides indeed," said Callias. "Harmodius and Aristogeiton. I have met visitors to Athens who think the Tyrannicides must have been gods, so honored is their place among the statues. But they were not gods, Nico; they were mortals, and they were lovers. These two were determined to end the tyranny by assassination, but not for any noble intention. Democratic freedom, my dear Nicolaos, began with a lovers' squabble. Harmodius was . . . how do I explain him? He was a simple man, and very, very beautiful." Callias sighed. "That was the thing people always noticed first: his beauty."

"You knew him," I said; not a question but a statement.

"I knew them both. No, I knew them all, every man and woman who was a player in that time. Harmodius was a few years older than I. What we had in common was we'd both lost our fathers at an early age. It gave us something to talk about at the gymnasium.

"Hippias the tyrant had a brother, younger by a few years, named Hipparchus. Hipparchus, being the brother of the tyrant, thought he could do whatever he liked with impunity."

"Uh oh."

"The moment Hipparchus set eyes on Harmodius, it was lust at first sight. Hipparchus took to following Harmodius around like a lovesick puppy. But Harmodius already had a lover: Aristogeiton. Hipparchus was intensely jealous of their happiness.

"It so happened that this was the year of a Great Panathenaea. The officials in charge decided that the sister of Harmodius should be the maiden who led the formal procession to the Acropolis, where the ceremonies are held."

I said, "That's a position of high honor."

"It is," Callias said. "I suspect Hipparchus, the rejected lover, had a hand in arranging it, considering what happened next."

"Yes?"

"The purity of the maiden is essential to the success of the ceremony. Hipparchus walked up, as it was about to begin, with all of Athens watching, and declared that the girl—the sister of Harmodius—was impure. It was tantamount to saying her own family had prostituted her."

"Dear Gods!" I said, shocked. "If I had a sister and someone said that, I'd kill him."

"Precisely. From the looks on their faces I could see the officials were as appalled as every other man and woman present, but after such an accusation, the officials had no choice but to order a change. Harmodius led away his sobbing sister."

"That was when the conspiracy began," I said with certainty.

"Of course. The insult to the family was mortal."

"But everyone knows his attack went horribly wrong," I said.

"Harmodius and his lover Aristogeiton gathered together other young men who wanted to end the tyranny. They formed a plot to assassinate both brothers in one rapid strike. Harmodius knifed Hipparchus to death but was killed in the attempt. Aristogeiton was captured. The other conspirators fled, leaving Hippias the tyrant unharmed. After that, Hippias was determined to destroy the other members of the plot; he realized—correctly!—that if he didn't, they'd try again. Aristogeiton was tortured to force him to reveal the names. He never talked," Callias said flatly. "Not even as they killed him."

"What happened to the little sister of Harmodius?"

Callias shrugged. "With her brother Harmodius gone, and his lover Aristogeiton captured and under torture, she had no male protector left. I expect Hippias had her killed. Don't look at me like that, Nicolaos! You know better than most men how these things work. Maybe family friends spirited the girl out of Athens. I like to think so. But the odds are her body lies in an unmarked grave outside the city walls."

"Was the girl's name Leana? That's the name on the other side of the blade."

Callias said, softly, "No, Leana was someone else again." He refused to say another word, but led me by the arm away from the statues of Harmodius and Aristogeiton. He led me out of the agora and along the Panathenaic Way, which wound south and then twisted up to the Acropolis. Callias led me all the way to the top.

The Acropolis was a disaster area of fallen pillars and charred timbers. The temples had been burned to the ground when the Persians sacked the city twenty years before. The Athenians had resolved to leave the place as a ruin for the rest of time, in remembrance, though recently Pericles had talked of a rebuild, an idea with which I agreed completely. I wanted to build for the future, not dwell in the past.

But the Acropolis as it stood was a ruin. A ramshackle temple had been erected to house the cult statue of Athena, and here and there among the black, rotted beams and fallen masonry were a few small statues that had survived the destruction. Callias led me to one of these.

It was a statue of a lioness, made in marble. The paint had blistered and peeled in the fires of the sacking, giving it a wretched color that would have made the figure look pathetic, were it not for the open, snarling mouth.

"Read the plinth," Callias instructed me.

I did. Etched into it was the name Leana.

"*This* is Leana?"

"This is her statue. Leana was the only woman member of the conspiracy against Hippias."

Callias rested against a fallen pillar that lay beside the lioness. The color had left his face again, as it had just before he fainted.

"After Aristogeiton died," he said, "Hippias ordered Leana arrested. I don't know how Hippias knew she was involved; perhaps she was seen during the assassination attempt, perhaps she was unlucky. One thing I'm sure of: Aristogeiton didn't betray her. In any event, she was arrested and bound, hand and foot.

"Hippias put the same questions to her as he had to Aristogeiton. Who else had plotted against him?

"Rather than betray her fellows, Leana bit through her own tongue and spat it out. She died shortly after."

I imagined what it must feel like, to press my teeth into that sensitive organ, and then to keep biting until I'd sliced it through, my mouth filling with the metallic taste of blood and the pain, and not stopping until I'd finished the self-amputation. My imagination carried me away and I gagged.

Callias continued in a calm voice, as if he were discussing some minor point of interest. "Have you ever noticed, Nicolaos, the sudden-death nature of Athenian politics?"

"It's come to my attention."

Callias said, "If you look in the lioness's mouth, within the statue, you'll see she has no tongue. The statue was ordered by the city authorities, but I commissioned it myself."

A lioness seemed fitting. I said, "A statue upon the Acropolis . . . you did her great honor, Callias."

"Not at all. One of the names she protected when she bit through her tongue was my own."

"*You?*"

"Me. I was one of the young men Harmodius and Aristogeiton recruited to help them destroy the tyranny," Callias said. The tears ran down his face. "You wanted to know who Leana was? Leana was my lover."

Chapter Eight

I left for Brauron next morning, before first light. I'd learned as much as I could in Athens, and been too long from whatever was happening at the sanctuary.

"What's *he* doing here?" was the first thing Diotima asked when I returned to Brauron. She pointed at Socrates, who stood behind me.

"Don't ask," I said. "It's a long story."

Socrates grinned and said, "Hello, Diotima. I got expelled from school!"

I ignored his obvious attention-seeking gambit and asked, "How did the search for Ophelia go?"

Diotima frowned. "Melo took control of the temple slaves, as Thea agreed he could. He had them scouring the countryside in regular sweeps. I must say, what Melo lacks in intelligence he makes up in energy. But he didn't turn up a thing. At least we know where she *isn't*."

"Which is?"

"Just about everywhere. It turns out Melo really does know this countryside. I watched the way he spread out the searchers, and I was impressed."

"What does Melo think now?"

"I don't know. After he turned up a blank, I made the same comment to him—about us knowing where Ophelia isn't. He took it as a slight on the way he'd led the search and got offended, which I hadn't meant, but I suppose I must have put it badly. He said he'd have to try something else and went away, and I haven't seen him for a couple of days."

"Maybe he's given up and gone back to Athens."

"Not him. But he might be sulking somewhere. Then again, I haven't left the sanctuary, and his presence here isn't exactly encouraged."

We walked as we talked. The best security from eavesdroppers was to keep moving, the sanctuary being such a crowded place, with so many nooks and crannies. At that moment we came to something I'd been thinking about, and stopped before it.

"There's one place we haven't looked for Ophelia," I said.

"Where?"

I pointed at the Sacred Spring. "In there."

IT WAS THE obvious conclusion. If everyone who guarded the sanctuary swore that Ophelia could not have passed them—and they all swore by Artemis that it was so—and if a thorough search of the sanctuary failed to find her—and it had—and if Melo's extensive search force had turned up nothing in the surrounding countryside—and I was prepared to believe he'd been thorough—then logically there was only one place left to look. We would have to dredge the Sacred Spring.

It didn't take long for a crowd to appear. First we needed the permission of the High Priestess. Doris sent one of the girls to fetch Thea, who came at once.

"Absolutely not," she said without a moment's hesitation. "This spring is the most sacred place in the entire sanctuary. It must not be polluted by swimming, particularly not by the body of a male."

"What about a female, then?" I asked, and the priestesses looked at me in astonishment, even Diotima. Thea said, "You're not suggesting a woman go in there, are you?"

No, I wasn't. Not now that I thought about it. It was obvious who'd be the one to go in, and I wasn't looking forward to it.

I said, "Thea, this needs to be done. If Ophelia's in there . . ." I trailed off, not wanting to say it. We all still hoped to find her alive.

Doris said into the uncomfortable silence, "Thea, think on this: Which is worse, to have a man swim in the spring, or to have the body of a child lie there forever? A child who, if she's in there—may Artemis avert it—was probably murdered? Which is the greater sacrilege?"

We were clustered about the edge of the spring as we argued. This inevitably caused passersby to notice and stop to listen. The small crowd nodded after Doris spoke. Thea must have seen the sentiment among her people and, more to the point, the irrefutable logic of the words. The High Priestess hesitated for a moment, then she too nodded, but it was clear she didn't like it.

It didn't take long for news to spread that a naked man was about to swim in the Sacred Spring in search of a dead body. Before I had stripped off, the few men at the sanctuary, and every woman and child, had gathered to watch.

As I pulled off my exomis and tossed it aside, I said nervously to Diotima and Socrates, "I hope I don't drown. I can swim, but not very well."

"You don't need to swim," Socrates pointed out. "You need to sink."

Terrific. But Socrates was right. I didn't need to go sideways, I needed to go down, and going down would be all too easy.

I stepped to the edge and looked in. The water was clear to a certain depth, but beyond that I couldn't see anything of interest—such as, for example, the bottom.

Standing around thinking about it didn't make the job any easier.

I dived in.

I came up spluttering. "*It's freezing!*"

"Oh, don't be such a baby," Diotima called from dry land, wrapped in her warm chiton. "Can you feel anything?"

I called back, treading water, "No, I'm numb all over!"

"No, you idiot. Can you feel anything *on the bottom*?" And before I could answer, she added, "Don't tell me about your bottom. Is there anything at the bottom of the spring?"

"My feet don't reach the bottom. I'll have to dive." With that, I took a deep breath, turned tail like a duck, and aimed for the bottom.

Except I didn't get there. Pressure kept pushing me back up. I couldn't kick hard enough to make my way, and after struggling for a short time I ran out of breath and had to return to the surface.

"Dear Gods, how does anyone manage to drown?" I said after the third attempt.

"Is it because they're weighted down?" Socrates suggested. "Maybe you could jump in wearing armor?"

"Thanks anyway."

But Socrates had given me an idea. I scrabbled out of the spring and up onto the surrounding grass.

In the audience, one of the older girls whispered something to the others and pointed at my crotch. I looked down. In the cold water, my penis had shrunk to the size of a pea. The girls giggled behind their hands—Doris ordered them to hush, but she herself was smiling as she scolded them—and Gaïs appraised me with a contemptuous smile.

Dignity demanded that I ignore them all. I walked to the base of the hills directly south of the temple. I selected the largest stone that I could comfortably lift and hauled it back to the Sacred Spring. With the water dripping off me, I shook uncontrollably, not from the weight of the stone, but from the wind against my wet skin. Suddenly I couldn't wait to get back in the water.

But there was one more thing to do. I took the length of rope that Zeke brought at my request and tied it about my waist. I handed the other end to Zeke's assistants.

"Pull me up if I tug on the line, or if I'm down there too long," I said to them. They nodded in a vague way and showed no signs of even paying attention, but I knew Diotima would see me safe.

I picked up my rock, waded back to where the ground fell away, and stepped over the edge.

The water that was so cold before now seemed strangely warm. My friend the rock carried me to the bottom. I was upside down, and I could feel that even my feet were thoroughly underwater. I let go of the rock, immediately began to float up, grabbed the weight again, and felt around with my right hand.

Slimy mud slipped between my fingers. I ignored it and kept sweeping in the dark. My fingers touched something hard. Not a rock—it felt man-made. Perhaps a weapon. I was beginning to feel the need to breathe. I got the fingers of my right hand around it, gathered up my rock-weight in the crook of my left arm, because I knew I'd be coming back, and tugged on the rope.

The first thing I did when my head broke the surface was suck in a lungful of air. The second was to toss my discovery onto the grass along the edge, where it rolled once or twice before coming to a halt on solid ground.

"Found that at the bottom! I think it's metal!"

I waded to the shallows while Diotima picked it up, whatever it was. She turned it over, and over again. I saw at once that it wasn't a dagger or a sword, which had been my first thoughts. It looked more like a plate.

"It's covered in slime," Diotima said. She used the hem of her chiton to wipe away the worst of the muck and algae. When she had finished, she said in wonder, "It's a statuette. It's a bronze statuette of a woman."

Diotima held the statuette at arm's length and considered. "It doesn't seem all that old," Diotima said. "If I saw this cleaned and polished and for sale in the agora, I wouldn't look twice."

I said, "So the priestess and the women supplicants threw all these things into the Sacred Spring as sacrifices to the Goddess?"

"Yes," said Diotima. "Mostly silver and gold. Some finely-wrought bronze."

Terrific. I would have to bring up every single item, because in the muddy depths I couldn't tell a murder weapon from a piss-pot. I took a deep breath and dived.

The ghastly business continued all afternoon. Piece by piece, two or three at a time when I could manage it, the Sacred Spring of Brauron gave up its secrets. It reached the point where I no longer cared what it was that I carried. I tossed them to the bank, and Diotima took each one and inspected it closely. If it was thoroughly covered in algae and mud, then it almost certainly wasn't of any interest, because it must have lain there for a long time. But she was careful.

At the very bottom, underneath all the other pieces, I came across something long and hard. At first I thought it was an oddly shaped rock, but when my fingers traced the outline of a hilt, I knew what I had. I hauled it up, and this one I handed over, so as not to accidentally hit Diotima.

"A sword?" Diotima said, puzzled. "That's an odd thing to find in a spring."

"Maybe it's something to do with us," I said.

"No, Nico," Diotima said, as she held it up in some disgust. "It's absolutely covered in slime. This thing's been down there since forever."

"Is it iron?"

"Yes." Diotima wiped at it with the edge of her chiton.

I dived again and swept the deepest part of the spring with eyes closed and arms outstretched.

My hand encountered flesh.

Even purely by feel I knew it for what it was, soft and resistant to my touch, cold but not at all slimy. My hand slid over the discovery and I clenched automatically; my palm felt a projection beneath it that my imagination said at once was the shape of a nose.

I resisted the urge to panic, in this dark, ice-cold place, in the presence of a corpse.

But was it? If I rose to the surface and raised the alarm and then was proven wrong, I'd look like an idiot. I opened my eyes; they were desperately sore from all the diving, but this was no time to worry about that. I could see nothing but a blur. I slid my hand down to feel what might be a mouth. I had to be sure. I pushed my fingers against whatever this was. They slid right in and I felt teeth and what could only be a tongue lodged between my fingers.

I gagged and choked on my own vomit. Underwater, I was in the greatest danger. I dropped my rock and swam to the surface, barely able to hold onto my heaving stomach. The moment my head breached the surface, I spewed my stomach contents across the Sacred Spring. I trod water, desperately trying to breathe and release the mess in my throat at the same time. I still could have choked to death.

"Nico!" Diotima screamed in alarm; she would have dived in had Zeke not grabbed hold of her. He motioned to two of the slaves, who splashed in, grabbed hold of me, and hauled me to land, where I pushed myself up on all fours and sucked in lungfuls of clean, precious air.

Diotima knelt beside me and said, "Nico, are you all right?"

"What happened?" Thea asked.

Calm at last, I said, "There's a body down there."

MY PRONOUNCEMENT SET off wailing among the girls for their departed sister, as was right and proper. The girls and the priestesses tugged at their hair and tore at their chitons. They would continue like this for days.

I ignored the noise as best I could. Feeling recovered enough now, I asked Zeke for a long rope, only to discover he'd already brought one. He was obviously a good man in a crisis, and I thanked the gods he was there.

I looped one end about me and tied it loosely with a simple knot. Zeke put a hand on my shoulder. "Are you sure you're all right to do this? You've been up and down a lot this day."

I nodded. "I can do it one last time. Have your men pull when I tug the line. I'll guide her body up so it doesn't snag."

I walked into the water—it felt like home—prepared myself for what I was about to touch, eased myself under, and kicked down. After so much practice, I no longer needed the rock.

For a moment or two, I thought I'd lost the body, but then I connected with a chest and then an arm. I pulled the end of the rope, and it came free to drift beside me. Luckily for me Poseidon had decreed that things in the water should be lighter than on land. It was easy to raise the body with one hand—there was a slight sucking resistance from the mud, easily overcome. I looped the floating rope around and under, across the chest, under the armpits, did it twice more to be sure, then tied two tight knots. As I tightened I thought to myself it might be too tight for her to breathe, then realized at once how stupid that was: this body wasn't breathing.

Though I'd worked as quickly I could, everything had been done by touch alone, and I was running short of breath. It didn't matter, I was done. I pulled on the rope going up until it was taut, then tugged three times, sharply.

At once the rope slipped through my hand and the body rose. I waited for it to pass by, then followed with both hands on the back, gently guiding it past the rocks and, when we neared the point where Ophelia would be dragged across the bottom, added my own force to save her corpse the indignity of being dragged through mud before her friends.

She broke surface the instant before me, and I heard the screams even through the thin layer of water above my ears that rose to a crescendo as I came up for air. Two men had been waiting, ready to grab the body and carry it to land.

I took my time getting relief with a few deep breaths. After all, there was no urgency to inspect a corpse.

As I waded through the last of the water, I saw only glimpses of the body between the legs of the people clustered about, staring, pointing, and arguing. Something about their reaction didn't seem quite right. I dripped my way across, the group parted, if only to avoid getting as wet as me, and I looked down into the very dead face of Melo.

"HOW IN HADES did *he* get in there?" I said loudly.

There was no point in asking. No one knew any better than I did.

"This is very depressing," I said.

"Especially from Melo's point of view," Diotima added, which was true enough.

I said, "We need to determine how he died."

"He drowned," said Zeke, frowning.

"Did he?" I asked. "We found him in the spring. It's not the same thing."

"Are we sure Ophelia's not in there too?" Doris asked.

"I'm sure," I said. "The spot where I found Melo was the last left on my sweeps. Why didn't he rise to the surface? I thought bodies did that."

"Not necessarily at once, I believe," Zeke said. "We live close to the coast. Every now and then I've been in town when a drowned man was brought in. They seem to stay under until they bloat. Then they rise."

"How long had Melo been in the water?" Doris asked.

"It can't be more than three days," Diotima said. "We spoke to him then, after we gave up the search."

"And how in Hades did he manage to drown without being seen, in the middle of a sanctuary full of girls and women walking back and forth?"

Then Diotima and I answered my question in unison. "He fell in at night."

"But Nico," said Socrates, frowning, "didn't you say it yourself?"

"Didn't I say what?"

"When you tried to dive. You said, 'How does anyone manage to drown?'"

It was a fair point. "You're right, Socrates. Something's . . . er . . . fishy. We'll have to inspect the body. But not here in front of the girls."

Zeke ordered the slaves to carry the body to the same storeroom where was stored the skeleton of Hippias. In the absence of a courtyard not inhabited by young girls, the storeroom would have to do for observance of the rites. The slaves would place Melo's feet toward the door, and the priestesses would clean his body and place the coin. I wondered if they'd find room enough for both bodies. If things kept on like this, the sanctuary might need to build an extension.

"What do we do with all this other stuff?" Diotima asked. She sat amongst a small fortune in gold and silver ornaments. No, not a small fortune: a large one. A family could probably live for a hundred years on the value of what she had scattered on the grass. Pots, vessels, statuettes, a whole pile of mirrors made of bronze, tarnished beyond repair, rings, gems, wooden spindles and spindle whorls, a case of sewing needles made of bone.

"Throw it back into the spring," Thea said.

"You must be joking!" I said it without thinking, before I could stop to think I was correcting the High Priestess.

Thea was not amused. "No, young man, I'm *not* joking. Everything you see lying on the grass was dedicated to the Goddess. Women long dead gave their most precious possessions to our Goddess, that she might grant them favor in life. They might be dead, and their psyches in Hades, but their gifts were forever, and I *will not see that undone*."

The lady had a point. I sighed and reached for the first, a beautiful statuette of a young child.

"I'll do this, Nico," Diotima said. "You go get yourself warm."

I smiled in gratitude, because I was shivering beyond control. As I left, I saw Diotima begin. Gaïs bent to help her, and together the two priestesses blessed each object with all their power before each was returned to its home.

It had been clever of me to strip. I used my exomis as a towel and then, in the absence of anything else to wear, put it on. I was damp, but at least I wasn't frozen and the shivers had left me.

I took Socrates with me to see the body.

A slave guarded the entrance. I told him there was little chance of the occupants escaping, and he replied that Zeke had ordered him to stay, not to keep the bodies in, but to keep the more curious girls out.

"They're already playing dare games to see who's willing to come closest," he said.

So much for protecting the children's innocence. I opened the door and we went inside. Socrates had seen death before, and I didn't expect such a clean body to be any concern.

He didn't disappoint me. But he stood back, looking somewhat askance, and said, "Nico, what do you look for? How do you inspect a body?"

"Like this." I knelt beside Melo and heaved him over. He'd been a light man in life, but in death he was heavy as a sack of rocks.

Despite having been in the water, the exomis he wore had nettles and seeds stuck to it. Well, that was no surprise. He'd spent his days wandering the countryside in search of his betrothed.

I pulled down the tunic and ran my fingers over his body. I said to Socrates, "I'm searching for any sign of a wound."

Socrates gave a moue of distaste. "Can't you just look?"

"With some wounds you have to find the broken bones beneath."

It was the idea of touching a dead body that upset him. We Hellenes have a horror of touching the dead. A man who's been in contact with a corpse is forbidden to eat or have sex or enter the holy places until he's been ritually cleansed.

"What's this?"

At the corpse's back, beneath the leather belt of his exomis, was something solid. I pulled it out, to find it was a piece of broken pottery. I held it up to Socrates and said, "Easy to see how a killer missed it."

"Nico, there are words on the other side."

I flipped it over. Socrates was right. Scratched into the fired clay were these words: *caves hills fields coast boats farmhouse*. A line had been scratched through the first four words. The final two were inscribed in the same hand but with slightly thicker lines. I guessed they'd been added later.

People used broken pottery to scratch notes all the time. This, it seemed to me, must have been notes Melo had scratched for himself. It didn't take much imagination to realize this was his checklist of places to search for Ophelia.

I said, "Socrates, don't tell anyone else about this, except for Diotima of course. All right?"

"Why not?" he asked.

"Because . . ." I was stumped for an answer. "Because you shouldn't give away information unless you need to."

Socrates nodded, but I could tell he didn't believe me.

My prodding and my close inspection of the body provided nothing more, either front or back. It was when I touched his head that I made progress. The bone beneath the hair moved. I poked around, gently at first, then more firmly, until I was certain. The skull at the back of his head had been broken. There was no blood, but then nor should there be, since the body had spent at least a day in cold running water.

I took Socrates out and returned to the spring for another look, and then we joined the others in Thea's office. It was crowded with everyone present, but at least the Little Bears couldn't hear us.

As I walked in, Thea was speaking. "The explanation is obvious," she said. "This annoying young man was in the habit of skulking around the sanctuary. Obviously, he fell into the water in the dark and drowned. It's happened before, and sadly, it will probably happen again."

They all stopped and turned to me as I entered.

Diotima said, "What did you find?"

"Melo was knocked on the head," I said. "From behind."

There was a pause before they understood the implication, then startled gasps from the women, except for Diotima. She'd expected as much.

"Are you sure?" Thea asked.

"It's certain," I said. "His skull is broken inward. Anyone can feel it."

Zeke nodded. He understood.

"Is there a chance he fell backward, knocked his head on a rock, and rolled in?" Doris asked in hope.

I shook my head. "Find me a rock on the edge with blood on it. You won't. I looked."

"Then Melo was murdered," Doris said sadly. "How long will this go on?"

Thea, Doris, and Sabina seemed upset, or if they weren't they acted it well. They pulled at their hair or clothing. Zeke clenched his hands in anger. Of them all, Gaïs seemed the least concerned. But that was consistent with her personality.

"Yes, Melo was murdered," I said. "I've touched a dead body, that makes me unclean. Ritually, that is."

Thea understood. Of course she did, she was a High Priestess. "We have plenty of cleansing water on hand," she said. "It's . . ." Her voice faded to a mumble, and she blushed. "I'm afraid our ritually clean water is the Sacred Spring. The spring from which you pulled the body."

It was an interesting theological point. Was I already clean because I'd had my head under sacred water for most of the day?

"Am I spiritually clean?" I asked Thea.

"Perhaps if you wash your hands, just to be sure."

Gaïs said, "High Priestess, is there not a larger question? Has the Sacred Spring been polluted by the presence of the body, or was the body cleansed of impurity when it touched the water?"

Thea, Doris, and Sabina all stood there, thunderstruck. "You know," Doris said at last, turning to her colleagues, "I don't think in all the history of the Hellenes there's ever been a case like this. A murdered corpse is the ultimate pollutant. A sacred spring blessed by a goddess is the ultimate cleanser. What happens when one touches the other?"

Sabina said, "If the spring's polluted, we have nothing to clean it."

In the background I could see Socrates frown. He began to mutter to himself and stared vacantly out the window. I knew that he was thinking about the priestess's question. We didn't have time for a long-winded explanation that no doubt wouldn't finish until midnight, so I took him by the shoulders and said quietly, "Socrates, pay attention to me, will you? Don't go bothering these people with your wild ideas."

"But Nico, don't you want to know the answer? The priestess asked—"

"I don't care what the priestess said—"

"I've solved it already, Nico. It's obvious."

"Socrates," Diotima said gently, "don't you think you should leave the ecumenical questions to the experts—"

But the priestesses had overheard us. They stared at Socrates in astonishment.

Thea said, "Did the child say he knows the answer? Yes? Speak up, lad. Is the spring polluted or clean?"

Socrates said, "Well, the water was polluted when the corpse hit it. So that water couldn't cleanse anything."

"This is your idea of a solution?" Diotima said, exasperated. "Socrates—"

"But that's a big sacred spring," Socrates plowed on. "*Some* of the water touched the corpse, and other parts of the water *didn't*."

Everyone nodded in unison.

"The water that *didn't* touch the corpse was never polluted. Which means the unpolluted water cleansed the polluted water."

"That's really very clever," Sabina said, half to herself.

"What made you think of such a thing?" Diotima asked.

"I remembered when Nico and I talked to that philosopher last year, the one who works for Pericles. Remember, Nico? He said everything was made of tiny particles? Well, if the water's all tiny particles, then obviously the tiny particles that never went near the body never had a chance to be polluted."

"What about the dead man's psyche?" Sabina asked.

Thea said, "It must still be here."

"Probably in the spring," Doris added. "It'll terrify the girls every time they go for water unless we do something about it."

I exploded. "Do we care more about the religious problems here, or the killing?"

Diotima looked at me coldly. "This *is* a religious community, you know, Nico. I suppose you noticed that big building out there? They call it a temple."

"Did anyone see anything in the night?" I asked the room in general. "Or hear anything?"

Silence. It had been a silly question—obviously if any innocent person had known something, they would already have spoken up—but I had to ask it to make my next point clear. Doris saved me the trouble.

"This means the murderer is among us," Doris said. "Whoever it is, they're here."

Thea put her head in her hands. "This could end the sanctuary."

"Permanent guards," Zeke said. "I'll set the men to guard every point. It means we won't get any work done, but . . ." He shrugged.

"But staying alive is more important," Gaïs said matter-of-factly. "I hope we can. Above all else, we must protect the girls."

THE MEETING BROKE up in confusion. The priestesses left the room in a daze. Diotima left with Gaïs to see to the girls, and to arrange matters so that no child was ever on her own. The absence of both women gave me a chance I'd been hoping would come.

I asked to speak to Thea privately. She looked at me oddly but nodded. We remained in her office as the others left. They went with backward glances, obviously wondering what I was up to.

When we were alone, I said, "I wanted to ask you, High Priestess, what it is between Gaïs and Diotima."

Thea had the grace not to look surprised at my question. "I thought I was the only one who'd noticed," she said. "I don't know. Perhaps it's something that happened when they were children."

"Gaïs said to me that something went wrong at Diotima's initiation ceremony." I was unwilling to repeat Gaïs's claim that Diotima had cheated; not until I knew what had really happened.

Thea frowned. "If it did, I don't know about it."

"Then could you tell me what the initiation ceremony truly means?"

Thea, who had been standing, put a hand out to the desk beside her and used it to ease herself down to a chair. She said, "I understand you have no sisters? Well, when a girl is born we call her *kore*, which means maiden. This you know."

"Yes."

"When she is ready to be betrothed she becomes a *nymphe*, and nymphe she remains until motherhood, when we call her *gyne*. These are the three phases of a woman's life: the maid, the nymph, and the mother. Every girl you see at this sanctuary is kore. They are children, we teach them as children, we treat them as children. Because they *are* children. But when they leave this place, they leave as nymphe. Brauron is a place of transformation."

"When does it happen?"

"At that rite of transformation you mentioned. Each child enters the temple with those girlish things that were important to her in childhood."

"You mean her toys?"

Thea gave one sharp nod. "The transformation to womanhood is one of the deepest mysteries in a woman's life. At the end of her year with us, she marks her new status by dedicating her toys to the Goddess. She is no longer a child, you see, so she no longer needs them. When she leaves the temple, she leaves as a woman who has left her childhood behind her."

"I see." I thought about it. It seemed harsh, perhaps as harsh as a man's time in the army, but at least it was over quickly.

"Don't the girls ever fight?" I asked. "Nasty tricks? Booby traps? I know what happens when you lump boys together."

"We've had catfights aplenty in the courtyard, when arguments overheat. We've had scratching and hair pulling and bared claws going for faces, but never, I say *never*, has one girl tried to kill another. Girls don't fight with their fists, as boys do, Nicolaos; they do it with cold words and ugly behavior."

"What do you do when a girl comes to you with such a problem?"

"I tell her to sort it out, and send her back to the other girls."

"You can't be serious!"

"I am. These girls must learn to deal with each other. It's essential. The girls we teach are destined to marry the most powerful men in Athens. I can't be there for the rest of their lives to protect the weak ones. Somehow they have to find that balance for themselves. No, Nicolaos, I want as many personal issues as possible sorted out here at Brauron, where I can keep an eye on things, and that means letting nature take its course."

I said, "You must end up with some unhappy girls."

"I'm not here to make them happy," said the High Priestess. "I'm here to turn them into the backbone of Athens. The men might make the decisions at the *ecclesia*, and they fight the wars, but where would the men be, where would we all be, if the women weren't running the homes and raising the children and nudging the men in the direction they need to go? There'd be no point to life, would there? Men might deny it in public, but in the privacy of their homes they listen carefully to their wives. Sons respect their mothers. Husbands respect their wives and care for their daughters."

I'd never thought of this before, but of course, the High Priestess was right. Out here, in the backwoods of Attica, at a tiny temple few ever thought about, this remarkable woman was inventing our future.

I said, "Gaïs was an orphan. Does the sanctuary take in many?"

"No. The sanctuary's taken in a mere handful of foundlings over the years. There are restrictions on whom we'll accept. To start with, the babe must be a girl! There must be no possible legal guardian for the child. There must be a high likelihood the child is born of citizens."

"Why?"

"Because nobody wants to encourage slaves to have illegitimate children and then abandon them on our steps. An awful ethical position."

"Oh," I said, taken aback. "Of course."

"Also, a girl-child raised by us has almost the same status as the daughter of a well-born citizen. A poor father with too many mouths to feed might be tempted to try his luck, to give his daughter a chance at a better life. One of the first things we do when a child turns up is check to see which local family is missing one."

"How is it that Gaïs isn't married?" I asked.

Thea raised her arms in despair. "We tried. Believe me, we tried. But every time a prospective suitor arrived with his father, Gaïs would run in and . . . well, you've seen how she looks after those wild runs. And then she says those strange things that often sound slightly threatening . . . The men can't wait to get away from her. One time I ordered her to be held down; we brushed her hair and made her put on a pretty dress. It didn't help. She still managed to scare away the suitor. You and I know there's no harm in her—"

"Of course," I said, certain of no such thing.

"But no father would risk such a daughter-in-law, and those that are desperate enough to take her . . . well, I wouldn't do that to Gaïs. I love her too much."

"Was Sabina an orphan, too?"

"Goodness me, no." Thea laughed. "Sabina's like Doris: a widow. I believe her husband died young and she had no children. She refused further offers—a woman doesn't have to remarry unless she's an heiress—and she's lent her facility with numbers to the temple. We're lucky to have her. A most unusual woman." Thea paused before she added, "None of this can have the slightest bearing on Ophelia."

Diotima and Gaïs returned from their work at the Sacred Spring, where they had rededicated every offering. I excused us and led Diotima away from the temple by saying, "Let's go for a walk." She looked at me oddly, but agreed. We went to the jetty, where the rowboat bobbed gently against the steps, and looked out to sea.

"Diotima, I've got a question for you." I said it hesitantly, because I had a feeling this might be a sensitive question.

"Yes?" she said, seeming puzzled.

"When we met, on that first case . . . at one time we were at your mother's house and you had to search for your bow. You opened a cupboard."

I paused.

She waited for me to finish the question.

"It's just that I remember all of your toys fell out."

Diotima burst into tears.

IT TOOK SOME time to calm her down. We sat on the jetty, our legs hanging over the side, almost touching the water. I had my arm around her while she sniffed away the last of the tears.

Diotima said, "I suppose you want to hear about it?"

I nodded. "Yes."

She said, "What a girl's supposed to do, when her bleeding starts, is go to the temple and dedicate her toys to the Goddess, because she isn't a girl anymore, you see, she's become a woman. So she gives all her toys to Artemis, and then goes home to wait for her marriage, with all the things of her girlhood gone. They take every single toy from you, Nico. I hated that. I loved my toys too much."

"Do all the girls feel the same?"

"Some of the girls can't wait to be women and have a husband. Not me."

"Terrific," I said, demoralized.

Diotima realized what she'd said. "Oh, Nico! That was what I thought when I was a child. I may have changed my mind slightly since."

"All right," I said, slightly mollified. "So what did you do?"

"What do you think? I cheated, of course! I didn't see any need to lose the toys I loved just to be a grown-up."

"But they'd know at once if you didn't hand over the toys."

"Which is why I handed over toys to the Goddess. It's just that the toys I dedicated weren't . . . er . . . they weren't mine."

"You *gave away some other girl's toys*?" I was shocked.

"Actually, I bought them from her." Diotima shrugged. "Sometimes it helps to be the spoiled child of a wealthy mother. I hid my toys, which I loved more than my parents, then took an expensive vase I knew Mother would never miss. I traded it for the toys of another girl. The other girl agreed! Father never looked, Mother didn't care, and I had something to fool the priestesses."

"What about the other girl? Didn't she get into trouble?"

"The other girl was Gaïs."

"Dear Gods!"

Diotima nodded. "She was a poor orphan. She didn't have much. I gave her a lot of money, Nico."

"So when Gaïs called you a cheat—"

"She'd be in a position to know," Diotima admitted. "Obviously, she's disgusted with me." She blushed deeply. "I never thought Gaïs would still be here. I thought I was safe to come back. Gaïs should have been married long ago and gone from the sanctuary. When you pointed her out, running in the woods, and then when she turned up at the sanctuary and Doris said she'd become a priestess . . . well . . . I thought I'd die. The funny thing is, it was because I cheated the Goddess that I became her priestess."

"That doesn't make sense."

"No, listen. The dedication is a very solemn moment for the girl. She stands before the Goddess and says a prayer. A priestess goes with her to make sure she says it right. With me it was Doris. The girl lays her toys at the foot of the Goddess, and drapes her hair ribbons over the Goddess's hand, and then she walks away, a woman.

"So when my time came, I stepped forward with the toys of Gaïs. Until that moment, I'd thought I had it all worked out, I knew I'd been smarter than all the grown-ups, but when I looked up I realized I'd made a huge mistake: I could fool my parents and the priestesses, but I couldn't fool the Goddess. The moment I laid down the toys, Artemis would know I'd cheated her.

"But it was too late to back out! I walked across the stones to the statue. It was early morning, chilly. I remember feeling the coldness of the stone under my bare feet. Doris and I stopped before the statue and I recited the prayer, word perfect of course. Doris said, 'Very good, Diotima, I knew you were one of the clever ones. Now lay your toys before her.'

"I hesitated then, sure that the moment I did so the Goddess would strike me dead, and I didn't want to die. I stood there for a long time. I can't imagine how silly I must have looked.

"Doris leaned over me and said, 'Do it, child. I promise the Goddess wants you to.'

"So I said my own silent prayer to Artemis and put down the toys. I was shaking so much I almost dropped them! I looked down at my dedication and saw at once how shoddy and simple it looked: a wooden doll with a rough face and no hair, a skipping rope of old rag—not at all the things of a girl with a rich father. I looked up into the face of Artemis, thinking she would come to life and strike me, but she didn't, in fact it was almost like she was smiling. So I placed my ribbons in her outstretched hand. I can't begin to tell you how relieved I was!

"I laughed then, because the Goddess had accepted me for what I was. Nico, that was the moment I knew I wanted to be a priestess. I didn't want to be a married woman, and I didn't want to be a prostitute, high class like my mother or otherwise; Artemis had selected me to be hers; it explained why I felt so different from the other girls."

"You got away with it, Diotima. Gaïs might not be impressed, but do you really care?"

"I'm scared, Nico."

"Scared of what?"

"That Gaïs is right. That Artemis is only waiting until I'm married before she wreaks revenge on me. I *did* cheat the Goddess, and at the very ceremony that made me a nymphe. What if our marriage is a disaster, Nico, and it's all my fault?"

I put an arm around her and hugged her tight. "It won't be a disaster."

"But what if it is?"

I sighed. "It won't be. You're the woman I want to spend the rest of my life with, and nothing will ever change that. Besides, if there's going to be a disaster, there's nobody I'd rather have it with than you."

"Is that supposed to make me feel better?"

I helped her up, and we walked back to the sanctuary to collect some dinner. We ignored Sabina's ugly stare and carried two bowls of lentils and bread out to the lawn. The moon was new, and the Temple of Artemis was a black shape.

As we ate, I told Diotima everything that had happened to me during the trip to Athens. Diotima, anxious to get her mind off her fears, listened closely.

"The man in the helmet said Hippias was wounded in the fighting?" she said.

"Yes," I replied. "Of course, there's no reason to believe him."

"But if he's telling the truth, then how did Hippias get from Marathon to Brauron?" Diotima asked. "Did he walk?"

I said, "Across what was effectively enemy territory? Surely someone would have spotted him."

"Well, I don't know then."

"We need a map," I said.

"We don't have one."

"We'll draw our own." I picked up a stick and began to scratch in the dirt at our feet. "Here's the coastline." I scratched in a rough outline of the coastline of Attica, the large area of southern Greece that was controlled by Athens.

"Here's Marathon." I marked the spot on the upper right of the map.

"The Persians landed their boats on the beach at Marathon, and that's where the army of Athens marched to meet them." I drew an oval to mark the beach, and a picture of a boat.

"The Athenians and the Persians fought." I drew an X in the oval that represented the beach. "Everyone agrees Hippias was at Marathon."

"All right," Diotima agreed. She stared down at the map intently.

"After the battle, the Persians boarded their boats. They sailed to Phaleron." I drew in another oval to denote Phaleron, a large expanse of beach to the south of Athens. I placed a pebble to show Athens on the left hand side of the map.

"Obviously the Persians hoped to unload at Phaleron and attack Athens before our army could return. But our men force-marched across all of Attica. When they got there, the Persians found lined up against them the same army that had whipped their asses at Marathon. The Persians gave up and went home."

"Hooray for our side," Diotima said. "But you haven't explained Hippias . . . oh, hold on . . . wait . . ." I could see Diotima's brain working hard. "Nico, Hippias was seen at Marathon, but *no one saw Hippias at Phaleron*."

"Right. To get from the beach at Marathon to the beach at Phaleron, the Persians had to take this route." I swept the stick in a long arc, from the top right of the map to the bottom.

"Brauron is here. On the coast." I placed an X a third of the way along the arc. Diotima said excitedly, "This is beginning to make sense. Hippias was dropped off at Brauron by the Persians on their way to Phaleron."

"Yes!"

"No," Diotima said, unhappily.

"*No?*"

"Wouldn't the people at Brauron have noticed a Persian warship pulling up at their dock?"

"Doris said that Hippias came from around here. Were the people of Brauron noticeably pro-Persian during the wars?"

"They can't have been *that* pro-Persian," Diotima said.

"No, you're right," I said glumly. "All right, they put him off nearby at a small beach. There must be lots of them around here."

"How old was Hippias?"

"I don't know. Fifty? Sixty? Seventy? They put him on a small boat and rowed him in."

"This is all supposition, Nico."

"But you know it's right," I said.

"Yes, I think it is. Why would Hippias split from the Persian force? They were the only ones who could guarantee his safety."

"Things can't have been too pleasant between them after that defeat," I said. "Maybe he was homesick?"

"That's idiotic, Nico." Diotima shook her head. "Failed

tyrants don't risk death to see their old homes. It would have to be something urgent."

It came to me like a lightning flash. "I've got it!" I yelled. "The man in the helmet said he almost killed Hippias during the battle. He said he struck the tyrant with his spear."

"So?"

"Don't you see? Hippias came ashore to a place he knew, because *he needed a doctor*."

TO FIND THE right doctor in Brauron was straightforward. There was only one. We obtained the address from Doris. Next morning, we walked into Brauron. Although it was a small town, we managed to get lost instantly. Brauron was an ancient settlement, and nothing was in the normal place. Eventually I stopped a passing stranger.

"Excuse me, can you tell me how to get to Sesamon Street?"

He pointed straight down, at our feet.

We were on it.

Brauron's main street ran parallel with the shore; Sesamon joined it at the middle, to form a T. The main wharf, the warehouse, the fishing boats, and pretty much everything else of value in Brauron was to be found at that corner, including the doctor's residence. It was on the side of the street opposite the water.

We knocked and were admitted by a slave. The doctor had converted the front rooms of his house to see patients. We walked straight into his iatrion, his surgery.

Diotima and I despaired the moment we saw Ascetos the Healer. He was a man in his midthirties. Not nearly old enough to have treated an injured tyrant three decades ago.

"Mostly I treat fishing injuries," he said, when we introduced ourselves. "You wouldn't believe how many hooks I've removed from flesh. Lots of broken bones, drownings, that sort of thing."

"Were you involved in the unfortunate incident at the sanctuary?" Diotima asked.

"The girl who died? I heard about that."

"Her name was Allike. The sanctuary didn't call you in?"

"No, why should they? The girl was dead. I'm a doctor, not a god."

"There's also a girl who's missing," Diotima said.

"Sorry, I can't help you."

We were getting nowhere.

"We're wasting the doctor's time and our own, too," I said to Diotima. To Ascetos I said, "I'm sorry, Doctor. We only asked about the children when we saw you wouldn't know about our real reason for coming."

"And what was that?"

"Whether Hippias the Tyrant had ever come here."

"Well, why didn't you say so?" he said. "I can tell you all about *that*."

NOW THAT HE had a story to tell, Ascetos called for wine and settled us on dining couches, as if we were honored guests.

"You should know my father was doctor here before me. Doctors' sons almost always take up the profession."

"The same thing happens with sculptors' sons," I said. It was my strong desire to avoid sculpture that had first moved me to take up investigation.

Ascetos said, "I was five years old, I think, but I already knew I was destined to become a doctor, so when the stranger bashed at the door in the dead of night, I took particular interest. Only the most interesting—that is to say, urgent—cases come at night."

"It was Hippias?"

"It was he. Though I didn't know that until my father told me later, and I didn't realize the fame of our patient, or the import of what had happened, until many years had passed. All I knew back then was, when Father opened the door, a stranger staggered in."

"How was he?"

"Except for the gaping wound in his throat, perfectly fine.

Father placed him on the examination couch. That's the one you're lying on at the moment, young lady—I've lost count of how many people have died on that couch . . . Where was I? Oh yes, the strange patient. He lay down, and there was a wound in the lower throat. Father peered in. So did I. I'm afraid I made rather a nuisance of myself.

"Hippias was unbelievably lucky. The slash that had opened the skin had missed everything vital. I could actually *see* the blood vessel pulsing. Sometimes when someone's been torn open by a ship's grappling hook, the blood pulses out in great spurts and then the man dies—sometimes the man lives long enough to reach me, but there's nothing anyone can do. Somehow, Hippias had managed to survive. The gods must have favored him like no other man. He could speak; he could eat. Amazing."

"Did he say how he came to be in Brauron?"

"If he did, it wasn't in my presence."

"What did your father do?"

"Closed the wound as best he could, and told his patient to lie still. Very, very still. For a very, very long time. Hippias asked if he was going to die—they always ask that—Father said it lay with the gods—the usual reply."

"How long was a very, very long time?"

"Until the flesh had healed and Hippias could stand up without the risk of bits of his throat falling out. Months, I should think, given what I know now."

"Surely Hippias didn't lie here all that time!"

"A few days later, men came and carried him away to recuperate."

"Where?"

"To a local estate."

A long pause, from both Diotima and me. This was the discovery we'd been looking for. I said, slowly, "You wouldn't happen to remember which estate he was taken to, would you, Doctor?"

"I was only five. Nobody tells a five-year-old anything. Father went to visit his patient from time to time, to check his recovery. I never accompanied him."

"Your father went to the estate where Hippias was hidden?" Diotima repeated. "*How long* was he away on each visit?"

Ascetos saw her point. "You want to find this place, don't you? Well, Father always left first thing in the morning and returned in time for his afternoon practice. I presume he ate lunch before he returned. A typical consultation would last the amount of time required to pray to the gods, perform a small sacrifice, and perhaps even inspect the patient. The place you're looking for is within half a morning's walk of this surgery."

"You said men came to carry Hippias. That's a long way to carry a man," I said.

"They used a board. It's a standard technique: the patient lies on a wide plank of wood; we strap him down so he doesn't roll off. With such an arrangement, men fore and aft could carry him forever."

"A board," Diotima said in an even tone. I knew what she was thinking. The bones of Hippias had been found laid out on a board. That board was now back at the sanctuary.

"I know this is a lot to ask," I said, "but is it possible you might recognize that board if you saw it again?"

"Surely it's rotted away by now, or been used for firewood."

"Just supposing."

Ascetos cocked his head to one side and puzzled. "It's possible. Father always used a particular size, and I never varied from his practice."

"So the boards you use now are the same?"

"That's what I said."

"Is there one here we could look at?"

"Look behind you."

Diotima and I both swiveled in our seats. Propped up against the wall was a wide plank. I decided not to inquire about the deep-red and brown stains that I observed in certain depressing locations. Instead I noted that the doctor's plank was close enough to the panel back at the sanctuary. I asked, "Why didn't your father tell anyone about this?"

"Talk about a patient? Good doctors don't do that, and my father was one of the best. Besides, what's it matter?"

Diotima and I traded a look. Ascetos didn't know about the skeleton found in the cave. Obviously word had not spread to Brauron, despite being common knowledge in Athens.

"Do you know where Hippias went?" Diotima asked.

Ascetos shrugged. "I presume a boat picked him up and took him back to Persia."

"How would a boat pick up Hippias?"

"If you look out the window, you'll observe a wharf. They're very convenient for that sort of thing."

"Let me rephrase that. How would a *Persian* boat retrieve him?"

Ascetos shrugged. "You'd have to ask the Persians. I'll tell you one thing: both before and after Marathon, this town was pro-Hippias. Maybe the only place in Attica that was for him. If a Persian boat *did* dock, the townspeople might have looked the other way."

"Is it possible Hippias died of his wounds while still here at Brauron?"

"No."

"You're sure about that?"

"Yes."

Diotima and I awaited an explanation. Ascetos eventually relented.

"Look, my father always got upset when a patient died. He was funny like that. Well, Father never got upset about Hippias."

"Any idea how Hippias died?"

"All I can tell you is, when Hippias left my father's care, he was still alive."

"IF WHAT THE doctor tells us is true, then Hippias might have died quite legitimately of war wounds," I said as we walked away.

"If Hippias wasn't murdered, after everything we've gone through, I'm going to scream," Diotima said.

"It doesn't explain the death of Allike, though," I said. "Nor find Ophelia."

"No, it doesn't."

We passed by the warehouse, toward the tiny agora that served Brauron. The smell of fish was strong in the air, and someone, somewhere, was making *garos* sauce. The pungent aroma of garos spread far in a light breeze, due to the sauce being made from fermented fish intestines. No meal was complete without garos.

"Do they sell eel here?" I wondered aloud. Eel in garos was my favorite meal. I'd never pass up a chance to have some. The only problem was, eel was expensive.

Just then my eye caught something, and I stopped abruptly. Then I backed up. Diotima carried on for five steps before she realized I wasn't with her. She turned to see me staring at the wall.

"Nico, what is it?"

I read a notice that someone had painted in bright white upon the dull wooden wall. It was a notice for a show in the local agora. For last month.

And the show's main attraction, written in larger letters than all the rest: a giant brown bear.

Chapter Nine

We rushed about the agora at Brauron in search of a giant bear, or at least, someone who could tell us where to find a giant bear. What we discovered was that the act had moved on.

"He's been gone this last month or two," said a vegetable seller, a thin man with a thin wife, and three hungry-looking children who stared up at us with big eyes. Diotima bought baskets of vegetables to take back to the sanctuary and overpaid the farmer.

"He did his show right here in the agora. Bear danced. Children loved it," the farmer said. "Fellow made the bear do tricks. If the fathers paid extra, he'd let the kids pat the bear." The farmer spat in the dirt. "I didn't eat that night. Every coin I earned that day went to the show. But me kids went to bed happy."

Diotima asked, "Was the bear tame?"

"It's one massive beast. But yeah, the bear seemed to like the children. I wasn't worried, if that's what you're thinking."

"Who was this man?" I asked. "The one who owns the bear?"

"Egesis by name. An ugly fellow."

"Ugly?"

"Scars. Like he'd been in the wars."

Well, that was common enough. Perhaps this Egesis had once been a mercenary.

"Any idea where he went?"

"Yeah. Athens."

We raced back to the sanctuary, where Diotima dumped the

vegetables in the kitchen, I collected a protesting Socrates ("But I only just got here!"), and Blossom surged off at a slow plod.

The funny thing was, this man Egesis was supposed to have left for the city a month before, yet I was sure there'd been no performing bear on show in Athens in the last month. The vegetable seller, however, had been quite definite, and others had repeated the same.

WE DISCUSSED THE case as we trudged along. I led Blossom. Socrates walked on the other side. He'd tried to climb onto the seat beside Diotima, but I'd hauled him off with a clear explanation that healthy men walk.

"It's important to note that everyone who's died has died at Brauron," Socrates said. He spoke with such a didactic air that I hoped he never became a schoolteacher.

"So?" I challenged him.

"So nobody's died in Athens," Socrates said. "Doesn't that mean the killer's at our backs? Someone we've left behind at the sanctuary?"

"It's a reasonable theory," Diotima said from the seat above us. "But now that we know the bear exists, we have to find it. Maybe the bear really did kill Allike."

"A bear didn't kill Melo," I pointed out.

"What about a man and a bear, working as a team?" Diotima suggested.

"Why?" I asked.

"You just don't want it to be anyone at the sanctuary," Socrates said, with surprising insight but unwelcome honesty.

Diotima had nothing to say to that.

"What if the killer strikes again while we're away?" Socrates persisted.

"Zeke's watching everything closely," Diotima said.

"What if *he's* the killer?" Socrates said.

I decided to ignore him. So did Diotima.

I said, "Hippias staggered into the doctor's surgery with a wounded throat. That's consistent with the story Socrates and I heard when we were kidnapped. Is it possible the crazy masked man was telling the truth?"

"Why wouldn't he?" Socrates asked.

"Because crazy masked men generally don't," Diotima said, absently.

"What about crazy naked priestesses?" I asked.

"Everything that Gaïs has said to us has turned out to be . . . er . . . true," Diotima said, obviously not wanting to repeat the story of her toys in front of Socrates. "Gaïs told us about a man in the woods and sure enough, there was Melo."

"Who, as it happens, is now dead," I pointed out.

WHEN WE ARRIVED at my father's house, I saw two dodgy-looking characters loitering on the other side of the street. One was scratching his behind. The other tossed a knife into the air and caught it by the handle, over and over, in a bored fashion. He wasn't even watching the blade as he caught it. Instead, he kept his gaze on the street, and as we rolled up, so did his gaze. It was the two characters who'd kidnapped Socrates and me.

"Not again," I said. I felt more confident this time because I'd spotted them in time to put a hand on my dagger, and they probably wouldn't expect Diotima to shoot them. This time we'd remembered to pack her bow on top.

"Relax," the leader said. He was the one who'd been flipping the dagger. "I got a message for you from my boss," he said.

"Well?"

"He says, 'Tell Nicolaos if he doesn't discover the conspirators, then I'll have him killed.'"

"Nice to know."

"I think he meant me and my friend here would be the ones doing the killing. Look, mate, if it comes to that, no hard feelings, all right? You know how it is. We're all professionals here."

"Sure."

"My boss says you should get on with the job. The soldiers of Marathon demand justice."

Exasperated, I said, "Why are you working for this man? He's obviously insane."

The professional thug shrugged. "A man like me's gotta take the money he can get. This fellow pays way over market rates. I don't know what he's up to, but he's hired a small army."

That little piece of information intrigued me. A small private army was something Pythax would want to know about.

"Do you have a name?" I asked.

"Not one you need to know." They turned to go.

"Hey, I've got another question for you!" I shouted as they walked away.

The leader stopped. "Yeah?"

"If I was a shifty character from out of town, down on my luck, and if I had a good reason to want to stay out of sight, where would I go for entertainment?"

"What makes you think I'd know?" he said, in a slightly hurt tone.

"Call it a wild intuition."

He thought about my question. "Try the warehouse district down by the docks," he said. "Why do you ask?"

"Just interested."

"Sure."

I WENT DOWN to the docks that night, having dressed as a poor laborer—it was only a short step down, unfortunately—and after having spent most of the afternoon arguing with Diotima.

"I'm going with you," she'd said.

"This is a men-only place I'm going to. So no, you're not."

"Yes I am."

"No you're not."

"Yes I am!"

"No you're not."

"You're not in charge here!"

"Actually, I am," I'd said coldly. "That's why they call us husbands."

Diotima had been close to tears. She said, "What have I done?" and stormed off. I heard the door bang upstairs. So too, probably, had every man in the deme. But I had to put my foot down on this, or we'd never get the marriage right.

Down by the docks, I saw at once what the street thug had meant. Within one of the warehouses behind the Emporion was what sounded like a loud party. Two men stood outside, guarding the entrance. They took one look at me and stepped aside to let me in.

The room stank of sweat, and stale wine, and fresh urine, and more sweat. And blood.

Men were clustered around a ring scratched into the hard dirt of the floor. I shouldered my way through, earning a few dirty looks, until I came to a layer of men willing to jab back when I tried to push past.

I peered over and under their smelly armpits to see what was so interesting.

In the center of the ring were two chickens. No, they were cocks. Huge ones. They strutted back and forth in an odd way, and it took me a moment to realize why: both birds had metal spurs tied to their feet. Those spurs looked vicious.

I'd walked into a cockfight. Lower-class Athenians loved a good cockfight as they loved few other things, except maybe drink and women.

The men around me studied the forms of the birds as they strutted back and forth aggressively. Then the referee called time, and suddenly everyone shouted for one cock or the other and threw money on the ground. All bets were even odds, one way or the other. Two men circled the inside of the ring; they took up the coins and remembered who'd bet what.

"You making a bet?" One of the bet takers appeared in front of me, a heavily bearded man.

Over the din I said, "No, I'm here to see a man about a bear. His name's Egesis. Do you know him?"

The bet taker jerked his head to the left. "Over there. The one with the scar on his forehead. You can't miss him. But listen here, mate, if you go causing trouble, or you interfere with the fight, the boys here'll tear your balls off."

"Right. Got it."

I edged my way left, careful not to cause trouble, but keeping a hand over the threatened parts, just in case.

I was so busy looking for a scar on a forehead that I walked straight into a young man.

"I'm sorry!" I said to him. "I was looking for—Diotima!"

"Shhh!" she hissed. "Don't shout it out!"

I lowered my voice and looked around to make sure no one had heard us. "What are you doing here?"

"If you think I'm letting you go after a killer without me, you can think again," she said.

She was wearing a full-length chiton, but in a man's style, not a woman's. And it had been carefully smeared with dirt. The chiton covered her arms to the wrists and legs to the ankles. No one would see her smooth woman's skin. She'd tied the belt loosely to hide her hips. Over the chiton she wore a cloak of the type used by itinerants to shield them from the weather, which would have been reasonable outdoors at midday, but indoors at midnight was of questionable sanity. She'd needed the deep hood of the cloak, though, to hide her long hair and womanly features. The overall effect was ridiculous.

I said, "Diotima. Women aren't allowed here. You have to go."

"I'm staying."

"It's not safe for you. When they find out you're a woman—"

"I'll make sure they don't. The longer we stand here arguing, the more likely someone is to notice, don't you think?"

"No. I'm your future husband. That makes me responsible for your safety, and I say go."

"I'll think about my own safety, thanks very much."

"Diotima, I said *go now*."

"No."

She was so dogmatically unreasonable, I was becoming angry. "I hope you don't think you can disobey me when we're married!"

"Relax, Nico," she said, cool as could be. "Everyone thinks I'm a man."

"There's a distinct lack of stubble."

"I know. I tried cutting a fake beard using old rabbit skin, but it looked like something furry had died on my face. It doesn't matter. I'll pass as a young man."

"What happened to your breasts?" Diotima was well endowed, but somehow her best feature—not counting her personality, of course—had disappeared.

Diotima grimaced. "A tight band of material, and believe me, it hurts."

"You better keep your voice low. Or better yet, don't say anything at all."

Diotima stared at the heaving mass of men's backs. "What are they doing?" she asked.

"It's a cockfight."

"Do I want to know about cockfights?"

"They tie spurs to the feet of cocks that fight each other, and bet on the winner."

"You mean, the one that survives?"

"Yes."

"Those poor chickens!"

"They're cocks."

"I don't care. Nico, you have to save those chickens."

I thought back to what the bet taker had said: that if I interrupted the fight, they'd cut off my balls.

"I don't think that's a good idea, Diotima. Anyway, what do

you care? I've seen you sacrifice animals at the temple, by your own hand even."

"That's different, Nico," she said in a superior tone. "A sacrifice is dedicated to the gods; it's a sacred rite that binds the higher powers to us. What those men are doing is unholy; they're letting animals rip each other apart for their *amusement*. It's disgusting."

"Well, you're the one who insists on walking into men's places. If you didn't come here, you wouldn't know about it. You could always leave."

"Where's Egesis?" she changed the subject.

I sighed. "I'm told he's this way." I took her by the hand, then thought better of it and let go. Instead I led her around the ring.

The bet taker was telling the truth. Egesis was hard to miss. He had a jagged scar across his forehead that was red and puckered. He looked like an ugly character.

Diotima quietly walked up behind him. I stopped in front.

I said, "Is your name Egesis?"

"Yeah. So what?" He tried to look around me, to see the cockfight that was about to start.

I continued on a firm note. "Your bear is responsible for the brutal death of a child. Pray to whatever gods you hold dear, Egesis, because the jury will have no mercy when those girls' fathers sue you."

After this fine verbal assault, Egesis looked at me blearily, as if he couldn't care less, and said, "Who in Hades are you?"

"Nicolaos, son of Sophroniscus, and your bear—"

"Yeah, yeah. I heard it the first time. I ain't got no bear. He was stolen."

"*Stolen?* Are you sure?"

Egesis held his arms wide apart. "Why don't you search me for the murder weapon?"

I was fairly sure Egesis didn't have a bear on him.

"You staked him somewhere outside the city," I said.

"Nope," Egesis said. "If I did, he wouldn't be there when I got back."

Somehow that sounded depressingly reasonable. My shoulders slumped. His voice and his utter lack of reaction or fear were enough to tell me we had the wrong man. That made me notice the scar all the more.

"What happened to your head?"

"I was kissed by the Furies," he said in a tired voice.

He certainly looked it. But I knew from the way he spoke that it was his stock answer.

"Oh. Sorry about that."

"I'm used to it. You say my bear killed a couple of kids?"

"One, at least. Maybe another."

"I don't believe it."

"Why not?"

"'Cause he's a tame creature, for all that he's damn near the size of a house. Sure, he'd kill if you poked him hard enough, but that's like anyone, you know? Do you know where he is?" he said hopefully.

"Sorry, no."

He spat in disgust, narrowly missing my foot. "Curse it, I was hoping someone might have him."

"So it's true, you did lose a bear?"

"Yeah. I've been doing the rounds, you know? I go from town to town. The bear does tricks while I collect coins." He shrugged. "It's a living. If you can call it that. I don't make much, and most of what I do goes to feeding the bear. Maybe I'm better off without the big bastard."

I guessed that Egesis cut a few purses while he was at it, but I wasn't about to suggest that; I needed this man's help.

"How do you catch a bear?"

"With a goat. You tie the goat to a stake and wait downwind, with men and a lot of nets. When the bear comes for the goat, well, then it gets exciting."

"What's the bear's name?" Diotima spoke in a low, gruff voice, but she couldn't maintain it and it rose to a high pitch.

Egesis turned to look at her. "Who's he?"

"A friend of mine. Ignore him. His voice is still breaking, and to tell you the truth, he's something of a village idiot. Never does what he's told."

Diotima stabbed me to death with her eyes.

Egesis spat in the dirt. "I've known a few men like that myself."

"The name of the bear?"

"I just call him Bear."

"Original."

"Look, it's a bear. It doesn't care what I call him."

"Did Bear get away at Brauron?"

"Yeah. Straight after the show." Egesis scratched vigorously beneath his tunic. He slept rough, beside a bear; he was probably covered in lice.

"I still don't know how the animal did it," he said, and scratched hard. "I chained him every night. He never got out before, but when I woke, he was gone. The collar just lay there empty. It wasn't broken. It was like he'd undone it." Egesis shrugged. "Maybe he learned one trick too many, but what I reckon is, someone took him. I reckon only a human could've undone that lock."

I said, "Why do I hear all these reports of bear sightings, yet no one knows it was you who lost him?"

Egesis sighed. "It's like this. I reckon he was stolen, but I can't prove it. So if my bear did damage on someone else's property, I'd be liable; they'd make me pay, right?"

"That's fair enough."

"All right. So if anything goes wrong on any farm anywhere near here—every goat that goes missing, every chicken that gets taken by a fox, every fence that gets damaged—they're gonna blame me, aren't they? Whether my bear did it or not, they're gonna look for every excuse to blame me, 'cause they'll squeeze me for every *drachma*. And I'll have to pay, 'cause if I took it to court, the jury would find against me anyway, 'cause I'm a Macedonian and they're Athenians. You see?"

"I see."

"So I figured the only safe thing was to lie low, you know?"

"Didn't you try to recover the bear?" Diotima asked.

Egesis spat again. "Of course I did. I staked out a goat in a couple of places and waited. Nothing. The accursed beast must not be hungry, or it really is eating the local livestock. I dunno. I figure it'll be easier to go back home and catch a new bear in the mountains, where they still got some. That's where I'm headed: back to Macedonia. But first I gotta make some money, or I'll starve on the way." He paused. "With any luck my dad's died by now. That's why I left, you know. The bastard wanted me to work on—" He shuddered. "On a farm."

"Sickening for you."

"You're telling me. Get up in the morning? No bloody way. How can I gamble all night and get up at dawn?"

"You could give up the gambling?" Diotima suggested.

Egesis looked at her in incomprehension. "Give up blood sports? What sort of a man are you?"

"How do you train a bear?" I asked, intrigued.

"With patience, and a big stick. You whack it when it doesn't do what you want."

"Is that a good idea?"

"It works for me. Of course, that's how I got the scar, so maybe it doesn't work all the time. Now shut up. The fight's about to start."

Egesis turned away from us. I didn't particularly care if animals fought, but like Diotima, I didn't need to see it either; I'd seen enough human blood to lose my taste for the sight of it. Instead I looked around at the crowd and—

"Uh oh," I said quietly to Diotima.

"What is it?" she whispered back.

"The two men who kidnapped me and took me to that meeting . . . they're over on the other side of the room, and they're circling. I think they're searching for me. They must have followed me here."

"What do they want, Nico?"

"Well, since I didn't give up the job, and I didn't deliver any names to the crazy man, I imagine they want to kill me."

There was only one door out of the room, and two routes to reach it. I looked along the other one. Two other men were heading our way, and though I didn't recognize them, I doubted they were here for the gambling.

We couldn't go right. We couldn't go left. There was only one other route.

The cocks were fighting furiously. Men shouted as the battle swayed one way then the other. They wailed or cheered, according to their bets, as one cock got in a good blow, and again when the same one struck again. The other cock staggered back but kept on clawing. He was game, but it seemed he couldn't last long.

I jumped onto an overturned crate, pointed at the bet taker, who crouched at the front, and shouted, "He's cheating! Him! I saw it! He threw poisoned grain into the ring!"

I had no idea what I was saying, but it didn't matter. With men's money on the line, tension was already running high. Everyone who'd bet on the injured cock was ready to believe me.

The bet taker stared at me in stupefaction for the briefest moment, then he stood to shout, "That's a lie!"

His denial instantly made everyone think he was guilty. Men waved their fists and demanded their money back. Other men waved their fists and demanded their winnings.

With so many fists waving, two of them connected.

That caused a scuffle.

The scuffle spread like spilled wine.

In the blink of an eye, every man in the room was fighting every other man.

I hauled Diotima up onto the crate beside me, so she wasn't accidentally caught by a flying fist, and stood ready to defend her. Across the sea of bobbing heads and swearing men, I could see our four pursuers. The two I knew had their backs to the wall; they edged toward us, pushing away any brawler who stumbled their way. The other two had been caught up in the fight; they stood back to back in the middle of a melee and threw punches. They'd certainly forgotten about us. That was our path, then.

"Come on." With my left hand I grabbed Diotima firmly by the wrist and dragged her along, keeping my right free to hit anyone who came at us. I pushed hard, keeping my left shoulder against the wall, until we came to a knot of men who'd forced another group against the wall and were beating them soundly. No way through.

"Keep your head down!" I shouted to Diotima, and pulled her toward the center.

We ducked under fists and made good progress. "I can see the door. Hold on, Diotima; we'll soon be there."

"Nico, wait!" Diotima broke free of my grasp. She ran into the ring, scooped up the fighting cocks, one under each arm, and turned back to me.

Except she couldn't return. A man jumped in front of her. The bet taker, who'd promised to take the balls of anyone who interfered with the fight. He came at Diotima with an evil grin and a sharp knife upraised.

He was going to be so disappointed when he lifted her chiton.

I couldn't save my girl; there were too many men between us.

Diotima stared at her attacker, retreating the few steps she had available until she was up against the wall on the opposite side.

She did the only thing she could. She threw the fighting cocks at him.

Two very angry cocks wearing metal spurs flew into the face of the bet taker, claws out.

The bet taker screamed. He shielded his face with his hands and backed off.

The cocks fell off him and at once strutted about in search of other victims to destroy, crowing their victory. The bet taker was still walking backward. I could see the blood seeping between his fingers. He tripped on a prostrate body and went over backward.

"Run! It's the Scythian Guard!"

Every head turned to the entrance. There, trying to push their way in, were two of the Scythian Guard of Athens, whose job was to enforce the peace. With batons if necessary.

The Scythians carried unstrung bows with which to beat unruly citizens, and they were known for their willingness to apply some stick. Right now, this gambling den looked like a good place for them to be doing business, and where there were two Scythians caught in a fight, you could bet there would soon be more.

Men scattered. Cockfighting wasn't illegal. Nor was gambling. But brawling was a serious misdemeanor. Anyone caught in this riot faced a court summons, followed quickly by a huge fine, one big enough to bankrupt a man; and that was *after* the Scythians had finished beating him senseless.

With everyone else worried about the brawl and the guardsmen, I saw Egesis break into the center ring, club a man out of the way, and shovel handfuls of coins into the material of his tunic. He tied a knot to stop the coins from falling out, then jingled his way toward the exit. Now he had enough money to get home to Macedonia. But his escape too was stopped by the mass of panicking men.

I grabbed Diotima by the arm. "Come on!"

She scooped up a rooster. I grabbed the other one.

"There's no way through!"

She was right. The jam of men struggling to get out now had to fight the Scythian Guardsmen struggling to get in.

I pulled her in the other direction, where lay workmen's tools. Among them was a mallet.

"Nico!" Diotima shouted at me in alarm over the din. "You're not going to hit people with that, are you?"

"No."

I swung hard. Right into the wall. Nothing happened, but I could feel the mud brick yield, ever so slightly. Everyone around us ignored me; they were all intent on getting out the door, so I swung again. And again. Every time on the same spot. I didn't tire. Years of assisting my father with the heavy stonework of his sculpting paid off now. It needed only a handful of blows to make a sizable dent.

Diotima, I noticed, watched me with some appreciation. My chiton was all but torn away. She could see the muscles of my upper arms and chest work. Diotima had always liked a strong male chest. The thought made me swing harder.

The first mud brick fell out. Immediately I attacked the one above it. It came out more easily. Then two to each side, a single blow for each. Soon I had a hole large enough to crawl through.

"Go!"

Diotima handed me her chicken and dived through. The cocks instantly attacked each other in my arms, and I got a face full of feathers. I threw both squabbling fowls out the hole, not caring if they ran off. I was about to follow them when a hand grabbed me by the shoulder and turned me round. I was too startled to resist.

"Not so fast." It was my two pursuers. I cursed myself for an idiot. When I'd led Diotima to the wall opposite the door, I'd taken us back to them.

I hit one of them with the mallet.

It wasn't much of a swing—there'd been no time to pull back—but the blow sent him tumbling into his friend. They both went down.

I jumped through the hole in the wall, to where Diotima waited for me, and together we ran into the dark night.

It would have been nice if the night hadn't been so dark. I ran straight into Pythax, standing in the middle of the road. My prospective father-in-law was more than twice my age, but he was built like a rock, and he wore the full armor of the Scythian Guard. I bounced off him and fell on my behind.

That was when I recalled that Pythax, whose permission I needed to marry Diotima, was chief of the Scythian Guard of Athens, the people we were trying to avoid.

"What are you doing here?" he growled. Then he saw the rooster under my arm. "Have you taken to stealing chickens?"

"It's a cock."

Then Pythax noticed my companion, also with a struggling fowl. He pointed at his own daughter and said, "Who's he?"

Diotima pushed back the hood of her traveling cloak. "Hello, Father!" she said. "Fancy meeting you here!"

PYTHAX STRODE BACK and forth while I stood at attention like a small boy before his schoolmaster. Diotima he had sent home, with a guard on either side to make sure she went, and with firm instructions to stay there until he calmed down, or possibly for the rest of her life, whichever came first. He had not even attempted to believe our explanation: that we happened to be walking down the street when we came across the fighting cocks, which had somehow escaped from the brawl in which we had had no involvement.

"What in Hades were you thinking!" Pythax stormed at me. "You took *my daughter* into a gambling den?"

"I swear I didn't, sir! Diotima got herself in there."

"You didn't stop her."

"I told her to leave, sir, but she refused."

"And you reckon you're fit to marry her, do you? Shit, boy. What sort of a man can't control his own wife?"

"Er . . ." I began, thinking of Pythax's inability to control his own wife's spending.

"If you answer that, I'll kill you," he said. He stopped his march, stared me in the face, and said, "What were *you* doing in there? You ain't the sort to go slumming with the lowlives."

"I was looking for a witness, Pythax. A man named Egesis." I explained about the bear sightings, and how they were due to a real bear.

"A bear wandering about Attica," he muttered. "And a murderous one at that. Gods, is there anything else that can go wrong?"

"Well . . ."

"Don't answer that. And don't make it happen, either, or my daughter'll be a widow before she's a wife."

"Yes sir."

"I suppose I'll have to send men to hunt down this bear. I can't have some bloody animal eating the citizens."

"No sir."

"You say there are men following you?"

"Yes sir. They're hired thugs. Their leader will have a large lump on his head, about the width of a mallet."

"I think we might have him. He was still unconscious when we picked over the bodies. Are you telling me you left an enemy alive? On purpose?"

"Yes sir."

"You're an idiot, Nico."

"Yes sir."

"Next time you got an enemy in your power, just kill the bastard. All right?"

"Yes sir."

"Dear Gods, boy, didn't I teach you anything?"

"No sir. Er . . . that is, yes sir."

"Do you want this thug?"

"It would be nice . . ."

"He's not a citizen; he's a metic," Pythax growled. "Just get him out of my sight, and out of Athens for that matter—I got no room for troublemakers in my city—and make sure he never comes back."

"Yes, Pythax. I can arrange that."

WHEN HE CAME to, he was bound with rope, wrapped around him so many times he looked like a fish. The winding finished at his ankles, whence the rope went up and over two tree branches. He hung upside down.

"Where am I?" was the first groggy thing he said.

I said, "Welcome to my farm. We thought this would be the best place to take you. Fewer people to hear you scream."

In the background, two roosters clucked and scratched about in search of seed. Diotima's first considered action on being released from her father's house had been to remove the spurs from the animals and tend to their wounds. We had to keep them separated—they had a tendency to want to kill each other—but they seemed happy enough. The slave Pericles had assigned had begun building a pen for each. We'd have to get a few chickens too. With two cocks and a few chickens we'd soon be chicken breeders. I'd always loved fresh eggs.

I said to our captive, hanging upside down, "We're all professionals here, right?"

"Right!" he said. "And as a professional courtesy, if you could get me down from here . . . the blood's rushing to my head, and I got a bad headache—"

"Tell me, how does one professional extract information from another?"

"Well, normally he beats the crap out of him, but in this case—"

"You see that woman over there?" I pointed to a figure fifty paces away. "That's my wife—fiancée rather—"

"Congratulations."

"Thank you. Diotima's quite a good shot with a bow. But I'm afraid she's a bit out of practice."

I grabbed hold of my victim, took two steps back, pulling him with me, then let go. He swung back and forth. The rope creaked slightly, and the olive branch bent under his weight, but he went with a more or less regular rhythm.

I said, "I'd like to know who you work for."

"You know I can't tell you that. It would be unprofessional."

I waved to Diotima.

She raised her bow, took careful aim, and fired.

The arrow whistled past and embedded itself with a solid thud, point-deep into the trunk of the olive tree. It had missed him by a whisker.

He twisted in a vain attempt to escape. "Hey!"

"I told you she was out of practice. Who do you work for?"

"You know a professional wouldn't tell—"

I waved to Diotima again.

This time the arrow grazed his head and went into the ground at the tree roots. The shot had drawn a scratch across his ear that quickly turned bright red and began to drip.

"Aaargh!"

"Sorry about that. I guess it's hard for a woman to get the pull right, them not being as strong as we men. It's a good thing you're a professional who doesn't talk. She'll have plenty more time to get her arm in."

I raised my arm to wave.

"I could retire from the professional ranks," he said quickly.

In the background one of the roosters crowed, and, not to be out-done, the other replied.

I dropped my arm. "Who do you work for?"

"Aeschylus."

"*The playwright?*"

"Yeah. It surprised me too when he hired us."

"Dear Gods."

Aeschylus was untouchable. He'd fought at Marathon. He was a war hero. He was the greatest playwright in the world; every contest he entered, he won. He practically owned the victory tripod of the Great Dionysia. And worst of all, his patron, like mine, was Pericles.

No wonder Aeschylus knew all about me. All he had to do was turn up at the latest symposium and ask the sources directly. No one would think not to tell Aeschylus anything he wanted to know.

"What does Aeschylus have to do with any of this? What does he want?"

"Hey, I just do what I'm told. That's what we former professionals do."

"Have you told me everything you know?"

"Yes. I swear it!"

I waved to Diotima.

"Hey, what are you doing?"

Diotima took up her bow once more and aimed. Even from a distance I could see her slightly unorthodox stance. Owing to the happy circumstance of her well-developed breasts, she wasn't able to hold the bow across her chest like a man; instead she had to extend her left arm for a slight angle and pull the string high, with her pulling hand at eye level. But years of practice had made her adept.

Our captive said, "Hey! We're all professionals here, right?"

"Sure."

"Then why are you doing this to me?"

"Well, I guess some of us are more professional than others. But if I could be persuaded that you'll leave Athens and never return, I might ask my fiancée not to use you for target practice."

"It's a deal. This town ain't safe for me anyway, not now I've betrayed my employer."

"Where will you go?" I asked, curious.

"I'm not sure. Do you have any suggestions?"

I thought about it. "How about Corinth? It's a rich place." Also, Corinth was the sworn enemy of Athens. I was very happy for him to cause trouble there.

"Good idea. Corinth it is."

I waved to Diotima. "You can shoot now!"

"Hey!"

Diotima released.

The arrow flew straight and true, with barely an arc. It whistled in and sliced through the rope just above his feet. The rope snapped. He fell to the ground head first, and was knocked out once more.

Diotima walked over.

"Good shot," I said to her.

"It was an effort to miss him the first few shots. Did you have to swing him?"

"I thought you needed the practice," I said. "Anyway, you missed him by a whisker, exactly as planned. Those were great shots."

"No they weren't. I really am out of practice. I was aiming to graze his legs."

THE PROBLEMS I'D had with Diotima had started to rankle. Pythax wanted to know why I couldn't control my own wife—or wife-to-be. The situation didn't bode well for the future. It was clear I'd have to do something to exert control, or our married life would be a disaster. So I sought advice from someone who I knew was an expert on how to run a happy household.

I found him in his workroom.

"Father, I have a question."

Sophroniscus looked up from his work. He was chiseling into a large block of marble, the first of his works destined for Olympia.

"Yes, son?"

I asked, "What do you do when Mother disobeys you?" Then, after a moment, I added, "Why are you laughing?"

"I'm sorry, son," said Sophroniscus, wiping away the tears. "I wondered how long it would be before you asked that."

"I hope I haven't disappointed you," I said, somewhat miffed.

"I thought it would be another two months before we had this conversation."

"Oh," I said, taken aback. "You expected me? Do all men have this problem?"

"You'll never find one who'll admit it."

"I'll take that as a yes. What's the answer? How do other men cope?"

"You've done your two years of basic training in the army. What did you learn?"

"Never volunteer?"

"Besides that."

"A lot of marching drills. I don't quite see the application to married life—"

"Did you spend time as a mess leader?"

"Of course. They rotate the position so everyone gets a turn to practice shouting at people."

"Good. So there you were with your friends, young men whom you've known since you were boys. You once played in the street together. You gave them a direct order, like . . . like . . ."

"Make camp?" I suggested, recalling one embarrassing incident. "Cut firewood, fetch water, pitch tents?"

"Just so," Father agreed. "You gave all those orders, and they laughed at you."

"How do you know?" I said.

"Son, unless young men have changed significantly since my day, I know *exactly* what happened. And after they laughed at you, and you couldn't make them obey orders even though you were nominally in charge, you lost all authority. From that point on, you had to ask your men to do things where the commanders would have ordered and expect to be obeyed."

"Are you sure you weren't there?"

Father shook his head.

"I guess I'm not leader material," I said sheepishly.

"Few are. The men of our family have always been upstanding citizens, but never in the public eye."

"I think that will change with my generation, sir."

"I hope you mean yourself and not Socrates," Father said.

We both shuddered. Socrates as a public figure didn't bear thinking about.

I said, "If my investigation work continues, I hope it will take me to a leadership position in Athens."

"Your ambition is foreign to me," Father said. "If you follow this course, then you must be aware your choice of wife will be an impediment."

"I'll manage."

"I see you're bent on self-destruction. Well, most young men are, I suppose. I asked for your army experience because it answers your question about woman management."

"It does?" I said, amazed.

"It does," Father said. "Simply this: don't give your wife an order she won't obey."

"That's it?" I said, incredulous. "That's all I need to know?"

"A marriage, son, is like leading a squad in the army. You're in charge, but the squad will only obey the orders they feel like. Get them in the habit of obedience by only issuing orders that make sense."

I said, "I see what you mean." I'd never thought about it before, but Father was right. I couldn't recall a time when my mother had disobeyed my father in public, but at home, Father toiled in his workshop while Mother made all the decisions and managed the household.

"I think I see," I said, excited. "Mother is like the commander of an auxiliary unit, such as . . . as . . . archers!" I said, inspired by my father's military analogy. "While you're the overall army commander."

"Exactly. The sub-commander is free to do whatever she likes with her troops—those are the house slaves—within the overall guidance of the supreme command."

"Thank you, Father. For the first time, I think I truly understand marriage."

"It's a pleasure, son. Come to me any time for advice."

"But sir, what if I want my soldiers . . . er, that is, what if I want my wife to do something she insists she won't do?"

Father scratched his head. "If you find the answer, son, let me know. It would help with your mother."

WITH THIS ADVICE in hand, I returned to the courtyard, where Diotima was sitting with my mother, Phaenarete. They were talking about weddings, so they barely noticed my presence. Socrates had made himself scarce.

A slave came from the front of the house. He addressed my mother. "Mistress, there are two visitors to see the lady Diotima."

Phaenarete said, "Why are you telling me?"

The slave blinked. "Because you're in charge?" he suggested.

Phaenarete sighed. "We may as well get used to the new way of things around here," she told him. "Very soon now we'll have another mistress in the house. Two of us! When she tells you to do something, it's as if I told you myself. Do you understand?"

"Yes, mistress."

"Then perhaps you might like to address your new mistress directly."

I don't think I've ever admired my mother more. She was making things as easy as possible for the woman I loved.

The slave looked at Diotima uneasily. A new mistress can upset even the most balanced of homes, and when Diotima and I wed, she would be second only to my mother in the running of the house. So many things can go wrong when a new mistress arrives. The mother and the bride might not get on, and if that happens it's a disaster for everyone, particularly the bride. Or the new mistress might prove a martinet, or worse, slack with the slaves in the hope they'll like her. Our slaves didn't know it yet, but they were in for a treat. Diotima had been running her mother's household for years, due in large part to Euterpe's indifference to everything but men. If there was anything that characterized Diotima's management style, it was ruthless efficiency.

The slave said, "Two women are here to see you, mistress. They asked for you by name. They're both gyne, matrons."

"Are they friends of the household? Do we know them?" Diotima asked.

"No, mistress. They have attendants, and they carry baskets."

Diotima and I shared a look. For a woman to visit a strange house without her husband was unheard of. Unless she was a working girl, and matrons with slaves didn't do that sort of work.

"Show them in."

As the slave departed, Diotima said to my mother, "Thank you, Phaenarete."

Phaenarete shrugged. "It's the way of things, dear. Just be good to the slaves."

"Of course."

"Your arrival makes me all too conscious of the passing of my years. A young mistress in the house . . . I remember when that was me, in this very courtyard. I was terrified."

Two women entered, almost the same age as my mother, followed by more attendants than I could quickly count. I was struck by the attendants—every one of them wore quality clothes that had been ripped to pieces—and even more so by the hair of one of the women: it had been cut roughly, almost to the scalp, and what remained stuck out in all directions. Her eyes were very, very red.

"My name is Aposila," said the lady with the shredded hair. "I am the mother of Allike." She paused. "I *was* the mother of Allike." She sobbed. Her friend put an arm around her to comfort her.

Diotima said, “We’re very sorry.”

“Aren’t you supposed to be at home?” I asked. Diotima threw me a nasty look, but I meant the question well. Women in mourning are not supposed to be out and about.

“This is the ninth day since the . . . since the funeral. I carried flowers and fruit and cakes and libations to Allike’s tomb, as the custom decrees. She always liked fruit cake. I made it with my own hands and left it by the urn.”

That meant Allike had been cremated, and her ashes lay in a pelike—a richly decorated jar—in the cemetery at Ceramicus.

I knew who the second woman was, because I had already met her. This was Malixa, the wife of Polonikos and the mother of Ophelia. I introduced her to Diotima and my mother.

Malixa said, “I pray to every god that will listen that I will not soon wear my hair like Aposila.”

Phaenarete made sympathetic noises and looked like she was about to cry.

“Our husbands think we’re going to the cemetery and then straight back home,” Malixa said. “We’d appreciate it if you didn’t tell them we were here.”

“Of course not,” Diotima said. “We knew Allike and Ophelia were friends, but we didn’t realize the families knew each other.”

“We don’t. Or we didn’t,” Malixa said, and shared a look with Aposila. Aposila said, “Malixa came to see me, to offer her sympathies. It was against the laws of proper mourning, but, well, it seemed very appropriate.”

“We discovered we have a lot in common,” Malixa said simply.

“Malixa told me—please tell me if it’s true—that you’re investigating my daughter’s death.”

“It’s true.” I didn’t tell her that as far as the powerful of Athens were concerned, Allike’s death was a side issue to the mystery of Hippias.

“She also told me that you said anything you can learn might help her lost daughter.”

"It's true."

"When I told Malixa what I'd seen, she convinced me to come see you."

"Oh?" I said, suddenly interested.

Aposila said, "We've come to you because our husbands—both of them—seem absolutely determined to do nothing about their daughters."

Polonikos, the father of Ophelia, had his financial problems with a dowry, but I couldn't imagine the coincidence of two fathers with the same problem. I said as much to Aposila, and she shook her head.

"At first my husband, Antobius, was furious. He demanded that the killer be caught. I'm not sure he had any idea how to catch a killer, but he said the sanctuary must know who'd done it. He said he would sue the sanctuary, take them to court, and expose them for negligence. That was on the day we heard the news." Aposila paused to wipe her face of tears. "Then, overnight, he changed his mind. He decided not to pursue the killer. It happened," she said bitterly, "after the stranger called."

Phaenarete called for refreshments. Slaves brought small bowls of figs, olives, grapes, goat's cheese and flat bread, and cups of heavily watered wine.

We wanted to know everything about strange visitors.

"It was late at night," Aposila went on. "Antobius and I were settling down for the night, when the house slave came to say there was a caller at the door. We never have visitors that late. Antobius would have told the slave to shut the door on him, but the stranger said it was urgent. Antobius went out to see him."

"Did you see him?" Diotima asked.

"They stood outside, in the dark."

"What did you do?"

"I watched out of the window. They talked for a long time. They were too far away for me to hear what they were saying; I heard voices but no words, and it was dark. But I could swear I saw the stranger hand my husband a bag. From the look of it, the bag was full and heavy. From the way Antobius hefted it, I think there were coins in it. Then the stranger walked away."

"When was this?"

"The day after we heard Allike had died."

Malixa spoke up. "The moment Aposila told me this, I knew you needed to know."

"You were right," I said with feeling. "Did the stranger return?"

"Not that I saw. But my husband acted differently."

"How so?"

Aposila shifted in her seat. "Antobius had been angry before, but next morning he was mollified. When I asked him about the strange visitor, he said it was business. I told him I'd seen the bag and asked him what was in it. He became angry and ordered me never to mention the incident again."

"Did you?"

"No."

"What did your husband do?"

"Nothing. After that night, he never again said anything against the sanctuary, nor blamed them for Allike's death." Now Aposila clenched her hands in anguish. "When I pressed him, he said he'd decided to let the matter rest."

"I'm confused," I said. "How does he explain the death of his daughter?"

In Athens, by law, a man was required to investigate the murder of any close relative. It was the only investigation that was guaranteed. Polonikos, the father of Ophelia, could argue that so far his daughter was only missing, but if Antobius, the father of Allike, refused to look into his own daughter's death, he'd be in flagrant breach of the law.

"My husband said that our daughter had been unlucky, that a wild bear had killed her. He said the stranger told him there'd been reports."

If true, that meant no crime had been committed. We knew

there really was a bear, which meant Antobius was permitted to make such a finding—technically.

"When Aposila told me this, I became desperate," said Malixa, the mother of Ophelia. "I had thought that perhaps when Allike's killer was found, it might bring us to my daughter. But if Antobius does nothing, then who will find the truth? Who will find my Ophelia?"

"If anyone can find your child, it's my son," Phaenarete said. "I promise you."

My jaw dropped. It was the first time my mother had ever said a word about my investigation work, and she'd begun with a promise I wasn't sure I could keep.

"What do you think?" Diotima asked Aposila. "What do you want to do?"

"What can I do?" Aposila said. "Tend the grave of my daughter and care for my family. I have two other children—sons—but I loved Allike best." Aposila paused, took a deep breath, then said, "I am determined to divorce my husband."

Diotima and Phaenarete gasped.

I asked, "Are you sure about this?"

Aposila said, "When I pressed him on the death of my daughter, he refused. Then, when I demanded that he do something, when I said I would go to the archons if he continued to do nothing, he struck me repeatedly."

"What!"

I could barely believe it, but now that I looked at Aposila, I could see the bruising about her left eye—there was a dark tinge to her cheek beneath the white makeup.

I had only one question.

"What are the rules for getting divorced?" I asked. It wasn't something I'd ever thought about.

"I don't know," Aposila said. "One hears of these cases, but no one ever talks about the details. I want you to find out," said Aposila. "Act for me as my agent, Nicolaos."

"*Me?*" I said, aghast.

"Yes. I'll pay you."

I scratched my head as I thought about it. "I don't know," I said. "This might be setting a bad precedent."

"Please," she begged. "My daughter is dead. My husband doesn't care. You're the only man who'll help me."

"Nico, we must help this woman," Diotima said. She didn't look at me as she spoke. She stared at the bruising beneath the skin of Aposila.

I didn't see myself as the sort of investigator who would take on family cases, but it was impossible to say no to a lady who'd lost her only daughter. Especially one with a black eye.

"Very well, Aposila. I'll do what I can."

But first, Diotima and I would have to interview Antobius, to see if he'd had anything to do with his own daughter's death.

CHAPTER TEN

ANTOBIUS, THE FATHER of Allike, lived in the deme of Phrearrhioi, which lies within the city walls in the southern part of Athens. Phrearrhioi was very much an upper-class neighborhood, and the house of Antobius was very much an upper-class house, as I could tell at once from the quality of the herm he'd placed by his front door. The bust of the god Hermes was made in bronze, in the latest fashion, and had been painted for realism. I marveled at the eyes, which seemed to watch me wherever I stood. In the case of Antobius, I thought it a pity the herm hadn't protected his own daughter.

Aposila was out of sight when we arrived, whether by coincidence or because she knew we were coming to interview her husband, I didn't know.

Antobius saw us in his courtyard, which was predictably populated with comfortable couches, had a well-paved floor of flat stones, and was surrounded by neatly painted columns in red and green. He was a thickset man in a chiton. I wondered if he'd done manual labor in his past, from the width of his forearms.

When I delicately approached the matter of taking a bag of money in the dead of night, I got a surprising answer.

"How do you know that?" he asked.

"You talked with the man out on the street. You were seen."

Antobius watched me, clearly waiting for the name of his accuser. I silently held his gaze until he got the message that I wouldn't be revealing the informant.

Antobius sighed. "A neighbor, no doubt. I hate nosy neighbors, particularly when they don't understand what they're seeing, and in this city, everyone talks. All right, I admit it," said Antobius. "I was paid money that night."

I gasped in shock.

"You took money to ignore the death of your own daughter?" Diotima said, her tone making it clear what she thought of that.

"Not at all," Antobius said calmly. He seemed oblivious to the reaction he'd provoked. "I'd already decided that my daughter's death was a misfortune sent upon her by the gods."

"You can't be serious," I blurted.

"I am. Allike was killed by a bear. Such a thing must have been ordained by the gods, perhaps by Artemis herself, since the bear is her special servant. I don't know what Allike did to deserve such a fate, but I for one am not going to take issue with the gods."

Diotima asked, "Did you see her body?"

"She was cremated and her ashes returned to us. They lie in the cemetery at Ceramicus."

"If you didn't see the wounds, how do you know a bear killed her?" Diotima said.

"Because everyone who saw her says so."

It was, unfortunately, a perfectly adequate answer. Even if I didn't believe it for a moment. Privately, I gave Aposila a mark of approval for wanting to divorce this man. I made sure I kept my face expressionless, reminded myself not to glance up to the women's quarters of the house, and asked, "Who was your visitor?"

"I rather thought it must be someone from the temple," Antobius said.

"You didn't ask his name?" I said.

"He didn't offer it."

"So when a man turned up, offering to pay you for the death of your daughter, you didn't think to ask any questions?"

"I saw it more as a monetary consolation for our loss. It was all according to the law, I assure you."

According to the law, my ass. I'd become a minor expert on homicide law, and I knew perfectly well it was illegal to accept blood money for a death. A man has an absolute obligation to prosecute the killer of any member of his family.

Antobius said to me. "I understand you act for the temple?"

"Yes."

"Then perhaps you should ask them the name of the man who came to me. I'm sure someone there would know him. You may also tell the temple that I hold them blameless. I expect they'll be relieved to hear it."

DIOTIMA STAGGERED FROM the house in shock. "Nico, he took blood money."

"I know that, and you know that, but can we prove it? Antobius will maintain the money was a gift. Did you notice he was clever enough to dispute the interpretation of what was seen, but not the veracity of the witness? He doesn't know who saw him, so he had to admit to what some reputable citizen might have reported."

"We have to help Aposila against him."

"Yes," I agreed.

"Why would someone pay to shut down an investigation?" Diotima said.

"Well, the murderer might have a vested interest," I said. "If that was him, then we're looking for a man."

Diotima said, "Have you forgotten what Socrates pointed out on the road back from Brauron? We all agreed we'd left the killer behind at the sanctuary."

"There's no chance that someone could have passed us on the road," I said, rubbing my chin in thought.

"And if someone was away long enough to bribe a father in Athens, their absence from the sanctuary would have been noted," Diotima added.

"Then it *wasn't* the murderer Antobius met," I said.

"Or he has a friend. Or an agent. Can we force Antobius to name him?"

I said, "The one moment when I actually believed Antobius was when he said the murderer didn't hand over his name along with the bribe money."

"Good point," Diotima said. "But Nico, we have to do something."

Was it possible to prosecute Antobius for taking blood money? I didn't know.

We needed to ask a lawyer. Unfortunately, Diotima had already killed the best lawyer in Athens. That had been last year, in the course of another case. We'd have to go see the second-best lawyer, assuming he was brave enough to talk to us.

I HAD NO idea about the law for divorce, but I knew who would: the man outside whose office lay the tablets of the law. I went to see the Basileus.

I had to wait a long time for my turn to see him. This was a private matter and I no longer had the letter from Pericles to get me past the queue. Bored, I sat on the steps and watched the other men who had business with him. These supplicants stood in the shade of the portico and argued; or they sat on the steps beside me and argued; or they crouched to play games on boards that had been scratched into the stone, with pebbles for playing pieces. Men stood about the game players and loudly critiqued their every move.

But the majority of the men around me argued over the coming elections.

"Philocles for Eponymous Archon, I reckon," one said.

Several heads nodded, enough to make me think Philocles was in with a chance.

"I like Glaucon for treasurer," the first man said. That got my attention.

"Glaucon is a nobody," a second man said.

I mentally dismissed Glaucon's ambitions. Unless it turned out he really had killed Hippias, in which case he'd become an instant celebrity. Perhaps that was why he'd been so quick to come see me. It occurred to me that Glaucon's career prospects depended very much on me.

"What do you think about Pericles?" I asked the group. They turned to notice me for the first time.

One of the men said, "He's going for strategos, isn't he? Pericles'll get voted in no matter what."

Every head present nodded glumly.

"Is that a bad thing?" I asked, intrigued.

"I guess not," the first man said. "But with him you know what the result'll be. That takes all the fun out. What's the point of turning up to vote when you know the result?"

Heads nodded again. Another man said, "It's like a race where one man's obviously the fastest. There's no interest in it. No one wants to watch. You know?"

Another man said, "Here, you look like a young fellow. You ever voted before?"

I shook my head. "No, I only finished my army time just last year. This'll be my first time."

"Well, don't let it faze you, kid. Just remember, voting's like sex. No matter what you do, you're gonna get screwed."

"Nicolaos, son of Sophroniscus!" Glaucon emerged from the offices within and shouted my name.

"I'm here!" I yelled at once, before he had time to assume I'd wandered off and selected the next man in line.

Glaucon said, "It's good to see you again. How goes the investigation?"

I shrugged, not wanting to tell him anything useful, but I had to state my business or the secretary wouldn't pass me through.

I said, "I need to see the Basileus about a divorce."

"Surely not for you," Glaucon said. He sounded surprised.

I spoke in a low voice, so only he could hear. "No, a client.

Aposila, wife of Antobius. They're the parents of the dead girl from the sanctuary at Brauron. Please tell the Basileus that. I'm sure he'll agree to see me."

Out on the steps of the stoa, one of the board-game players suddenly accused the other of moving a piece while he wasn't watching, in a loud, screeching voice. The other angrily denied it.

Glaucon opened the door. "Come inside."

As I went inside, the board-game players were grappling with each other and rolling in the dust, fighting over who had cheated.

"You again," said the Basileus when he saw me. "Don't you have anything better to do than take up my time?"

"I'm sorry, sir," I said. "I need to ask how someone gets a divorce."

"I thought you were only just about to get married?"

"I am."

"Aren't you getting a little ahead of yourself?"

"It's not for me, sir. I ask for a client."

"Oh?" I could see he didn't believe me. "Well, it's simple enough, in any case. A man need only declare his intention to divorce. The wife is then required to leave her husband's household and return to her closest male relative. By law her dowry must go with her, every last drachma, and all property attached to her. There are obscure situations where the archons might disallow a divorce—if there's not yet a legitimate heir for the lady's property, for example—but those needn't concern us in general."

"Yes, sir, that's for a man," I said. "What if it's a woman who wants to divorce?"

"This is *a client* you ask for?" he said, clearly disturbed.

"The mother of the child who died at Brauron," I told him.

"Young man," he said sternly, "I think you had better tell me everything."

So I did. The Basileus had a reputation for honesty, which was rare enough in Athens, and of the greatest integrity—during his term he had actually prosecuted other officials for taking bribes—but he was also known as a very strict follower of the law.

As I told my tale, the expression of the Basileus became angrier and angrier.

When I had finished, the Basileus said, "So this husband and father, Antobius by name, refused to follow up the death of *his own child*?"

"Yes, sir."

"I don't care if she was only a girl. The law gives him no latitude in this. He's *required* to pursue the killer."

I said, "Then perhaps you could tell me, sir, is it possible to prosecute Antobius? I know he can legitimately declare that the girl's death was an accident, but what if we can prove he took money to ignore her death?"

The Basileus slumped on his stool. He said, "Unfortunately, such a prosecution is likely to fail."

"Why?"

"Because the law sets no time limit on the duration of an investigation. Your hypothetically bribed man could claim he intends to prosecute, but that he's still collecting evidence. He could do this for decades and stay within the letter of the law."

"Even if everyone knows it's a deliberate delaying tactic?"

"Even so. Of course, the rest of society would cut him dead—a man who behaved so badly could forget about ever holding public office—but if the bribe is sufficiently large, perhaps he doesn't care."

This was depressing news. It meant a man could murder someone and then buy his way out of trouble, as long as his wealth was deep enough, and the victim's family venal enough, to take money for their loved one's demise.

There was another implication, too: this killer who had visited Antobius, whoever he was, must have a source of wealth great enough to tempt a man.

The Basileus added, "But this Antobius *could* be prosecuted for beating his wife."

I snorted but was too polite to say what I thought.

"Yes, all right," the Basileus conceded. "A jury is more likely to take the husband's part."

"What about divorce for the wife?" I asked. "Is it possible?"

"You act on the wife's behalf?"

"Yes, sir."

"I must say, this is very generous of you. I warn you, young man, that your legal standing in this matter is dubious. You're no relative of the victim; if anything goes wrong, you'll be exposed to prosecution."

I said, "If Antobius can't be punished for his crime, sir, perhaps he can be punished for his behavior?"

"I see the thread of your reasoning now. Yes. To divorce, a lady must simply present herself to an archon and declare her intent."

"That's it?" I asked, incredulous. It seemed too simple.

"Restrictions apply with respect to heirs."

"She has two sons."

"Then there's no possible objection. Technically she should go to the Eponymous Archon, since he deals with matters of citizenry, but the law permits any archon to perform the service. I suggest that she come to me instead; any other archon will demand to know why she wishes to divorce; I know her case and can save her the pain."

"That's kind of you, sir. I'll bring her as soon as possible."

"No," the Basileus said, horrified. "That's what you *mustn't* do. No matter what, you *must not* come with her. If a man accompanies the wife, it will bring her motives into question. It's not unknown for a man to lure a woman away from her husband in order to gain the wealth that comes with her."

"Does that happen?" I asked.

"More often than you might think," the Basileus said grimly. "It's completely illegal, of course; to steal the affections of another man's wife is a listed crime on the tablets outside this office. But some men will do anything for money, and women will do anything for love."

"What happens then, after Aposila comes to see you?"

"I must ask after the cause of the divorce. If the lady has been suborned, I must refuse to hear her request, and thereby prevent the divorce. This is for the lady's own good. Women, as you know, are easily misled by unscrupulous men."

"Yes, of course."

The door slammed open. Antobius stood there, his chest heaving, the sweat pouring from his brow—he was slightly overweight—his mouth curved into an angry scowl.

"What has this man been telling you?!" Antobius shouted at the Basileus.

"Who in Hades are you?!" the Basileus shouted back. "And what do you mean bursting in here—"

"My name is Antobius, and this man"—he pointed at me—"this man has been interfering with my wife."

The Basileus looked from one to the other of us. I could tell he was trying to decide which of us to believe, because by his own words, the Basileus had more than once had to deal with unscrupulous fortune hunters. How did he know I wasn't one of them?

"That's not the story I hear," the Basileus said at last.

"What do you hear?" Antobius demanded.

"I make no accusation I cannot prove. But I will ask you a question. Tell me, Antobius, if I were to visit your home this instant this instant and ask to see your wife, would I find her bruised, or with black eyes, or a crooked nose?"

"I deny you permission to see her, as is my right," Antobius said at once.

The Basileus nodded. "That's your right," he agreed.

Then Antobius made a mistake. He said, "What a man does in his home is his own business."

"The law does *not* permit you to beat a woman, even if she's your wife," the Basileus said sharply. "I warn you, Antobius, that there's plenty of precedent for wife-beaters being fined large sums."

Antobius said nothing.

"Now I require you to leave this office," said the Basileus. "As is *my* right."

The Basileus stood, and the two men faced each other.

I thought for a moment that Antobius might actually strike an elected archon. But instead he turned and walked. We could hear the sound of his departure as he hit things and people on the way out.

When all was quiet, the Basileus turned to me and said, "I will assist you this much: I will clear the offices when the lady is to come, and give orders that she's to be admitted at once. I will not have a lady of Athens stand in the agora like a common supplicant."

"That's kind of you, sir."

"No, it's merely the most that the law permits me. I believe your words, but that's not enough. An archon must be seen by the people to have enforced the law fairly, *especially* when he's asked to separate a woman from a man who doesn't wish to lose her. This Aposila must be seen by the people of Athens to walk alone, and to speak to me alone, so that all of Athens will know that the customs have been observed and that it is her own wish that speaks. If there's any deviation, with all the people watching, no matter how much I may agree with you, I will refuse to hear your client."

Chapter Eleven

APOSILA STEPPED FROM the house of Malixa and Polonikos, where she had stayed since the episode in the office of the Basileus. Antobius had sworn his wife would not divorce him, which meant Aposila didn't dare go home. He could have locked her in.

Malixa had offered her own home as refuge, telling her husband that Aposila was a friend whose husband was off with the army. It was common for wives to come together when their men were away; Polonikos had accepted the story without question. Nor did the two husbands know each other, so that Antobius had no way of knowing where his wife was hiding. All Antobius could do was ring the agora with watchers and wait for her to appear. We would have to escort Aposila through whatever cordon Antobius had devised, and do it without being seen to help her.

I watched Aposila out of the corner of my eye, from the opposite side of the street, where I leaned against a wall as if I were just another out-of-work laborer with nothing better to do. I wore the heavily sweat-stained exomis that I always used when my father needed me to help him with blocks of stone. If any civic-minded citizen asked me my business, I would tell him I was a laborer out looking for work.

The Basileus had made it clear I couldn't accompany Aposila; he hadn't said a word against guarding her from afar. The question was, did Antobius know that today was the day? Probably he did. And did he know where Aposila would begin her journey? Probably not.

Aposila wore a chiton of the type worn by many matrons, doubled over at the shoulders to give two layers of material for extra modesty, this one dyed in somber green and red, with a simple key pattern about the edges. She wore no jewelry, and her hair was braided and tied up in a simple knot of some sort. On her feet were strong leather sandals. Good. She'd need them for this walk.

Malixa appeared in the entrance behind Aposila. Aposila turned, and the two women hugged—the mother of a missing child and the mother of a dead one.

As she closed the door behind her friend, Malixa saw me standing across the road. She gave me the briefest nod of recognition before she shut the door.

Aposila set off down the road.

She passed by Diotima, who sat in the dirt at the corner and wore the tattered cloth of a beggar woman. It was a futile disguise, for Diotima had no hope of passing for a beggar. Her skin was unmarked by disease, her teeth were perfect—not one of them was black—her face lacked the thinness of starvation, and her hair refused to do anything other than fall in enticing curls. I tried to tell her this, but she put it down to my prejudice.

Aposila turned the corner. Diotima swiveled to watch her. I pushed off from the wall where I leaned and turned the corner after our client.

This was our plan: to leapfrog each other all the way, to keep an eye out for Antobius, who we were sure would do everything in his power to prevent his wife from reaching the archons. Diotima and I would do everything in our power to maintain a safe corridor down which Aposila could walk.

I passed by Aposila. She stepped at a steady, average pace, as we'd asked her. Well ahead, I stopped at the next corner and peered around it. I saw in the street to come the usual people going about their business—men walked along, women stood outside their doors and talked with one another—nothing that looked a threat. I nodded to Diotima as she hurried up. The moment she reached the corner, she slowed to a shuffle. She called for alms as she went down the street. Five men stopped to place coins in her bowl. All five made suggestions that, were we not in disguise, would have caused me to knock them down. Diotima smiled and pretended not to hear them and walked on.

After Aposila passed me—we'd warned her not to acknowledge us in any way—I waited for her to make it halfway along while Diotima stood at the other end. Then I took off, and we did it again for the next street. We continued like this all the way to the city gates, because Polonikos and Malixa lived outside the walls, like at least half the city.

The city gates were open—as they should be, it was the middle of the day—and when the gates were open the guards had nothing better to do than watch the traffic flow past and argue about women and sport. Strictly against regulations, they leaned against the gateposts and did exactly that.

Yet when Aposila approached, they stood up straight and asked, "Can we help you, madam?"

I had to give them credit for doing their job. Aposila might have been a citizen in distress. A respectable woman on the road with nary a slave nor a servant nor a man to accompany her was almost certainly a woman in need of help. Yet I winced, because they'd drawn attention to our client when I would have preferred her to slip through quietly and anonymously all the way to the agora.

Aposila smiled a brittle smile and told him that all was well. The squad leader stepped back, obviously not believing her assurance, but with no right to interfere.

The guards weren't the only ones to have noticed Aposila. Across the way a small, thin man in the dress of a slave took note of the conversation between Aposila and the guards. He stood up and walked into Athens, and I knew right away he'd been sent by Antobius to watch out for his wife.

Diotima, who had preceded Aposila through the gates, saw it

too. She sat on the other side with her begging bowl in her lap. She shot me a worried look, a feeling I shared, but there was nothing we could do.

Diotima and I had agonized over the best route to take once Aposila entered the inner city. The fastest, most obvious route was to go straight up Tripod Road. It was a wide and open major road that passed by the Acropolis to its left and then fed into the agora on the opposite side to the Stoa Basileus. The problem was, Tripod Road was *too* obvious; I was sure Antobius would be waiting for us there. The other choice was to turn hard left, pass the Acropolis on its southern side by taking back streets, and then turn right up Piraeus Road to enter the agora on the same side as the Stoa Basileus.

Diotima worried that Aposila would become lost in the twisty narrow streets, streets that I knew well, but down which the wife of a wealthy landholder never had to venture. On the way to her divorce was probably not the best time for Aposila to learn Athenian geography. I, on the other hand, worried that such a route might look too sneaky. The Basileus was a punctilious man, and his words rang in my ears: Aposila had to be seen by the people to obey the customs.

It had to be Tripod Road. Which meant we had to get Aposila up the most visible road in Athens, and now the opposition knew we were on the way.

I dumped our plan on the spot, pushed my way past Aposila and then Diotima and took the point. I wouldn't let Diotima take the lead when I knew that was where the threat lay. I wished I'd thought to bring a club. I worked my way up the right-hand side of the road; Diotima took my meaning and did the same on the left. I tried to keep one eye ahead and the other eye on Diotima, in case she struck trouble first.

Someone stopped Diotima to try to give her alms. She pushed him out of the way. Then she realized why he'd stopped her and threw away the begging bowl.

It didn't take long for Aposila to attract attention. There were few reasons a woman of her station would be out without a single attendant, and all of them were interesting. A few people trailed behind her to see what she would do. Our client ignored them; she walked on with a determined step. She looked neither left nor right; she didn't need to, since Diotima and I were doing that for her.

I jumped onto a nearby tripod, the better to see what lay down the road. Tripod Road is so called because all along it are the victory tripods erected by winners at the Great Dionysia, the great arts festival of Athens. Just as the commanding general of a victorious army will erect a tripod upon the field of battle, so the *choregos* of a winning production at the theater would commission a brazier upon three legs and inscribe into it his name, and the names of the author and the deme that supplied the chorus. They were set upon plinths for all to see and remember the great art. Some tripods fell into disrepair after their choregos had died, but this one was recently polished. I looked down at the inscription. I'd jumped onto the tripod erected by Pericles for his victory with the tragedy *The Persians*, which had been written by Aeschylus.

Ahead of us the road passed between buildings on each side, the homes of wealthy men who could afford townhouses so close to the agora. Two men peered around the corner of one building. They stood in a narrow alley between homes. I knew at once that they waited for Aposila. They looked anxious; I could see one of the men point straight at her.

These would be men who worked for Antobius. I could hardly approach them from the front, not one against two, not in full view of the street. Nor could I deal with them from behind, because they'd chosen well; I knew the alley in which they stood was a dead end. That gave me an idea.

I stepped off the plinth and ran to the other side of the house. This place was unusual in that it had *two* alleys alongside it. I jumped on top of crates and discarded building material that someone had dumped beside the wall years ago and forgotten to remove. From there I jumped and barely caught the eave of the roof. I swung a leg over the edge and hauled myself to the lowest part. What I did now was illegal. Crouching low, to hide my profile from the street, I crept across to the other side. The roof was thatched, like most houses in Athens, which was all to the good. My footsteps made no noise.

I stopped at the other edge. There they were, right below me. With a dead end behind them, they felt perfectly comfortable; they never looked back. I'd spent too long climbing; Aposila was almost upon us. I could see them tense to run out and grab her. If they did, and if they carried her back to the home of Antobius, it would be illegal, but Antobius could square that away with a fine, and Aposila would never again have a chance to make this walk.

I took a deep breath, then let it out, as Pythax had taught me; *never* jump with your breath held.

I landed behind them, knees bent to cushion my fall and letting out an "oof" despite my best efforts, stood, got my hands to each side of them, and smashed their heads together.

They fell like rocks.

I laughed to myself. Maybe I'd learned something from Pythax after all.

Someone knocked me over. The two I'd brought down hadn't looked behind them, and *I* hadn't checked to see whether there was a third man opposite. He'd seen me attack his friends, run across the road, and knocked me over. He was a big, burly man, and he stood over me and snarled while I sprawled in the dirt. He could easily have kicked me unconscious. Then he'd be the last man standing, ready to snatch Aposila.

"Aaargh!" A high-pitched scream.

My assailant was spun about by a blow to the head. A lump of wood had come spinning out of nowhere.

The big man fell at my feet, unconscious, to reveal Diotima

standing behind him, with a vicious-looking piece of building material clutched in both hands. The end was smeared red.

"Are you all right?" she asked solicitously.

"Thanks." I got up and dusted my hands.

"I saw you climb the house," she said.

I dragged the three unconscious bodies farther into the alleyway.

It seemed like everyone was having a bad day for looking behind them. I made sure the error didn't continue by checking behind Diotima. There were no more threats, but Aposila was well past us and about to enter the agora, and she was unprotected. Now there was a crowd about her, watching her progress. They'd worked out what she was about. Not one of them had noticed Diotima and me on her flanks.

I said to Diotima, "Stay with her."

I ran ahead. I was amazed Antobius hadn't joined the fight in the alley. The fact that he hadn't worried me.

I ran about the edge of the agora, jumping constantly to see over the heads of the people, in search of our main opponent.

There he was.

Antobius stood on the steps of the Stoa Basileus, waiting for his wife to appear. He'd picked the one spot to wait that Aposila *couldn't* avoid.

The great arc I'd run around the market had taken me to the same steps, but from the side. His back was to me, his full attention on his wife. He could easily nab her as she came up the stairs.

There wasn't a thing I could do. If I attacked him there, in full view of the agora crowd, I'd be up for assault. Nor would it help Aposila if I did, because it would show a man had intervened in her divorce.

At that moment Aposila saw Antobius upon the steps, waiting for her. Her steps faltered.

Unable to be seen to help, but desperate to save her, I mouthed a single word, straight at Aposila: "RUN."

She saw me, nodded imperceptibly, picked up her skirts, and ran.

The spectacle of a middle-aged matron sprinting across the agora grabbed everyone's attention. Everyone, that is, except the invariable board-game players outside the Basileus's office—the same ones as before, whom I'd last seen fighting over a trivial point.

While everyone watched Aposila, I edged up behind Antobius and gave him a good shove.

He'd been balanced on the top step. He fell forward, down the steps, straight into the board game. The pieces scattered; the game was ruined. The two players were enraged. Both struck out at Antobius. He struck back by sheer reflex. At that, the gamers began to pummel him furiously.

Meanwhile, Aposila was almost flying across the agora. I'd never seen a middle-aged woman run so fast. The crowd had seen Antobius on the steps, standing like an enraged bull; they'd guessed what was happening and they cheered her on.

Antobius had an even better idea of what had happened. He knew I'd pushed him. He disposed of the game players with two massive, double-handed blows that sent both players spinning through the air.

Aposila had reached the bottom step. But Antobius could easily catch her before she reached the door.

I jumped between them. Antobius ran into me.

"Get out of my way!"

"No."

I couldn't hit him, but I could stand between them.

The last thing I saw was Antobius's fist going into my face.

WHEN I CAME to, there were three Diotimas floating above me.

"Did she make it?" I asked all three of them, groggily.

"She made it. Aposila is divorced."

Diotima raised my head to give me water, but it hurt so much she quickly lowered me. The whole world spun, and I had to shut my eyes.

"Antobius was so busy pounding you that he let Aposila slip past. Well done, Nico."

"Yes, very clever of me." My head throbbed.

"Antobius tried to force his way into the stoa offices. The Basileus had him thrown out. When he tried again, they called the Scythians. They escorted Aposila to a friend's house; a friend whose husband doesn't like Antobius."

"Lucky the Scythians were close by."

"No luck whatsoever. I suggested to Father he might like to keep this area well patrolled today."

That was the advantage of marrying a clever woman. I told myself I would never, ever give Diotima cause to make that walk to the archon's office.

I lay in the dirt of the agora. The excitement over, everyone had gone back to their business and completely ignored me.

Diotima had sent a Scythian for help. He returned with a couple of slaves and a board. They put me on the board and carried me home.

THERE SHOULD BE a rule that when a man is married, or about to be, his mother isn't allowed to scold him anymore.

Unfortunately there isn't, so Phaenarete shared her views on my stupidity as she washed and bandaged my cuts and bruises.

She finished with, "Dear Gods, Nico, look at the state of you. It's a good thing Diotima is joining us. It's going to take the two of us to keep you alive. You obviously can't do it on your own."

I refrained from pointing out it was Diotima who'd gotten me into this state, when she talked me into taking on a divorce case.

I wondered about this as I toiled away on an urgent domestic task that couldn't be put off any longer. I was in the women's quarters of our house, a place in which I had not spent any significant time since I was a boy. Every house has its women's quarters, always on the second floor, usually on the side of the house that gets the most sun. The women's quarters of our house was one open rectangular space. Since I didn't have any sisters, the only inhabitant was my mother. But that was about to change.

When Diotima moved in, she would share this space with my mother. But no two women can share the same room every moment of their lives without any privacy, particularly not when one is a new wife and the other her mother-in-law. Tradition and domestic harmony both required me to partition this room: a space for my mother, one for Diotima, and a sitting room to share.

Scattered about me were a mallet, two drills, two saws—one for rough cutting and the other for finishing work—and chisels of varying widths, all borrowed from my father's workshop. The advantage of belonging to an artisan family was that you never lacked for the right tool. When I borrowed the tools, I'd asked Father if he'd care to help me, expecting him to say yes. Instead he'd given me a look I couldn't interpret and told me that he already had.

The house slaves had carried Mother's precious possessions —her bed and dresser and cupboard and her fine chairs—down to the courtyard, dropping them fewer times than I would have, so that I was left with a totally empty space in which to work. Phaenarete sat in the courtyard, on furniture that was set out in imitation of the women's quarters, while I tore apart the room she'd lived in all her married life.

I began by pulling down the panels of the inner walls of her room. They were attached firmly with holding pegs and had to be pried off with a crowbar. Most of the pegs snapped with age when they came away, but I was prepared for that. I had a whole basket of new pegs that I'd bought from the local carpenter's workshop. Apprentices turned them out by the bucket load.

When the walls had been stripped, I saw, to my surprise, that cut into the support beams were insets for joists. I stood back to judge the position of the joist insets. They were perfectly positioned to create three rooms from one. It was as if some psychic builder had put everything where I would want it placed decades later.

It was impossible.

Then the answer hit me: I wasn't the first man to remodel this room. Forty years ago, my father had performed the same service for his bride, my mother Phaenarete. When he'd said he'd already helped me, he wasn't joking. He'd left me to do this on my own, so I could discover an interesting lesson about the cycle of life.

When my grandmother had died, Father must have converted the room back into one large space, removing the internal walls and replacing the paneling, but leaving everything necessary in place for his own son to do it over again. I wondered if my father might be smarter than I'd thought.

Father had partitioned the room much as I planned to do, with a small bedroom at each end and the common room in the middle. That was when I realized that all the windows overlooking the courtyard had been placed so that there'd be one for each bedroom and two for the common room.

I decided I'd be a fool to change Father's original layout. I set to work. What I'd thought would take four or five days now would be done in one. I had the walls up before sundown.

The women's quarters had seemed quite large when it was empty. Now that it was partitioned, the rooms all seemed cramped. Diotima's room was adequate, no better than that. But it was the best that a middle-class artisan family could do. I wondered again if we should have moved into her father's old home, but it would have been so against custom that it would have caused more trouble than it was worth. Besides, we could rent the place for extra income.

I awaited Diotima's reaction to my handiwork with some trepidation. She was a young woman used to the best, courtesy of her birth father, and what I had to offer her was a step or two below that.

Diotima arrived to see how I was going. She was amazed I'd achieved so much in a day.

"It's not what you're used to," I said. Better to get it out of the way at once.

"I don't care," she said. "There's something here much more important than space."

My expression must have told her that I couldn't imagine what it was.

"A family that's more or less normal," she told me. "I've never had one of those."

One thing in particular she noticed.

"Why is this wall so thick?" she asked of the wall that separated her room from the rest.

"I thought it might be a good idea. For privacy."

"But it takes up so much room, and there's so little to spare. Make it thinner, Nico."

"Has it occurred to you we'll be having sex in this room, with my mother right next door?"

The look on her face told me that Diotima hadn't thought of that. She fingered the new party wall. "Make this wall soundproof," she ordered. "Very soundproof."

"Good idea."

As I worked I talked about the case. "There are too many contradictions," I said. "The murderer must be old enough to have been at Marathon. He must be rich enough to bribe Antobius. He must be placed at the sanctuary at Brauron when the children disappeared. He must have a motive for killing Hippias. He must have a motive for not wanting anyone to know he killed Hippias."

"Who fits all those?" Diotima asked.

"Nobody," I said, pushing the frame into place. I had spent ages with the hand drill, to create holes in the woodwork where the pegs were to be hammered, to hold everything in place. The holes aligned perfectly. I pointed this out to Diotima with some pride, but she barely noticed.

"Then what are the essential facts?" Diotima asked as she passed me the first peg. "What *must* be true about the killer?"

"He took the missing scroll," I said at once. "Something written in it must be incriminating evidence, else why take it?" I hammered in the peg.

"But everything in the scroll is ages old."

"Then it refers to a crime that's ages old. The obvious candidate is that signal after the battle."

Diotima passed me another peg. "Yes. Hippias knew the names of the signalers. He wrote them down. That's a perfect reason to remove the evidence. It means the killer must be a veteran."

"There are no veterans of Marathon at the sanctuary," I pointed out while I hammered. "And the sanctuary's where the killer must have been."

I missed with the hammer and hit my thumb.

"Ouch!"

Diotima nodded glumly, ignoring my pain. "Perhaps a conspiracy of two?" she suggested.

"Which two?" I said, sucking my thumb. "Find a combination that works."

"Three, then?"

I snorted. "Why not go all the way then, and say that all the suspects did it together in one large, weird conspiracy?"

"That would obviously be ludicrous."

I said, "There's only one other person we haven't looked into enough, and that's Aeschylus."

"I thought we agreed he was deluded?"

"He's a writer. Staring at words all day probably turns your head."

"I don't know, Nico—"

"Aeschylus was present when Glaucon announced the discovery of the skull. Aeschylus fought at Marathon. Aeschylus has buckets of money with which to bribe Antobius."

"Aeschylus has a reputation as a solid citizen," Diotima added.

"He's also the only individual who fits more than half the criteria."

"If we accuse the most popular playwright in Athens, it might cause a riot," Diotima said. "We promised Pythax we wouldn't do that anymore."

"Name someone else then."

Diotima opened her mouth, thought better of it, probably realized she had no better idea, then nodded reluctantly. "All right, it's agreed," she said. "We go after Aeschylus."

I completed the framework, keeping the party wall as thick as when Diotima first saw it, with space in the middle. Meanwhile Diotima left to collect old rags from around the house and, when it was clear there wouldn't be nearly enough, hurried down to the agora to buy up cheap rags and several rolls of canvas. Together we stuffed the material down into the wall before I attached the outer boards with more wooden pegs.

I left Diotima in her bedroom and walked across the new sitting room into Mother's new bedroom. I would spend extra time in here to do it up as nicely as I could, by way of apology for taking away so much of her living space.

I shouted out, "Diotima, can you hear me?"

"Yes!" she shouted back.

"Have an orgasm," I shouted again.

"What? *Now?*" Diotima screeched at me through two walls.

I shouted back, "I want to know if Mother will be able to hear us. For our privacy!"

A voice floated up from the courtyard, through the open windows. "Nicolaos, if you want Diotima to have an orgasm, instead of letting the whole house hear about it, perhaps you could ask her quietly while you're in the same room. For her privacy."

It was my mother.

I NEEDED TO know more about Aeschylus before I approached him. You can't go after the foremost playwright in Athens without knowing what you're doing. I couldn't ask Pericles; he and Aeschylus were close friends. Instead I decided to call on someone who'd always helped me: Callias. I had to take Socrates along because, unfortunately, I had promised to include him in the investigation.

Callias invited us in at once, and I told him the story. He laughed at the image of Aeschylus wearing a helmet to hide his identity, but sobered considerably when he heard about the thugs who'd followed me, whose leader had admitted they worked for him.

I asked, "Might Aeschylus have had some involvement with Hippias?"

Callias frowned. "The idea's ridiculous."

"I don't know what to do, Callias."

"I do. We must confront Aeschylus head on."

"We?"

"I'm going with you. We have to get to the bottom of this."

"Aeschylus has hired thugs," I warned him. Callias was an old man. I didn't want to see him hurt.

"Then I'll take thugs of my own," Callias said. "If Aeschylus had anything to do with the death of Leana, he's a dead man."

It seemed there was nothing you could say to these old men of Marathon that wouldn't set them off.

Callias clapped his hands and called for his bodyguards. He'd made much of his early money with a rent-a-slave business, an innovative idea no one had ever thought of before, in which he bought slaves wholesale from the markets at Piraeus, then hired them out to the state to work the silver mines that kept Athens rich. The state liked it because they didn't have to deal with all the capital expense and Callias did all the man management. This had earned him so much money that in the end he'd bought his own mine, an incredible thing for any man.

It was the simplest thing for Callias to handpick from this large pool the largest, toughest men for personal guards. Not that he called it that. "Handyman" has a much more pleasant ring.

Callias and Socrates and I walked the streets of Athens with these handymen at our back. The smallest was half as big again as I, and twice as wide. Any one of them would have been a fine addition to the Scythian Guard, except Pythax would have looked askance at any man he hadn't trained to do things *his* way. This lot had the look of former soldiers. Callias confirmed it.

"Most of them are prisoners of war," he said to me as we walked. "Given a choice of serving me or going down a mine, only the dumbest hesitate for a moment."

"What if they hesitate?" Socrates asked.

"Down the mine they go. Who needs a dumb bodyguard?"

There was a certain unreality to talking with Callias. Most of the time he seemed like anyone else, but then he'd say something that reminded me that here was a man who *owned* a silver mine. If it were legal, he could have issued his own currency. There were minor cities with less wealth than him.

I said of the bodyguards, "These are the smart ones, then."

"Yes, but don't push their limits, Nico. If it comes to it, just point and say 'kill.'"

"Right. Got it," I said. But I was more worried than I let on. I'd come to Callias for advice on how to approach Aeschylus in a diplomatic manner. I hoped I hadn't started a street war.

AESCHYLUS KEPT A townhouse in Athens, like most successful men. We marched straight to his street. It was no surprise to me when we rounded the corner to see a group of ugly men waiting for us. Ugly not so much for their looks as for the clubs they carried.

We stopped before them.

The door of Aeschylus's home opened and a man stepped out. An old man, by his beard, but one with a strong step. He wore armor, and pushed back a helmet on his head to expose his face for better sight as a soldier will before a battle.

"I am Aeschylus, son of Euphorion, of the deme Eleusis," said the man below the helmet. "I know you, Callias."

"As I know you, Aeschylus. I've heard surprising news. News that disturbs me. That you impede the investigation into the death of the tyrant. That you threatened an agent of Athens."

"I wouldn't have thought it of you, Callias," said Aeschylus, and he shook his head in disgust. "A man like you, associating with the revolting spawn of Hippias."

"I do no such thing."

"Then why do you stand beside *him*?" Aeschylus pointed at me.

"What?" I said.

"What?" Callias repeated.

"That dog beside you works for the traitors who plotted to return Hippias."

"Who told you that?" I asked, dumbfounded.

"See, he admits it. Stand aside, Callias, so I can kill him."

"I'm sure you're wrong, Aeschylus. I've known Nicolaos some small time. He'd do no such thing."

"I have it on good authority," Aeschylus insisted.

What was this about?

Callias said, "We both fought at Marathon, Aeschylus. I hope this won't be another battlefield we share."

"If it is, it'll be your last, Callias."

The combined ages of Callias and Aeschylus couldn't be less than 130. But that minor detail wasn't going to stop these two. I pushed Socrates behind the line of our men and told him to stay there.

Callias raised his hand, his index finger extended. He pointed straight at Aeschylus and said—

"What's going on here?"

The voice belonged to Pythax. I breathed a huge sigh of relief.

Pythax was panting slightly. Well, my father-in-law-to-be was getting on in years—his beard was streaked with gray—and he'd probably run all the way from the guard barracks. Behind him stood eight Scythians. They weren't panting at all. They looked relaxed and in tip-top condition, their bows unstrung and held in their hands, at the ready to break some heads.

It was a lucky slave who could get away with beating his owner. The Scythians, being state-owned slaves, were not only allowed but *required* to beat unruly citizens. I'd trained with them; I knew it was the part of their job they relished best.

The combatants all eyed one another.

This would be a three-way battle that only the Scythians could hope to win. There were 292 more where this lot came from, and Pythax was no fool; he surely must have sent for reinforcements from among his command. Indeed, even as he spoke another ten Scythians appeared from down the street and fell into line beside their comrades.

Pythax turned to me. "Why is it, little boy, that whenever there's a riot, you're in the middle of it?"

"It's all a misunderstanding, Pythax," I said. "Honest."

"Yeah, sure." Pythax looked as if he didn't believe me. "You lot, and you lot," he pointed at the mercenaries of both Aeschylus and Callias. "I want to see your backs, walking down the street. Now."

One of the men behind Aeschylus pushed past, stuck his face in front of Pythax, poked him in the chest, and said, "Listen up, barbarian, you don't give orders to an Athenian citiz—"

Pythax backhanded him, and he went flying into the wall headfirst.

"Anyone else?" he asked.

Both groups looked to their employers. Callias and Aeschylus, without taking their eyes off each other, nodded as one. Both of their groups turned and walked, leaving the Scythians to hold the field. I wondered if they'd later erect a victory tripod, as was the custom.

"Now," Pythax said. "What in Hades is wrong here? You first," he said to Callias.

Callias pointed at Aeschylus and said, "Gods know why, but he's protecting the secret followers of Hippias."

Pythax turned to Aeschylus.

Aeschylus pointed at me and said, "He's plotting with the followers of Hippias."

Pythax turned to me.

I said, "Don't ask me, Pythax. I'm completely ignorant."

"That," Pythax growled, "is the first thing I've heard today that I can believe."

PYTHAX ORDERED US all into the andron of Aeschylus's townhouse. He sat us in a row like naughty schoolboys: the richest man in Athens, our greatest playwright, and me. Socrates stood to the side. For once, he wasn't the one in trouble. He tried and failed to suppress a grin. I knew my brother wouldn't let me forget this anytime soon.

Pythax stood before us, folded his arms, and tapped his foot. "Well?"

Callias said, "Nicolaos has information that proves Aeschylus is interfering with the investigation into who killed Hippias, or at least, the remains of what we think is Hippias. It was Aeschylus who sent thugs to attack him."

Pythax turned to Aeschylus. "Those were your thugs following Nicolaos?"

Aeschylus nodded, and didn't look embarrassed in the slightest. "For a good reason. I've received information that this fellow Nicolaos has been working with traitors."

"What do you mean?" I demanded angrily. I was mortally offended. I might have reached for my knife except that Pythax was in the room.

Aeschylus said, "I was told by someone who was well informed."

"Who? Who told you?"

"An anonymous source."

That made Pythax, Callias, and me all stare at Aeschylus.

Aeschylus blushed. He said, "A man knocked on the door one night—"

"Let me guess," I said. "He refused to come inside where there was light. Instead, the two of you stood in the dark street, and he spoke in a low whisper."

Aeschylus nodded. "He told me that you're an agent. An agent for hire."

"That's true," I said.

"He told me the remains of Hippias had been discovered." He paused to look each of us in the eyes. "This I already knew. You see, I was present when the Basileus was informed. The fact that this man was privy to the same information told me he had access to confidential sources."

Callias nodded. "A reasonable deduction."

"He knew about the signal that flashed on the mountain behind us after the battle at Marathon."

"That's common knowledge," Callias said.

"He said a scroll was removed from the case found alongside the body."

"That's supposed to be a secret," I said. "How did he know that?"

"You perceive the reason why I found his story credible. He then said the men who flashed the signal at Marathon were the ones who took the missing scroll, to hide their identities."

"That's one of the theories we're running with," I said. "It may even be the best theory."

"He said you were in the pay of those traitors. To make sure their names never emerged."

"That's a lie!" I said, outraged.

"Perhaps. Perhaps not," said Aeschylus. "Yet you *are* an agent, by your own admission. Such men will do anything for money, and who better to hide the truth than the man assigned to uncover it?"

I was exasperated by his assumption that as an agent I must be dishonest. "All I can say, Aeschylus, is that you've been lied to."

"If so, it's a lie immersed in a great deal of truth."

I had to concede that Aeschylus had a point. In his position, I too might have believed the entire story.

"Did this stranger have anything else to say?" I asked.

"He knew Hippias had been at Brauron. He knew that it was I who wounded Hippias."

Callias snorted. "So you've always claimed. I know of no one who saw it."

"No, Callias, it's true," I said. "I've met the son of a doctor who treated Hippias. The tyrant was wounded just as Aeschylus claims."

"What's this?" Aeschylus and Callias both exclaimed.

I explained the evidence of the doctor at Brauron, how as a boy he had seen Hippias stagger into his father's surgery. "The doctor's evidence places Hippias in Brauron, near to where the skeleton was found. With the diary found beside the bones, we can conclude that the remains are the tyrant."

"So I *did* wound Hippias," Aeschylus said in triumph, half to himself.

"Yes, Aeschylus, you did," I said.

"Perhaps it was my blow that eventually killed him," Aeschylus said hopefully.

I shook my head. "I don't think so, not according to the doctor." Then, in a spirit of tactful diplomacy, I added, "But it was your blow, Aeschylus, that forced Hippias to retreat to the place where he met his fate."

Aeschylus brightened at that happy thought and sat back on the couch.

There was something about Aeschylus's tone as he spoke, a note of confusion. I began to consider the possibility that he might be entirely innocent.

I said, "Aeschylus, you need to know that the man who approached you also bribed the father of the murdered girl not to complain about her death."

I described the circumstances and finished with, "If you compare notes with Antobius, I'll wager you'll find that you spoke with the same man."

Aeschylus thought about that, while the rest of us awaited his verdict.

"It seems we've been working at cross-purposes," he admitted.

"Because someone's been feeding us false information," Callias said. "Someone who'll face a jury when we catch him."

"Not all false, but a combination of false and true," I said. "Whoever he is, he's a good liar."

That would make him harder to uncover.

Callias leaned forward in his seat and said, "The stranger told Aeschylus that the soldier who flashed the signal was the same man who took the missing scroll." Callias paused, then asked, "Was that a true part, or a false?"

"Probably true," I said. "The odds are that we're looking for a veteran of Marathon, and across this entire case, there's only one other man who might fit."

They all looked at me questioningly.

I said, "At the sanctuary there's a man named Zeke. Did Zeke fight at Marathon? He's old enough."

"You think this Zeke might be the man who approached Aeschylus?" Callias asked.

I shrugged. "He knows about the skeleton. He lives in the right place to have been involved. He's had command experience, I'm sure of it. He reminds me of my officers when I was an ephebe."

Callias looked at Aeschylus. Aeschylus looked at Callias.

Aeschylus said, "Wait here."

He left the room. The rest of us stared at each other and wondered what Aeschylus was about.

He returned with a large sheet of faded papyrus in his hand. It was covered in tiny letters. Aeschylus said, "Honors were awarded to every man who fought in the battle, their names read in assembly for all to hear. I did the reading, and I was meticulous about including every man, even the slaves who fought alongside us and the fine men from other cities. This is the sheet from which I read. There is no Zeke."

"That settles it, then," I said. "Zeke wasn't at the battle. You see, sirs, why I centered on Aeschylus. He's the only old soldier to be present for both the current deaths and the signal thirty years ago."

Socrates frowned. "Nico, I don't think this can be right."

"What do you mean?" I said.

Socrates said, "I don't think a soldier could have sent the signal at Marathon."

To our combined astonished looks, he asked, in his inquisitive way, "Do soldiers really flash signals?"

"Yes, boy, they do," Aeschylus said. "Soldiers use their shield to flash signals in the sunlight all the time. It's a standard trick."

"Over such a distance?"

"Usually across a battlefield."

"Do they use the inside of the shield, or the outside?"

"The outside, of course. The inside is all wood and leather. Surely you've seen your father's armor."

"Socrates," I said, "leave this to the adults."

Socrates scratched his head. "But Nico, I can't imagine it working here."

"Whyever not?" I said, annoyed. Somehow Socrates had taken control of the conversation.

Socrates said, "Well, this man, whoever he was, stood on the mountain behind the army."

"Far behind. Yes," said Aeschylus.

"And high up?"

"High up. Yes."

"This was after the big battle?"

"Yes."

"Then the sun must have been high in the sky, to the south at least, maybe even the southwest."

"Of course."

"But the battle happened to the *northeast* of where this man stood. It's impossible. You can't reflect light like that. Not with the curved face of a shield."

We all absorbed that thought for a few moments.

"What does it mean if the signal was *not* sent by a soldier?" Callias asked.

I said, "It unlinks the action at Marathon from the murders. It opens up the possible suspects, because we're no longer definitely looking for a veteran."

"Are you sure about this, boy?" Aeschylus asked Socrates.

"No, sir, I'm not. But I don't think light could reflect off a curve like that, not at that angle."

"Then there's only one thing we can do," I said. "We must go to Marathon. I'll climb the mountain with Father's shield. Socrates and Diotima can look for a flash."

Socrates scratched his head again. "You mean . . . actually try it? To see what happens?"

"Yes," I said.

"That's really very clever, Nico. I never thought of that."

"You won't use your father's shield," said Aeschylus.

"Why not?" I asked.

"Because you'll use mine," he said. "I'm coming with you. I've been tricked, and what's more, whoever tricked me is a traitor to Athens. He must be found. He must be destroyed."

I suppressed a silent groan. Aeschylus was an old man. He was sure to slow us down.

MARATHON IS WELL north of Brauron, and even farther from Athens. It's a coastal town, right on the beach.

The heroes of Marathon had force-marched the distance in less than half a day, but they were men in good condition, not a woman and a child and an old man. I put Diotima on the cart while Socrates and I walked beside Blossom. The donkey and I had spent so much time together on the road I'd come to like him. Aeschylus rode his horse, and therefore was the fastest of us. I watched him sourly, and thought it must be nice to have so much money to be able to afford such a fine beast.

Three quarters of the way between Athens and Marathon is a great mountain. The road goes up one side, through a pass, and down the other side. It slowed us enough that we arrived at Marathon in the late afternoon. It was too late to perform the test that day. It had to be done at the same time as the end of the battle, which Aeschylus and Callias both remembered as after midday.

We stayed overnight in the best local tavern, which wasn't saying much, a hostelry where they wiped down the tables once a month, whether they needed it or not. At least there was straw on the floor to catch scraps, though it looked like it hadn't been swept in ten days or more. The scuttling sounds from beneath the thicker parts in the corners did not bode well.

We all picked at our food that evening. Diotima and Socrates went upstairs to our room early—it would have been unseemly for a woman and child to tarry amongst the rough men with whom we shared the table. Aeschylus opened his travel bag to remove some old papyrus, a small jar of ink, and a thin brush of the kind used by scribes. He pulled one of the tavern's lamps close, smoothed the papyrus out before him, dipped the brush in the ink, and began to write words.

I watched him do this.

"Is that a play?" I asked, unable to restrain my curiosity.

"Yes," he said, without stopping the movement of his brush across the papyrus.

I'd seen plays at the theater, but this was the first time I'd seen one written down.

"I write military adventure," Aeschylus said as he scribbled. "*The Persians*. *Seven Against Thebes*. They're all war stories. That, and family drama like this trilogy I'm doing now. Dysfunctional families slaughtering one another. You know the sort of thing." Aeschylus shrugged. "It's what people like."

"You never thought about doing serious work?" I asked. "Like Pindar does? I met him at Olympia." Pindar was the foremost poet of the Hellenes and deeply revered.

"People say they admire Pindar, but in the contests what they vote for is my stuff." Aeschylus paused. "Did you say you know Pindar?"

"Yes."

"A decent writer, if a little stuck-up."

I was beginning to wonder if that was a common trait among writers.

"What's this one about?" I asked.

"It's called *Agamemnon*," he said. "I'm writing this for the next contest."

He hadn't stopped scribbling all the time we'd been talking. I peered over his shoulder to read the words.

"You just misspelled ΚΑΤΑΚΑΡΦΟΜΕΝΗΣ."

"I'm not surprised," he said calmly. "There're a lot of letters in it."

But he didn't go back to correct his error. Aeschylus continued to scribble new words.

"Aren't you going to fix it?" I prodded after a moment.

"I'll catch it in the edits," he said, and ignored my helpful correction.

I got the impression Aeschylus wanted to be left alone, so I resolved to remain silent. I watched over his shoulder while he wrote a few more words.

"You just used the wrong declension of ΔΥΝΑΤΟΝ." I leaned across him to point out the mistake. Unfortunately my finger slipped and I smudged the line.

Aeschylus threw down his brush. "Perhaps I'll write later," he said. "I'm not concentrating well at the moment."

"Oh, don't mind me!"

"Not at all."

Aeschylus called to the innkeeper for his best wine, in the forlorn hope that it might be drinkable.

"So what happens in your play?" I asked as we drank.

"It's in three parts. In the first, Clytemnestra, the wife of Agamemnon, murders her husband with an axe. That's in revenge for him using their daughter as a human sacrifice before going off to the Trojan War for ten years. Also, she's very angry about a slave girl that he brings back with him."

"Yes, I've had that problem too," I murmured, half to myself.

"Your wife took an axe to you?" Aeschylus asked solicitously.

"No. Diotima and I aren't married yet. The bit about the slave girl." I explained that Diotima had once been very displeased to find me in the company of a beautiful slave by the name of Asia. It had all been entirely innocent, but convincing Diotima of that had been tricky.

Aeschylus shrugged. "Wives can be irrational about such things."

"What happens next in the play?"

"In part two, Orestes, the son of Agamemnon and Clytemnestra, slaughters his mother in revenge for her taking an axe to his father. He also offs his mother's lover."

"Fair enough."

"Then in part three, the Furies attack Orestes as a kin-slayer. He's saved at the last moment by the goddess Athena. The gods hold a trial over the whole affair. Orestes gets off on a hung jury. Athena invites the Furies to live in Athens forever by way of compensation, since they're not allowed to tear Orestes into little bits. The play closes with women and children singing the praises of the gods and the mysterious workings of destiny."

"Seems a bit flat on the climax," I said.

"What's wrong with it?" Aeschylus said. For some reason he seemed defensive.

"After all that murder and mayhem, it ends with a not-guilty? Your fans will never go for it, Aeschylus. Also, it's obvious Orestes did it. I have an idea to fix the plot—"

"If you can do better, young man, I look forward to seeing you at the next contest. Come with your own play, then we'll see who's got the plot."

"I might do that," I said. Now that I'd seen how Aeschylus did it, the writing seemed very simple, and I knew I could spell better.

THE PLAN WAS for Aeschylus to stand where he'd stood all those years ago, when he saw the flashing signal. We would try to reflect light using his shield, from the direction in which he said the signal had come. At the end, we would know whether it was a soldier or someone else who had talked to the enemy. The answer would narrow our field of suspects.

There was nothing to distinguish Marathon from any other Hellenic fishing village. The people lived on the coast, beside a spring where a stream of fresh water flowed. Their homes were small and designed for shelter from the wind more than comfort. They didn't bother with a jetty. Each morning the fishermen hauled their craft off the sands and straight into the sea.

We ate a simple breakfast of figs and bread and watered wine, before Aeschylus led us out of the town, through a grove of olive trees that grew behind the houses, and onto the open field. It was a short walk. Aeschylus stopped at the edge.

The plain of Marathon didn't look like a battlefield. It looked like a good place for a camping holiday.

"This is the first time I've been back," Aeschylus said to us as he surveyed the scene for long moments. "It's been thirty years."

We could only imagine what Aeschylus must be feeling.

"Has it changed much since you saw it last?" Diotima asked.

"There are fewer Persians," Aeschylus said shortly. "It's a distinct improvement."

He stepped forward and we followed behind, not wishing to disturb his memories with our talk.

I'd always thought of Marathon as being a small place, but it wasn't. The open land before us was roughly rectangular in outline, some two thousand paces across the short side, and perhaps three times that in length, stretching along the coast to the northeast. From where we stood, the village lay in the bottom right-hand corner of the field of battle.

Before us, two hundred paces away, was an enormous mound of dirt, upon which grew grasses. It was easy to see that the dirt had been shoveled there by men, because it was perfectly round at the base and rose evenly on all sides. A monument of marble stood at the top. That mound was in the perfect location for a good view.

Aeschylus strode toward it. The soil underfoot was rich and soft and covered with fennel plants that grew to knee height. It was like wading through a sea of yellow and green.

I thought that, like me, Aeschylus wanted to climb it for the view, but instead he stopped short, careful not to tread upon its slope. He held out an arm, to prevent our passage.

"My brother lies in there," he said, simply.

"Your brother, sir?" Socrates asked.

"You see before you the burial mound of the heroes of Marathon."

I canceled my plan to enjoy the view from the top.

Aeschylus said, "The memorial stone displays one hundred and ninety-two names." He pointed to the far end of the field. "And in that direction you will find the trench where we buried the Persian dead. All six thousand four hundred of them."

I already knew those incredible numbers; that facing an army almost ten times their own size, the Athenians had killed *thirty-two* enemies for every one of their own who had fallen. But seeing now the sheer scale of it, my mind boggled.

The plain of Marathon was ringed by mountains to landward. Aeschylus pointed to the southernmost of these and said, "That's where we camped, on the slopes."

Then he pointed to the mound of the dead. "And this . . . this is where we began our attack. We thought the dead would wish to lie where their victory began."

Socrates spoke up. "Our father fought here."

I knew what Socrates was thinking. My brother and I had always considered our father to be the mildest of men. Yet he had stood upon this plain with his spear and shield, and he had hewn down enemies with the best of them. I wondered how many of those Persian dead were my father's work. I knew, because he had told me, that he hadn't expected to survive that day.

Diotima, Socrates, and I pressed on, leaving Aeschylus alone for a few moments with the funeral mound. We walked in silence, absorbing the atmosphere of the place. I wondered how the villagers felt about living so close to what was practically holy ground.

Aeschylus called to us when we were about halfway across the plain. We waited for him to catch us up. He was barely out of breath after the long walk.

"This is where we began our charge," he said. "Up to this point, we'd marched in close formation."

"Where were the Persians, sir?" I asked.

Aeschylus pointed to a location about eight *stadia* distant. He said, "They formed a line over there, at the far end."

"They didn't come out at you?" I asked.

"No. They had archers waiting for us to come within range. Their soldiers were still getting into line. It was at this point we saw the first of their cavalry arrive. We'd moved at first light, you see, before their side was ready, and their horses were still out to paddock. It took them until we were halfway across the field to get mounted."

We moved on.

"Ouch!" I hopped on my left foot while I held my right and swore. "There's something sharp in the sand."

Socrates thrust his hand into the dirt where I'd stepped. His hand emerged with a small bronze object with a pointy end.

"Arrowhead," said Aeschylus. "This is where they hit us with the arrows as we charged in."

"Didn't anyone clean up afterward?" I said, rubbing my foot.

"Young man, when the archers let loose, there were thousands of those things in the air raining down on us. I remember them bouncing off my shield. Every time one landed, it was like someone had hit me with a hammer. The arrows ricocheted all over the place. The villagers were bound to miss a few when they picked up."

"Where were you, Aeschylus, in the line?" I asked.

"Right flank. Not far from Kallimachos, who was the Polemarch that year, our war leader. He was a good fellow, old Kallimachos. The Persians stuck him so full of spears that his body didn't even fall over. We found what was left of him after the battle, still upright." Aeschylus sighed. "Ah well. There were plenty of dead at his feet. He took enough of the bastards with him."

Aeschylus pointed to the far left corner.

"The first few mounted Persians were over there, only a handful, but as soon as we saw them, we knew the time had come. We had to get to close quarters before there were enough cavalry on the field to make a difference."

"What did you do, sir?" Socrates asked, enthralled.

"We ran at the enemy, lad. We *ran*."

There is a race at the Olympics—it's the last event—in which the competitors run two lengths of the stadium—two stadia—in soldiers' kit. The men of Marathon had run four times that distance, knowing that at the end they would have to fight for their lives against an enemy almost ten times more numerous.

"It was mad, but it worked," Aeschylus said. "We'd known what it would be like before we attacked. We'd all shed our loads down to the minimum. I myself fought in sandals, with only shield and helmet. I gave my body armor to a poor farmer who hadn't even a spear to fight with. He'd come to fight for Athens with a broken plowshare. Later on I saw him crushing Persian skulls with it.

"The Persians were so surprised when we rushed them that they gave us time to reform our lines right in front of them, and then the fighting began. Man for man, their infantry were no match for us. The problem was that there were so damned many of them."

Aeschylus walked on another five hundred paces. He stopped at a single pillar of fine marble that rose from the field. I didn't have to ask what that was. It could only be the trophy set up to commemorate the victory.

"This is where we won," Aeschylus said.

"We deliberately thinned the center of our line and moved extra men to the flanks. Our men in the middle didn't have to survive," he said, coldly pragmatic. "They merely had to live long enough to give those of us on the flanks time to defeat the enemy."

I knew my father had served in the middle of the line. I resolved at that moment to listen to my sire more, and argue with him less.

"As it turned out, our center fought a brilliant fighting retreat," Aeschylus said. "They gave up ground only when they were forced, a step or two at a time. The Persian center pressed forward. We'd hoped to win on one flank or the other, but we won on both, at almost the same time! We pushed them back on both sides until our left and right flanks met in the middle, at the enemy's rear. The Persians were caught in a circle ringed by our men. It was like slaughtering sheep," Aeschylus said with quiet satisfaction.

"Then they ran," I said.

"They broke and ran," Aeschylus agreed. "This way."

He walked to the northeastern end of the beach, out onto the sand. The waves washed about our feet.

"The Persian fleet anchored here," Aeschylus told us. "About six hundred ships. The cavalry had ridden onto the boats when they saw how the battle must go. The infantry of theirs that had evaded us followed, and soon the Persian boats would escape."

Aeschylus choked back his emotion.

"My brother Cynegirus grabbed my arm. We had fought as a pair, you see. We had always been close. Now Cynegirus pointed to a particular Persian boat. There was Hippias, leaning over the side, watching the battle from safety.

"Cynegirus yelled, 'Come on!' He chased after the boat, and I chased after him. We had to wade to reach it; the sea was up to our hips.

"We were maddened by the bloodlust of the battle. I don't know how we were supposed to fight a whole shipload of men, but that was our plan. Cynegirus reached his arm to the gunwale to haul himself up. A Persian ran from the stern, carrying an axe. He brought it down and chopped off my brother's hand at the wrist, clean through. Cynegirus yelled and fell back into the water. Hippias recoiled, but not before I'd thrust my spear. I tore his throat and he staggered back, clutching the wound."

"Did you think you'd killed him?" Diotima asked.

"I did for a moment. But he was still standing as the boat glided away," said Aeschylus sadly. "I saw him clearly. I didn't have time to curse. I found Cynegirus under the water and dragged him back to the beach. My brother bled to death before my eyes. There wasn't a thing I could do."

Aeschylus swept down his arm in a rapid motion of anger. If he'd been holding a sword at that moment, someone might have gotten hurt.

"The signal," I prompted him, to get his mind off the subject. "Where were you when you saw the signal flash?"

"Kneeling beside my dead brother. Cynegirus spoke to me

as he bled out. He left messages for his wife and his newborn son. He asked me to care for them, and to be as a father to his son. He made last bequests. He said that he was cold. I wrapped him in my cloak. When he breathed his last, the sand about us was red with his blood.

"I looked up, and there, across the plain, some traitor was flashing a signal. It could only have been to the enemy. I resolved, then and there, to destroy that traitor, whoever he was. But I never discovered him."

Aeschylus looked about. He stared at the three largest mountains that ringed the plain. He took several steps to the right. "I was right about here," he finished. "I remember it well. And the signal came from . . . there."

He picked up a stick that had been washed in by the sea. He pointed with the stick, the better for us to see where he meant. Diotima and I both stood behind his shoulder and peered along the direction. Aeschylus had pinpointed the southernmost of the nearby mountains, the one closest to the coast. A road wound past that exact spot.

It was almost midday. Time to conduct the test.

Diotima and I left to flash the shield. Aeschylus and Socrates remained on the beach to see what happened. As we walked away, Aeschylus began to regale Socrates with more war stories.

It was faster up the mountain than I expected. The road that Aeschylus had pointed out was a good one, and the slope gentle enough that we reached the spot as the sun passed its zenith.

Fortunately, it was a sunny day. I judged the position of the sun against the spot on the beach where Aeschylus and Socrates stood—they were two tiny figures on a white background—then I angled the shield as I thought best to send down the light. I wobbled the shield to produce seven flashes.

"Try this too," Diotima said. She passed me her hand mirror.

"It's small," I said.

"It's the best we've got," Diotima pointed out.

She was right.

With the mirror I sent five flashes.

"Did anything happen?" I asked after a while.

"How should I know? Wait, I have an idea," Diotima said. She walked down the path a hundred paces.

"Do them both again," she called out.

I tried the shield again, angling it this way and that.

Diotima watched intently.

"Nico, I'm pretty sure nothing's being reflected my way."

I said, "Let's try the mirror again."

"I see flashes as you wobble it," Diotima called, as I moved the mirror about.

We repeated the two different signals over and over, and then, when we were sure the others must have seen something, we packed and returned. Aeschylus and Socrates waited on the beach.

Socrates spoke at once. "We saw flashes of fives, but they were dim."

"Five was Diotima's hand mirror." I said. "Seven was the shield. We did our best with both. You never saw seven?"

"No," Aeschylus said. "We watched most closely."

"That means I was right, Nico!" Socrates said. "It's all because of the curvature of the reflecting surface. You see—"

"Don't let it go to your head," I interrupted.

But much as it pained me to admit it, Socrates had indeed been right. The signal the men had seen at the battle had come from a large mirror. Whoever had sent that message was *not* a soldier.

"The signal we saw after the battle was much brighter," Aeschylus said.

"The mirror we used was quite small: Diotima's hand mirror," I said. "The real mirror must have been much larger."

"This changes things." Aeschylus rubbed his chin. "I admit my view of what happened on the day of the battle has changed. But now I'm confused. We were hard-enough pressed to march fast with the minimum equipment. I'm positive no one in our force carried a large mirror. Where would a man get such a thing?"

"Good question," I said.

CHAPTER TWELVE

OUR ODD LITTLE caravan pulled into the sanctuary at Brauron next day, in the late afternoon. Aeschylus had ridden all the way, but as we approached the sanctuary he insisted on marching in with his spear in his hand and his shield on his back, as a soldier should.

We pulled up in front of the courtyard, under the astonished gaze of Doris and Sabina. They hadn't been expecting us. For good reason: when we left Athens for Marathon, we hadn't expected to come here. But after the mirror test, I insisted.

A girl was sent running into the stoa, and shortly after Thea emerged.

"Yes?" Thea asked. At that moment Zeke appeared from the fields. News of our arrival had spread.

"We've come from Marathon," I said.

Sabina said, "We weren't expecting you. I've made no preparations for you at all."

I told the priestesses of the experiment with the shields and ended with an introduction. "This is Aeschylus," I said.

Doris and Sabina looked uncomprehending. Gaïs was startled; she appraised our companion with a knowing stare, and I wondered if in the course of her life Gaïs had managed to get to Athens to see some plays. Of the assembled habitués of Brauron, Gaïs was the only one who seemed to know or care who he was. She looked Aeschylus square in the eye and said in a clear voice, "For the gods plant in mortal man a fatal flaw, when they wish to destroy his house utterly."

Gaïs said these words as if it were the most natural thing in the world to pronounce a curse on a stranger, then she turned and walked away.

Aeschylus watched Gaïs depart. He might be old, but he was still young enough to appreciate her perfect legs and taut buttocks as they swung into the distance. So was I.

"What that young lady with remarkably few clothes said . . . she quoted from my play, *Niobe*," Aeschylus said in wonder. "Has she memorized my work?"

Doris shrugged. "Gaïs says these things. I've given up wondering about it."

"What happens in *Niobe*?" Diotima asked.

"The goddess Artemis slaughters the children of the heroine, because Niobe boasted she had so many." Aeschylus was clearly disturbed.

"None of this has anything to do with our girls," Thea said. "What are you doing to help them, Nicolaos? Do you mean to say that in the time you've been away, this nonsense about Marathon is what you've been doing?"

"Nicolaos has been investigating a matter that goes to the heart of Athens," Aeschylus spoke up. "There can be no greater good."

The High Priestess turned her attention to the playwright. "I know of you, Aeschylus. I know you to be one of those men who count honor the greatest virtue. Let me tell you, when men think only of honor, it's the little people who suffer. The families, the wives, the little girls. Especially the little girls. Believe me, I know." Thea turned back to me. "A child might be dying, and you amuse yourself with ancient history. I must insist you drop this nonsense and return to what we're paying you for."

"I think I know the answer," I announced.

That stopped them dead.

"You know who attacked our girls?" she said.

"I think so. Yes."

"Then tell us," Thea said. "End this agony."

"There's something we have to do first." To their horrified expressions, I said, "It's important, believe me."

Diotima and I had talked over our plan on the way to the sanctuary, in quiet whispers at night so that Aeschylus wouldn't hear. I pulled out a wax tablet and a stylus. I wrote a message in small, careful letters. It was most important that this message be clear.

I handed the tablet to Thea. "Could you please make sure this goes to Athens at once?" I asked her.

Thea nodded reluctantly. "I'll send it by runner. Will there be a return message?"

"Yes, but it will take some time to arrive."

Thea frowned at this state of affairs. Gaïs snorted in disgust, as if it confirmed something she'd always thought. Doris was disconcerted, and Sabina looked worried and angry. None had any choice but to accept my decision.

Dinner that night was a silent and cold-shouldered affair.

NEXT MORNING, BEFORE dawn, Diotima and I tried to sneak out of the sanctuary.

We failed. Doris was up early and saw us.

"What are you two doing?" Doris asked. "You both look too guilty for it to be anything innocent."

I felt like a child caught stealing from the kitchen.

"We're going on a bear hunt," Diotima told the priestess.

"We're going to catch a big one," I added.

Doris stared at us before she said, "Diotima, my dear, when you were a child, I confess I thought you'd never find a man to match you. I was wrong. You're both as strange as each other. Are you sure this is safe?"

"Don't worry Doris," I said. "We'll be fine."

The expression on Doris's face said she didn't believe me. She peered at Diotima's companion. Her companion other than me, that is. "Is that a goat?" Doris asked.

"I believe it may be," Diotima admitted. She gave the lead a tug and the goat bleated. "We . . . er . . . borrowed the goat from the sanctuary's farm. I'd appreciate it if you didn't tell Zeke."

"I never tell lies, though perhaps I could avoid Zeke this morning. By then it'll be too late. Possibly too late for you, too. You'll be back today, won't you?"

"Either that, or we'll be bear food," I wanted to say, but I saw no need to worry her.

"Why do you have a goat?" Doris asked.

"Because that's how you catch a bear," I said. "A professional bear keeper once told us that." I thought it better not to tell her the professional was the man who'd lost the bear in the first place.

Diotima and I walked south, she leading the goat, which we kept happy by feeding it as we walked. I hoped it would survive the adventure. When we were out of sight of the sanctuary, I pulled out the broken pottery that I'd found on the drowned body of Melo. Diotima produced a map of the local area, one that she'd drawn the night before by mercilessly drilling Zeke on every piece of land, every feature, every landmark within walking distance.

I read Melo's search list to Diotima. "Caves, hills, fields, coast, boats, and farmhouse. In that order, I suppose. The last two words were added later."

Diotima nodded. "I know he covered the first four when he had use of the sanctuary slaves."

"Those are the ones scratched out. We know he found nothing, but surely he was killed for something he knew."

"Or discovered," Diotima added. "Yet Melo was killed *after* we gave up our search of the countryside."

"Therefore this discovery, whatever it was, must have occurred after the search," I said. "We know the nearby boat can't be rowed by a girl on her own. Therefore it must be the farmhouse."

"Farmhouse, singular. That's what he wrote," Diotima said. "Yet there are many farmhouses in the area."

"Therefore we're looking for a singular farmhouse. We're looking for the one and only farmhouse about which there's something unique."

In the satisfied silence that followed, I said, "We're starting to sound like Socrates."

"That's a bad habit we'll want to watch," Diotima said.

We'd deliberately left Socrates behind, fast asleep in the men's hut, because, frankly, I knew it would annoy him. If we ran into what I expected to find, my all-too-inquisitive brother would be safer away from the scene. Also, he was sleeping right next to Aeschylus, and I didn't want to wake the playwright, or he'd insist on coming with us.

Our path took us to the main road. If we turned right, the way would lead us to Athens; if we went left, to Brauron in short order. We did neither. We crossed the road into the fields beyond. Straight toward the copse from which a bowman had shot at us on the day we first came to Brauron.

We passed by the copse, rather warily. All the while we kept a close eye on the goat. If the goat suddenly became scared, it would be time for us to worry about bears.

Soon the copse was far at our back, and we were well into the next field. We arrived at a line of horos stones, the white-painted rocks that Pericles had explained were used to mark boundaries in the country.

I read the first one we came to. This horos stone said, I BELONG TO GLAUCON.

Diotima and I shared a glance. I said, "He did tell me he had property near here."

"But so close?" Diotima said.

I shrugged. "It's a coincidence."

We carried on across fields that were rich in corn, fields that belonged to Glaucon, the first man to confess to killing Hippias. We saw no one, which was no surprise this early in the morning. On the other side, we passed by another row of white-painted stones. They announced that we were now leaving Glaucon's estate.

Before long we'd reached the middle of the neighboring property. We picked up an uneven dirt track into which dry, tough grass was determined to encroach. We followed the track until we saw at the end a farmhouse.

Diotima consulted her map. "This is the place where the farmer died."

Doris had told us, when we first met her, that a farmer had been found dead in his fields. There was nothing suspicious about his death—he'd been an old man—but Diotima and I had agreed that it made his farmhouse singular: it was the only one in the area that was empty.

Which made it a good place to hide.

The building—the sole structure but for a pen beside—was more than a hut but less than a house, built of age-grayed wood that had seen better days. The windows had no shutters. It took no great imagination to see it was once the home of a lonely man.

From where we stood, the place looked empty. That was a disappointment. We'd hoped to find Ophelia here before trying the surrounding countryside with the goat in search of the bear.

The goat was bleating again. Diotima tied it to a shrub rather than have it warn anyone within the farmhouse as we approached. The goat instantly took a bite out of the shrub and munched contentedly.

We left the goat behind and, when we came close to our target, we split up. Diotima stayed on the near side, and I circled around to the other with some caution. I was all too aware that someone had taken potshots at us the day we first arrived at the sanctuary, and that the attacker had run in this direction.

I crept quietly through the long grasses, bent low, sometimes crawling when the ground rose, determined not to give away my position. When I reached the other side, I pushed aside the barley stalks to see through the open window. What I saw within took my breath away. With even more caution, I made my way back to Diotima. From the look on her face, I knew she'd seen what I'd seen.

"There's a bear in there," Diotima whispered.

"And a chair as well," I whispered back. "I can see it from the other side. Diotima, someone's sitting in the chair. I saw them from behind."

"What sort of crazy person would sit in a house with a bear?"

We crept up slowly. When we reached the wall, with the greatest caution, we poked our heads up over the window base to peer inside.

All our caution didn't do us the least good.

The bear got down on all fours to lumber through the doorway. He must have smelled Diotima and me, because he turned the corner and came straight at us.

"Don't turn your back," I said to Diotima.

She didn't. We stepped backward, away from the approaching bear. In the distance I could hear a goat bleating. That was the goat we'd brought along to distract any bears; the goat we'd tied up a hundred paces away.

The creature was massive, like a walking wall of fur. Its beady little eyes fixated on Diotima and me, and I knew he wouldn't let us escape. I thought of Allike, torn to shreds, and wondered if it had hurt for long.

"We could run in opposite directions?" Diotima suggested.

"With a one-in-two chance of either of us being the victim?" I said. "Thanks anyway. What say you turn and run right now?"

"Leave you here? No."

I hadn't expected any less. But it left us with a problem.

I was suddenly aware of fencing to both our sides. We'd retreated into the pen beside the house. Three steps later and our backs were against a wall.

The bear kept coming, and I prepared to fight for our lives. I pulled my knife and my backup, a blade in each hand. If I could keep it busy, perhaps Diotima might run past.

"Don't you hurt Rollo!"

Rollo?

A child slipped past the bear. We hadn't seen her behind him. She flung her arms protectively around the creature five times her size and a hundred times her own weight. The bear hugged her back, with the greatest delicacy.

Diotima and I stared at the bear and the girl. The girl and the bear stared at us. I understood then that the bear had been protecting the girl.

I put away my knives.

"Hello, Ophelia," I said, "I thought we might find you here."

WE SAT IN the abandoned farmhouse. Dirty bowls lay piled on the one small table. It was the leftovers of many meals. The deceased farmer had stored food against the coming winter, in *amphorae* Ophelia had broken open with a hammer. Mostly barley and lentils, and weak wine, and from somewhere she'd found some milk. The shards of the broken amphorae had been pushed into a corner. It seemed Ophelia wasn't one for housework.

Rollo lay on the floor with his head resting on his enormous paws. Ophelia shoved at his torso, to no visible effect, until she was satisfied, then settled back against the bear, who ignored the indignity. Diotima and I kept our distance. We knew the bear was tame. We knew Egesis, his owner, had assured us that the bear wouldn't hurt anyone. We knew he was gentle with Ophelia. And we knew he had threatened us when he believed Ophelia was in danger.

One thing I was now certain of: Ophelia didn't need our protection.

"Why did you run away?" I asked her.

"After Allike died? I knew whoever had killed her would kill me too. They said the bear had killed Allike, but I knew for sure it wasn't Rollo. Rollo's tame," Ophelia explained. "I know, because he's . . . ah—that is, he's . . . er—"

"Is 'stolen' the word you're looking for?" I suggested.

"Oh, you know about that," she said, crestfallen. "Will I have to give him back? His owner was very cruel. That's why we saved him. Allike and I saw him in Brauron. He hit Rollo over and over until the poor thing danced, so people would throw coins. Poor Rollo's feet were so sore, too. There was blood where he stepped. Look!"

With both hands she turned over one of the bear's massive rear paws. They were indeed scarred and crusted with blood.

"I think it's because the bad owner made him walk so far," Ophelia said. "Allike and I knew we had to save him. So we waited till that night to release him."

"Weren't you scared?" Diotima asked.

Ophelia stared at Diotima as if she'd suggested a crazy thing. "No, why would we be? Everyone knows the Little Bears were founded when a girl played with a friendly bear. We knew the Goddess would protect us."

It seemed the Goddess had. Either the two girls were unbelievably lucky, or they really did have divine protection.

I said, "So you didn't believe Rollo killed Allike."

"I screamed when they brought Allike in. That was my friend, lying there, and she was . . ." Ophelia shuddered. "And I imagined myself lying there like that, and I got very scared. I was shaking so much I could barely stand. That night I crept out of the rooms and came here. Allike and I brought Rollo here when we got him. Well, when I came that night, Rollo was still here, waiting for us to bring food, like he always did, and there was no blood on him, and I knew *for sure* Rollo hadn't hurt Allike, and I knew *for sure* someone else had, and whoever it was had made it look like our bear had killed Allike, which meant I'd be next. But if I told the priestesses, then I'd have to confess we'd stolen Rollo, and besides, no one would believe me. Not even Gaïs."

"Not even Gaïs?"

"Gaïs is nice, she's not like the others, and she likes me. She's more like a big sister than a priestess."

"Big sister. Right," I said.

Ophelia shot me an angry look. "It's true! I cried every night when I came to the sanctuary. You don't know what it's like to lie in your bed and listen to your fears."

"Oh yes I do. Believe me," Diotima said with feeling.

"Gaïs held me and told me how wonderful the sanctuary was. She told me the sanctuary was started by a princess whose father wanted to sacrifice her, but the Goddess wouldn't let the girl die. She saved the girl and sent her here."

"Gaïs was right," Diotima said. "The girl's name was Iphigenia. Her brother was Orestes and her sister was Elektra. Their father was Agamemnon, who led the Greeks at Troy. This all happened long ago, obviously, when the gods still walked the earth. Artemis commanded Iphigenia to settle here and found the temple. She was the first High Priestess."

"Gaïs is always so sure of herself," said Ophelia, wistfully.

Diotima's mention of Elektra reminded me of the last scroll in the case. The one in which Hippias had written that he didn't need another Elektra. The tyrant had said that in reference to a child of fifty years ago, one whom he'd listed to die. I hadn't realized until Diotima said it that the sanctuary had been founded by Elektra's sister.

"Does Gaïs know you're here?" Diotima asked. "Does she know you're safe?"

"No. I wanted to tell her, but how could I without returning?"

Suddenly I realized why Gaïs spent so much time out running. Like Melo, she was in search of Ophelia. Then Ophelia thought to ask the question I'd been expecting. She said, "How did you know where to find me?"

"We deduced it from Melo. He thought to look here."

"That idiot!" she said with contempt.

I thought this was a trifle harsh, considering the lad had died trying to help her.

"If you didn't like him, why did you sneak out of the sanctuary to meet him?" Diotima asked. "More than once, even?"

"I was trapped. It's not like a girl gets much choice who she's to marry. I thought I might as well make the best of it. At least I could find out what he was like before I had to . . . you know . . . with him."

"You're not interested in boys?" Diotima said.

Ophelia shrugged. "I can take them or leave them."

No wonder Ophelia wasn't in with the popular crowd.

"As it turned out, Melo's nice enough," Ophelia went on, blithely unaware of what had happened. "He's a lot easier to get on with than my father. I guess I can stand him."

"There's only one problem, Ophelia," I said. There obviously wasn't any need to break the news gently. "Melo's dead."

Chapter Thirteen

"Well how was I supposed to know she'd get upset?" I complained. "She was acting like she didn't care about him at all."

"Oh, Nico, that was mere pretense," Diotima said. "Girls do that. Obviously she was desperately in love with him."

"Oh yeah. Right."

I didn't believe it for a moment. But Ophelia had wailed, and tugged at her hair, and beat the ground with her fists, until the bear, who'd been becoming increasingly nervous throughout the conversation, decided once again that I must be a threat to the child and advanced on me. I faced a large wall of angry fur and backed away until I was caught in a corner. It was only when Ophelia ceased her wailing long enough to save me that I escaped. She took one of the bear's giant paws and stroked his arm and led him back to the entrance. The bear followed her obediently.

I'd learned an important lesson: never upset a girl with a bear.

Diotima and I returned to the sanctuary, without Ophelia, to find a small convoy of carts and horses. I shot Diotima a triumphant look. The answer to my urgent message to Athens had arrived.

Callias stood in the grassy courtyard, where he spoke to Thea. When I approached he greeted me and said, "Nicolaos, I've brought everyone you asked me to bring."

Callias gestured behind him. Standing amongst the columns of the stoa were Aposila, the mother of Allike, and Malixa and Polonikos, the parents of Ophelia.

Callias might be aged, but his management skills hadn't slowed one whit. The man who ran a mine with a thousand slaves had rounded up three citizen parents with admirable speed.

Callias said, "They're as puzzled as I am. Why are we here?"

I said, loudly enough for Polonikos and Malixa to hear, "I have some good news for you—"

"The bear! The bear's come to eat us!"

One of the girls screamed and pointed at Rollo, who lumbered his way over the hill south of the sanctuary. A moment later Ophelia was visible beside him.

This was why we'd returned without Ophelia. She'd insisted that Rollo must return with her, and then only on condition that Rollo the bear's good name be cleared of murder.

"Or I will never, never, never go back," Ophelia had finished, not realizing that now that we knew where she was, I could return with enough men to force her home. I had solemnly sworn upon Artemis that I would clear Rollo of the false charge against him, and Ophelia had agreed.

WHEN OPHELIA CAME down from the hills, leading behind her a large brown bear, it caused utter chaos, fear, consternation, panic, and wonderment. Women gasped. Aeschylus, Callias, and Zeke all swore mighty oaths. Socrates explained his new theory of bears, to which no one listened. Malixa cried, "It's my baby!" and fainted dead away.

Ophelia acted like a girl possessed, unaware of the spectacle she posed. She was sure footed as she stepped down the slope, and upon her face was a smile. In her left hand was a thin chain, and on the other end was Rollo. The bear could have snapped the chain in an instant if he wished. He could have torn Ophelia apart in a trice. He could have swallowed her in three gulps. But instead he followed the girl, as docile as a lamb. Rollo followed Ophelia because he chose to.

"It's like something out of the legend," Doris said in wonder.

"The legend of how the Little Bears began. Do you think this is how it happened?"

"I think the Goddess is close," Diotima said.

"You think the goddess Artemis inhabits the body of Ophelia?" I said in awe.

"No, you idiot. *The bear.*"

Behind me I heard a woman sob. It was Aposila, the mother of Allike.

Ophelia stopped in the courtyard of the sanctuary. Rollo stopped behind her. She faced the assembled Little Bears. I knew she was anxious about what sort of reception she faced. The assembled Little Bears were silent for a long, uncomfortable moment. Ophelia understood the problem. "He won't hurt you," she said. "He's very gentle."

Then Malixa rushed forward to envelop her daughter Ophelia in—appropriately enough—a bear hug. Rollo stood and watched over them. When Rollo failed to eat Ophelia's mother, the girls saw that he was safe and rushed forward to mob Ophelia, squealing.

Rollo watched in calm approval.

THE CELEBRATIONS CARRIED on for some time. In fact they went on for so long that they threatened to stretch well into evening. Rollo was tied to a tree behind the stoa, and the girls took turns daring to go near him. The only person who managed to contain her joy was Sabina, who carried on with business as usual and pulled over a slave to send him running with a message—no doubt to let the Basileus know the latest developments before anyone else could claim credit. I waved my arms until people began to notice me.

"We need to talk," I announced. "All of us."

The children looked at me quizzically.

"All of the adults," I amended. "There's still a crime to solve."

"You mean the names of the conspirators at Marathon," Aeschylus said.

"He means who killed Hippias," said Sabina. "And who hid him in that cave."

"No, he means who murdered my daughter," said Aposila.

"I mean all those mysteries," I told them. "Each one caused the next, and if I read this right, there's one other mystery here, buried so deep that no one's even noticed it. It might be the most important of all."

We filed into the temple. It was the only space large enough to accommodate every adult. Slaves lit torches to brighten the relative dark of the inner room. Then the slaves were ordered to depart. The torchlight flickered over our faces. It made for an eerie experience.

There was nowhere to sit. It was obvious from the frosty silence what everyone thought of the arrangement, but when they heard what I had to say, they'd thank me for leading them to the only place where the children couldn't overhear. At least, some of them would thank me.

"When Allike and Ophelia discovered the skeleton of Hippias," I began, "it unleashed anxieties that had lain unresolved for thirty years. Not in one person, but in many. The result was a sequence of disastrous mistakes.

"Hippias was supposed to have died at Lemnos, on the way back to Persia after the defeat at Marathon. The presence of Hippias at Brauron, even dead, was a blow to our peace of mind. The subsequent death of Allike clearly implied that someone among us felt threatened by the discovery, thirty years after the fact."

I paused for a moment, to see what they thought of this. Aeschylus scowled. Callias was attentive. Thea clenched her hands in concern. Zeke stood beside her. He placed a hand on her shoulder. Doris looked puzzled. Sabina's face was blank, and Gaïs apparently bored. Of the parents, Aposila had tears in her eyes, Polonikos was plainly uninterested, and Malixa too happy at the restoration of her daughter to care about anything else.

I continued. "Most of us assumed that any man who felt threatened must be a traitor. And when we think of traitors and Hippias, we think of the signal at Marathon that flashed to the enemy from behind the backs of our men. Pericles himself mentioned the signal straight away when he gave me this job."

"This is obvious," said Aeschylus. "After the battle the traitors signaled to Hippias. Perhaps their message told the tyrant to meet them here at Brauron. It's true I wounded him, but probably Hippias was coming to Brauron anyway. Hippias knew the names of the men he was about to meet, and he wrote them in his diary. That's why they had to remove the fifth scroll. This is all very reasonable—"

"But it's also wrong." I spoke over the playwright. "The death of Allike had nothing to do with the signal at Marathon. Once you get that out of the way, the rest of the mystery becomes much clearer. What's more, the signal at Marathon had nothing to do with Hippias being at Brauron."

"What do you mean?" demanded Callias. "It must have."

"No. We all assumed the flashing signal was sent by a soldier. But Socrates proved a soldier's shield couldn't reflect light that way. The sunlight had to have been reflected by something flat. It was a mirror."

This was the inspiration that had struck me on the sands of Marathon: that only a large mirror would answer. The source of the mirror was vital.

"Men don't use mirrors," Callias said.

"No, but women do."

Aeschylus frowned. "What woman? There were no women with the army, we ordered our families to stay in Athens."

"Perhaps a local lady?" Callias suggested.

Aeschylus scoffed. "Where would a local woman find a mirror the size of a shield?"

"How about just over here?" I said. I walked across to the temple entrance. I lifted the mirror off the wall, the one that the girls used to touch up their hair before their womanhood ceremony.

I held it up for all to see. The angle reflected light from the entrance, and the room brightened.

"This mirror, ladies and gentlemen, is the right size to have flashed the signal at Marathon."

They stared at it in silence for a moment, then Callias spoke up. "You're saying the signal was sent by someone from the temple."

"Yes. To explain why, I must delve into an entirely different mystery. It's the key to removing all the irrelevant clues. The moment I met him, I was intrigued by the question of who Zeke was."

Every eye turned to Zeke. He stood beside Thea with a face like stone.

"No one knows where Zeke came from," I said. "He won't say. Thea won't say. Have you wondered about his accent? I have. Then there's the sword that I dredged up from the bottom of the Sacred Spring. It's Persian. How did it get there?

"This put me in mind of an interesting idea: that Zeke might be from Persia. I remarked to Diotima, very early on, that the way Zeke had set guards around the sanctuary was up to the standard of a top-notch camp commander. How did a man whose last thirty years had been spent as a jack-of-all-trades at a temple acquire such expertise?

"Fortunately there was an event that explained everything. It's called the Battle of Marathon. You'll recall I asked you, Aeschylus and Callias, whether Zeke had been at Marathon. You told me he wasn't on the memorial list. But Zeke did fight at Marathon. *He fought on the Persian side*. And given his expertise, I suggest he was an officer. Notice, too, that Zeke appeared at Brauron some time after the battle, but well before the second invasion ten years later. The timing fits."

Gasps from about the temple. Zeke stared at me, expressionless, as one might an enemy.

"Are you indeed a Persian?" Callias asked Zeke.

Zeke turned to Thea.

"We may as well tell them, dear," Thea said, and she held his hand. "We've nothing to be ashamed of." She paused, then added, "And even if we did, we're too old to regret it now."

"Then I admit it. It's true," Zeke said, with obvious reluctance. "I was once an officer of the Great King. After Marathon I decided to settle here, to be with Thea. For obvious reasons, I couldn't do so openly. For thirty years I've been Zeke the maintenance man, and that's how I intend to remain. I've committed no crime."

"No crime? You fought against Athens!" Aeschylus almost exploded. He advanced on Zeke and Thea. Zeke, seeing the threat, stepped in front of Thea to protect her and prepared to strike Aeschylus. I quickly put myself between them and pushed them apart. Callias grabbed Aeschylus by the arm.

Aeschylus spat. "My brother died in the rush to take their ships. This Persian might have killed him."

"As a soldier of his own country," I said. "Zeke's right, Aeschylus. That's no crime."

"If it's any compensation, I couldn't have killed your brother," Zeke said. "After our line broke, I was cut off and had to retreat south. I took no part in the ship action. As it turned out, I was lucky. It meant when I saw Thea's signal, I could go to her."

"It was I who flashed that signal," Thea said. "To tell Zeke that I loved him. To ask him to come to me, if he would."

"How did you meet?" said Callias, intrigued. "How could a woman who spent her whole life in this sanctuary manage to meet a Persian officer?"

"I should imagine a scouting party?" I said. "This is, after all, the hometown of Hippias, the safest place to land advance scouts."

Zeke nodded. "When the Great King decided to attack Athens, he sent an advance force to scout the path."

"No doubt," said Callias.

"I led that force. We landed at Brauron, because it was the home of Hippias, as Nicolaos says. He told us of places where a team might land quietly. One of these was the bay close by the temple. I landed with eight men in the dead of night. There, as the gods would have it, my force of Persians ran straight into a priestess, a woman of the greatest beauty. It was Thea, walking by the seaside in the moonlight, and I loved her the moment I saw her," Zeke said quietly. "My men hid while I spoke with her."

"You had to learn Greek," Aeschylus pointed out.

"I already spoke it. That was why I was chosen to lead the advance. My father, who was a senior officer of the Great King, married a Hellene woman of Ionia." Zeke smiled. "It seems the men of my family have a fondness for Hellene women.

"She saw in me what I saw in her. I know this only happens in the songs of peasants, but the truth is, we fell in love that night. Thea never gave us away."

Thea held Zeke's arm and said, "I couldn't support the Persians. I could never do that. But nor could I give Zeke away."

Zeke said, "In the days that followed, my men and I hid during the day and moved about in the dark, scouting paths for the coming invasion."

"Where did you hide? Surely not at the temple."

"No. In a nearby cave that we discovered."

"Not—"

"Yes, in the same cave in which the remains of Hippias were found."

Thea said, "I went to visit him there, often. We sat and spoke of our different lives, and what we'd do after the war. Zeke said he would have to return to Persia. He asked me to go with him. I refused."

"We argued about it," Zeke said. "The only time we have argued in thirty years." The old soldier and the old priestess smiled at each other.

Thea said, "Nothing could cause me to join the Persians. Not while they supported Hippias. But Zeke was honor-bound to return to his own army. It seemed fate would separate us."

"I told her that I must return," Zeke said. "But I thought long and hard, and I confess my heart was not in it. I told Thea that if she still wanted me after I had fought against her own people, then she should signal from the mountain."

"Which I did," Thea said simply.

Callias and Aeschylus both gasped. Aeschylus said, "It was you I saw?"

Zeke ignored them, intent on his story, now that it was revealed. "I expected our side to win at Marathon," he said. "But if I disappeared at once, straight after the fighting, men would assume I had perished in the fight, and there would be no stain on the honor of my family. As it happened, our heavy defeat made it that much easier to desert my country. When Thea flashed the light, I could see where she was, and I joined her. We made our way back here."

"Zeke couldn't join us at Brauron immediately," Thea added. "It would have been too obvious. We waited months while he camped out."

I said, "You see, Aeschylus, the signal at Marathon had nothing to do with political conspiracy. It was a love letter."

Aeschylus rubbed his chin and thought, and then said, "I must believe you. But don't think this means Athens trusts you, Persian."

I said, "This leads us to the next question, the one for which Pericles and the archons commissioned me. Who killed Hippias, and why?"

"You're about to tell us that Hippias recognized Zeke in Brauron," Aeschylus said, "and to protect his identity, Zeke killed Hippias."

"That certainly *could* have happened," I said. "But I don't think it did, because of the evidence of the knife and the scrolls. The fifth scroll is missing. That must be because it incriminates someone still with us. But whoever took the fifth scroll left the first four. In the fourth, Diotima found these words. She read them to me before ever we came to Brauron. I'll read a part to you now." I opened the fourth scroll and read.

Have discovered via local source that the girl was hidden near my own estates. She will go on the next execution list. The last thing I require is another Elektra.

I closed the scroll. "There's an execution list that follows shortly after. In it, there's a line that reads merely 'the girl.' Hippias didn't know her name, despite which he wanted her dead. Who is this girl, to threaten a tyrant? In the legends, Elektra, the daughter of Agamemnon, grew up to avenge her father. Elektra could only be a reference to the sister of Harmodius. Hippias feared that the sister of Harmodius would grow up and return to avenge her brother."

"So the sister of Harmodius was indeed killed," Callias said sadly. "I always thought it."

"This note comes at the very end of scroll four," I said. "Shortly before the second rebellion—organized in part by you, Callias—had succeeded in overthrowing Hippias. It's possible that last list of victims was never executed. Maybe "the girl" survived. Let me speculate for a moment on who she might be. Where were the estates of Hippias?"

"Here at Brauron. But they were sold immediately after he was expelled."

"Even so, this girl was hidden near his estates, which means Brauron, yes?"

"Yes."

"Elektra was the sister of Iphigenia. Iphigenia founded the Sanctuary of Brauron. If Hippias was thinking of the sanctuary, it's only reasonable this would put him in mind of Iphigenia, and thence her sister who wreaked revenge for murder, particularly since that's his own fear."

"It's possible," Aeschylus said. "People allude to the characters in Homer all the time. I've been known to do it myself."

"Just so. And who here at Brauron today was also here that long ago? Who was raised here as an orphan?"

I put my hand on Thea's shoulder. "I introduce you to the sister of Harmodius, whose expulsion from a public ceremony in Athens, when she was seven years old, commenced the series of assassinations that brought us to this pass."

Thea sat mute. When it became clear that she had nothing to say, Callias asked, "Is this true? Are you the sister of Harmodius?"

Thea sighed. "It's true, Callias. You knew me when I was a child."

"I wish I could say you haven't changed at all, but I didn't recognize you," Callias said sadly.

"Age does terrible things to us all, my friend." Thea gripped Zeke's hand even tighter.

"This is an enormous coincidence," Aeschylus said.

I said, "Not so! In fact, when you look at the facts, it was almost inevitable. You said to me, Callias, that you didn't know what had happened to the little sister of Harmodius."

"She disappeared."

"But you hoped someone had smuggled her out of the city."

"A forlorn hope."

"But that's exactly what happened. Thea was hidden in the most obvious place possible. All they had to do was change her name, and Thea became one girl among many. Better yet, the sanctuary has a history of caring for orphans. Like Gaïs, for example."

Aeschylus said, "I concede you're right, Nicolaos. That does seem inevitable."

Callias clasped Thea's left hand. With tears in his eyes, he said, "I cannot tell you how much it pleases me that you survived. I only wish you'd come to me before. I could have helped you."

Thea shrugged. "I've tried so hard to forget those times. To this day, I still have nightmares. I see myself ejected from the ceremony, and then I see my brother cut down. It's kind of you,

Callias, but I had everything I needed here. The sanctuary succored me, and I've served the Goddess."

I said, "We now come to the next part of the sequence. Hippias was dropped at Brauron because he'd been wounded at Marathon. He needed a doctor, and quickly. The evidence of the doctor proves Hippias survived the battle. He probably even survived the doctor.

"Tell me," I said, "what do most people do to get their strength back when they recover from a wound?"

"They go for walks," Aeschylus said. "They start with short ones, then make them longer as they become stronger."

"Yes, and if you were Hippias, in Attica, after the battle at Marathon, when would you go for a walk?"

"On the darkest nights possible," said Aeschylus grimly. "The tyrant would hide for fear that I or someone like me would run into him."

"Correct! And who did we just hear was walking about the countryside at night?"

Aeschylus frowned. "Zeke?"

"No, Zeke scouted the countryside *before* the battle. Afterward, he was in hiding, waiting for the Athenian army to disperse. There was one very important find that came with the skeleton, one that Sabina didn't send along with the scrolls. If she had, everything might have turned out differently. Among the ribs, hidden amongst them and the dirt, was a knife. Scratched into one side were the names Harmodius and Aristogeiton. Scratched into the other side was the name Leana. It's overwhelmingly likely that this was the murder weapon. Those names were the killer's motive. Now that we have discovered the sister of Harmodius, the name of the killer is obvious."

"Not Thea!" Callias exclaimed.

"Thea," I said.

"Is this true?" Callias asked. "Are you, Thea, the true Tyrannicide?"

Thea said in a small voice, "It is as Nicolaos says. One evening

I was walking back from visiting Zeke—I went to see him every spare moment—when I saw coming in the other direction an old man. He shuffled along. It was dark, I didn't recognize Hippias until he was upon me, and he never recognized me at all." She stopped and looked at us each in turn. "You must remember, I was thirty-one then, and in my prime. He hadn't seen me since I was seven."

Several heads nodded at her explanation.

"Hippias said, 'Good evening, Priestess.' I'd never thought to have such a chance. He shambled, like a sick, weak, old man. I boiled with anger that welled up until I couldn't control it. I drew my knife and I stabbed him in the heart. I stabbed him over and over." Thea shuddered. "Then, when he was dead and I'd come to my senses, I scratched into the blade the names of the people I'd avenged. I wanted his shade to know why he'd died. I pushed the knife back into him and then I went to tell Zeke what I'd done. Together we carried him to the cave where Zeke and his men had hidden. That's the entire story. I only regret that I couldn't kill him before he destroyed my family."

Callias said, "With your permission, Zeke?"

Zeke nodded.

Callias wrapped Thea up in a massive hug.

"All of Athens owes you a debt, lady, and I look forward to paying it. I shall commission your statue and have it raised upon the Acropolis. You shall stand next to my Leana, whom you avenged."

Thea pushed Callias back in horror. "Please, no, Callias! I'd prefer no one to ever know. I want my brother Harmodius and his friend Aristogeiton to be remembered as the Tyrannicides."

"But it's not true," Callias said, puzzled. "You know it's not. This makes no sense."

"They died for it; I didn't. Leana too. I remember her." Thea stopped to wipe away a tear.

"What of my Allike?" Aposila said. "Did you kill her, too?"

Thea shook her head violently. "No! Of course not. I'd never harm a child. Not after what I went through."

"Thea's right," I said. "It's impossible for either her or Zeke to have hurt Allike. Neither has the strength to dismemb—" I realized Allike's mother was in the room. "That is, to hurt someone. But luckily for us, the answer to the worst of crime of all—the murder of a child—becomes simple once we remove all the distractions of those other mysteries. There can be only one person who hurt your daughter, Aposila. It had to be a man. It had to be a man who knew of the discovery of the skeleton. That narrows the suspects. What's more, it had to be a man who stood to lose from the discovery.

"I asked you before, Callias and Aeschylus, what would happen to the man who killed Hippias. You said he'd be a certain winner in the elections."

"Yes."

"But what if the man who protected Hippias was up for election? What if we could prove it?"

"He certainly wouldn't win any election," said Callias.

"Dead men can't," Aeschylus added grimly.

"I thought as much. Then tell me, who is the only man in this case who knew of the skeleton, who has property in Brauron, and who might have hidden Hippias?"

Thea got there first. "Glaucon?" she said.

"Glaucon. Glaucon must have harbored Hippias. It's the *only* explanation consistent with everything we know. When Glaucon saw the message from Sabina, he must have opened the scrolls and seen his own name prominently displayed at the end of scroll five. The discovery would have destroyed his chances at the election. In fact, it would have killed him! Glaucon pulled the fifth scroll."

Callias scratched his head. "But you told me Glaucon confessed, and you didn't believe him."

"Glaucon confessed to killing *Hippias*. When I mentioned

the girls, he acted like he'd never heard of them. But that had to be false, because he was the first one to read the report Sabina sent to Athens. Glaucon lied to me. He took credit for a killing he didn't commit, and then denied all knowledge of the perfidy he did commit."

"Raiders! Raiders!"

The voices came from outside. Girls screamed.

"Dear Gods, it's happening again," Thea whispered.

CHAPTER FOURTEEN

I WAS FIRST OUT the door, but only because I was closest. Sabina was right behind me. Everyone piled out behind us in an untidy heap.

Sabina ran to the end of the bridge. She stood there, staring open-mouthed. On the other side, about to cross, were men, ten or more, and they were armed with spears. Bringing up the rear was—

"Is that *Glaucon*?" Callias said, shocked.

"It is," I said.

"Amazing how he arrives just as he's revealed to be the murderer."

"Isn't it." My mind was working furiously, and no doubt so was Diotima's. We exchanged looks, and I knew we were thinking the same thing.

To a man, the temple slaves rushed to the bridge to defend it, and to a man, they went down. The attackers had been prepared for the first rush. Three of the slaves took spear thrusts to the stomach. They rolled on the ground in agony. The other two slaves weren't so badly hurt. They turned and ran. I couldn't blame them. No one expects a slave to die for his owners; that they'd tried to protect the girls at all was to their credit.

But now we were exposed.

"Get the girls into the stoa!" It was Gaïs. Everyone looked at her in shock. For possibly the first time in her life, Gaïs had said something that made sense.

Gaïs spread her arms like a net and pushed the girls back into the stoa. Doris joined her. The girls heeded them and ran for cover.

"What do we do now?" Aposila asked.

"We fight," Gaïs said.

"What have we got to fight with?" I asked Zeke.

"Nothing," he said bluntly. "This is a sanctuary, not a barracks." Zeke turned and ran. I stared in shock for a moment. I hadn't expected that.

I said, "Diotima, take your bow and get up on the roof. Lie low and pick off targets when you see an opportunity."

"No, Nico. I'll stay here and—"

"Don't argue with me," I said, and I meant it. "I don't have time to deal with it. Get up there and shoot."

Diotima blinked, and looked at me as if she'd never seen me before. Then she said, "Yes, Nico."

I hauled the sanctuary's only ladder from where it lay against the shed and set it against the back wall of the main building. As I did, Diotima picked up the skirt of her chiton to stuff the material beneath her belt so that her bare feet were clear to climb. She hooked her sleeves over the brooches at her shoulders and scampered up. I handed up her bow and every arrow she owned.

"Are you safely up?"

"Yes, Nico."

I pulled the ladder away to let it fall to the ground. I grabbed the sanctuary's axe and used it to smash every rung of the ladder. Good. Even if the enemy broke in, Diotima would be out of their reach.

I dropped the axe to return to the bridge. As I did Aposila ran up from behind, grabbed the axe and followed me. She'd die instantly if it came to real combat, but there was no time to argue with her. Besides, Aposila wasn't Diotima; Aposila wasn't my problem.

"I'm ready." Aeschylus strode into the courtyard. He was dressed in his hoplite armor: the huge round shield painted with the face of a snarling gorgon, the sharp spear in his right hand, and the helmet that covered his face and made him look like a remorseless automaton.

Except that I knew different.

"You can't be serious," I blurted. "You're a sixty-five-year-old man."

"So am I," Zeke returned. "And I too am ready for combat." From wherever he'd hidden them all these years, Zeke had retrieved the dress of his former life, an officer of the Persian Immortals. He wore heavy scale armor of a type I'd only ever seen in Ionia, where the Persians ruled: hundreds of small metal plates attached to a leather jerkin. In his right hand, he wielded the sword I'd retrieved from the Sacred Spring. It had lost the leather of its handle, but that wouldn't stop a veteran. In his left he held a wicker shield.

Callias had nothing but his dagger. He drew this and stood beside them in the only order that made sense for the armaments they carried: Zeke on the left with his smaller shield, Aeschylus in the middle where his large hoplon gave them the best protection, and Callias in the place of honor on the right, where the dagger in his right hand was free to strike. Aeschylus called the time.

"March!"

They marched.

It was ludicrous.

They were going to be slaughtered. The greatest playwright the world had ever known was about to die, and when it happened, Pericles was going to blame me.

Then I reflected that these were heroes of Marathon, even if Zeke had been on the other side. These three ancient men would fight until they'd been torn to shreds, and even then, with their last breath they'd struggle to win.

The veterans didn't break step. They met the enemy on the green verge of the sanctuary's lawn. They clashed their shields against the invaders, then with great shouts to unnerve their opponents they sought to drive their swords through the enemy shield wall. The weapons bounced. The brigands tried the same, but nor could they find a gap. After that both sides settled to the deadly business of armored combat.

Glaucon stood behind the line of raiders and urged them on. He made no attempt to help his men. A look at the attackers told me they were mercenaries. Hellas was full of them, all looking for work. These ones were armed with shield and spear and probably short sword for emergencies. The shield barrier made it hard for our men to touch them.

I looked for some way I could come at Glaucon.

"Callias is dead!" one of the women screamed.

I whirled around.

Callias was thoroughly unconscious. Blood flowed from his head. Aeschylus and Zeke fought on. I thought about carrying Callias to cover, then realized there was no point. If we lost here, no one was safe.

Gaïs took Ophelia by the shoulders and looked her in the eyes. She said, "Ophelia, if those men break in here, even if we're still alive, *especially* if they kill the men but capture us priestesses, you're to lead all the girls to the farm where you hid. Can you find it again?"

"Yes, Gaïs," Ophelia said.

Gaïs kissed Ophelia on the lips. "Good girl."

When the brigands had decided to attack a girls' school, they probably hadn't expected to face heavy infantry. Their surprise told in the caution of their attack. I knew it was only two old men, but the raiders didn't: the armor covered the faces and chests of Aeschylus and Zeke, and anything else that might give away their age. Certainly neither of them moved like old men. I could see the slowness of their counter-strokes, but only because I was looking for it.

But their skill would eventually count for little when it was two against so many. They gave ground; it was only a matter of moments before they were flanked. Aeschylus and Zeke turned to fight back to back, each moving in one fluid motion. My old drill instructor would have smiled to see it.

An arrow flew over my head. It came from behind. Diotima had found her perch, and now she was trying for targets. The first shot missed, but her second elicited a painful yell from someone in that melee.

I had to do something to help, but with only my dagger and no armor to protect me, I knew that like Callias I wouldn't stand for long. I needed a better weapon.

Then I realized where I could get one.

I turned and ran.

Rollo had been tied to a tree out back of the sanctuary. Zeke had replaced the light chain Ophelia had used with a heavy one that even the enormous bear couldn't break. Then he'd secured the chain with a wooden lock too heavy for a child to lift.

I grabbed the lock with both hands and shoved upward. The lock came off. I unwrapped the chain from the tree trunk.

"Come on, Rollo," I said. I tugged on the bear's chain, but he didn't move. I tugged harder. The bear didn't budge. I pulled with all my might. Rollo looked at me with contempt.

"What do you want?"

It was Ophelia. The girls had gathered out back, ready to run, and they'd watched me free the bear.

"I'm taking Rollo into that fight," I said. "We'll lose without him."

"He won't go with you," Ophelia said. "But he will with me." She took hold of the chain and said gently, "Come along, Rollo."

The bear lumbered after her.

I couldn't take a child into a battle. But I couldn't not take the bear. I drew my breath, drew my dagger, and took the lead.

"Where are we going?" Ophelia asked.

"Aeschylus and Zeke are surrounded," I told her. "We're going down the west side of the sanctuary, past the Sacred Spring, and through the gap between the temple and the stoa. The buildings will hide us from view until we're right on top of them. We'll hit them from behind before they see us."

I didn't know if Rollo would fight, but I did know that having a giant bear at your back was a good reason to run away.

The raiders had left two men at the bridge. They saw us first. One yelled, the other turned, and both leveled their spears and came at us.

The first man thrust his spear at me with both hands; he put his weight behind it and sent the sharp metal tip straight at my stomach. He grinned as he tried to kill me; if he connected I'd soon be seeing my bowels.

His technique was correct but slow. I swiveled my hips a heartbeat before the spearhead could skewer me, and at the same time I used my free left hand to bat away the shaft, hitting it just behind the spearhead with my open palm.

The spear slid right past me. The look of surprise on the spearman's face made me laugh.

It was a trick Pythax had taught me. Now I was turned side-on to my enemy for minimum profile, and my knife hand was at the forefront.

The spearman had expected resistance when the spear sank into my body. He wasn't braced to stop. He practically ran onto my upraised blade. It took him in the throat.

I breathed a thanks to Pythax. A year ago, that attack would have killed me.

The second man, meanwhile, had made the mistake of running at Ophelia. The bear didn't even break stride. Rollo clubbed Ophelia's attacker with one of his massive paws. The man flew backward to land on his behind, and blood splattered where the bear's claws had scarred him. The raider dropped his spear to scramble backward with both hands, then, when Rollo kept coming at him, the raider picked himself up and ran across the bridge, down the road, and into the darkness.

"Quick," I said to Ophelia. I was astonished she hadn't shown fear, but with that bear beside her the girl was fearless. We passed between the Temple of Artemis and the stoa to see Aeschylus and Zeke hard pressed. Diotima was a dark figure on the roof behind them. She stood to shoot, which exposed her. As I watched, a man threw a spear her way, but Diotima didn't flinch. She shot back. The raider was ready; he blocked her shot with his upraised shield. But that didn't save him. As the arrow hit his shield a figure shot out of the darkness and dragged a short blade down his unarmored arm.

It was Gaïs. She was using her speed to run at the enemy, slash them, then run out of range. Gaïs wielded a priestess knife, the same type that Diotima carried. Those knives were very short, but they were sharpened to slit the throat of a sacrifice in an instant.

They were working as a team. Diotima was pinning the armored men with her shots, and Gaïs was slashing the immobilized targets. Gaïs couldn't kill an armored man with her knife, but it's hard to fight when your arm's shredded.

"Now!" I pulled on Rollo's chain, and this time he followed me.

Rollo lumbered into battle. His giant paw came down upon the first of the raiders and crushed him to the ground. His next swipe tore off the armor of the next man in line. The man was spun around and he came face to face with the hot breath of a giant bear. The man screamed, dropped his spear, and ran. His shield impeded his running, so he flung it away. He disappeared over the bridge and round the bend, and we never saw him again.

Rollo roared. The other raiders noticed that a bear was about to kill them. They turned as one to confront the new threat.

Zeke and Aeschylus didn't waste the opportunity. They both plunged their blades into the backs of attackers. The rest didn't wait to die. They followed their comrade over the bridge and probably out of Attica.

Now my only fear was that Rollo might take down my own side.

The gods must have been on our side, because the bear turned toward the man who'd caused it all. Glaucon had no one to protect him.

Glaucon ran, pursued by the bear.

THE SANCTUARY LOOKED like every battlefield after the fighting was over. Aeschylus and Zeke both sagged to the ground. The fight had taken it out of the old men, but they'd given a display that would have done credit to men half their age.

I picked up Callias in my arms—he was disturbingly light—and carried him into the stoa where Doris had set up an aid station. Gaïs was already sprinting for Brauron as fast as her incredibly swift legs could take her to bring the doctor.

Before she left, I'd said, "You did well, Gaïs, in that attack."

"Well, I had to do something. That idiot Sabina was going to stand there slack-jawed while those men attacked us."

"You're not insane," I said, wondering.

"Of course I'm not."

"I thought you might be pretending to be mad as part of some subtle plan to catch the killer."

Gaïs looked at me strangely. "What sort of a crazy person would do that? No, I've got a much better reason for making people think I'm touched in the head. Can you think of a better way to avoid having to get married than to say crazy things and run through the woods naked? Besides, it's fun."

"Glaucon got away," Diotima said.

"We can pick him up easily," Callias said. He lay propped up against a column with a bad headache and a wet rag pressed to the gaping wound in his skull. "Now that we know who to look for, he can't get away."

Aeschylus walked up to me, slowly. "If you ever tell anyone that I fought alongside a Persian," he said, "I will personally tear out your entrails."

"Your secret's safe with me, Aeschylus," I said, barely suppressing a grin.

"Good." He turned on his heel and walked away.

Doris ran over, her chiton picked up to let her run. "Has anyone seen Aposila?" she asked.

Aposila was missing.

"Who last saw Aposila?" I shouted, then when no one replied, I realized the answer was me. She'd picked up the axe after me and run into the battle.

Dear Gods. Had Aposila followed her daughter to Hades?

I ran to where the bodies of the raiders still lay and pushed them over. Aposila wasn't underneath.

One of the smallest children pointed down the road.

I started running. Diotima wasn't far behind.

Rollo had bailed Glaucon up against a tree. That was where Aposila had found them.

Aposila held a bloodied axe in her hands; at her feet was the splayed body of Glaucon. She'd split him almost down the middle, from the top of his head through the neck and halfway down his chest before the ribs had brought the axe to a halt. She was covered in blood. Drenched in dripping red.

"For my Allike," she said.

Then she dropped the axe, buried her face in her blood-red hands, and wept.

CHAPTER FIFTEEN

"WHAT HAPPENS TO the bear?" Thea asked the next day.

"The bear goes wherever Ophelia goes," Diotima said, and Gaïs nodded. She understood. For the first time ever, the two of them had agreed on something.

"Ophelia can't take a bear home with her!" Sabina objected. "What would her father say?"

"She isn't going home. She's staying here," Gaïs said. "No, let me rephrase that. Ophelia's already home. She's priestess-born; it's obvious." *Unlike you, Sabina,* were the words Gaïs didn't say, but we all heard.

"You don't rule here," Sabina snapped at Gaïs.

"Oh yes, that's right," Thea said. "Let me fix that. Gaïs, kneel."

"What?" Gaïs said, perplexed.

"I said kneel before me, girl. The games are over for you. It's time to do some real work."

Gaïs stammered. "High Priestess . . . no. You can't do this . . . I can't do this . . ."

Thea said, "We all saw, when the crisis was upon us, how you commanded and everyone else obeyed."

"I only said what had to be done," Gaïs protested. "And I only said it because no one was doing it."

"Welcome to management," Thea said to her.

Gaïs slowly went down on her knees.

Thea placed her hands on Gaïs's head. "By the power given me by the Goddess, I name you, Gaïs, the High Priestess of Artemis

Brauronia. May the Goddess ease your path, because the girls certainly won't."

Thea removed her hands. Gaïs, still kneeling, looked up at her.

"That's it?" Gaïs said. "That's the entire ritual? You're completely altering my life with thirty words?"

"I'm making this up as I go, child. Which pretty much sums up how I've ruled here for the last twenty years. If there's a special ritual for this, I don't know it. I got the job myself by default. The old High Priestess never had a chance to pass on a thing to me. Compared to mine, girl, your handover is a luxury."

"Shouldn't we be doing this in the temple, in the presence of Artemis?" Gaïs said.

"There's the bear," Diotima pointed out, and everyone turned to look at Rollo, who stared back in calm equanimity. If Artemis did inhabit the body of the bear—and all the legends said it could be true—then the Goddess clearly didn't object to Gaïs as her new High Priestess.

Gaïs said, "High Priestess . . . Thea . . . I don't know what to do."

"You'll have Doris to help you with the day-to-day running. She's been doing most of the work for years now anyway." Thea added, gently, "And if I read the signs right, you'll have Ophelia to support you in the years to come. I can't begin to tell you, dear, how important it is, to have someone there for you."

"You'll be here, won't you?"

"You don't need your predecessor looking over your shoulder. I'm retiring. You'll need a new maintenance man. Zeke's retiring too."

Well, that surprised no one.

"Away from here?" Gaïs asked.

"Yes."

"Stay with us, Thea," Gaïs said.

"No."

Gaïs said, "Doris should be High Priestess."

Doris laughed and shook her head.

"She's not a leader," Thea said. "Doris knows this about herself, child. At Delphi they have a saying inscribed in the stone: *Know thyself*. You've never been to Delphi, have you? You'd better go before you get too settled in here. The Pythoness at Delphi is your peer now. It's always good to know your professional colleagues. You won't be alone, Gaïs. Doris will be here to help you for as long as you need it, which I suspect won't be long."

I nodded at that, and so did Diotima. Knowing Gaïs as we now did, even though she couldn't read, we knew she'd memorize every part of the running of Brauron before the month was out. In two months she'd be making changes to protect the sanctuary as she thought best.

But still Gaïs tried to avert her fate. She said, "Thea, I'm not worthy."

"In the attack, your first thought was to protect the sanctuary, not yourself," Thea said.

"Of course it was."

"You're worthy."

Sabina said, "High Priestess, you can't mean this. The girl's ignorant."

Thea grinned. "Oh, but I do, Sabina. I know what you're thinking, that you were next in line. But there's no line here; there's only excellence, or the lack of it."

Sabina turned on her heel and walked out, without another word.

"It's unworthy of me, but I confess I enjoyed that," Thea remarked.

Gaïs said, "Sabina wants the job. She'll cause trouble."

"Sabina whines a lot. Deal with it," Thea said without a trace of sympathy. "Anyway, she's bound to die eventually, and then you'll have some peace. In the meantime she's an honest treasurer, which is more than you can say for most types like her.

Trust me, child, once Sabina realizes she has no hope, she'll fall into line."

I KNEW SOMETHING Thea didn't, and this was the time to deal with it. Diotima and I left Thea's office, which was also her bedroom, and would soon be the bedroom of Gaïs. We left the old High Priestess and the new with their lieutenant Doris as they talked in animated fashion about sanctuary administration.

We went in search of Sabina and found her by the edge of the Sacred Spring. She stood there, staring into the waters.

"It was all for nothing, Sabina," I said.

She looked up, startled. Her eyes were red. "What? Oh, it's you."

"What did those young people do that they deserved to die? Why, Sabina?" Diotima said.

"Glaucon killed them."

"Glaucon killed Allike," I said. "But it was you who made it possible. Out of all the children in this place, how did Glaucon know which two had found the scrolls? Your note didn't give their names, Sabina, and even if it had, how would he recognize two girls among many? Someone must have pointed out the victims. That person was you."

"You're guessing—"

"Almost the first thing you said to us, as soon as we met, was that you're a trusted assistant of the Basileus. I thought it was a boastful claim at the time—I still do. I've since met the man and I know he'd never trust a woman with money—but you've been sending reports to his office, haven't you? The assistant who received them at the other end was Glaucon, and he, no doubt, sent you back instructions. Of course you knew each other. You're even both treasurer types. You're probably the only person here at Brauron that Glaucon knew."

"Proves nothing," Sabina said shortly. "It's not a crime to know a killer."

"But it's a crime to be a killer. Glaucon can't have killed Melo, Sabina. He was in Athens then. I know it because I saw him there. But we *know* Glaucon murdered Allike, and we *know* Melo's death was related, and we *know* it was someone at the sanctuary who did it.

"You killed Melo, Sabina. You met him by this spring, maybe exactly where we stand now. Maybe you crept up behind him. You hit him on the head then pushed him in, where he drowned."

"Why would I do such a thing?"

"Because he found Ophelia, and he was unlucky enough to tell you about it. You're always patrolling the grounds, aren't you? You caught Diotima and me holding hands quickly enough. Melo ran into you first. Melo told you where to find Ophelia, then you got rid of him. You didn't dare let anyone find Ophelia before you did. She might have told them what she knew. So you murdered Melo, and I'm guessing then you went to that abandoned farmhouse."

I searched her face for confirmation, and I saw it.

"Why didn't you go in and attack Ophelia?" I asked.

"The bear," she said. "I didn't think the sightings were true until I saw it for myself. It was protecting her. I couldn't see a way around the bear." Sabina looked back into the running waters of the spring. "All I ever wanted was to be High Priestess of this place," she said.

"You're not fit," said Diotima.

"I don't see why not. Thea got the job by default. Why not me?" She sounded like a petulant child.

"When did you decide to murder Allike?" I asked.

"I didn't. I was as shocked as everyone else. You see, when I forwarded the scrolls to Athens, to the Basileus, I sent five."

I said, "But Glaucon was assistant to the Basileus. He opened the case before anyone else saw it."

"Yes," Sabina agreed. "Glaucon read all the scrolls. When he came to the fifth, he was horrified. Hippias had named Glaucon as the man on whose estates he stayed while he recovered from his wound. That scroll would destroy any chance of Glaucon ever gaining high office. In fact it would probably get him killed when the people found out. There was no chance to scratch out his name without it being obvious. So he did the only thing he could: he removed the scroll."

"That was when the conspiracy began," I said.

Sabina nodded reluctantly. "Glaucon started it. I received a note by courier, asking me to meet him in town," Sabina went on. "I knew him, of course; Glaucon's a wealthy landowner in these parts. I'd always been careful to make sure the well-known and the wealthy knew of me. Glaucon made his proposal in person: that if I helped him get elected in Athens, he would help me become High Priestess in Brauron. Well, I knew Thea didn't have long to go. How could I say no?"

With the greatest of ease, I thought, but I didn't bother to say it.

Sabina said, "Glaucon couldn't suppress the discovery. Too many people knew about it. But he thought to turn it to his advantage. Glaucon reasoned that with the fifth scroll out of the way, all he had to do was claim to be the man who killed Hippias. It wasn't that big a lie, you know, and it was only to get one miserable man a single year in office. Glaucon probably only wanted to be treasurer so he could embezzle state funds, but that wasn't my lookout. The so-called statesmen in Athens do worse every day."

I said, "So he suppressed evidence of his own perfidy and then took credit for someone else's crime. What happened to the fifth scroll?"

"Glaucon destroyed it. There was nothing we could do about the gap within the case. Too many people had seen that case to get rid of it. But with any luck, no one would care about the contents, and even if they did, who was to say there hadn't always been four scrolls? It should have worked. No one should have been hurt."

"Except a girl died."

"Allike blurted out to me that she knew there were five scrolls. She'd tried to read them. I doubt she understood a word, but merely knowing of their existence was a danger. I warned Glaucon. I never intended for him to kill her. Please believe me."

"Glaucon tortured the child," Diotima said, and I could hear the vile taste in her mouth as she said it.

"There'd been so much talk of a bear loose in the countryside. Glaucon probably thought it was the most natural thing to make it look like Allike had been killed by a bear."

"Probably?" Diotima said.

"That's what he said, later," Sabina admitted slyly.

With Glaucon dead, we'd never know whether it was his idea or Sabina had told him to make it look like a bear attack. One thing I was sure of: it was Sabina, not Glaucon, who was the smart one in that partnership.

"Then Ophelia disappeared," I said.

"That wasn't my doing! How was I supposed to know she had a tame bear?"

I said, "Ophelia was the only one who knew *for sure* that the bear hadn't killed her friend. She knew it was a human killer. She didn't know who, but she guessed she'd be next. She ran."

"It was the bear that started this, you know," Sabina said bitterly. "Or those gods-accursed children, rather. If they hadn't discovered the cave, I wouldn't be a murderer. And who would have thought a bunch of old men would get so excited about one thoroughly dead body? All that talk of flashing signals and traitors and other nonsense. Men can be very stupid about such things."

"There was murder in your heart anyway, or you would never have done it," Diotima said.

"Why did you tell us there were five scrolls?" I asked. "If you'd said four, it might have muddied the trail."

"I had no choice," Sabina said, as if it had been a difficult move in a child's game. "I knew Allike and Ophelia had looked inside.

They knew there were five; I didn't know who else they might have told. If I'd said four and someone else at the sanctuary swore to five, it would have pinpointed me at once."

Sabina scuffed her bare feet in the soil and stared once more into the pond. Her eyes had a faraway look. Was she recalling what it had been like to push Melo in at this very place, to watch him drown?

"I suppose you're going to turn me in," Sabina said, self-pityingly. "They'll execute me, you know."

"No, Sabina," said Diotima. "We won't say a thing. You'll stay here."

Sabina looked surprised. She hadn't expected mercy. "Why?" she asked.

"Gaïs doesn't know numbers," Diotima said. "She can barely read. Doris reads well, but she can't add. Gaïs must have someone who understands money if she's to succeed here, and I'm going to make sure it happens. I sentence you, Sabina, to be the best treasurer this sanctuary has ever had."

"*Help* Gaïs?" Sabina said, aghast. "And if I refuse?"

"Then you're a dead woman. You'll serve Gaïs as if your life depended on it. Which it does. That's the deal, Sabina, and it's far, far better than you deserve. Take it or leave it."

Diotima stopped abruptly, as if she'd suddenly remembered something. She looked up at me, and said, "If my husband-to-be approves, of course."

It was my turn to be surprised. I hoped I didn't show it.

In the past, I'd been appalled at Diotima's readiness to blackmail whenever it suited her, and she knew how I felt. But Diotima was right about Gaïs, and nobody knew the temple finances like Sabina did.

Besides, I had a point to make.

I said. "Diotima, whatever you think best, that's what we'll do."

"Seriously?"

"This is your field, Diotima. Only an idiot would question

your judgment. I hope I'm not an idiot." I was starting to see this marriage would be more complex than either of us had thought, but I could also see we'd find a balance, if we kept trying.

Diotima smiled at me, then she turned back to Sabina. "One more thing. Gaïs might not know numbers, but I do, Sabina. I'll be back here on a regular basis, and when I am, I'll be checking your books. If I find one *obol* out of place, or the slightest problem, or if I hear one word that you've caused Gaïs trouble, then you're dead. Do you understand me?"

"I could throw myself on the mercy of the High Priestess," Sabina said. "Then we'll see what your threats are worth."

"Does Gaïs strike you as the forgiving sort?" I asked.

Sabina was silent. We all knew that Thea might forgive human weakness; she'd endured her fair share. But Gaïs was younger, and Sabina had put her ambitions above the good of the sanctuary. Gaïs would be merciless.

"One final thing," Diotima said.

"*Another* thing?" Sabina said. I could see she was already wondering if death might not have been easier.

"Yes," said Diotima. "This is non-negotiable. From now on, when Nico and I visit the sanctuary, we get our own room."

Sabina said at once, "Very well. I accept."

I DON'T KNOW what made me wake up that night. Perhaps it was the full moon, because when my eyes opened its bright light was shining in my face. Whatever it was, I stood and tiptoed over the sleeping bodies in the shed and out into the sanctuary.

I walked about, curious to see the place in the dead of night. In moonlight it seemed eerie. It was as if everyone had died, or we'd all been transported to the underworld in our sleep.

I stepped around the sacred pond, careful to give it a wide berth—if I fell in now, no one would find my body till at least the morning, maybe not for days—and that was when I noticed torchlight within the Temple of Artemis.

At this time?

It flickered, and the movement of the shadows told me someone was within.

I crept, slowly, careful not to disturb whatever was happening. I edged up to the entrance and peered around the corner, not knowing what to expect.

There, with her back to me, standing before the statue of the Goddess, was Diotima. Her arms were raised, and she intoned a prayer to Artemis.

I stood up and walked in, not bothering to hide my steps, which echoed in the nighttime silence.

I was only three steps across the small temple when Diotima turned and said, "Help me, Nico."

Lying at her feet were three balls of different colors; two drawing slates of the kind used by children, on which a child's pictures were still drawn in fading chalk; a wooden pull-along toy of a puppy, the wheels of which had seen long use; a doll; and, in a brightly painted box, a set of doll's clothes.

I stopped alongside her and held her hand. She gripped me back and held on hard. She whispered to me, "I collected them from my cupboard when we were back in Athens."

She spoke to the Goddess.

"I am Diotima, the daughter of Ephialtes, the stepdaughter of Pythax. I stand before you, Artemis of the Sacred Spring, before my wedding, to dedicate to you my doll and her pretty clothes, my bouncing balls, and the slates on which I drew so many pictures; my gift to you, Goddess, before I am a married woman."

Diotima let go my hand. She picked up each toy and placed it on the wall beyond the statue, where hung hooks to accept offerings. When she came to her doll, she hugged it tight, and there were tears in her eyes. But she placed the doll, too, upon the wall, and with a final gesture smoothed down the doll's tiny dress.

Then my fiancée took my hand once more, and together we left the temple.

"The usual formula is to say it's a virgin's gift," she said to me. "But it's a bit too late for that."

"Better late than never. The Goddess won't mind."

"No, I don't think she will. I feel better, but sad, Nico. Very sad."

I didn't return to my bed that night, and nor did Diotima. We spent the night in each other's arms, on the soft grass beside the Sacred Spring.

Chapter Sixteen

"NOW IT'S BACK to school for me," said Socrates mournfully. He'd have sounded more cheerful if someone had sentenced him to death.

"Don't you like school?" Diotima asked.

"I like learning. I don't like school. The two things are totally different. School's boring. It's a drag having to wait for the teacher to catch up with me."

"The solution to that's easy," said Diotima. "I'll teach you, Socrates."

"*You?*" I said, astonished.

"I'd appreciate it if you said that with some more confidence. Why not? I'm better qualified than all those clapped-out soldiers who take up teaching, aren't I?"

"Well, yes, of course. But—"

"It's not like I won't be around the home. We're living in the same place now. He won't have to travel to school."

I could already see Socrates scheming to get around her.

"Don't think this means you get to slack off," she told him. "The difference between Karinthos and me is, *I know what you can do, and I expect you to do it.* If I catch you working one bit below your ability, my brother-in-law, I'll have the slaves beat you."

"Terrific," Socrates muttered.

"Do you know your Homer?" she demanded.

"Of course," Socrates said confidently.

"Excellent. Then we can move on to the good stuff. I think we'll start with Sappho."

"*Sappho?*" Socrates said, aghast. "You want me to learn *girlie* poetry?"

"All of it."

"It'll be good for you, Socrates," I said, grinning. "It'll help you later with the girls."

"Then why don't you learn it?"

"I don't need to. I've already got a girl," I told him.

He glared at me.

"Your idea's brilliant, Diotima," I said. "I'll talk to Father about it as soon as possible."

Diotima rubbed her hands in anticipation. "This is going to be fun."

DIOTIMA AND I drove Aposila to her brother's farm, to the far northeast. She'd said her goodbyes to Malixa back in Athens, and also to her sons, who by law remained with their father; and so Aposila left with us to begin her new life as a divorced woman.

With Glaucon dead, and with all the talk of who killed Hippias finally dying down, the elections would be free and fair. Pericles was already talking about next year's vote, making noises about standing again.

It was hard, stony land we rode through. The farms we passed looked as if they could barely scratch a living. When we came to the farm of Theoxotos, I saw it was no different.

I led Blossom into the yard that surrounded the farmhouse. Naked children ran about, the owner's children and the slave children together. They chased the chickens, which squawked and flew away, and the children laughed. Men and women toiled at their tasks about the yard. They looked up as we arrived. They'd been expecting us.

A man rubbed his hands against his tunic and walked over from where he'd been threshing corn. He stopped before me and said, "I'm Theoxotos, the brother of Aposila."

"Nicolaos, son of Sophroniscus. I bring you your sister."

Theoxotos handed down Aposila from the cart. Aposila smiled at me, at Diotima, but said nothing. She walked into the farmhouse.

Theoxotos watched her go in, then said, "We'll care for her. I know this place doesn't look much, but no one goes hungry."

The laughter of the children had told me that. I said, "I know."

"It was you who helped my sister get her divorce, wasn't it?"

"Yes."

"You did her a great service. How much do I owe you?" he asked.

These people were so poor, I didn't have the heart to take his money. They were poorer than my own family. But like my father, I knew Theoxotos would be a proud man. If I refused to be paid, he'd be more insulted than if I overcharged him.

I searched about the yard desperately for something that might expunge the debt without crippling the owner. Over the other side, I noticed the chicken coop, and stacked beside it, canvas sacks. I had a fair idea what was in those sacks. It gave me an idea.

"Could I have a few of those, please?" I said.

Theoxotos followed my pointing finger.

"You want to be paid in chicken feed?" he said.

"Maybe a few chickens, too, if you can manage it. You see, I've started a farm."

Theoxotos turned to his head slave, whose thin frame stood naked but for a tiny loincloth, his skin burnt by the sun. "Give this man as many sacks of grain as will fit on that cart, and all the chickens he wants."

"Yes, master."

He turned back to me.

"Thank you, Nicolaos."

IT WAS THE night of a full moon, always a night of good luck, but this particular moon was especially lucky to me: it was the night I would get married. Married, that is, for the last, final, officially approved time.

My family went on ahead to the house of Pythax, while I remained with my friend Timodemus, who I'd asked to act as best man. His duty would be to drive my bride to her new home. Together we slowly drove the cart through the narrow streets of Athens, taking care to avoid the worst of the mud, to keep the cart clean.

By the time I arrived, my father, my brother, and Pythax were in the courtyard. Diotima and her mother, Euterpe, were upstairs in the women's quarters. My mother, Phaenarete, had gone up to join them. We men waited for Diotima to make her appearance, and thus begin the ceremony.

There was only one thing missing.

There were no guests.

"What happened?" I whispered to my father.

"We were never able to resolve all the arguments," Sophroniscus whispered back. "Say nothing, son, for the insult to Pythax is severe, and I don't wish to make it worse."

Severe indeed, and Father didn't need to explain. The respectable families—the friends of Sophroniscus and Phaenarete—had refused their invitations to the home of an ex-courtesan whose new husband was a former slave. The friends of Pythax . . . well, he had no friends among the citizenry, and all his old friends were slaves.

The door of the women's quarters opened. All we men—my father, Pythax, Socrates, and I—instinctively looked up to see Diotima standing there, in a dress of flowing red silk. It was the satin she and I had brought back with us from Ionia. Upon her head was a fine yellow veil. Diotima came carefully down the steps, I took her hands, and she smiled at me through the veil. I couldn't be sure, but I thought her eyes were red.

The courtyard seemed empty with only the seven of us. Every time we spoke, the sound echoed off the walls. It reminded us there were no guests, which no one was brave enough to say, but everyone was thinking. It made us all the more reluctant to say anything at all. Euterpe seemed close to sobbing. She knew the embarrassing no-shows were because of her dubious reputation.

We sat and ate and drank in silence. Very little, for no one had an appetite, except for Pythax, who drank the wine.

Pythax knocked back the last of his wine. "Well," he said in the echoing room. "You may as well get going."

I stepped from the house, to check that all was ready. Awaiting us right at the door was the wedding chariot—actually, it was Blossom and his cart—fresh-painted in white with blue facings and decked out in flowers. Holding the reins, ready to transport my bride to her new home, was Timodemus. He favored his good leg, but he was more than able to manage the steady drive. He gave me a broad grin.

The donkey's mane had been combed and tied in ribbons. The donkey gave me a sour look as I stepped out the door, as if to say his embarrassment was all my fault.

But then I myself stood, stunned. For there, standing in two lines before the donkey, ready to lead the procession, were the Little Bears of Brauron. All of them, decked out in their finest dresses, and since they came of the wealthiest families of Athens, their finest was fine indeed. They'd woven flowers into the braids of their hair, and the moment I emerged they began to sing panegyrics in praise of Artemis.

For the first time ever, the Little Bears had come to lead one of their own to her wedding.

Doris stood to the side.

"You arranged this," I said to her.

"It was the least I could do," Doris said.

Standing along both sides of the road was a crowd to admire the spectacle. A sizable crowd that stretched down the street, full of people I didn't recognize. Then it hit me: the parents of the Little Bears had come to watch their girls, as they should. Euterpe had got her wish: the best families of Athens were here to attend her daughter's wedding.

Phaenarete stared in amazement at the assembled personages. My mother clenched her hands and said in dismay, "We can't possibly feed all these people." I thought she might be about to cry.

"I've seen to that," said Callias, the richest man in Athens. He stepped out of the crowd. He sported a bandage wrapped tightly around his head, which couldn't hide the massive lump beneath.

"The city owes Nicolaos a debt, and so do I. He put to rest a personal agony that's plagued me all my life. When you come to your home, Phaenarete, you'll find the best food my estates can provide. Also extra slaves to serve." He paused. "I'm afraid there wasn't enough room in your courtyard, fine though it is. I ordered my staff to block off the street so the party can spill out."

"Won't the archons object?"

"That's them over there." Callias nodded in the direction of three harried-looking men and their plump wives. "They won't say a thing. Not if they want to eat tonight."

One of those archons saw me. The Basileus waved in my direction and called his best wishes across the heads of the crowd. I waved back.

The door opened again. Diotima stood waiting. Pythax handed her out into the street to be admired. Then Pythax, too, saw what awaited us, and stared in amazement, before a slow smile crossed his face.

Diotima seemed barely to notice; she was too busy being the center of attention. It was the first time the women of Athens had ever seen silk. Female gasps could be heard from all over the crowd. From the looks on the men's faces as they stared at Diotima, I knew that for months to come, complete strangers would be stopping me in the street to congratulate me on my good fortune.

Leading the Little Bears was Ophelia on the left, and on the right, a girl who I knew for sure was *not* a Bear. Speechless, I walked over to her.

"Hello, master," said Asia.

"I'm not your master. What are you doing here?"

For Asia was the survivor of a previous adventure. After what she'd been through, I'd thought she'd never want to see me or Diotima again. Yet here she was, to wish us good fortune.

Asia glanced over to where Diotima was being admired by the crowd.

"She's lucky," Asia said. "And so are you."

"Yes."

"Go back to your bride, master."

So many friends.

Pythax took Diotima by the wrist and led her to me. He said, in a voice loud enough to be heard by the many people about us, "Before these witnesses, I, Pythax, give this woman, Diotima, to you, for your wife."

Did I hear a catch in his voice?

Pythax offered Diotima's wrist to me. I took her wrist to lead her to the cart. I handed her up onto the back, where she would stand for the coming journey, for all of Athens to see.

The Little Bears led the way. As they walked they sang the traditional praise of marriage.

"*Io Hymen! Io Hymen! Hymenaeus Io!*"

Timodemus took Blossom's reins. Not that Blossom needed any guidance; he knew the way to his new home already. He set off in an easy glide before Timo had a chance to move him.

I walked behind. I passed up to Diotima a quince, which she ate, as custom demands. People we passed wished us good luck. Our guests followed.

When we arrived at our home, Socrates and Timodemus

unhitched Blossom while I handed Diotima down. I raised her veil then, for she had come to her new home, and set the thin material back over her head, to see that she'd been crying beneath the veil. I smiled at her, probably like an idiot, and she smiled back and was lovely. I presented my bride to my parents, officially. They stood by the entrance to our home. Sophroniscus opened the door. Phaenarete invited Diotima within.

I took the axe that had been left conveniently by the front door. No one who watched knew it, but this was the axe that Aposila had used to dispatch Glaucon. This I hefted, and in a series of hard swings used it to destroy the cart, so that it might never be used for any lesser purpose than to bring my wife to me. Also so that Diotima couldn't change her mind and go back home.

I threw the dismembered axle to Socrates, who put it on the waiting bonfire. As the night wore on, he would feed the rest of the cart into the fire, to give the guests light by which to party.

Which they proceeded to do.

It seemed like half of Athens was at our home. The Little Bears ate in a group isolated from the rest, under the highly protective eye of Doris. At least, when Socrates tried to chat them up, she sent him running. Other young men eyed the Bears from a safe distance. The girls knew it and giggled and played up to them in their pretty dresses. With all the parents present, I wondered how many negotiations might be underway before the night ended.

Down the far end of the street had gathered those of the Scythian Guard who weren't on duty, and the thugs of Aeschylus and Callias, and a large swathe of disreputable-looking men with shifty eyes. They played drinking games together and sang and swore. The ones with shifty eyes were probably most of the professional thieves in Athens. In any case, they all seemed to know each other, and called the Scythians by name. Predators and prey taking a break. I sent them extra amphorae of our cheapest wine.

Pythax, who had his back to me, turned to look their way, with a strange expression on his face.

"Do you miss it?" I asked him.

"No, lad," he said. "I was thinking it's funny that I *don't* miss it. I guess I'm getting old."

"Pythax? You didn't call me little boy."

"Yeah, that's a habit I've got to break now." He punched me in the shoulder, then returned to the animated discussion he'd been having with the archons, over wine and roast lamb, about funds for equipment purchases for the guard.

Doris raised her arms, and the Little Bears rose with her, as one, to sing the epithalamium, the praise song for the happy couple. But this wasn't the traditional song. This was something I'd never heard before, and they sang of Diotima by name. The song praised her beauty and called her high in the regard of the divine Huntress. What was this?

"I hope you like it," said a voice beside me. I turned to see Aeschylus.

"I'd be upset if you didn't like my work," he added.

"*You* wrote our poem, Aeschylus?" I said. "That was kind of you."

"Least I could do," he said gruffly. "Think of it as an apology for trying to kill you."

"Apology accepted."

"I've decided to leave Athens. There are too many memories for me here. I'll go to Sicily, to the rich new lands. I find that Athens has become a place for young men. Maybe it always was, but I used to be young once and I didn't notice. In any case, you don't need old men like me."

"You'll be missed," I said, and I meant it. "What about your estates? Won't they fall to ruin without you?"

"No. I've recently hired a new estate manager. A very competent man, an honorable man, with much experience."

"I see."

Aeschylus shrugged. "He won't have to do any work himself. He'll have many slaves to carry out his commands, and the house is comfortable. I think he and his wife will be happy."

The girls sang to the crowd, many of whom stood before them to listen.

Married love between man and woman
is greater than any mortal oath,
for love is a rite of nature.

All the grown-ups cheered and whistled at those words.

Aeschylus the playwright observed the crowd's reaction with a critical eye.

"I was rather pleased with that line myself," he said. "I might use it in my next play."

"Isn't that the play with all the murder in it?"

"Yes. So appropriate for your marriage, don't you think? In any case, only half your song is mine. I sent a runner to the poet Pindar. It seems he once wrote you a praise song that you didn't stay to hear. That was exceedingly rude of you, lad."

"Yes. I feel bad about running from him, but at the time there were a bunch of people trying to kill me."

"Does this sort of thing happen often? That's a bad habit you've acquired. I suggest you break it."

"Good idea."

The tune of the Little Bears abruptly changed. Now they sang about me, and the words of the song brought a blush to my cheeks.

"That's Pindar's praise song," Aeschylus said. "I've been rehearsing the children all day."

I took Diotima's hand and led her between the two columns

of Little Bears. The girls threw confetti over us as they sang our song. I led my wife to our room, then shut the door behind us.

Half of Athens waited outside our door. I knew for sure their every ear was bent, to hear what happened next.

Fortunately, the room was well soundproofed.

Author Note

THIS AUTHOR NOTE talks about the true history behind the story. All of the places and most of the people are real, and quite a few of the events really happened. That means this note is full of spoilers, so if you haven't read the book yet, turn back to the front, and I'll see you again in a little while.

THE SANCTUARY OF Artemis at Brauron was one of the world's first schools for girls. The great poetess Sappho ran what amounted to a finishing school for young ladies in the century before. I know of no school for girls before those two.

The sanctuary itself was ancient. There's been a settlement there since Neolithic times. Evidence of the worship of Artemis goes back to at least the eighth century BC.

The girls who attended the sanctuary really were called the Little Bears. In the play *Lysistrata* by Aristophanes, the heroine describes the high points of her childhood with these words:

At seven years of age, I carried the sacred vessels;
At ten, I pounded barley for the altar of Athene;
Next, clad in a robe of saffron,
I played the bear to Artemis at Brauron.

Nothing is known about the staff who looked after the Little Bears. It's possible, however, to make some educated guesses. It's inconceivable that an Athenian father would have entrusted his highly marriageable, nubile, upper-class, teenage daughter to the care of a strange man. The ethics of the time forbade it. In fact, modern ethics largely forbids it too. The teachers of the Little Bears must therefore have been an all-female crew.

It was the nature of those times that, since virtually all women married, most of the carers were probably older widows, such as Doris and Sabina, with possibly a core of professional priestesses, like Thea and Gäis. Anyone who's been involved with a girls' school will realize there are certain challenges. I assume the priestesses at Brauron were not only religious figures, but also teachers, and probably dorm mothers driven to their wits' end.

THE REMAINS OF the sanctuary still exist. If you visit, you'll find standing columns holding up impressive-looking stone crosspieces. They haven't been upright for more than two millennia—that would be a remarkable achievement; they were restored by the first modern excavators, using the stone blocks that they found on the ground.

The stoa at the sanctuary is the site's most impressive ruin. Its size places a limit on how many girls and staff could have lived there at any one time.

The bridge at the sanctuary is the *only* surviving example of a stone bridge from classical Greece. That this small temple complex had such an extravagance speaks entirely to the fact that this was a finishing school for well-born young ladies. Their doting fathers were the men who controlled the state budget. It would be reasonable to assume the sanctuary got the best of everything.

Though the bridge is still there, the small river it crossed is gone. The water was diverted long ago. Back then, the sanctuary sat by the sea. These days it's about four hundred paces inland. The intervening space has been filled by silt.

I made the Sacred Spring larger and deeper than the small surviving spring, purely to force Nico to dive into it. It does seem possible, however, that the spring was deeper and a lot larger in classical times than it is today. The treasure that Nico hauls out of the spring, and which Diotima throws back in on the orders of Thea, is entirely real. It's been recovered by archaeologists and is now on display at the nearby museum. Among the recovered treasure are many rings, scarabs, vases, and other womanly adornments, including some well-preserved mirrors. At least some of it appears to have been tossed in to save it from being plundered by the Persians, while other items date to hundreds of years before the time of Nico and Diotima.

For the treasure to have survived more than 2,500 years, it must have been well hidden. Archaeologists generally assume that the spring was filled in at the time of the Persian invasion, because no dedicated items have been recovered from after that period, but it might equally be because the Greeks changed their practices at that time. In any case, I have the Sacred Spring open and functioning twenty years after the invasion.

Oddly, even as I wrote this book, archaeologists working at the site made a new discovery that was reported in the news. They found buried treasure at an unexpected location, and the treasure dated to about the same period as my story. This left me biting my nails, wondering if they were about to find something that would destroy my plot, and I sat with fingers poised over the keyboard, ready to alter my story in real time as news came to hand. Luckily, nothing went wrong (yet . . . but new discoveries are one of the occupational risks of writing historical fiction).

What the archaeologists found were more items like the ones Nico discovers at the bottom of the Sacred Spring. These new items had been buried north of the spring, in an out-of-the-way place. In fact, Nico and Ophelia must have walked over that spot when they led the bear into battle.

It seems likely that the treasure had been buried to hide it from the incoming Persians. That it wasn't recovered indicates that whoever buried it didn't survive the sacking.

ONE THING I definitely did *not* make up is that girls were required to sacrifice their toys.

I once gave a talk at my daughters' school about ancient Greece. I talked about hairstyles, how children dressed, about ancient schools and how children took part in the festivals and how girls went to the sanctuary at Brauron. Then I mentioned in passing that ancient Greek girls, before they married, were required to dedicate all their toys to the goddess Artemis.

Fifteen minutes later, I was still fielding questions as the girls desperately looked for ways around this evil rule. They were *shocked*.

It was instantly obvious to me that Diotima would have cheated the system.

The dedication of the toys is obviously a coming-of-age ritual. A maiden puts away her childish things before she becomes a wife. More accurately, it worked like this: When a girl was born she was a kore, which means maiden. When she was betrothed she became a nymphe, and nymphe she remained until motherhood, when she became a gyne. This is obviously the source of our modern word nymph, but the meaning has changed somewhat. The closest modern equivalent for the ancient nymphe would be the highly respectable debutante.

The dedication of the toys was part of the transformation. The girl went to the temple, no doubt with her family, where in a ceremony she placed her toys within the temple. Then she left without them, no longer a girl, but a young woman.

There are a few surviving dedications that we can read today. The clearest I know of is this one:

Timareta, the daughter of Timaretus,
before her wedding,
has dedicated to you, Artemis of the Lake,
her tambourine and her pretty ball,
and the net that kept up her hair;
and her dolls too, and their dresses;
a virgin's gift, as is fit, to a virgin goddess.

THESE DAYS WE think of becoming an adult as a gradual process, but to the Greeks it was an instantaneous event. The adults in this book refer to the girls at the sanctuary as children. Which they are! But at the end of their time at the sanctuary the girls perform their dedication, and from that instant they are marriageable adults.

A proud father would commission a statue of his girl to commemorate the occasion. This was like the graduation photos that families take these days, only back in classical Athens they did them in solid marble. The great majority of statues of girls from the ancient world come from Brauron. The surviving statues are very beautiful and lifelike, so that we have an astonishingly good idea what the girl children of classical Athens looked like.

This instant graduation system might seem tough on the girls, but oddly the boys had the exact opposite problem. Men didn't obtain their legal majority until their fathers had passed away. It was possible for a sixty-year-old man to still need his father's permission to do anything (and indeed this happened to the unfortunate son of the playwright Sophocles). This is why in the book Nico, despite having served in the army, must ask his father for permission to leave the city. He will have to continue this practice for as long as Sophroniscus lives.

NICO AND DIOTIMA have a slight problem when they inspect the bones of Hippias: forensics won't be invented for centuries to come, and there isn't a thing they can learn from a pile of musty old bones. I'm afraid *CSI: Athenai* is not a concept. The Greeks held the bodies of the dead in very great respect; even to touch the dead was considered ritually polluting, and human dissection was absolute anathema to them, as it was to virtually every culture until quite recently.

The Greeks believed that a person's psyche continued after death. It was the psyche that descended to Hades. "Psyche" means breath—in this case the breath of life, in the sense of the soul—and, quite obviously, it is the source of our modern words psyche, psychology, psychiatry, etc. To release a psyche from its mortal remains required a proper burial and, famously, the coin under the tongue with which to pay Charon the ferryman to take you to the underworld. If the proper forms were not observed, the psyche was doomed to remain on earth. Nico and Diotima take it for granted that the psyche of Hippias is hanging around close by.

DIVORCE LAW WORKED exactly as the book describes. A man needed only to declare his intention. A woman needed only speak to an archon, one of the elected officials.

The wife was then required to leave the marital home. She would have to go and live with her closest male relative, who typically would be her father if he was still alive, or else a brother. But there was a kicker to this. Not only did the wife leave, but her dowry went with her. Every last drachma. Or if it was property, every last little bit of land. Athenian law was rock solid on this point.

The Greek dowry system was like the ancient version of a trust fund in the lady's name, to be administered by her husband for her benefit. In the normal course of a happy married life, it was all in the family, and when the wife died her dowry would be inherited by her sons. But in the event of divorce, the dowry did not belong to the husband. It was the woman's retirement fund, supplied by her father. This meant that the larger the dowry, the less likely an unhappy marriage was to break down. There was more than one man dependent on his wife's dowry property for most of his income.

Though divorce was much easier—or at least simpler—back then than it is today, the divorce rate was far lower than in modern times. Also, there was no such thing as gossip rags back then (we've definitely gone downhill on that one). Consequently, there are only a handful of documented divorce cases. The cases however make it clear that women could divorce simply by seeing an archon.

This rule led to the most bizarre divorce case in the city's history.

There was a general and politician by the name of Alcibiades, fifty years after the time of this story, whose wife Hipparete despaired of him because he constantly consorted with prostitutes. Unable to take it any more, she began the walk to see an archon to declare divorce. Her husband, Alcibiades, got wind of this. He turned up just as she was crossing the agora, picked her up bodily, and carried her home. She never tried again.

Alcibiades's actions were far from the norm—so much so that people were still talking about it hundreds of years after his outrageous behavior. This true story is the basis for my scene in which Aposila makes the same walk, also with a husband prepared to stop her. The difference is, Aposila has Nico and Diotima to protect her.

APOSILA AND MALIXA, the mothers of Allike and Ophelia, strike up a friendship in the face of their common woes. Wives socialized by visiting one another's homes, where no doubt they nibbled on snacks as they gossiped about their friends and complained about their husbands. This was the ancient world's equivalent of sitting around the kitchen table with a cup of coffee. The other very frequent activity was going to the agora together, no doubt with a few slaves to carry the purchases.

There were no cafés or clubs, but there were the temples, and it's known that some religious festivals were women-only affairs. The men were probably intensely curious about what their wives got up to during those. Likewise, there are surviving decorations that show women partaking in athletic games.

It's perfectly viable and easy for Aposila and Malixa to fib to their husbands about where they're going when they consult Nico and Diotima. They need only say they're going shopping, and their husbands grunt and ignore them.

It's likely that wives whose husbands were away on active service moved in with friends, if only for the company. They all had slaves to do the basic household chores. So when Aposila is about to divorce and stays with Malixa, Malixa's husband probably doesn't even notice.

If Antobius had divined Aposila's location and turned up demanding her back, Polonikos would have handed her over in an instant. But Antobius doesn't know where his wife's gone. His only chance to stop his wife from divorcing him is to ring the agora with watchers and wait for her to turn up.

ANTOBIUS, THE FATHER of Allike, considered suing the sanctuary for damages after his daughter was killed.

Classical Athens was highly litigious. The comic playwright Aristophanes makes lots of jokes about it. It was almost impossible for any citizen to get through life without suing or being sued several times. Far from being a modern curse, vexatious litigation is as old as civilization.

IT SUITED MY story to make this the first year in which Pericles stood for election. Pericles was well and truly established as the foremost man in Athens by 460 BC, which was the year before. Historical sources usually give 458 as his first elected year, but it makes sense to me that he would have run for an official position as soon as possible.

These days we tend to think of Pericles as a wise statesman in a flowing white robe. The truth is, his day job was running the army. Pericles went on to win twenty-nine elections, all of which were free and fair. I believe that remains the world record for any leader of a democratic nation.

WHEN GLAUCON WORKS through his list of record tablets, he calls out some strange-looking names for the days. The Athenian calendar had lunar months. Every month began with the new moon and ended on the last day of the cycle. An Athenian need merely look up at the night sky to know what day of the month it was.

As you surely know, the moon waxes and wanes. The Athenians named the days of the month to match. The first day of each month was called Noumenia, which means "new moon." After Noumenia, the next day was called 2nd Waxing, then 3rd Waxing, and so on to 10th Waxing. Then the system changes to 11th, 12th, 13th . . . 19th, and then Earlier 10th. The *earlier* is very important, because the following day was *later* 10th. Yes, they had two 10ths in a row: earlier and later. After Later 10th it counted down: 9th Waning, 8th Waning, down to 2nd Waning, and ending with *Hena kai nea*, meaning "old and new."

The definition of "day" was a bit odd. For the Greeks, the old day ended and the new one began at dusk. This makes perfect sense for people working to a lunar calendar. But it creates a terminology problem for me. Nicolaos could say at midday, "I'll meet you early tomorrow," and mean that night, leaving you, the reader, totally confused. I solved this problem by completely ignoring it. I stuck to modern convention.

—

THE VAST MAJORITY of Greek priestesses were married and did their priestessing on a part-time basis. People tend to think of ancient priestesses as being like the Vestal Virgins, but the Vestals were purely Roman and had no Greek counterpart whatsoever.

There was no requirement for either chastity or virginity among the Greeks, except probably in a few special cases. One special case would surely be the Pythoness who uttered prophecy at Delphi. I assume another would be the Priestess of the Sacred Games.

Thus there's nothing shocking or sacrilegious in the relationship between Zeke and Thea. It also means Diotima loses none of her priestessly character now that she's a married woman.

Where I have traduced Zeke's character is in making him a deserter from the Persian army. There were many real cases of Greeks going over to the Persian side, but I don't know of a single instance where a Persian officer deserted to the Greeks. The Persians were men of remarkable integrity. Of course, Zeke did it for love, and his family assumes that he perished at Marathon, so his good name remains secure.

BEARS DEFINITELY USED to live in southern Greece, but as Nico points out they were hunted to extinction. There were still wild bears in northern Greece. One of the royal tombs in Macedonia shows a hunt scene in which a bear is part of the action.

The Greeks never practiced bear baiting, but they did have cockfights. They seem to have been popular among lower-class men. The great General Themistocles was once invited to a fight, and he was so horrified by what he saw that he tried to have the practice banned. He failed miserably.

THE MARATHON CONSPIRACY is the fourth book in the series, and the first book in which characters from previous adventures appear in cameos. You may have noticed during the wedding that Nico mentions two people who otherwise play no part in the story: Asia and Timodemus. These two were important to Nico and Diotima in the second and third books respectively (*The Ionia Sanction* and *Sacred Games*). Asia and Timo are both Athenians, and it would be strange indeed if they didn't turn up for the wedding of their friends.

The Athenian marriage ceremony was much as I give it, with a lot of detail removed because otherwise the book would never end. There were a lot of rituals involved, and the party could go on for days.

Confetti is a very ancient tradition. It's known that classical wedding guests threw it. The veil was also definitely worn. A white dress for the bride is much more recent. The silk for Diotima's bridal gown was acquired on a previous adventure. Silk had reached Persia by this date but no further. When she appears at the door, Diotima becomes the first woman in Europe ever to wear a silk dress.

The epithalamium was a song written especially for a newly married couple. It was a standard part of every marriage ceremony, though it would have been a rare marriage song that was co-authored by Pindar and Aeschylus. When you're an historical novelist you can get away with these things. Believe it or not, epithalamium remains a valid word in English to this day.

THE PLAY THAT Aeschylus is writing during the story, for which Nico so helpfully offers plot ideas, is known today as *The Oresteia Trilogy*. Aeschylus will go on to win first prize with it at the next major contest. It will be one of the last things he writes. It's said that he was killed when an eagle dropped a tortoise on his head.

Aeschylus wrote his own epitaph:

> *Here lies Aeschylus the Athenian, son of Euphorion,*
> *who perished in the wheat-bearing land of Gela.*
> *Of his fighting powers the grove of Marathon can speak,*
> *and the long-haired Persian knows it well.*

Today we honor Aeschylus as the founder of modern drama, the genius inventor of tragedy, but in the epitaph that he wrote for himself, he spoke only of his ability to slaughter Persians. It never occurred to him to mention that he'd written a few plays.

THE BATTLE OF Marathon changed the course of history. It's probably the most famous battle ever. Despite which, modern historians can't even agree on which direction the opposing lines faced, let alone details like whether the Persian cavalry took the field.

I'm convinced that the version Aeschylus gives is the most likely approximation of the truth. But a lot of people have written a lot of books about Marathon, and if you want to learn more about this vastly important battle, I recommend reading Herodotus and one of the modern texts for comparison.

The story of the signal that flashed to the enemy from behind the Athenian lines can be found in Herodotus. The identity of the traitors caused a lot of wild speculation back then, and continues to do so to this day. The problem of light reflecting off a curved shield, which Socrates points out in the book, was in fact pointed out by a modern historian.

In describing the battle, Herodotus said this of the Athenians:

> *If they bow down before the Medes, it is clear from past experience what they will suffer when handed over to Hippias; but if this city prevails, it can become the first among all Greek cities.*

THE STORY OF Harmodius, Aristogeiton, and Leana is as Callias gives it in the book. I find it interesting that the first people in history to give their lives for democratic freedom were two gay men and a woman.

The original statues of Harmodius and Aristogeiton were taken by the Persians when they sacked Athens. The Athenians made replacements when they retook their city. It's the second version that Nico sees in the agora. Alexander the Great returned the originals to Athens after he conquered Persia, and the two pairs stood together for centuries. The Romans made copies of the second pair. Some of these copies survive—probably the best copy is at the museum in Naples—which means we have a fair idea of what Harmodius and Aristogeiton looked like. As Nico reports, they stand close together, pressing forward but turned so that they're almost back to back, and in each hand they wield a sword.

Incredibly, Leana gets lost in modern retellings of their story. The bias isn't ancient. All the ancient sources, including Herodotus, Plutarch, and Pausanias, are united and fulsome in their praise of her. It seems to be modern writers who've lost track of the female hero.

The social status of Leana is a bit of a mystery. She's usually described as the mistress of Aristogeiton. I think this highly unlikely, because the one thing everyone agrees on is that Harmodius and Aristogeiton were as gay as can be. Also, given the praise heaped upon her, Leana must surely have been a citizen. I fudged it by making her the unmarried sister of Aristogeiton. This also helps me to explain the deep admiration Callias had for her.

Leana is the only mortal woman ever to be given a statue atop the Acropolis. In those days it was illegal to erect a statue in honor of a woman, but Callias insisted, and then paid for it himself.

Pausanias reports seeing the statue three hundred years later. I copied his description of Leana's memorial: a dangerous lioness who roars without a tongue.

CALLIAS WAS THE first culturally modern European, to my mind, even more so than Pericles or Socrates. Callias was instrumental in the second, successful plot to overthrow Hippias.

It's my own idea, but I think as certain as such things can

be, that Callias was one of the original plotters recruited by Harmodius and Aristogeiton, one of those who had to flee when the conspiracy went wrong at the last moment. Callias must have been almost the same age as Harmodius. That he was at the forefront of the next plot shows he was of a like mind. That he went out of his way to honor Leana demonstrates a connection.

Callias went on to make himself the richest man in Greece through his business acumen, his management expertise, and his people skills. Athens had a number of good military men, but when it was peace they wanted, it was to Callias that the Athenians turned for the negotiations.

He eventually fell madly in love with Elpinice, the sister of Cimon, who happened to be the mortal enemy of Pericles. Elpinice and Callias had several sons and three daughters.

Callias asked each daughter as she came of age who she wanted for a husband. Each girl in turn checked out the local talent and then made her selection. Callias offered the father of the target young man a dowry so large that no sane father could refuse. This turnabout of the usual process was so talked about that it even made it into the ancient histories. It also showed the extent to which Callias valued his womenfolk.

In his final years, Callias pulled off his greatest coup. The non-aggression pact that finally ended the Persian Wars is called the Peace of Callias, because he engineered it.

Callias, then, was a man who, at enormous personal risk, was instrumental in the birth of democracy. He was a self-made millionaire who didn't hesitate to fight in the ranks as a common soldier when his state needed him. He was the city's premier diplomat. He had a gloriously happy home life and then, to top it off, he successfully negotiated peace in the Middle East.

THAT HIPPIAS KEEPS a diary is something of an innovation. Paper was an expensive luxury item. However, it's reasonable that Hippias had access to a lot of paper and might have written because of an odd fact: the works of Homer were first recorded thanks to the father of Hippias, a man named Peisistratus, who was also a tyrant. Up until then the entire *Iliad* and *The Odyssey* had been passed down as oral tradition. Peisistratus feared the works would be garbled generation by generation, so he caused scribes to write down the whole thing.

It's quite likely that Hippias had a hand in the recording of Homer's works. He could have picked up the scribbling habit then.

NOBODY KNOWS WHAT happened to the sister of Harmodius, the girl whose public shaming led to the first plot against the tyranny. Since she had no remaining male protector after her brother died, there's every chance that the real child filled an unmarked grave. In the story I give the much more pleasant possibility that friends helped her escape to the sanctuary, where she flowers to become the High Priestess.

This book is intertwined with a famous legend of Homeric revenge.

Hippias refers in his diary to the sister of Harmodius as a future Elektra. The tyrant would have been intimately familiar with the legend that when King Agamemnon returned from Troy, his wife took to him with an axe. Aeschylus mentions this unfortunate incident when he describes the play he's writing about Orestes.

Elektra and Orestes were the children of Agamemnon. They grew to avenge the death of their father, just as Hippias fears that Thea might grow to avenge her brother.

Elektra and Orestes had a sister named Iphigenia, whose fate was quite different to theirs.

There are two stories about Iphigenia. In the Homeric version, her father sacrifices her to the gods in return for fair weather on the trip to Troy. The Athenians had an alternative ending, where the goddess Artemis appears at the last moment to save Iphigenia. Iphigenia then travels to Brauron, where on the instruction of the Goddess she founds the Sanctuary of Artemis and becomes its first High Priestess. Her body is said to be buried there.

Thus not only does Thea act the role of Elektra when she avenges her family against Hippias, but as High Priestess she's also the direct successor of Elektra's sister Iphigenia.

A MINOR EVENT occurs toward the end of this book that is going to change the world. The characters have no way of knowing it, but they were present at the birth of modern philosophy, and so were you. It happens when Diotima decides that from now on, she will teach Socrates.

The real Diotima was the teacher of the real Socrates. You might be amused to hear that Diotima succeeded in her plan to make Socrates read girlie poetry. In Plato's *Symposium*, Socrates—now an old man—stands to explain his philosophy and the meaning of love, and he says right away that everything he knows he learned from Diotima, a priestess of Mantinea.

I SWORE WHEN I began this series that it wouldn't take me three books to get Nico and Diotima married.

It didn't. It took me four.

Nico can finally cross off marrying Diotima from his list of life ambitions. Now he can turn his attention to the first two ambitions that he listed to Pericles, at the start of *The Pericles Commission*: to win an official position in the running of Athens, and to find a way to make investigation pay.

Yet for now the happy couple have a chance to settle down. Their friend Aeschylus will be putting on his final play next year, at the greatest arts festival of the ancient world, the Great Dionysia of Athens, to which thousands came from across the civilized world to see the best plays ever written. Nico and Diotima will be there to see them too.

Which will entangle them in the theatrical disaster of *Death ex Machina*.

Timeline

THE TIMELINE LISTS the dark and bloody deeds that lead up to the Marathon conspiracy. This book is fiction, but everything the characters talk about that happened in *their* past is real history.

You don't need any of this to enjoy the book, but if you'd like to know how the characters got to where they are, here are fifty-five years of murder and mayhem, plus a certain amount of conspiracy, plotting, justified paranoia, and unrequited lust:

515 BC	Athens has been ruled for many years by a tyrant named Hippias and his younger brother Hipparchus. In those days, the word "tyrant" didn't have the negative meaning that it does today. But that's about to change.
514 BC	Hipparchus, the brother of the tyrant, falls desperately in love with a young man named Harmodius. But Harmodius already has a lover, an older man named Aristogeiton. Harmodius rejects the advances of the tyrant's brother. Out of the pure spite of his unrequited love, Hipparchus publicly slanders the young sister of Harmodius, so badly that the child's life is ruined.

514 BC	Harmodius seeks revenge for the damage done to his sister. But he and his lover, Aristogeiton, know that to harm the brother of the tyrant means death, unless they can bring down the whole tyranny at the same time. They gather together men who wish to end the tyranny, and also a young woman named Leana. They conceive a plot to kill both brothers at the next public festival. The plot goes horribly wrong at the last moment. Harmodius knifes Hipparchus to death, but is himself killed in the attempt. Aristogeiton is captured. The other conspirators flee, leaving Hippias the tyrant unharmed. With his brother murdered, Hippias is determined to find and destroy everyone who opposes his rule. Aristogeiton dies under torture a few days later, without ever revealing anything of the plot. Hippias orders the arrest of Leana, whom he guesses was involved. Under torture Leana bites out her own tongue, to stop herself from revealing the names of the other conspirators. In so doing she saves their lives, but loses her own.

~ Four years of increasingly paranoid rule pass ~

510 BC	Hippias is overthrown by a second plot against him. He escapes with his life, and runs to the Persians. The Athenians erect statues of Harmodius and Aristogeiton, to stand side by side in the agora. They'll be known forever after as the Tyrannicides. Leana becomes the only mortal woman in history to be awarded a statue atop the Acropolis.

~ Twenty years of self-rule pass ~

490 BC	Hippias convinces the Persians to re-install him as Tyrant of Athens. In return he'll make Athens a client-state of Persia. The Persians land an army on the beach, at a place called Marathon. The Athenian citizen-militia marches out to face the enemy. The Athenians are outnumbered almost ten to one, but they won't have Hippias back at any price. In the ensuing battle, the grossly outnumbered Athenians totally thrash the Persians. Athens takes only 203 casualties, to 6,400 Persian dead. After the battle, the Athenians see someone on the mountain behind them flash a signal to the enemy. It looks like there are traitors prepared to deal with Persia. Speculation is wild, but the identity of the signalers is never discovered. Hippias dies shortly after the battle.

~ Ten years pass ~

480 BC	The Persians make a second attempt. This time they invade Greece with the largest army the world has ever seen. In desperation, the Greeks unite. Athens falls and is sacked. The Persians carry off many treasures, including the statues of Harmodius and Aristogeiton. They also send a small force, to sack the treasures of a sacred Sanctuary of Artemis, at a nearby town called Brauron. Incredibly, after a great sea battle at Salamis, the Persians lose again. This is becoming a habit.

480 BC	The Golden Age of Greece begins. At that very moment, as the Athenians reclaim their ruined city, a boy named Nicolaos is born to a sculptor and his wife.

~ Twenty-one years pass, during which Nicolaos grows up and democracy begins ~

459 BC	Fifty-five years have passed since those first bloody deeds, when Harmodius and Aristogeiton and Leana died to bring down the tyranny. A man who was young in those days would be an old man now. Such a man would have spent his entire life in the Persian Wars. He risked everything in the great sea battle at Salamis. He saw Athens fall and then rise again to become the greatest city in the world. But most of all, he would remember the day of the desperate Battle of Marathon, when the future of Europe hung on the point of his spear. He would remember the secret signal from behind the lines, which flashed to the enemy, even as the Persian dead lay about him on the blood-red sands, so that now, in 459 BC, when the skeletal remains of the tyrant Hippias are discovered in a cave not far from Athens, it will trigger the unfortunate events of *The Marathon Conspiracy*.

Acknowledgments

THANKS FIRST AND foremost to my family, Helen, Catriona, and Megan, who were remarkably patient while I wrote this book. Blossom the donkey owes his life to Catriona. He would like to take this opportunity to thank her.

Helen reads and checks everything five times throughout the course of producing each book. I'm not sure where that item appeared in the marriage vows, but she nevertheless takes it as a sacred duty.

Juliet Grames made this book a whole lot better with her excellent editing. I discovered after I'd submitted the manuscript that she'd previously edited an academic text on the Battle of Marathon, thus making her the perfect editor for *The Marathon Conspiracy*.

Stefano Vitale has produced the covers for all my books, each a lovely work of art.

Janet Reid, world's best literary agent, made all this possible by selling the series, and then using her people-management skills to keep everyone around her calm and more or less sane.